What a group of suspects!

"Would you like more tea?" Winnie Cantrell asked, motioning Riley toward the kitchen. But Jack knew what the older woman was doing. It was a technique cops used all the time—isolate the suspect and question them separately. In the meantime, Jack was left with the three other women who belonged to Winnie's bridge club. One of whom, he realized with a start, was beaming at him.

"If you don't like that tea, I'd be happy to invite you over to my place," Prue Fielding said, batting her eyelashes. "I make a wicked pot of coffee."

"Ha!" her sister Gert said. "It'll be wicked, all right. There's no telling what she'll put in it. She's blind as a bat."

Thankfully, Riley chose that moment to enter the room with a tray. "Have another cookie. It'll help take the edge off the tea."

Taking a cookie, Jack wondered ruefully what would take the edge off his growing attraction for his prime suspect—Riley herself!

For more, turn to page 9

Ryan tried for his best I'm-not-a-pervert smile.

Suddenly the woman's arm whipped out from beneath the shower curtain and she squirted him right in the eyes with some sort of gel.

"Ouch! That stings!" Squeezing his eyes shut, Ryan felt along the wall for the towel rack. "Look, I think—"

Another blob of gel landed on his cheek. He wiped it off and barely dodged two more missiles. The woman had an aim like a major league pitcher. And she was dangerous! Bending over, she snatched up a pink safety razor and brandished it like a sword. "If you come near me, I'll cut you to shreds," she said in a fierce voice.

Ryan looked at her, one white-knuckled hand holding the razor, the other clutching the curtain around her. Obviously she hadn't noticed that the curtain's wide stripes—one of which ran across her chest—were transparent.

Her breasts were as centerfold-worthy as her behind.

Forcing his gaze back to her face, he couldn't help feeling bad for her. She was clearly very frightened. She was also wet, almost naked and...he squinted at her...*familiar?*

For more, turn to page 197

HARLEQUIN DUETS

ISBN 0-373-44122-3

THE LIFE OF RILEY
Copyright © 2001 by Carolyn Hanlon

NAKED IN NEW ENGLAND
Copyright © 2001 by Jacquie D'Alessandro

This edition published by arrangement with Harlequin Books S.A.

® and TM are trademarks of the publisher. Trademarks indicated with ® are registered in the United States Patent and Trademark Office, the Canadian Trade Marks Office and in other countries.

Visit us at www.eHarlequin.com

Printed in U.S.A.

The Life of Riley

Cara Summers

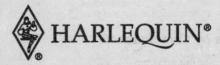

HARLEQUIN®

TORONTO • NEW YORK • LONDON
AMSTERDAM • PARIS • SYDNEY • HAMBURG
STOCKHOLM • ATHENS • TOKYO • MILAN • MADRID
PRAGUE • WARSAW • BUDAPEST • AUCKLAND

Dear Reader,

I love writing romantic comedy, because it seems to me that when two people fall in love, the opportunities for laughter spring to life—especially when those two people have no business falling in love in the first place!

And that is exactly the situation my hero and heroine find themselves in. Jack DeRosa shouldn't even be thinking about kissing Riley Foster, certainly not when he expects to arrest her at any minute. And Riley definitely shouldn't be thinking about kissing Detective DeRosa back, at least not while she's hiding stolen jewels.

But of course, Jack does kiss Riley, and that's just the beginning of the adventure. I hope you have as much fun as I did with these two characters. And I hope you will look for my next Harlequin Temptation novel, scheduled for release late this year.

Love and laughter always!

Cara Summers

P.S. I love to hear from my readers. You can write to me at P.O. Box 718, Fayetteville, NY 13066.

Books by Cara Summers

HARLEQUIN DUETS
40—MISTLETOE & MAYHEM

HARLEQUIN TEMPTATION
813—OTHERWISE ENGAGED

To the Condren Women and all of their descendants.
Especially to my great-aunts, Judy Vanda,
Ethel Linehan and Ann Langton,
who have been three of my biggest fans.
You will always be an inspiration to me.

1

"SOMETHING IS ROTTEN in Denmark!"

"You've got that right." Riley didn't even bother to glance at the parrot who was perched on the back of a nearby kitchen chair. The Bard had a comment for nearly every situation as long as he could sum it up with a quote from Shakespeare, and this one seemed particularly appropriate.

She'd just pulled two packages out of the bottom of her duffel. The plastic bag with the greenish-colored sandwich merely meant that her brother Ben had taken her duffel by mistake again. It was the small brown paper bag that she was curious about.

"Something is rotten in Denmark!"

"All right. All right. I'll get rid of it."

The moment Riley lifted the sandwich by the corner of the plastic bag it was growing in, the mountain of fur lying in front of the refrigerator raised its head, then slowly lumbered to its feet.

"No, Beowulf. Don't even think about it." Moving quickly, she deposited it in the trash under the sink and shut the door. "Decaying bologna sandwiches are definitely not meant to be doggie snacks." Patting the mountain on its head, she turned her attention back to the brown bag.

"To be or not to be. That is the question," the Bard stated firmly.

"No, the question is, should I look in the bag or not?" She didn't like invading Ben's privacy. Her brother and her uncle both worked part-time at Foster Care, her pet-care service. For the sake of efficiency, they each had their own duffel bag filled with a schedule, instructions, snacks for the pets and a set of keys that allowed them access to clients' apartments. But in the six months she'd been operating Foster Care, she'd learned one thing. She was organized. Her brother and uncle were not. Frequently, the bags became mixed up, which was why they each contained duplicate items.

Except for the brown paper bag. She always used plastic. Lifting it, she tipped the contents out onto the table, then stared at the diamond brooch. Curiosity gave way to anxiety as she studied it. She was almost sure she'd seen it before. Four of the people whose pets she cared for had been burglarized in the past few weeks. And just yesterday the two detectives assigned to the case had informed her she was their number one suspect. Her uncle Avery was urging her to hire a lawyer, but that was out of the question. Besides, not one of her clients suspected her of stealing from them. Leaning closer, she lifted the brooch just as the phone rang.

Grabbing the wall extension, she moved closer to the window and held the pin up to the light. "Foster Care Pet Service."

"Captain Duffy here," the voice barked in her ear. "Is that you, Ms. Foster?"

"Yes," she said. It was at that moment that she recognized the brooch. Tiny pinpricks of light cascaded down the opposite wall as it slipped through her fingers and clattered to the floor.

Beowulf barked at it.

"Something is rotten in Denmark," squawked the Bard.

Riley merely stared at the diamond pin she'd seen Hattie Silverman wearing on several occasions.

"There's been another robbery. One of your clients, Hattie Silverman, just called it in. I want to see you in my office at one-thirty sharp," Captain Duffy barked.

Riley sank to her knees, trying to remember the last time she'd seen Hattie wearing the brooch, but there were too many questions spinning around in her head. How had it gotten into her bag? How in the world was she going to explain it to the police?

"Captain Duffy," she managed as she lifted the brooch. "You're not going to believe this—"

"No excuses," Duffy said. "If you're not in my office at one-thirty, I'll send some uniforms to get you. Got that?"

"But—"

"Hattie Silverman claims you had nothing to do with the robbery," Duffy said. "But she says you were in her apartment yesterday. You walked her dog while she was at a doctor's appointment. Is that right?"

For the second time in as many minutes, Riley fingers went numb and the brooch spun to the floor. Once again pinwheels of light swirled across the walls and ceiling. "That's right," she lied. Because she hadn't walked Hattie Silverman's Chihuahua yesterday. Her brother Ben had.

"One-thirty," Duffy said before he cut the connection.

Riley pressed a hand against her stomach where the knot of fear had tightened and made herself take a deep breath. She was being ridiculous. Granted, she and Ben had been having their differences lately. But a few heated discussions about whether or not he should go to college didn't mean that he would steal from her clients. How could she even entertain that thought for a second? There was some other explanation for the fact that Hattie's jewels had found their way into her duffel bag.

"Something is rotten in Denmark."

She frowned down at the diamonds. "Exactly."

THE MOMENT she heard the sound—the cry of an animal in distress—Riley Foster did a quick about-face and walked smack into the man behind her. She had a quick, vivid im-

pression of pressing against a rock-solid wall with no give
to it.

"Sorry," she murmured, as she glanced up at him. *Tough*
was the word that went through her mind. She was aware of
the lean, hard lines of his face and the longish, dark hair that
curled below his ears, but it was his eyes that she couldn't
glance away from. She didn't think she'd ever seen eyes that
intense or that cool. And she recognized the look. It was the
same one a jungle predator might give its prey while it considered attacking.

"Are you all right?"

The deep, sand-papery voice only reinforced the image
she'd formed in her mind. Shoving aside an urge to turn and
run, she remembered why she'd turned back from the corner—that cry of distress. "I'm fine," she assured him. And
she was, though she couldn't remember the last time she'd
had such a strange reaction to someone she'd bumped into
on the street. Very curious, she thought as she circled around
him, then dodged and jostled her way out of the stream of
pedestrians pushing their way toward the green light at the
corner. A sunny spring day had lured most of Manhattan's
workers out of their office buildings for the lunch hour, and
now they were scurrying back to work.

Reaching the haven of a store entrance, Riley glanced at
her watch. One-twenty. She had ten minutes before her appointment with Captain Duffy, and she couldn't afford to be
late. She still hadn't decided what she was going to do about
Hattie Silverman's diamond brooch. Handing it over to the
captain was risky. He'd probably arrest her for stealing it.
The woman detective who'd questioned her had thought she
was behind the burglaries.

Glancing down the street, she listened intently. A symphony of noise assaulted her ears—the staccato bleating of a
horn, disjointed scraps of conversations, the long gasp of a
bus door opening. Then she caught it again—the faint wail

of a frightened animal. It had to be coming from the alley she'd passed halfway down the block.

Tightening her grip on her duffel bag, she hurried toward it, pausing for only a moment when she reached the entrance. For a few seconds, she couldn't see a thing. The bright April sunshine was totally blocked by the tall buildings that rose on either side. Five steps in, she spotted a movement near the wall of the building. Moving closer, she saw the kitten, and a few feet away from it, she squatted down. "It's all right," she said in a soft voice. But the moment she started to inch her way forward, the kitten hissed and streaked away.

Rising, she hurried after it, relieved when it ran into a dead end in the corner a Dumpster formed with the brick wall. "It's all right," she repeated as she slowly dropped to her knees again.

The kitten let out a screech.

"Yes, I know you're frightened. You've been in a fight," she said, noting the missing patches of fur. But the eyes were bright, the body rigid and trembling. "I wonder what the other guy looks like," she said in a soothing tone. Slowly, still talking softly, she slipped her hand into her duffel and pulled out some dry pellets of food. "I bet you're hungry," she said, moving her hand slowly closer to the kitten. She dropped one pellet about a foot away, then left a trail of them back to her knees. The kitten stepped forward, sniffed the first one, then ate it greedily. Pleased, Riley watched it eat its way closer and closer. The final pellet lay in the palm of her hand. "I learned this trick the first time I saw *E.T.*," she said as the kitten lapped it up. Then, still talking softly, she gathered the kitten close to her body while she unzipped a compartment of her duffel. Finally, she eased the kitten in. She knew from experience that she had to secure it or it would leap away at the first loud sound.

"There," she murmured, checking to see that it had plenty of room to breathe.

"Hand over that bag, lady."

Riley jumped, then scrambled to her feet and turned. One look at the two men had the fear arrowing through her. They were big, and as they moved closer, she could see their features clearly enough to determine that they were young. The smaller one couldn't have been more than twelve or thirteen, the larger one no more than fifteen or sixteen, her brother's age.

"Don't even think of screaming," the older one said.

With fear lodged tight in her throat, she wasn't sure she could.

"Hand over the bag and your jacket," the younger one said.

A SANE PERSON did not walk into an alley. Not in Manhattan, Jack DeRosa thought grimly as he started after the woman who'd just entered one. Bad things happened in alleys. Sweat, cold and clammy, broke out on his forehead even as the image of that night formed itself in his mind. Quickly, he shoved it away. Better to think of the woman. What if he hadn't been watching her? What if he hadn't given into that strange compulsion to stare at her after she'd walked into him? For an instant, while her body had been pressed against his, he'd felt so...aware of her. It wasn't that she was blatantly attractive. Her blond hair was cropped shorter than his, and she wore no makeup. It was her eyes. They were a deep, clear shade of blue, and for a moment, when he'd looked into them, he'd completely lost his train of thought.

What the hell was she doing in that alley? With a frown, he increased his pace, ignoring the twinge in his thigh. The way she'd turned back from the corner and headed straight for it told him it was her intended destination. Was she meeting someone there? A lot of business was conducted in New York City alleys, none of it good.

The instant he turned into it, he spotted the three figures

near the Dumpster. Years of experience as a cop had him automatically flattening himself against the wall and reaching in the back waistband of his jeans for his gun. His hand came up empty before he remembered that it wasn't there. A cop on sick leave wasn't supposed to carry.

Moving forward, he ignored the increasingly sharp twinges in his thigh and assessed the situation. Gang members. They'd both have weapons. Not guns, he figured, or they would have drawn them already. So it would be knives. And there were two of them, only one of her. With no weapon, he needed surprise on his side.

As he moved slowly closer, he saw the smaller one grab the strap of her bag. Then to his surprise, she yanked it back! What was she thinking? Hadn't anyone ever told her not to argue with muggers? Pushing himself from the wall, he ran forward, trying to ignore the pain that seared with more force through his thigh each time his foot pounded down on the pavement.

"Two against one," he said, stopping a few feet away. "Doesn't seem fair."

The bigger kid whirled toward him, and the moment Jack saw light flash off the steel of the knife, his vision began to blur. The alley suddenly grew darker, the stench of the garbage more ripe, and the memory of that night struggled to push its way into his mind. Fear iced his veins, just as it had then, slowing his reflexes so that he barely dodged the first downward slice of the blade. The second swipe cut through the sleeve of his jacket. Dodging to his right, Jack felt his leg nearly give out on him. As he switched his weight to his good leg, he felt as if he were moving in slow motion. But the kid was moving at regular speed, and this time the blade was going to rip through him, just as it had... At the last minute, the scream—a terrified howl of fear and pain—freed him.

Jack lunged to the left, pivoted, and delivered one swift

blow to the side of the boy's neck. As the guy pitched to the ground, Jack reached for his cuffs, then swore when they weren't there.

Another scream from behind him had him whirling. The woman stood with her back against the wall, holding a gun aimed at the other kid. His hands were clutching his eyes as he backed away.

She ran forward then to Jack's side and aimed the gun at the bigger kid who had scrambled to his knees. "I'll give you three to get away. One, two..."

The kid was on his feet and streaking away. The younger was still howling. She moved toward him. "It's only vinegar," she said. "You can rinse it away. You'll be fine."

For a moment all Jack could do was stare at her. *Vinegar!*

"There are some tissues in my bag," she said, unzipping it.

"Tissues?" Jack grabbed the boy and twisted his arm behind his back.

"What do you think you're doing?" she asked, pressing some into the boy's free hand.

"The precinct station is just two blocks away. I'm going to march him over there."

"No. Just let him go."

Jack looked warily at the gun she still had in her hand. This close he could see it was a water pistol, but she had it aimed at him, and he didn't relish getting an eyeful of vinegar. "This kid and his buddy just tried to rob you. You should press charges."

"I won't do that. Please let him go. Can't you see he's just a kid?"

Later, he would ask himself what he'd been thinking. As a cop, he'd always prided himself on doing things by the book. Maybe it was the look in those incredibly blue eyes. Maybe it was the fact that her special brand of insanity was contagious. Or perhaps it was because the kid's eyes were still streaming, but they were open, wary and frightened.

"This is your lucky day," he said, dropping his hands and stepping back.

The boy streaked down the alley in the direction his buddy had taken.

"Thank you," she said.

"If you want to thank me for something, thank me for this." He plucked the water pistol from her hand and slipped it into his pocket.

"Hey, I need that for protection," she protested.

"If it gives you false courage, it doesn't protect you," Jack said as he took her arm and drew her with him toward the mouth of the alley.

"I think it did a pretty good job. It got us both out of a tough spot, didn't it?"

"Just because you were lucky this time—" Stumbling, he swore under his breath.

"You're hurt. Did he get you in the leg with that knife?"

"No. It's an old injury." He wasn't sure how it happened, but her hand was in his. Her grip was strong. That didn't surprise him. What did was the fact that he didn't pull away automatically. For a moment, the same awareness that he'd felt before moved through him again.

"Do you need to see a doctor or go to an emergency room?"

"No." He wasn't sure whether he was more irritated with himself or with her as he withdrew his hand and limped with her toward the end of the alley. He'd had enough of doctors and hospitals. And he knew from the pain in his leg that he'd be limping for the next day or so. Just what he needed.

"You really shouldn't go into any more alleys until that injury heals," she said as they stepped out onto the sidewalk.

"*I* shouldn't go into an alley? I followed *you*."

"Well, you shouldn't have. It's dangerous. Now, if I could have my gun back…"

Jack stared at her outstretched palm. Then he glanced once more into those bottomless blue eyes of hers. A big mistake. "Look," he finally said. "This is the way it's going to go down. I'm going to leave your pistol with the desk sergeant at the police station up the street. When you bring proof that you've completed a self-defense class, you can pick it up."

"A self-defense class? I don't have time—"

He gave her his best cop stare. "Make the time. Or your next stroll into an alley could be your last."

THE TWO-BLOCK WALK to the station had taken Jack longer than it should have, and though the pain in his thigh had dulled somewhat, he was still limping. And he was breathing too hard. The physical therapist he'd worked with twice a week since the injury had told him the muscles were strong, the tendons healed. The leg should be fully rehabilitated. But this pain was real. It couldn't be just in his head. Pausing for a moment, he rubbed his hand over his thigh. The last thing he needed was to limp into his captain's office. All he could hope for now was that Duffy wouldn't notice it. Right, he thought. And maybe one day pigs would fly.

Hesitating before the door to the detectives' division on the second floor, Jack drew in a deep breath. Somehow, he had to convince his boss to let him return to work. If he had to stare at the walls of his apartment for thirty more days— hell, if he had to stare at them for one more day—he was going to go nuts. Maybe just as nuts as that woman with the vinegar-filled water pistol.

Closing his eyes, he drew in another breath and let it out. He wasn't going to think about her. When he'd first arrived at the station, he'd noticed that she'd followed him, so he'd introduced her to the desk sergeant, instructing the man to give her whatever brochures he had on self-defense classes.

At least she'd taken his advice. Maybe she wouldn't turn into another number in the crime statistics. Drawing in one last deep breath, he pushed through the frosted glass doors and entered the detectives' room.

The smell of burnt coffee, stale food and old cigarette smoke assaulted his nostrils. Home, he thought as he made his way past rows of desks pushed nose to nose. Some were manned, others were empty. His was occupied. He stopped short and stared at the complete stranger, sitting at his desk, using his phone. He'd started toward the intruder when a voice distracted him.

"DeRosa!"

Inwardly, Jack groaned as he turned to watch a slender brunette dressed in a tan-colored designer suit hurrying toward him. On paper, Alexandra Markham was one of the best detectives in the room. It was her methods that bothered him. She was so focused on her own personal advancement that she'd do almost anything to make an arrest. The bright smile she flashed at him only reminded him to watch his back.

The moment she was close enough, she pitched her voice low. "Duffy was out here bellowing your name about ten minutes ago. He didn't look too happy when he didn't find you."

Jack swallowed a sigh. His boss was an abrupt, irascible man who valued promptness almost as much as he valued thorough investigative work. "Yeah, well, I'm not happy to see someone sitting at my desk."

Alexandra gave his arm a quick pat, falling into step beside him as he walked down the short corridor to the captain's glass-walled office. "It's only temporary. His name is Carmichael and he's here on loan for a month. Unless you're going to have to be out longer."

"I was hoping to talk the captain into letting me come back today."

She turned to look at him, her eyes wide with surprise. "What about your leg?"

"It's coming along just fine." It would have been a hell of a lot finer if he hadn't run down that alley. And he would have been on time, too.

"You shouldn't rush it, Jack," Alexandra said, a worried frown on her face.

Oh, she was worried all right, Jack thought. Worried that he'd get the promotion she wanted.

"Markham?"

They both turned to see that Carmichael had risen from Jack's desk. "A call from that pawn shop we visited yesterday. He's got something he wants us to see."

Alex turned back to Jack. "I know how much you hate advice, and I don't suppose you'll take it, but I don't think you should come back until you're one hundred percent." She smiled then. "I gotta go. Good luck with the captain."

Jack watched her until she left the room, grateful that he didn't have to reply to her advice. What he didn't want to articulate, not even to himself, was his fear that he might not ever be one hundred percent again. He'd very nearly frozen in that alley just now. If that kid hadn't screamed…

Behind him a door opened and Duffy growled, "DeRosa."

Turning, Jack walked carefully into the office.

Duffy gestured him into a chair. Then, after closing the door, he propped his hip on the corner of his desk. "You're late, and you're still limping, I see."

"Guilty on both counts," Jack said. He wouldn't offer an excuse. Relating what had happened in that alley was not going to endear him to the captain, especially since he hadn't managed to bring either of the young thugs in.

"And…?" Duffy prompted, holding out his arm and tapping his finger on the face of his wristwatch. "You've got about five minutes left of the fifteen I scheduled for you."

Jack met his boss's eyes steadily. "I want to come back to work."

Duffy made a noise that sounded like a grunt. "I've spoken with your doctors. Physically, they say you're ready. It's the police psychologist who's holding back on releasing you."

Jack knew quite well what the psychologist's report said—that the continued pain in his leg was probably due to issues he had to work through surrounding his young partner's death in that alley. What he couldn't make the head doctor understand was that going back to work was the only way he knew of dealing with the so-called issues.

"If I have to stay in that apartment another day—" Jack cut himself off before he finished the sentence, but the words he hadn't said hung in the air.

Duffy raised his hands and dropped them. "Until you receive a clean bill of health, my hands are tied. Unless..."

"What?"

"I've got a matter that needs delicate handling. Officially, I can't assign anyone to it because I don't have that kind of manpower at my disposal."

Jack studied his boss. The man was scowling—he always scowled—that wasn't what bothered him. It was the quickness with which Duffy had come up with his "delicate matter." Jack smelled a trap. Yet, as the silence stretched between them, he couldn't prevent himself from asking, "Undercover work?"

"Right. And no one except for Markham and Carmichael can know you've taken the assignment. They're working the case."

Taken the assignment. The presumption in the phrase set off little alarms in Jack's head. "Whoa, slow down. Just what is it we're talking about?"

Moving behind his desk, Duffy picked up a folder. "I've made a copy of the file. We've had a string of burglaries in some high-rent apartments in the Central Park area. Jewelry mostly. It's stuff that's out in the open. None of the safes have been broken into.''

"Amateurs," Jack said.

"That's what Markham and Carmichael are thinking. The first three were in the same building, and the three ladies who were burglarized belong to the same bridge club. They meet every Thursday afternoon. We figured one of them was getting sticky fingers. Then the same kind of thing occurred two days ago at another address ten blocks away. And since the ladies are in their seventies and eighties and don't get around much, we had to modify the theory. Long story short—the one thing all of the victims have in common is they use the same pet-care service, an outfit called Foster Care. A Riley Foster runs it. She has an uncle and a teenage brother who work for her part-time. They each have keys to the apartments. It's all here in the file.''

Jack stared at the folder his captain was holding out to him. "What exactly am I supposed to do with it? It sounds like you've got your jewel thieves.''

Duffy scowled at him. Then setting the folder down, he opened a drawer and pulled out a box of cigars. "We haven't caught Ms. Foster with the goods. We can't even get a search warrant unless we can find something more in the way of evidence. Her customers are very loyal, and yesterday, I got a call from the commissioner who had just received a phone call from his godmother, the victim who runs the bridge club. It seems that she doesn't want the police harassing her pet-care service provider. Since then, I've been giving the commissioner hourly updates on our progress.''

Clipping off the end of the cigar he'd selected, Duffy rattled off an uncensored version of what he thought of police commissioners who had eccentric old ladies for godmothers. Just before lighting up, he nudged the box of cigars closer to Jack. "Care to join me?''

Jack stared down at the cigars, then at his boss. Duffy had never before offered him a cigar. The man was clearly desperate—desperate to suck Jack into solving his political problem for him. He waved away the cigar offer and said, "Just what is it you want me to do?"

"I want you to work on the case from the inside. Foster Care is going to hire you on as an assistant. And once you get some solid evidence on someone who works there, you'll make an arrest."

"And if I don't get the evidence?" Jack asked.

Duffy stubbed out his cigar. "You will. I'm sick to death of the commissioner breathing down my neck on each and every investigation. I want this case off my desk. Markham and Carmichael think this Riley Foster is guilty. I want evidence. It would help if you could catch her in the act. Second-best scenario would be to find the jewels on her or one of her relatives or in her apartment. And then the commissioner's precious godmother can damn well find herself another pet-care service provider!"

Instead of reaching for the file, Jack stuffed his hands in his pockets. "And as soon as I make the arrest, I get to return to work."

The captain's eyes narrowed. "You're bargaining with me?"

"Take it or leave it."

Duffy's phone interrupted his pithy reply. Reaching for it, he barked, "Yeah?" Then glaring at Jack, he said, "Yes, Commissioner, I'm handling the matter just as we agreed. I've got one of my best men on the case." Placing a hand over the receiver, he said, "Take the file out with you and bring yourself up to speed. I'll be with you shortly."

THE MOMENT he closed the door behind him, Jack sank down into one of the chairs outside his boss's office and quickly flipped through the file on Foster Care. The meeting hadn't gone exactly the way he'd hoped, but the case looked like a piece of cake. By the time he'd finished skimming through Alexandra Markham's reports, he was convinced that someone at Foster Care had to be behind the robberies. The owner, Riley Foster, was twenty-three years old, a graduate of an expensive girls' college, a pampered Park Avenue princess, he figured. Her mother had died when she was twelve. Then she'd found herself penniless after her father had died in a plane crash nine months ago.

Alexandra's research had been thorough, as usual. She'd even included the fact that the FAA hadn't ruled out suicide as the cause of the plane crash. Ms. Foster's father was about to be charged with embezzling money from his investment firm when the accident had occurred.

Following the funeral, Ms. Foster had moved in with her uncle who, from the looks of his Park Avenue address, could support her in the style to which she'd become accustomed. Within three months she'd developed a pet-care service that catered to the rich. Her clients loved her, recommended her to their friends, and everyone seemed to trust her implicitly.

Closing the file, Jack considered the possibilities. Foster Care could provide a perfect front for the burglaries. And Ms. Foster could be the thief. But the teenage brother who worked as her assistant after school and on weekends was also a possibility. As was the uncle, a semiretired actor whose career had slumped lately. Mentally, Jack gave himself three or four days to make an arrest. And, at least, he'd be out of his apartment.

Leaning back in his chair, he closed his eyes for a moment. In the office behind him, the rumble of his captain's voice grew fainter. The pain in his leg had already subsided into a manageable but steady throb. It was the tiredness it had left in its wake that disturbed Jack more. But it would pass, he told himself. It had to.

RILEY FLASHED her best smile at the desk sergeant as she scooped the kitten off his desk and tucked her carefully back into the duffel. The young man had reached for his gun when the little stray had suddenly leapt out onto the pages of his daybook.

"I'm so sorry. She's a stray and they scare easily."

"Yes, well…" The sergeant paused, clearly embarrassed that he'd nearly pulled his gun on a kitten.

"Thanks for the brochure on the self-defense class," Riley hastened to add. "And I'd appreciate it very much if you could direct me to Captain Duffy's office. I have an appointment with him that I'm already late for."

"Right up those stairs at the end of the hall," the sergeant said. "And Ma'am…"

"Yes?"

"I don't think it's a good idea to take that kitten into his office. He's very…particular about his things."

"Right. Thanks," Riley said as she hurried toward the stairs.

What in the world was she going to do with the kitten while she talked to Captain Duffy? And there was still the question of Hattie Silverman's diamond brooch. It was the second problem that had her stomach sinking further and further with each step she climbed.

Honesty was the best policy. It was something her father had repeated often enough to her while she was growing up. But then, he'd never followed that particular maxim himself. She was the daughter of a thief, a man who'd gambled away people's life savings. Wouldn't the police expect her to be following in her father's footsteps?

But if she was going to prove them wrong, wasn't her only choice to be perfectly honest with them? Reaching the top of the stairs, she moved directly through the open door in front of her. A quick glance around the room packed with desks told her that the woman detective who'd questioned her the day before wasn't there. She wasn't sure whether it was relief or disappointment she felt as she headed toward the glassed-in office with Captain Duffy's name on the door.

And then she spotted a familiar face—the man who'd followed her into the alley. Immediately, the plan formed in her mind. She just might have the solution to one of her problems.

IT WAS A meowing screech that brought him fully alert, and Jack found himself staring into the eyes of the pistol-packing woman he'd followed into the alley.

"I'm sorry I woke you," she said.

Jack frowned at her. "I wasn't sleeping. I was resting my eyes."

"Right. I won't tell anyone if you'll do me a favor. I have an appointment with Captain Duffy and I was wondering if you could just take Abra off my hands for a few minutes."

"Abra?" Jack stared at the small animal she was lifting out of her duffel bag. A rat was his first thought. But most of the rats he'd spotted in New York City looked a lot healthier than this scrawny creature.

"Short for abracadabra. She has a tendency to materialize suddenly out of my duffel bag when it's least convenient. The desk sergeant went for his gun, and I don't want to upset Captain Duffy."

Somehow, while he'd been trying to follow the thread of her conversation, Jack discovered that she'd transferred the creature to his hands. He felt the brush of a tiny tongue on his wrist.

"Hold her close to your body. Underneath your jacket would be best. Strays are so nervous, and I don't know how long she was in that alley before I found her."

"You went into that alley after this…this…what is it anyway?" he asked as she unzipped his jacket and gestured him to tuck the animal inside.

Jack resisted her prompting until she glanced up at him. Then he was once more struck by the color of her eyes. This time the blue reminded him of the ocean at its deepest and darkest, inviting…fascinating.

"She's a kitten, and she could be startled by the least little noise. If she gets away from you, there's no telling how long it might take me to corner her in this place. The desk sergeant warned me that Captain Duffy might not be pleased by that scenario."

"Is that right?" barked a voice behind her.

As if on cue, the kitten leapt from Jack's hands, streaked between Duffy's legs and disappeared into his office. The woman was after it in a flash, and Jack found himself rising quickly to shoo his angry boss back into the room so he could shut the door. The kitten was cowering in a corner, screeching, and he found himself watching in admiration as Abra's protector approached her slowly, talking softly. He could picture her doing the same thing in that alley. Her hands were inches from their goal when the kitten screeched again and shot past her. Jack dropped to his knees, wincing as the pain arrowed up his thigh. He made a grab for the kitten as it raced by and missed. It leapt onto the captain's desk and sent a shower of papers cascading to the floor.

"Damn it!" shouted Duffy.

The kitten shot off the desk and disappeared behind it.

"Not so loud, please," the woman said in the same soothing tone she'd been using with the kitten. "Can't you see she's terrified?"

"She has good reason to be. She just destroyed a whole morning's work! DeRosa, get that thing out of here," Duffy growled.

"Hush," Riley said. "You'll scare her." Then, still on her knees, she moved over to Jack. "You go around the back of the desk, and I'll take the direct route. But don't make any fast moves. Okay?"

Though he felt like a fool, Jack did as she directed, trying to ignore the pain in his leg. His route was longer, his progress slower, and she was only a few feet away from the kitten by the time he spotted it. As he watched, she took pellets out of her bag and made a little trail of food from her hand to a spot a foot away from the animal. Smart move. All the while she kept talking to it softly in much the same way a cop might talk to a panicked man with a gun. Hardly daring to breathe, he watched the kitten eat its way slowly toward her. She had one hand around it when it bolted. This time he was ready. With both hands, he scooped it up, pulled it close and got part of his jacket around it.

"Excellent," she said, smiling as she rose to her feet.

"DeRosa, have you got the…situation contained?" Duffy asked, keeping a wary eye on Jack's jacket as he edged himself behind his desk.

"Yes, sir," Jack said. As he shifted his weight onto his bad knee, he winced. Suddenly, the woman was at his side, gripping his elbow.

"Lean on me," she said.

"I can manage," he said curtly as he rose to his feet. When he turned, he caught the captain observing him closely.

"You sure you're up to this assignment?" Duffy asked.

"We have a deal," Jack reminded him.

With a nod, the captain turned his attention to the woman. "I take it you two have met."

"No." They spoke at the same time.

"Riley Foster, this is Detective DeRosa," Duffy said.

"Foster?"

"Detective?"

Once again they spoke in unison, and Jack found himself staring at her. *This* Riley Foster didn't look anything like the Park Avenue princess he'd pictured in his mind.

"Until we get to the bottom of who's stealing from your clients," Duffy continued, "Detective DeRosa will be working undercover as your new assistant. From now on, he's going to be your shadow."

2

SHADOW! As a bright bubble of panic blossomed within her, Riley stared at Captain Duffy. "And just why do I need a shadow?"

"Because you are the prime suspect in a series of burglaries that have been plaguing your clients," Duffy said.

"Suspect?" Riley felt the panic begin to spread.

"You have motive, means and opportunity," Duffy said. "According to Detective Markham, you are planning on opening a day-care center for pets, but you need cash to complete the renovations. That's motive. You also have keys to all the victims' apartments and easy access to their buildings. That's means and opportunity. The only reason we haven't made an arrest yet is because, so far, we haven't been able to link you directly to any of the stolen property."

Riley tightened her grip on her duffel bag. "I didn't steal anything."

"You can help us prove that by cooperating and hiring DeRosa here as your new assistant."

What in the world was she going to do? He might have a bad leg, but he was sharp, maybe even sharper than the two detectives who had been questioning her for the past two weeks. Until she could figure out how the diamond brooch had ended up in her bag and what in the world she was going to do with it, she couldn't afford to have someone dogging her every step. Walking forward, she planted her hands on the captain's desk. "I think—no, I'm sure—that your plan would violate my rights." She waved a hand. "Somehow."

Duffy leaned toward her until they were nearly nose to nose. "I thought you were innocent. You say you are. Your friend Winnie Cantrell says you are, and she called up her godchild, the police commissioner, and told him that we were harassing you. So now, my boss is convinced that you're innocent, too, and he's telling me to make this case go away ASAP. Detective DeRosa's going to do that. Right, De-Rosa?"

"Right," Jack said.

"And what if I refuse?"

"Then I'm going to call in Markham and Carmichael, the two detectives on the case and tell them to watch your every move. They'll be questioning your clients, even the ones who haven't been robbed. Your present clients may be very loyal, but it won't take long for rumors to spread that you're under investigation. That will make it tough for you to increase your business."

Riley swallowed as the picture he was painting formed in her mind. "What happens if I cooperate?"

"I'll call Markham and Carmichael off. Unless there's another burglary, they won't be bothering you or your clients anymore. In exchange, you're going to provide a cover for Detective DeRosa here and let him investigate the thefts from the inside. If you cooperate, I expect him to make an arrest by the end of the week."

Riley frowned. "Provide a cover? Just what would that entail?"

Duffy frowned right back at her. "You're going to hire him as your assistant and rent him one of the spare rooms in that rambling, penthouse apartment you live in."

"Rent him a room? I can't do that. How would I explain that to my uncle?"

"I just arrived in town," Jack suggested. "You're putting me up until I can find a place of my own."

"Exactly." Duffy shot Jack an approving look before he returned his gaze to Riley.

"I don't have to do this," she said.

"No," Duffy agreed. "But it's *your* clients who are being burglarized. Don't you want to put a stop to that?"

Riley drew in a breath and let it out. "Okay. He can be my new assistant on one condition."

Duffy's eyes narrowed as his color heightened. "Young lady, you're in no position to make conditions."

"I don't want my uncle or my brother to know anything about this. They have enough to worry about without thinking that you're going to throw me in jail."

"No one but you will know Detective DeRosa's a cop." Duffy's face grew redder and his volume increased with each word he bit out. "In fact, no one but you *can* know that he's a cop. That's what providing him with a cover *means!* Get it?"

"Yes. Okay." Riley backed up a quick step as she shot Jack a glance. "I guess I agree to the plan." She turned back to Duffy. "As long as it only takes a week. He has to be out in a week."

"Young lady—" Duffy began again.

"It probably won't take that long," Jack interjected before his boss could blow up. "Why don't I start this afternoon?"

"Just what I was going to suggest," Duffy said, taking a deep breath and letting it out.

"If you wouldn't mind letting us use your office for a few minutes, Captain, I'm sure Ms. Foster and I could work out the details."

"You've got five minutes," Duffy said as he strode toward the door. Then he turned back to them. "Five minutes, and then I want my office cleared. And I don't want to find any trace of that…that…whatever it is that you've got stuffed under your jacket, DeRosa. Understood?"

"Understood," Jack said.

As soon as Captain Duffy slammed the door of his office, Riley drew in a deep breath. Then she turned to face Detective DeRosa. Her biggest talent lay in handling animals, but she was good at handling humans, too. She'd just have to find a way to handle this one. Even seated, he looked very big and very self-contained. Like a gunslinger in an old western, if he wanted to stop you, he would. And those eyes. The way he was looking at her now was enough to convince her that he would soon know all of her secrets. A quick sliver of fear shot up her spine. She had to say something quick. Anything. "I don't suppose I could talk you out of this."

"No."

She tried a smile. "Do you do this kind of undercover work often?"

"No."

She studied him for a minute as annoyance began to push down the fear. "You don't say much."

"No."

"My uncle has a bird that talks more than you do."

"That a fact?"

"Yes." Keeping her eyes on him, she let the silence stretch. Two could play that game. They had at least four-and-a-half minutes until the captain would barge through the door again. She could shut up that long if he could. At least she hoped she could. By the time she counted ten seconds off in her head, she decided that keeping quiet wasn't the problem. The problem was going to be staring into his eyes for that long. Shifting her gaze to the kitten, she saw that Abra had pretty much settled herself into one of his hands. It was large enough to hold her. The other one was stroking her gently. Strong hands, she thought, recalling how he had used just one of them to strike down that big kid in the alley. They wouldn't be soft, yet they were gentle now. She tried to remind herself that those same hands had gripped a gun, they'd probably taken a human life. He was a cop. She had to be on her guard against him. But as she watched those long, tapered fingers move over the kitten, she couldn't seem to prevent herself from wondering if they would move over a woman in just that way.

Move over a woman? The unexpected turn in her thoughts had her lifting her eyes to meet his. *Bad move.* What if he could tell what she was thinking?

No, that was ridiculous. No one really had X-ray vision. Still, the longer she stared at him, the less she was able to deny the strange sensations moving through her. There was a funny feeling of warmth spreading from her stomach downward. And her blood had suddenly grown thicker; it seemed to be moving much more slowly. Even her arms seemed to be affected. She wasn't sure she could lift them. But she wanted to. She wanted to move closer to him, to reach out with her hands and...

"You win," Jack said.

Riley blinked. She felt as if she'd suddenly been released from some invisible, magnetic beam. "What?"

When the corners of his mouth slowly lifted, she blinked again. This man was dangerous enough when he had that serious, gunslinger look on his face. Smiling, he was absolutely lethal. Another realization struck then—the worst one of all. She was beginning to like him. A bubble of panic bloomed in her stomach.

"I'll talk first. We should get the details settled before the captain returns."

"Details." She licked her lips, annoyed when she found them dry. "Right. You know, it's not too late to call this off. I mean, if you're really going to be my assistant, you should know that caring for pets is physically demanding, and...no offense, but you don't seem to be in any shape to..."

Her words faded the moment the smile disappeared from his face and he rose from his chair. She felt as if someone had suddenly turned off a light. Then she realized that he was merely blocking the sunlight pouring in through the windows.

"There's no way out of this for either one of us. If you cooperate, it will go faster."

In the back of her mind, Riley thought she heard the ominous clang of a prison door closing. It could be over just that quickly if he found out what she had in the duffel bag. Quickly dismissing the thought, she tried to focus on the problem at hand. She was good at that. She was going to stop letting this man intimidate her. She'd handled those two kids in the alley. She was going to handle this...cop. "Where are you from?"

"My apartment's on the West Side."

"Wrong. Detective DeRosa lives on the West Side. But my *new assistant* has just arrived in the city. So where are you from?"

Jack nodded at her. "Point taken, Ms. Foster. I'm from California."

"Riley. Everybody calls me that. What about your family? Occupation?"

"No family. And I've worked at a lot of things—everything from construction to short-order cook."

Tilting her head to one side, Riley studied him for a moment. "Do you *really* cook?"

His eyes narrowed. "Sure. Nothing fancy."

It took her only a second to decide. If she was going to have to put up with a cop in the house, she might as well make the best of it. "My uncle and my brother and I take turns cooking meals. If you're going to live with us, you'll have to take a shift. It would be part of your cover."

He studied her for a moment. "I could do that."

"Great. And what about your name? What should I call you?"

"Let's keep it simple. I'll stick with my real name. Jack DeRosa."

"Nice to meet you, Jack." Smiling, Riley held out her hand, and she was pleased when he hesitated for a second. She was definitely getting control of the situation. When his hand finally closed over hers, it was just what she had anticipated. His palms were hard, his grip strong. And it was just an ordinary handshake. People did this every day. When he released her, she decided to ignore that her hand felt as if she'd just passed it over a flame.

"I have a busy schedule this afternoon," she said. "Why don't we discuss the rest of the details on the way?"

"What are your plans for this?" He held out the kitten who was still snuggled in his palm.

Riley frowned. "I should really take her to the apartment."

"Fine," Jack said, holding the kitten out to her. "We can swing by my place on the way, and we can move in together."

When Riley reached out to take her, the kitten hissed at her and then screeched. "I think you're stuck with her."

It was Jack's turn to frown. "I'll take my turn in the kitchen, but I don't do kittens."

Riley smiled up at him. "As my new assistant, you're going to have to do a lot more than kittens."

"I DON'T DO KITTENS," Jack said, frowning at the cat on his bed.

The kitten didn't even open its eyes to acknowledge his comment. But it was only pretending to be asleep, just as it had on the taxi ride to his apartment. It would wake up soon enough if he lifted it up and took it out to the living room where Riley was waiting for him. He'd tried three times now to give her the kitten and each time the little rascal had put up a fight, hissing or screeching.

Riley was getting a huge kick out of it. He wasn't. She'd said that he'd better get used to it. The kitten had bonded with him.

Abra stretched, sighed and settled herself more comfortably on his pillow.

"You've picked the wrong person to bond with." Jack's frown deepened as he studied the kitten. He'd seen homeless people who looked better fed and groomed. But the little thing had spirit. He couldn't prevent himself from admiring it.

Just as he couldn't prevent himself from admiring Riley Foster. And that was a problem. She was a problem.

Turning, he pulled underwear and socks out of his drawer and placed them in his bag. As he continued to pack, selecting and folding clothes from his closet, he kept his mind focused on sorting through the problem. It was a technique he'd honed to perfection in his years on the force. Some of his best insights into cases had come while he was performing some routine ritual. In this case, the prime suspect didn't impress him as a jewel thief.

As a cop, he'd learned to trust his first impressions of people. More often than not, they were accurate. Riley Foster seemed guileless, and there was innocence in her eyes. But in this case...he just wasn't sure.

Moving to the bathroom, he packed shaving equipment into his travel kit. The truth was he was attracted to Riley Foster. He'd known it when she'd first bumped into him on the street. There'd only been that brief moment of contact, but the sensation of her body pressed against his had lingered, even after she'd pushed past him. His own body had tightened, and he'd felt the tug of attraction that sometimes occurred instantly between a man and a woman. That hadn't surprised him. What had was his desire to grab her back into his arms and just hold on.

That was new. Unprecedented, in fact. It was why he'd turned to watch her walk away. Who was she and why had he reacted to her that way? She wasn't anything like the type of woman he was usually attracted to. In a crowded room he wouldn't have given her more than a passing glance. It was usually more polished, sophisticated women who drew his attention. Riley Foster didn't look as if she spent any time at all on her appearance. She didn't wear makeup. Her hair looked as though she'd hacked it off herself with scissors. And she didn't smell like any manufactured aroma that came out of a bottle. No, he'd had plenty of time in the taxi to try to put a name to her scent, and the closest he could come was spring. An image slipped into his mind then, one that he'd invented as a child. Riley Foster reminded him of the elfin creatures his Aunt Rachel had spun endless stories about when he was growing up.

His hand stilled as he dropped the razor into his travel kit, and he faced himself in the mirror. It wouldn't do to dwell on his memories of Aunt Rachel and how he'd failed her. The nightmares that had been plaguing him since his injury only grew worse when he did.

"Concentrate on the case," he said to the man who stared back at him. It was his ticket to salvation. Riley Foster was just another assignment. The robberies were merely another puzzle to solve. And he knew how to remain objective, detached. He'd spent his life honing that particular skill.

Moving back into the bedroom, he dropped his shaving kit into his duffel bag, then went to his dresser and found his gun. When that, too, was packed, he pulled the zipper closed.

The kitten immediately opened its eyes, stood up and scrambled over to his bag.

"Faker," he said as he scooped it up and strode out of the room.

KNOW YOUR ENEMY. Riley wasn't sure who'd said it first. Shakespeare probably. Either that or someone in the Bible. And, surely, a man's apartment should reveal something about him. But at first glance, Jack DeRosa's apartment hadn't told her squat. Frowning, she took a second look. The furniture consisted of a couch, a chair, two end tables with lamps, a coffee table and a TV. There were no bookshelves, no magazines scattered about, no clutter whatsoever. The place was as anonymous as a motel room.

Moving to the end of the room, she spotted the CD player sitting on a cabinet. One of the chairs had blocked her view. Squatting down, she glanced over the albums lined up neatly on shelves. There had to be over a hundred, she guessed. Jack DeRosa liked classical music, jazz and blues. The fact that her own taste ran in the same direction gave her a moment's pause. It wouldn't have occurred to her that she could have anything in common with him.

Rising, she headed toward the kitchen, which was separated from the living area by a counter and two stools. *Two*, she mused. Did that mean he entertained an occasional guest? A woman, perhaps? The idea made her pause again—because she didn't like picturing a woman seated on one of those stools, laughing at something Jack DeRosa was saying, and leaning closer....

Get a grip, Foster! She didn't care one bit about who Jack DeRosa entertained on his stools. He wasn't, he couldn't, be someone she was interested in that way. He was the enemy. And she had to get to know him. Walking purposefully toward the cupboard, she began to open them one by one. There were matched sets of everything—dishes, glasses, even the silverware in the drawer matched. She wondered if it had all come with the apartment. Opening a door under the counter, she found a few staples: cans of soup, tuna fish, sugar and coffee. Very few staples. Where were the cookies? With a sigh, she stood up. This was proving to be a decidedly unfruitful little exercise. So far she knew that he shared her taste in music and he liked his coffee with caffeine. Sherlock Holmes might be able to make something out of that, but it stumped her.

The refrigerator had to reveal something. *We are what we*

eat. She couldn't blame that little nugget of wisdom on Shake-speare. She could lay it at the door of Daryl, the health food nut she'd dated in college for about two weeks. And she didn't doubt for a moment that he was right. With her hand on the door of the fridge, she paused. Then hoping for the best, she pulled it open.

Nothing. The light was on, the motor was running, but the shelves were absolutely bare. Desperate, she jerked open the door of the freezer, then breathed a sigh of relief when she saw the quart of chocolate ice cream. Her relief faded the moment she realized that it was not only her favorite flavor, but her favorite brand as well. What was she supposed to make of that? she thought as she stared at it. Know your enemy because he's like you?

"If you're looking for jewelry or money, you're out of luck."

Riley jumped, then whirled. "I didn't hear you."

"I can see that. Just what were you doing poking around in my freezer?"

His face was grim. So was his tone. And his eyes... To escape that penetrating gaze, Riley turned and busied herself with closing the cupboard doors, wincing as she caught her hand in one of them. "I didn't..." She paused to extract her hand. "I wasn't..."

"You most certainly were. A lot of people hide their money and their jewels in the freezer. Burglars are well aware of that."

Riley felt the heat flood her face. Usually she took the time to count to ten when her temper rose. Not this time. Striding around the counter, she stood toe to toe with Jack DeRosa. "I am not a burglar. I have never stolen anything from my clients." She wanted very much to poke him in the chest, but he had the kitten tucked under his arm, and she didn't want to frighten it. "And I'll have you know that I would not steal anything from your freezer. Not even a taste of my very favorite ice cream. So…'' Once again she stifled an almost overpowering urge to poke him. ''So…there!''

''What were you doing in my freezer then?''

''I was looking for clues…something about you.'' She threw up her hands. ''And there aren't any.''

''You didn't find anything?''

''Nothing except we like the same music and the same kind of ice cream.''

''That's something.''

Riley shook her head. ''It has to be a fluke. We're not anything alike. And there should be more…stuff here. This place is so anonymous. There's no clutter.''

''I'm neat.''

Her eyes narrowed suddenly. ''You're laughing at me.''

''No.''

This time she did poke him, aiming well away from the kitten.

Abra hissed and gave a little screech.

''Hush,'' Riley said, giving the kitten a stern look. ''This is between him and me.'' Then returning her gaze to Jack's, she continued. ''Your mouth may not be laughing, but your eyes are.''

''I'll…'' He paused to clear his throat. ''I'll try to keep them under control.''

Riley bit down on the inside of her cheek to keep from smiling. The amusement that shone so clearly in his eyes was contagious. This close, she could see that his eyes were gray, a smoky color that turned lighter when he was amused. Even as she watched, the color seemed to darken, just like she'd seen the sky darken before a storm. The air seemed to change, too, just as it might in those breathlessly still moments before lightning crackled across the sky. Suddenly, she was aware of how close she was standing to him. Their bodies were nearly brushing, just as they had when she'd first bumped into him on the sidewalk. Heat. She could feel it now just as she had then. It was coming from him…or was it coming from her? She could certainly feel it moving through her, radiating from her center downward and outward. It was different from what she'd felt before. This was edgier, hotter. Her gaze dropped to his mouth. His lips were narrow, masculine. They wouldn't be soft—when they pressed against hers—they would be hard, demanding—

Not *if,* but *when.* It was the significance of her word choice that finally penetrated the little fantasy she was losing herself in. She wanted Jack DeRosa to kiss her. She wanted it enough to let it happen, maybe even enough to make it happen. Before she let herself seriously entertain that option, she took a quick step back. This time her whole body felt as if she'd backed away from a flame. She could practically feel the smoke in her lungs.

"Well," she said, trying to gather her scattered thoughts. His eyes told her nothing except that he didn't seem to be amused anymore. Well, he could have had a really good laugh if she launched herself at him and kissed him. He probably would have laughed for days.

"Shall we go?"

"Sure," she said. But she didn't move. She didn't trust her legs yet. *Stall,* she told herself. "Just one more thing. I thought you said you could cook."

"I can."

"Your kitchen contradicts you."

Jack didn't say anything for a moment. "I haven't cooked lately."

Riley's eyes widened. Of course, he hadn't cooked lately. His leg. She recalled the pain she'd seen in his eyes more than once. "I'm sorry. Of course, you haven't. I didn't mean… I'm usually not so insensitive."

The ringing of her cell phone put a halt to her babbling apology. Whoever it was, she was going to hug them, she thought as she hurried over to her duffel bag and pulled out her phone. "Foster Care... Winnie? No, I'm not at the police station. Yes, I spoke with Captain Duffy. Well, I haven't exactly been cleared."

Jack was at her side, his hand over the mouthpiece of the phone before she could blink. He spoke in a whisper. "Remember, I'm your new assistant. Nothing else."

"She just wants to know if I've been cleared," she whispered back. "Surely, I can tell her—"

"Tell her you can't talk right now. You'll call her back later."

The moment he removed his hand, she said, "Winnie, I don't want to talk about this on the phone. I'll stop by right after I make my afternoon rounds, okay?... See you soon." Tucking the phone away in her duffel, she turned to Jack. "This might be a good time to tell you that I'm not very good at lying. I think I can handle telling everyone that you're my new assistant. Winnie has been after me to hire someone because my brother Ben has been taking a film class and he hasn't had much time to help me out lately. She worries about me like she's my grandmother. And as soon as we get to her place, she's going to want to know everything that went on in Captain Duffy's office. I don't like lying to her."

"Then stick to the truth as much as possible."

"So I can tell her I haven't been cleared. I'm still under investigation."

"The problem with that is that Markham and Carmichael won't be bothering you or them anymore. So she's going to start wondering who's doing the investigating. If she's a smart lady, it's not going to take her long to suspect that I might be that person. And then my cover is blown."

Riley thought for a moment. Everything he said made sense. "Okay, what do we tell them?"

"You can stick pretty close to the truth. The best liars always do that. Tell everyone that since the police haven't been able to find any hard evidence to connect you to the burglaries, they're pursuing other leads. Can you do that?''

"Sure. It's the truth in a way, isn't it?"

"In a way."

Riley studied him for a moment. "You're really good at what you do, aren't you?"

"I try."

Great, she thought to herself. A smart cop was just what she needed while she was carrying around stolen loot in her duffel bag!

3

"WE'LL JUST drop off your bag," Riley said as she twisted her key in the lock. "But we'll have to take Abra with us. I don't trust either Beowulf or the Bard with her."

Jack searched his memory of her file and drew a blank on the names. "Beowulf and the Bard?"

"A dog and a bird. Their previous owners passed on, and I couldn't let them go to an animal shelter. Uncle Avery says, that's it—no more pets." She slanted him a look as she opened the door. "It's a good thing that Abra's taken a shine to you."

"Now wait just a minute. I don't do pets."

"She's only a kitten," Riley pointed out as she led the way into the foyer.

A series of barks punctuated by some other noise that Jack couldn't quite identify distracted him from making a reply. Then a huge mound of canine fur came barreling down the hallway, leapt up on Riley and sent her crashing into him. He grabbed her shoulders, then teetering, he stepped back into the wall and managed to keep them both balanced as both his bag and her duffel slid to the floor. The kitten was out in a flash, streaking down the hall with the dog in hot pursuit. Riley grabbed his hand, dragging him with her as she raced after them. "We have to save her."

In the kitchen, a cacophony of sounds greeted their ears. Above it all, one voice was making itself heard.

"Alas, poor Yorick!"

After a quick scan of the room, Jack decided that the large

bird cowering on the top of his cage was the one squawking Shakespearean quotes—although his first guess had been the tall, elderly man. Dressed in a red velvet robe and wearing his mane of hair swept back from his forehead, he looked every inch the seasoned actor that Alexandra had described Riley's uncle to be in the file. Three sharp staccato barks erupted from the mountain that had attacked Riley in the foyer, but the hissing and screeches emanating from the kitten who had taken up residence on the kitchen table seemed to be holding both the bird and the dog at bay.

In the brief beats of time that weren't filled with the din of barks, screeches and squawks, he could just make out the laughter of the tall, young man who was leaning against a counter, nearly doubled over with mirth. He had to be Riley's younger brother.

Abruptly, the dog stopped barking, gave one whine and dropped its paws from the table. The boy broke out into a fresh wave of laughter as the kitten turned and screeched at the bird.

"Out, out, I say!" squawked the bird.

Then except for the laughter of the boy, and one final whine from the dog, silence descended on the room.

Avery Foster pointed a dramatic finger at Abra. "That kitten cannot stay. I told you, no more pets. You are turning this place into a menagerie!"

"She's not going to stay, Uncle Avery," Riley said, going to him and giving him a quick hug. "I'll have a home for her in a few days. I promise. And once I open the Foster Care Pet Center, I know that someone will see Beowulf and the Bard and want to adopt them."

"Right," Avery said, rolling his eyes and waving his hand. "Everyone in New York City wants a mutt the size of a small horse and a bird who slaughters Shakespeare every time it—"

"Alas, poor—" the Bard began.

The kitten let out an ear-piercing screech, and the bird squawked, flapped his wings and subsided.

"That kitten is awesome," the boy said. "He's got the Bard and Beowulf totally freaked out." Then he turned to Jack. "And who are you?"

"This is my new assistant, Jack DeRosa," Riley said.

Jack found himself pinned by two pairs of eyes. He read curiosity in the boy's, assessment in the older man's.

"Thought you were dead set against hiring anyone," Avery said, keeping his gaze on Jack.

"I didn't think I could afford anyone, but Mr. DeRosa is in need of a place to stay, and we were thinking about renting out the guest room. So I made him an offer he couldn't refuse."

Avery's eyes swept toward Jack, his gaze narrowed. "Do you have any references?"

"Captain Duffy vouched for him," Riley said. "He was visiting the captain when I dropped by the station."

Avery turned back to Riley with a frown. "Why were you at the police station?"

"There was another robbery. Hattie Silverman, this time. Captain Duffy asked me to stop by."

"Because they suspect you." Avery began to pace. "You need a lawyer. Someone to protect your rights." Pausing, he pinned Jack with another look. "Perhaps you can talk some sense into her, Mr. DeRosa."

"I—" Jack found himself at a loss for words.

"The sense we have to worry about is dollars and cents," Riley said in a very calm, matter-of-fact voice. "I'm not going to dip into Ben's college fund to hire a lawyer. Besides—"

"We live in a litigious society!" Pacing to the counter, Avery whirled, his hand raised, his red robe flowing out from him. "Everyone needs a lawyer!"

"And I won't need that money if I don't go to college," Ben said. "I don't need a degree to become a filmmaker."

"You're going to college first," Riley said. "That's the plan. And then you can become a filmmaker."

"That's your plan. Uncle Avery didn't have to go to college to learn how to act."

"Whoa!" Avery threw up his hands. "Hold it right there. I told you that I won't be dragged into the middle of this particular family feud."

Ben turned to Jack. "What about you? Did your family make you go to college?"

"No," Jack said. Immediately a memory filled his mind—his Aunt Rachel urging him to take the money she'd saved, arguing that he could go to the police academy after he'd earned his degree. The pain cut through him, as fresh and sharp as it had been on the day of her funeral. Before he could add anything to his curt denial, Ben turned to Riley.

"I want you to use my college money to hire a lawyer."

"I'm not touching it," Riley said. "And besides, I found out today that the police are going to pursue other leads. They can't find any concrete evidence to connect me to the burglaries."

"That's great news, Sis," Ben said.

Avery turned to Jack. "And how did you happen to be visiting the good captain?" Avery asked.

"My father and Captain Duffy go way back. They fought in Vietnam together." Jack said. It was the truth and it fit perfectly into the story that he and Riley had come up with on the way to the apartment. He hoped it would be enough to convince Riley's uncle, who, in spite of his flair for the dramatic, had very shrewd eyes.

"I notice you're favoring that leg," Avery said.

"Car accident," Jack explained. "Since I'm on disability, I thought it was a good time to seek my fortune in the big city."

Avery had his mouth open to ask another question when Riley edged her way between them, hands on hips. "Uncle Avery, please. This isn't the third act of your play. And you are not really Sherlock Holmes."

"On the contrary," Avery said with a wave of his hand, "if this play of Harold's gets enough backers to open, I *will* be Sherlock Holmes."

Riley took a step forward. Her uncle took a step back. "How long have you been after me to hire an assistant? Do you want to run him off before he even starts?"

"I'm Ben," said a voice at Jack's elbow. "And don't mind my uncle. He tends to make a scene out of everything. Isn't he amazing?"

Jack turned his attention from the discussion Riley was having with her uncle to the young man standing at his side. He was taller than his sister, but he had her coloring, except for the eyes, which were a lighter shade of blue. "Yes. And I don't mind. He's just concerned about your sister. You got anything you want to ask me?"

"She said you were going to live here?"

"That's the plan," Jack said.

"Do you cook?"

"A little." Riley had asked the same question, he recalled, and he noted that her brother's eyes lit with anticipation just as hers had at his answer.

"Spaghetti?" Ben asked.

"I can do that."

"Did I hear spaghetti?" Avery glanced over Riley's head to meet Jack's eyes.

"He can cook it," Ben said, his enthusiasm clear in his voice.

"With meatballs?" Avery asked.

Suddenly, Jack became aware that he had the undivided attention of everyone in the kitchen. The three humans along with the dog, the kitten and the bird were all looking at him as if he had been sent to lead them to the promised land.

"Sure. I can make meatballs."

"He's not cooking on his first night," Riley said. "We have to give him time to settle in. Besides, it's my turn to cook tonight."

"I'm getting together with Jeff and Henry this afternoon," Ben said. "We're going to be up all night at Jeff's house studying for a big math exam."

"Isn't it Jeff's turn to come here?" Riley asked. "I wanted to talk to you later."

"His mom's making lasagna," Ben said, then turned to Jack. "Maybe you could make spaghetti tomorrow?"

"Yes, Saturday's excellent," Avery said. "I won't be meeting my friend Harold until around nine." To Riley, he said, "I'm on my way over to Harold's now. We're working on the third act, and I'll be staying over." Then he turned back to Jack. "Welcome aboard."

"Yeah," Ben said, flashing Jack a grin as he followed his uncle out of the kitchen.

"Nothing clears the place faster than the news that I'm cooking," Riley said.

"Is it really that bad?"

"Worse. But theirs isn't much better, and I, at least, make an effort to eat whatever they're serving."

"Why don't you hire a cook?"

"Can't afford one."

"Your uncle has an apartment on Park Avenue, and he doesn't have the money to hire a cook?"

"No. He made a bad investment." Riley turned quickly away, but not before Jack saw the laughter drain completely out of her eyes. She glanced at her watch. "And we won't even be able to afford groceries if I miss getting the Zimmermans' St. Bernard out for his walk on time. C'mon."

Jack frowned thoughtfully as he followed Riley out of the

apartment. She was definitely not what he'd pictured in his mind when he'd first read her file. And she wasn't the only Foster who might have a motive for stealing from her clients. Avery needed backers for his play, and Ben could certainly use money if he wanted to begin a career as a filmmaker. And then there was the apartment. Even if it was rent controlled, it would take some money to maintain the place.

It was during the ride down in the elevator that Jack realized something. He didn't want Riley Foster to be guilty.

"YOU'VE GOT yourself one gorgeous hunk of an assistant, sweetie."

Glass jars lined the counter, and Winnie Cantrell selected a pinch of leaves from one, a full teaspoon from another and dropped them into a teapot. Late afternoon sun slanted through her kitchen windows lightening her peach-colored hair by about three shades. She brewed tea with all the concentration of a scientist in a lab. Finally, she whirled to face Riley, her navy chiffon caftan billowing out around her.

Sabrina, the senior citizen witch, Riley thought.

"I want to know all about him," Winnie said.

Resigned, Riley climbed onto one of the stools across the counter from her friend. Winnie had whisked her off to the kitchen the moment she and Jack had arrived at the apartment, leaving Jack to be entertained by the three other women in her bridge club.

"Well?" Winnie prompted.

"We met in an alley. He...helped me rescue a stray kitten," Riley said.

"How romantic!"

Riley didn't view Jack DeRosa as romantic. He was becoming more and more of a threat. For one thing, she hadn't been able to stop herself from thinking about what had almost happened in his apartment. She'd wanted to kiss him. And nothing that had happened during the course of the afternoon had pushed the idea out of her mind. Not even when he'd taken charge of her duffel bag. She'd set it down on a park bench for just a second so that she could tie the lace on her sneaker. And the Zimmermans' St. Bernard had chosen that particular moment to break away and race after a squirrel. By the time she'd caught him, Jack had her bag slung over his shoulder. It was the least he could do, he'd said, since he hadn't been much use in chasing down the St. Bernard. And he still had it. At any minute he could find the evidence that would put her behind bars, and she still wanted to kiss him!

"He reminds me of my second husband, a truly splendid specimen," Winnie said as she sprinkled fennel seeds into the pot. "No money. But of course, I had plenty of that from husband number one. I was ready for a more physical kind of relationship."

"My relationship with Jack DeRosa is not what you're thinking. He's a…" Riley bit down hard on her lip just in time to keep herself from blowing Jack's cover. "He's just my assistant. I hired him because he's good with animals. The stray kitten he helped me rescue has already bonded with him."

"Sounds to me like that stray's got better sense than you do."

"You of all people know that I don't have time for a man right now. I need every second I can find if I'm going to open up the Foster Care Pet Center by the end of the year." Saying the words out loud was helping, Riley discovered. By the time she had to walk back into Winnie's living room and face Jack, she wouldn't be thinking about kissing him anymore.

"My offer still stands. I'll lend you the money and you can open up tomorrow."

"And my refusal still stands. If the business goes under, it will be only *my* money that's lost."

"You aren't your father. You're not responsible for what he did."

"And I don't intend to repeat his mistakes. I won't use other people's money."

Winnie squeezed Riley's hands before she released them. "Okay. I'll quit lecturing you on that topic. But you're going to have to learn that you need help in this world. Everyone does. Now tell me more about your assistant. I thought you couldn't afford one. What made you change your mind?"

Riley was prepared for this question. It was one she'd been expecting Winnie to ask since they'd entered the kitchen. "Because he's new in town, he's willing to take room and board as part of his wages."

"He's living with you? And here I was giving you advice about fitting a man like that into your life." Moving around the counter, Winnie gave her a big hug. "I take back what I said about that stray having more sense than you." Then drawing back, she said, "This is the start of something good. I felt it when I read the tea leaves this morning, and the call I got from the police commissioner only confirmed it."

"What did he tell you?" Riley asked.

"That since the police didn't have one shred of evidence to connect you to the burglaries, they'd decided to pursue other leads." Interrupted by the shrill whistle of the teakettle, Winnie turned back to the stove. "You've got to be so relieved. And then to have the good luck to run into Mr. DeRosa! This is your lucky day!"

Riley tried to control the little bubble of panic in her stomach. It could turn out to the worst day of her life. If Jack DeRosa discovered that brown paper bag in her duffel... Right now he could be slipping his hand into it. She could picture those long, lean fingers closing over the bag, lifting it... Clearing her throat, she said, "Winnie, I need to tell you something. You're the only person I can trust."

"Ask me anything, my dear. After seven husbands and

I'm not really sure of how many lovers—I never did keep track, not like some women I know who actually carved notches in their bedposts—anyway, there's not much that I'm not aware of. So go right ahead. Shoot.''

"This isn't about men," Riley said. "It's about the burglaries.''

"But you don't have to worry about that anymore.''

"Yes, I do. This morning when I went to clean out my duffel bag, I found a brown paper bag with a brooch in it. I have no idea how it got there. I thought of turning it over to Captain Duffy, but he said that the only reason they hadn't arrested me was because they didn't have any hard evidence to connect me with the stolen jewels.''

"What kind of brooch? Can you describe it?" Winnie asked.

"I'm pretty sure it's Hattie's. It has one diamond in the center with a spray of smaller diamonds around it. I think I've seen her wearing it.''

"Yes," Winnie said with a sigh. "It sounds like hers. I was afraid of this.''

"What?" Riley asked, studying Winnie closely.

"It was my dear godchild, the police commissioner, who started me thinking. He told me if I really wanted to help you, I should make a list of who else the thief might be. But I didn't have to make a list. Hattie popped right into my mind.''

"No." Riley shook her head. "That's just not possible. Besides, she doesn't need the money.''

Winnie leaned closer, dropping her voice as she said, "The only money she has is her social security check. And Hattie Silverman isn't her real name. She changed it when she was released from prison.''

Riley stared at Winnie. "Hattie was in prison?''

Winnie nodded and pitched her voice even lower. "Fifteen years ago, I met her at a halfway house one of my charitable foundations was running, and I invited her to live here in my building. She used to rob banks with a man who had mob connections. His name was Louie 'the Rock' Mancuso, but she always called him Rocky. Needless to say, he was a bad influence on her, and he was released from prison four weeks ago. That's when the burglaries started, right?"

Riley nodded.

"He called her right after he got out. Just that one time, I think, and she's been acting oddly ever since."

"Maybe she's just depressed because he hasn't called again."

"Or," Winnie's voice dropped to a whisper, "maybe he's trying to pull her right back into a life of crime. You remember what they did to Michael Corleone in *The Godfather?*"

Try as she might, Riley couldn't picture a less likely mobster than Hattie Silverman. The woman walked with a cane and was forever nodding off to sleep. "She's gone straight all these years and, besides, she's not very mobile. How did she get herself over to Cora Simpson's apartment? It's ten blocks away."

Winnie sighed again. "We took a taxi to Cora's for lunch on the Monday she was robbed."

Riley shook her head. "Hattie would never steal from you or Gert or Prue. She wouldn't want to hurt you."

Winnie waved a hand. "She knows quite well that we're not going to be hurt financially if she swipes a few of our baubles."

"Even if you're right, it doesn't explain how or why her brooch ended up in my duffel bag."

Winnie leaned even closer to Riley. "She knew that I was calling the police commissioner and she was afraid with you out of the picture, the police would start suspecting her. She panicked!"

Riley took Winnie's hands in hers. "I think you're wrong."

"There's one way to find out," Winnie said. "You sneak that brooch back into her apartment and then we'll see what she does. If she suddenly announces that she's found it, then you're right—she's innocent. But if she tries to plant it on you again, then we'll know she's the jewel thief."

Riley opened her mouth, and then shut it. She knew better than to argue with Winnie once she got something into her head. Besides, her suggestion had some merit. What better way to get rid of the pin than to return it to its owner?

"Okay," Riley said. "I'll try to get it back to her tonight."

"Good girl. Need any help?"

"No. I think I'd better handle it alone."

After giving her a conspiratorial nod, Winnie hefted the tea tray and led the way through the swinging door.

"WOULD YOU LIKE more tea?" asked the woman introduced to Jack as Winnie Cantrell. There was something about the way she looked in that swirling navy blue outfit that made him think of a witch. And she'd insisted on preparing one of her special healing teas the moment she'd noticed he was limping. As an act of kindness, it hadn't fooled Jack for more than the amount of time it had taken her to request Riley's help in the kitchen. It was a technique cops used all the time. Isolate the suspects and question them separately. If Riley wanted to come clean with Winnie Cantrell, she'd had her opportunity.

"No thank you," Jack said. "I'm still finishing this."

Winnie peered into his cup and made a tsking noise. "It won't work its magic unless you drink up."

Feeling a little like a child who hadn't cleaned his plate, Jack took another sip. In addition to dried grass and licorice, he detected a hint of dill.

Winnie gave him an approving nod before she fluttered on to her next victim.

There were plenty of them seated in the parlor. From the

moment that Winnie and Riley had disappeared into the kitchen, he'd been surrounded by the three other ladies who belonged to Winnie's bridge club. The fact that they each resembled their dogs was the only way he'd been able to keep them straight.

Hattie Silverman, a tiny birdlike woman with silver hair was the quietest of the group, mainly because she nodded off to sleep every few moments. She had the smallest dog, too, a Chihuahua named Baby. Both of them were presently taking a snooze. Gert and Prue Fielding were twins. They had positioned themselves in the wing-backed chairs that flanked him on either side. Both were built along the same stocky lines as the bulldogs named Frick and Frack who had settled at their feet. But the personalities of the two women were as different as night and day. Gert was a grump who alternated between shoving her glasses up on the bridge of her nose and complaining about anything her sister brought up in the conversation. Prue never seemed to take offense, and Jack was beginning to wonder if anything disturbed what he suspected was a permanent smile on her face.

He realized with a start that Prue was presently beaming at a spot just past his left shoulder.

"If you don't like that tea, I'd be happy to invite you over to my place," she said, batting her eyelashes in his general direction. "I make a wicked pot of coffee."

"Ha!" Gert said. "It'll be wicked, all right. There's no telling what she'll put in it. She's blind as a bat without her glasses."

Jack lifted his cup. "The tea is fine."

"Attaboy," Gert said. "I like a man who can hold his tea."

Winnie Cantrell, in contrast to her friends, was tall and slender. She was also a cat person. And the animal didn't look anything like her. It was huge and black, the kind of cat one might expect to find riding on the back of a broomstick, and it was appropriately named Beelzebub. Jack guessed that it could have taken on both bulldogs and won easily. Right now, it was on the back of the sofa, its paws only inches away from his shoulder.

He recalled from the file he'd read that each one of the women was a client of Riley and each had been victimized by the burglar. To judge by the hugs they'd lavished on her when she'd arrived, none of them believed she was the jewel thief.

"I imagine you're feeling a bit like Alice at the Mad Hatter's tea party." Riley pitched her voice so only he could hear it as she sat down on the arm of the sofa next to him.

Jack bit back a smile.

"Have another cookie. It helps to take the edge off the tea."

Jack glanced down at his cup. "Do I dare ask what's in it?"

Riley grinned. "Winnie doesn't give away her secrets, but I suspect eye of newt."

"I was afraid of that." Jack slanted her a look. "How'd it go in the kitchen?"

She shrugged and glanced away. "She doesn't suspect you're a cop."

What wasn't she telling him? he wondered as he took another sip of his tea and wished for one of the pain pills that he'd left in his bag at Riley's apartment. He hadn't allowed himself to take one for over a week now, but the pain in his leg hadn't eased even though he'd been sitting down for over half an hour. Before they'd dropped in for tea at Winnie's, they'd finished Riley's afternoon rounds, gathering up five dogs for an afternoon walk, then delivering them back to their homes. All the walking on top of the run down the alley was going to cost him sleep tonight. Jack was sure of it. With his palm, he rubbed the side of his thigh.

"We can leave soon," Riley said.

Chimes rang, and Winnie hurried down the hall to answer the door accompanied by all three dogs and the cat. The moment the voices drifted in from the foyer, Riley stiffened.

"Problem?" Jack asked softly.

"No, not really."

The blond man who followed behind Winnie had preppy good looks, and the moment he spotted Riley, he crossed immediately to her side.

"How is everything?" he asked, taking her hand. "I've been so upset ever since Aunt Winnie told me the police suspected you in these robberies. Why didn't you return my calls?"

"I've been very busy," Riley said.

The young man frowned. "I want to help. Please let me."

"I've taken your advice and hired myself an assistant," Riley said. "This is Jack DeRosa. Jack, this is Winnie's nephew, Charles Cantrell."

Jack rose and extended his hand, forcing Charles to free Riley's. The handshake was brief, Charles's grip firm, and the moment it was over, he had his hand back on Riley's arm. Jack could have sworn that Riley stiffened again. He was considering his options when Winnie floated over.

"Has Riley told you her good news?" she asked. "She's finally hired an assistant."

"We've met," Charles said.

"Well, I haven't met him."

Jack turned to watch a slender blonde move toward them.

"Ah, here you are Christina," Winnie said. "I thought you were right behind me."

"I had to make a quick phone call. What did I miss besides meeting Riley's assistant?"

"She's no longer a suspect," Winnie announced. "The police have finally come to their senses."

"What? What happened?" Hattie asked, coming out of her

nap and shooting up from her chair. "What did I miss? Was there another burglary?"

In the ensuing deluge of explanations in which Riley's status as a suspect faded more and more with each retelling of the phone call Winnie had received from the police commissioner, Jack learned that Christina was Charles's sister and that he and Riley had dated a few times. And Charles wanted to date her again, Jack decided when he noticed that the two of them were heading up the hallway to the foyer.

"Yes, I'll make sure that Frick doesn't get himself involved with any designing females in the park," Jack said to Gert, who had been lecturing him on the care and feeding of her bulldog. Privately, he wondered if anyone would be able to stop Frick once he put his mind to something. Certainly, nothing seemed to stop Gert from rattling on and on about her pet. Desperate, he flashed her a smile. "My boss is on her way out the door. I don't want to lose my job on the first day."

Gert gave him a sly wink. "Well, we certainly wouldn't want that, would we?"

"But I haven't had a chance to tell him about Frack." Prue reached out to lay a hand on Jack's arm and missed.

Gert grabbed her sister and steadied her. "Down, girl! We don't want the man to get fired."

Just as he stepped free of the twins, Hattie blocked his way. Studying him with a puzzled frown, she asked, "Have I introduced you to Baby?"

"Yes," Jack said as the Chihuahua bared its teeth at him.

"He doesn't seem to remember you," Hattie said. "Perhaps he was asleep."

"Watch it," Gert said with a frown. "That dog is a real man hater."

Baby barked just as Winnie took his arm and ran interference for him as they headed down the hall. One thing was becoming clear to him. Caring for people's pets involved caring for the owners as well. He'd developed a new respect for Riley Foster during the course of the past hour. It faded the moment he and Winnie arrived in the foyer and saw Riley kissing Charles Cantrell.

What he felt then was a mix of emotions, but one feeling hit him like a blow, leaving him slightly disoriented. For some reason he couldn't quite grasp, he felt like grabbing Charles Cantrell and slamming him into the nearest wall.

"DAMN!" Riley said the moment she stepped out onto the sidewalk.

"What is it?" Jack asked.

"I wish I was more experienced at handling men." As they started toward the corner, she made the mistake of glancing at his face. It had the same unreadable expression that it had had when she'd managed to ease herself out of Charles Cantrell's arms in Winnie's foyer. She had no idea what he was thinking, but the fact that he'd seen her kissing Charles had made her see what a mistake it had been. "You must have had a lot of experience with women."

"What?"

His expression had gone from unreadable to incredulous.

"Don't worry," she said. "I'm not asking for details. I don't suppose it would help much anyway. Handling women must be different than handling men. I think there should be a course you could take in it. Or some kind of way you could hook up with a mentor. Maybe you could give me some tips."

"You and your dad never talked about it?"

Riley shook her head. "He was always at the office or off giving a seminar on investments. His business always came first. Not that I think that was a bad thing. I put my business first, too. It's probably in my genes. And that's why I shouldn't have let Charles kiss me."

"Why did you then?" he asked as they paused at the corner for a light.

"Because he'd just asked me for another date, and I had to say no. I've tried to explain that I don't have time for a relationship right now. But I could tell he was hurt, so I let him kiss me."

"That was stupid."

"Thanks," she said dryly. "It's always nice to have one's self-diagnosis confirmed." Out of the corner of her eye she was almost sure she saw his lips curve. She wasn't sure why, but her mood suddenly lightened. When the light turned, she led the way across the street so that they could walk back to her uncle's place along the edge of Central Park. A cool evening breeze carried the scent of lilacs and magnolias. At six o'clock, the traffic had thinned, and even most of the pedestrians had gone home. It was one of her favorite times of the day.

"Why did you go out with him if you don't have time for a man in your life?"

"Pressure. He's Winnie's nephew, and she was pushing it. Haven't you ever felt you should do something simply to please the people who care about you?"

"No."

She turned then to find him looking at her, and in the split second before he glanced away, she was sure that she saw pain in his eyes.

"You and Winnie Cantrell are pretty close," he said.

Riley nodded as they paused again for another traffic light. "She and her bridge club ladies are the reason I was able to build my clientele so quickly. Once they started using me, they spread the word to everyone they knew. I owe them all a lot."

"I take it they're all very well off."

"I always assumed so. Though it's hard to tell really. Winnie was just saying…'' Letting her sentence trail off, she turned to face him. ''Why are you asking?''

''I'm doing my job. If you're not the jewel thief, then someone else is.''

''Not one of them,'' she said firmly. But mentally she was kicking herself. She'd let herself forget for a moment that he had a job to do. And it might very well include tossing her in jail. Or maybe it was Hattie Silverman that he'd arrest. Somehow she had to make sure that neither of those scenarios came to pass. But how? Now that she had a cop as a shadow, how was she supposed to get the jewels that could convict her back into Hattie's apartment? The second the light changed, she stepped off the curb. She didn't see the taxi trying to race the yellow light until it was too late. Suddenly an arm gripped her hard and yanked her backward. She felt a rush of wind push at her as the taxi raced past and then suddenly she was lying on top of Jack on the sidewalk, trying to catch a breath around the fear that was still lodged in her throat.

The grunt he made as he shifted her off him told her that he was in pain. She scrambled to her knees, concern shoving away the fear that had paralyzed her. ''Are you all right?''

''It's just this damn leg,'' he said, grunting again as he sat up. Two pedestrians walked by, giving them a wide berth. ''I must have twisted it.''

''Let me help you up,'' she said taking his arm.

''I can manage. I just need a minute.''

''I'm sorry,'' she said as she watched him massage his thigh with one hand. ''I didn't look before I stepped off the curb. I know better. If you hadn't grabbed me…'' Acting purely on instinct, she put her arms around him and hugged him close. ''Thank you.''

In the few seconds her cheek rested on his, she was aware that his skin was scratchy with the growth of a day's beard. His scent was a mixture of soap and sunshine and something undeniably male. Then she felt his arm wrap around her, and the desire moved through her to stay where she was—to hold and be held. When she tried to pull back, she felt his hand move to the back of her neck.

"This is a bad idea," he said.

Their faces were so close she could feel her skin heat and then chill as his breath moved over it. She couldn't seem to take her gaze off his mouth. Bad idea or good, she wanted him to kiss her. She'd been wondering about it—even when she'd been kissing Charles.

She wasn't sure who moved, but suddenly his lips brushed against hers. The contact was broken almost instantly, but not before a wave of heat shot through her.

"A very bad idea," Jack murmured. But his grip on her remained firm.

More. She wasn't sure whether she said the words aloud or merely thought them, but his lips pressed against hers again, and this time they didn't withdraw. His mouth was warm and impossibly soft, offering a sharp contrast to the hard press of his fingers against the back of her neck. There were other sensations, too—a flood of them. She heard the sound of a horn, a snatch of laughter from a passing car, and the thud of her heart growing faster with each beat. She tasted the flavor of Winnie's tea and the hint of something darker and much more unsettling just beneath it. And there was heat—rushing through her, melting her, draining away her thoughts and any secrets she might have.

Secrets. She had plenty of them that she didn't want him to know! She drew back at the same moment that he did. But neither one of them spoke. Lord help her, she wanted to kiss him again. He was a cop, she was his prime suspect, and sitting right next to him was a bag containing the evidence that would convict her. What was she thinking?

"You're right," she said. "It was a very bad idea. Now that we know, I don't think we should do it again."

She watched something flash in his eyes, and for a moment she was sure he was going to kiss her again. She wasn't sure what shocked her the most—the thrill that raced through her or the disappointment she felt when he merely said, "You know what they say about knowledge? A little is a very dangerous thing."

When he shifted away and got to his knees, Riley was very careful not to touch him again. Instead, she used the opportunity to grab her duffel and sling it over her shoulder. He winced the moment he put his weight on his leg.

"Don't you have something you can take for the pain?"

"I packed some pills in my bag. They just make me sleepy."

While they waited for the light, a plan formed in Riley's mind. She knew exactly how she was going to manage to get the brooch back in Hattie Silverman's apartment.

4

RILEY STARED at her reflection in her bedroom mirror. The woman who stared back at her didn't look like a criminal. But she was. She'd just drugged a cop.

Lifting her hands, she saw they were still shaking, just as they had been when she smashed up one of Jack DeRosa's pain pills and stirred it into his tomato soup. She'd nearly dropped the bowl when she'd carried it to the table.

And he'd eaten every drop. He'd even complimented her on the thyme she'd crumbled into it.

That's what had really gotten to her. No one had ever complimented her on her tomato soup before. And it was one of her safest recipes—open the can, add water. She hadn't even known what she'd crumbled into it. She'd just grabbed something from the spice drawer, hoping to hide the taste of the pill.

He'd mentioned again how much he'd enjoyed it right before he'd passed out on the couch.

That hadn't been part of her plan. He was supposed to get gradually sleepy and decide to lie down on his bed. Instead, he'd fallen asleep on the couch in the library, a room that opened off the foyer. Only one thin door would separate her from him when she slipped out of the apartment. She'd taken the precaution of putting the animals in her room, so if they went at it again, Jack wouldn't wake up.

"Out, out, damned spot," the Bard said.

Riley managed to tear her gaze away from her hands to stare at the bird. She hadn't heard him say anything since

Abra had arrived. And now he was back to quoting from Lady Macbeth's sleepwalking scene. How appropriate! "What are you, psychic?"

"Out, out, damned spot."

She frowned at him. "It's not the same thing at all. I didn't kill him. I just drugged him." Even as she said the words, she imagined repeating them in front of a judge. If Jack DeRosa ever figured out she'd doctored his soup, he was going to lock her up and throw away the key.

He'd certainly never kiss her again. And it had occurred to her as she'd sat across the table from him, listening to him compliment her cooking, that she very much wanted Jack DeRosa to kiss her again—and again. She sighed. No one had ever made her feel that way. In her head, she knew perfectly well that not only was the idea of kissing Jack DeRosa again bad, but it was absolutely impossible. A smart woman should not want to kiss a cop who was investigating her. That was tantamount to sleeping with the enemy.

Not that there was going to be any more kissing now that she'd drugged him.

"What other choice did I have?"

The Bard stared solemnly back at her from his cage.

Beowulf whined sympathetically, but he didn't lift his head from her pillow. "Don't get too comfortable," she warned him with a frown. "As soon as I get back, you're going back to your own bed in the kitchen."

From her position at the bedroom door, Abra let out a screech. She'd been emitting them like clockwork since Riley had shut her in. "Shhh," Riley said, moving quickly to squat down in front of her. "I know you want to be with him." She could sympathize far too well with the feeling. "But I have to get those jewels back to Hattie Silverman's apartment before anyone discovers that I have them."

Abra let out a very loud screech.

Riley raised her hands in a gesture of surrender. "Okay, I

hear you. But if I let you out, you have to promise not to wake him up.''

The kitten stared back at her in silence.

''Okay.'' Rising, she twisted the door handle and let the kitten out. Then she turned back to Beowulf and the Bard. ''Sometimes it's like that. Love at first sight.''

The noise Beowulf made sounded suspiciously like a snort.

''Great,'' Riley said, throwing up her hands. ''Of all the animals in the world, I'm stuck with a love-sick kitten, a cynical dog and a parrot who thinks he's psychic.'' Then she took a quick look at her watch. Nine-thirty. It had taken her longer than she'd thought to round up the animals, and she didn't know how long the pain pill would keep Jack sleeping. Pressing a hand against the butterflies that were whipping around in her stomach, she hurried toward the bathroom. One quick pit stop and she'd be on her way.

THE STENCH of garbage nearly smothered him as he moved forward, peering into the darkness. There was no moon, and the streetlights couldn't penetrate this deep into the alley. The gunshot still echoed in his mind, but there was no sound now. And nothing he could see. He broke into a run. But the heat pressed against him, slowing his movements. He had to be in time. Then suddenly, he saw two shadows darker than the others—two men locked together, struggling. Stopping, he raised his gun, steadying it with both hands. But he couldn't shoot, not until he could tell which man was which. Out of the corner of his eye, he caught the movement and pivoted toward it.

The knife slashed down and pierced him in the side. As the pain burned through him, he discharged his gun, saw the flash of fire as the weapon slipped out of his hand. The sound was still ricocheting through his mind when the knife plunged into him again, ripping through his flesh. Another shot pierced the silence. He was too late, he thought as the blackness swallowed him. Too late.

Struggling for air, Jack sat straight up. Then he began to shiver uncontrollably. Glancing around, he concentrated hard on the details. Experience had taught him it was the quickest way out of the dream. All he could hear was the sound of his own ragged breathing. And his vision seemed blurred, his mind fuzzy. Shutting his eyes, he opened them and tried again. Drawing in a deep breath, he caught the scent of old leather and lemon wax. A small lamp sat on the table beside him, its light softened by a leaded-glass shade. Gleaming wood floors framed a faded carpet. The wall in front of him held shelves of books.

He was in the library of Riley Foster's apartment. It had been the last room she'd shown him when she'd taken him on a brief tour after dinner.

He must have fallen asleep on the job. He'd never done that before. Frowning, Jack glanced around the room again, trying to remember exactly what had happened when Riley had brought him here. After the abuse his leg had suffered during the day, he'd resigned himself to a sleepless night. That was why he'd lingered in the library. A good book would keep him occupied until everyone was asleep and he could search the place. Since there was no method to the way the books had been arranged on the shelves, he had browsed for a while before selecting one.

The movement of the library door swinging open had his muscles tensing. He was halfway off the couch when he registered the kitten. It skidded to a stop and rolled over. Then righting itself, it dashed into the room and leapt onto the coffee table in front of him.

He met its gaze directly. "I don't do kittens."

Undeterred by either his tone or his glare, the kitten made its way slowly forward, then leapt to the cushion beside him.

"You don't give up, do you?" he asked, frowning down at it.

The kitten inched closer until it could settle against the side of his thigh.

"Stupid," he said. But he ran one finger down the scrawny bundle of bones and fur. Riley had been right about one thing. It had definitely begun to bond with him.

The thought of Riley had him frowning again and glancing at his watch. Nine-thirty. They'd finished dinner at about eight, and after she'd taken him on a quick tour of the apartment, they'd settled in the library. She'd claimed she had at least two hours of book work to catch up on.

His gaze moved to the desk tucked into one corner of the room. The last time he recalled glancing up from his book, she'd been hunched over a ledger, scribbling away. The house had been quiet just as it was now. All he could hear was the occasional scratch of her pencil on the paper or the sound of a page being turned. He recalled feeling peaceful, the way he had as a child in his home. And he'd begun to feel drowsy.

Opening his eyes, he realized that he'd leaned his head back against the couch. He was feeling drowsy again. He never felt this way unless...

As the suspicion grew in his mind, he levered himself up off the couch and tested his weight on his bad leg. There was a twinge, nothing like the pain that had been plaguing him earlier in the evening.

He hadn't taken a pain pill because he'd known that it would make him sluggish and sleepy, just the way he'd felt right before he'd dozed off, and just the way he was feeling right now. It didn't take his years of experience as a detective to figure out that she'd drugged him. He'd told her he had pain pills in his bag; he'd even confided that they made him fall asleep—right after he'd kissed her.

The kiss had not only been a bad idea, it had been a huge

mistake. He was a cop. It went without saying that he couldn't get involved with a suspect. And yet, he'd kissed Riley Foster. He'd been attracted to her almost from the first. But the moment he'd accepted the case and discovered that she was the prime suspect, he'd known he could never act on that attraction. That should have been that. After all, he'd been attracted to women before and not acted on it.

Yet he had with Riley. Why? he wondered as he headed down the hallway toward the kitchen. Oh, he'd told himself it was to get her out of his system. But maybe it was because she was…different?

She was *different* all right. She'd snuck under his guard and dosed him with his own pain pills! When he reached the kitchen, not only was there no sign of Riley, but there was no sign of the dog or the bird, either.

For one brief second, he felt a skip of panic move up his spine. But he quickly dismissed the idea that she'd flown the coop. He hadn't known her long, but she was loyal. She'd never leave her brother or her uncle. Suddenly, he found his lips curving. If she had by some chance taken off, she wouldn't get far with that mountain of fur and a bird that shouted lines from Shakespeare every few minutes.

He glanced longingly at the coffeepot. She'd filled it after dinner, and he was tempted to turn it on. But first, he and Ms. Riley Foster were going to clear a few things up. He was turning to leave when he felt the kitten rub up against his leg. "Why don't you lead the way?"

His own bedroom was at the very far end of the hall, but that wasn't the one that the kitten led him to. The moment he opened the door, he caught her scent. It reminded him of the flowers his aunt had brought home whenever she could. The dog and the bird stared at him silently as he and the kitten entered the room. He felt the same little skip of panic that he'd experienced in the kitchen. Had she stashed Beowulf and the Bard here so that she could take off and…?

Behind the closed door of the bathroom, he could hear the water running. She was still here.

A breeze was pushing her bedroom curtains out from the window, and the sounds of traffic drifted up from the street below. The room had originally been decorated for a man, Jack guessed. The furniture was dark wood with clean, spare lines. A sofa and a chair were upholstered in navy and white stripes that matched the spread. Still, Riley Foster had left her unique stamp on it. The walls were filled with photos of animals in colorful frames, some professionally done, some candids. He recognized the three dogs he'd met at Winnie Cantrell's apartment that afternoon, along with their owners. And then there were the pillows she'd tossed carelessly on the bed and the sofa, each in a different shade of the rainbow. The room was incredibly neat, nothing out of place, no litter on the dresser. He inspected the drawers, one by one, and found the same neatness inside as out. Nothing was out of place.

Then he spotted the duffel bag on the far side of the bed. Though he'd carried it half the afternoon, he'd had no chance to inspect it until now. Lifting it to the bed, he unzipped it. Immediately, Abra leapt onto the bed, and Beowulf scrambled up from where he was resting on the pillow. The dog immediately stuck his nose into the bag again, snuffling around until he finally pulled something out.

"Something's rotten in Denmark," the Bard said.

Beowulf dropped what was in his mouth and stuck his nose back into the bag. This time, he retrieved a plastic packet of treats. Abra raced to his side, but Jack's eyes never left the brown paper bag that the dog had discarded on the bedspread. Sticking halfway out was what looked like a brooch. When he lifted it, a rainbow of color shot against the wall.

He was staring at it when he heard Riley open the bathroom door and step into the room. Looking up, he asked, "Do you want to explain this?"

She said nothing. But as he watched, her eyes grew huge, her skin paled and she slid silently to the floor.

"COME ON. Snap out of it."

The voice came from far away. And she was aware of a hand at the side of her face. Sighing, she turned her head.

"Attagirl. Come on. Open your eyes."

The voice was deep, familiar and so persuasive. She did what it asked and found herself staring up at Jack. His face was close. She must be dreaming about that kiss. And any minute now she would relive those feelings that he'd stirred up in her, the heat, the quick spiraling of desire. Only the sun wasn't beating down as it had been before. But the heat was the same, and she wanted more than anything to bring his mouth down to hers. It had to be lust she was feeling. Pure and wonderful, she thought as she lifted a hand to his shoulder to bring him closer.

"Am I dreaming?" she asked.

"No."

"Even better," she said on a sigh.

"You fainted."

She blinked and the memory came flooding back—Jack standing there next to her bed holding Hattie's diamond brooch in the palm of his hand. She squeezed her eyes shut, praying that the whole thing had been a dream. But when she opened them, he was still leaning over her. "I'm still alive?" she asked.

"I'd say so."

"My whole life just passed before my eyes. I thought you were supposed to die after that."

The corners of his mouth lifted. "Apparently not. Why don't we see if you can sit up?"

"Aren't you going to handcuff me first?"

"You don't look like you're in any shape to make a run for it," he said as he gripped her shoulders and settled her so that her back was against the side of the bed and he was sitting next to her.

"You're probably wondering about that diamond brooch."

"Yeah."

She shook her head. "You're never going to believe me."

"Why don't we give it a try. We'll start with something simple. Does it belong to you?"

Riley thought for a moment. In spite of the fact that she'd spent the day with Jack DeRosa, searched his apartment, kissed him, doped him with pain pills and lusted after him, she really didn't know that much about him. Except that he was neat. Frowning, she tried to think of something else. He said he could cook. Winnie and the ladies in her bridge club liked him. He'd been good with the animals. Turning, she saw that Abra had settled herself in his lap. Clearly, the kitten had fallen in love with him. Balanced against that was the fact that he was a cop. And he'd just discovered the evidence that would connect her to the burglaries.

"Just tell me the truth," Jack urged her in that deep voice that had coaxed her out of her faint.

"No, the brooch doesn't belong to me. It belongs to Hattie Silverman."

"I believe you. See? That was easy."

"Okay, try this. I didn't steal it. And I don't know how it got into my duffel bag."

"Something is rotten in Denmark," the Bard said.

Riley drew away from the bed to glance over her shoulder at the bird. "He thinks he's psychic." When she turned, she found Jack studying her closely, his expression unreadable. "You don't believe me, do you?"

"What I need is some coffee." His eyes narrowed. "And you could probably do with a shot of brandy. Do you keep any?"

"I don't have time for…"

"Yeah," he said as he set the kitten on the floor, then got

to his knees. The moment he winced, she scrambled into a squat and grabbed his arm to help him. "You stay put," he said. "I don't want you fainting again."

"But your leg—"

"My leg's much better," he said as he got to his feet. "Those pain pills you slipped me really did the trick."

As she rose, Riley felt the color rush to her face. "You know?"

"A good cop always knows when he's been drugged."

AND A GOOD COP should also know when he was being lied to. But as he watched Riley Foster wrinkle her nose and take a cautious sip of the brandy he'd just poured her, he realized that he was afraid to trust himself on this one.

And rightly so. He'd always prided himself on his ability to keep his emotions locked away when he was on a case. But his feelings had been involved from the moment he'd seen her cornered in that alley. That had to be part of the reason he felt this almost overwhelming need to protect her.

He wanted to believe her, and that was interfering with his objectivity. Hell, the truth was, he just plain wanted her. As much as he didn't intend to act on the attraction between them, it was there, tugging at him when he least expected it. He'd wanted very much to kiss her when she'd come out of that faint. He'd wanted to touch her. Hell, he'd wanted to cover her body with his and take her right on the floor of her bedroom. And she'd wanted it, too. He'd seen it in her eyes. And when she'd touched his arm to pull him down, he'd very nearly given them what they'd both wanted. Lifting his mug, he drained the rest of his coffee and crossed to the table to sit down across from her. It was high time he started thinking and acting like a cop.

She shivered and made a face as she swallowed another sip of the brandy.

"You're supposed to enjoy that stuff," he said.

She shook her head. "It always reminds me of medicine. When I was little, I had an Irish nanny who used to smash up my pills in a mixture of whiskey and sugar. It was almost enough to turn me completely off alcohol."

"I can understand that. I'm never going to feel quite the same way about tomato soup again."

Color stained her cheeks. "I'm sorry about that. I was hoping you wouldn't figure it out."

"Why did you do it?"

She met his eyes then. "I have to get that brooch back into Hattie's apartment."

"Why?"

"It's complicated."

Rising, Jack moved to the counter to pour himself another cup of coffee. He had a feeling he was going to need it. "It'll save time if I don't have to figure it out for myself."

Riley took another sip of the brandy. "Winnie thinks that Hattie is the jewel thief."

"Isn't Hattie the one with the Chihuahua who uses a cane and drifts off to sleep?"

"Exactly."

"She's not exactly prime suspect material."

Riley leaned forward. "I don't believe it, either, but she's an ex-con. And her old bank-robbing partner was just let out of jail about a month ago. She has the means, the opportunity and a motive—she needs the money."

As Jack listened to Riley explain the plan she and Winnie had come up with to sneak the brooch back into Hattie's apartment, he began to get the same sensation as he had at Winnie Cantrell's apartment—that somehow he'd fallen down a rabbit hole.

"So I was going over there tonight to put the brooch back and to take a look around to see if she had any of the other jewels. There might even be some evidence that she's seeing this Rocky person."

Jack studied her for a moment. None of this interesting background on Hattie Silverman had been in Alexandra's file. "That is just about the most implausible story that I've ever heard in my life, and I've heard quite a few."

She met his eyes without blinking. "It's the only one I've got."

Setting down his mug, he stood up. "Okay, let's go."

"Oh." She sat perfectly still, staring at him.

He took her arm to help her to her feet.

"But…I'll have to leave a note with some instructions for Uncle Avery and Ben."

"Why? They're both out for the evening."

"I have clients. Someone has to take care of their pets while I'm in jail."

Jack stared at her. "I'm not taking you to jail. I'm going to help you put the brooch back in Hattie Silverman's apartment."

"You are? Then you believe me?"

"Let's just say I believe in good police work. The best way to find the real thief is to eliminate the suspects one by one. We can start with your friend Hattie."

"YOU'VE GOT A PLAN, I presume," Jack said as they arrived at the apartment building that was home to Winnie Cantrell's bridge club. Through the glass doors, he could see that, at ten-thirty at night, the lobby was well lit and a uniformed security guard was reading a book behind the desk. He spotted a security camera on the far wall.

"Sort of," Riley said, using her key on the outside door.

The moment the guard glanced up, a wide smile brightened his features. "Good evening, Ms. Riley. That advice you gave me about my grandson's dog worked like a charm."

"I'm glad, Tommy." Walking quickly to the desk, she said, "I want you to meet my new assistant, Jack. Jack, this is Tommy Nesbitt."

"I didn't expect you to be back so soon. I imagine Ms. Cantrell is in bed by now."

Riley leaned on the edge of the desk. "I'm not here to see Winnie. I promised Hattie that I would stop by and put some drops in Baby's eyes. She's afraid she'll forget, but she didn't want the other ladies to know. I know you won't mention it to them. Hattie is so sensitive about the fact that she forgets things."

Tommy's grin spread even wider as he winked at Riley. "I won't breathe a word. I'm getting a little sensitive about that myself. You want me to ring her that you're on your way up?"

Riley shook her head as she headed for the elevator. "If she's sleeping, I'd rather not wake her. I can be in and out, and she can get a good night's sleep."

Jack waited until the elevator doors closed and they were speeding upward before he said, "That was smooth." In spite of those innocent eyes and her words to the contrary, she was a good liar. It wouldn't do to forget that.

"I hate lying. I'm always sure that my nose is going to shoot out a mile in front of my face, or that I'm going to go cross-eyed checking to see if it has."

He couldn't prevent a smile. "For someone who hates it, you're very good at it."

"You think so? I guess the talent runs in my family."

Jack watched in surprise as the amusement faded abruptly from her eyes. Before he could press her to explain, the elevator door slid open and she was leading the way down the hall. He caught up just as she inserted the key into what he supposed was Hattie's door. "Maybe you could fill me in on the 'sort of' plan?"

She turned to him then. "Are you good at searching a place?"

His brows rose. "I've had some experience."

"I'm going to try and get the brooch into Hattie's bedroom. Winnie's sure that's where she kept them. While I'm doing that, you look around and see if you can find any of the other stuff that's been stolen.''

It occurred to him as she opened the door that nothing they found would be admissible in court. Not that he really expected to find anything. He'd barely shut the door behind him when teeth bit into his ankle.

"Damn!" he grunted.

There was a growl somewhere near his other foot, and the teeth struck again.

"Something's biting me," he said as he ran his hands along the wall and flipped the switch.

There was Baby, two feet away and poised to leap in for another taste. Jack leapt first, and came down hard on his bad leg. "Get that thing away from me," he managed as he felt his knee buckle and his shoulder crashed into the wall.

Riley dropped to her knees. "Baby, it's just Jack and me."

Baby barked, racing a few feet away, then pivoting on a dime and streaking back.

"Shhhh," Riley said, holding out her hands. Baby skidded to a halt, sniffed her fingers frantically, then turned on Jack and began to bark again.

A light went on at the end of the hall. A cane thumped on the floor. "Who is it, Baby? Who's there? Is that you, Rocky?"

Baby raced down the hall at the sound of his mistress's voice.

"Rocky…? All right, whoever it is, I've got a gun."

Jack heard the unmistakable sound of a rifle being cocked. "She really has got a gun." Reaching behind him, he opened a door with one hand and grabbed Riley's arm with the other. The cane thumped closer. Baby skidded out of a doorway he'd disappeared into, slid into a wall, bounced off and streaked toward them.

"We're getting out of here." Dragging her with him, Jack

stepped backward. The moment he shut the door, he realized that they were trapped in a closet. Baby was barking. He hit the door with a thud and began scratching. The cane was getting closer.

"Quick!" he said, pulling her with him as he pushed clothes aside and burrowed to the back. Every inch of the floor was covered with boxes of various sizes. Finally, he found a space for them between a row of clothes and the back wall.

"Are you all right?" she whispered.

Jack realized that the only reason he could hear her above the din was because she was standing on something and so close that her cheek was pressed against his and her mouth was right against his ear. Of course his body was way ahead of his brain in coming to this realization, and every single part of it had hardened. He made an attempt to set her away, but discovered they were really wedged in.

In some part of his mind, he was aware that a mad woman with chronic memory loss and a loaded rifle was bearing down on them. The rest of his mind was totally focused on the fact that he couldn't go another minute without kissing Riley.

"I think I'm going to sneeze," she whispered.

Turning his head, he covered her mouth with his. She didn't sneeze, and she didn't protest. Impossible as it was, she seemed to press even closer as if she were melting into him. And then her taste poured into him—the tart-sweet flavor only deepening as it warmed. She was so soft, so pliant. He felt her breasts yield against the hardness of his chest. Even as he slid his hand between them to touch her, he told himself to stop. He had to, and he should have been able to. But her arms were around him, her lips parted. Through the thin fabric of her sweater, he could feel her heart beat in rhythm with his.

And then all he knew was that he was drowning, in sensations, in longings, and he'd lost any desire to save himself. For a moment, as the blood pounded in his brain, he forgot everything except that he could have her now. As the power streamed through him, he shifted her against the wall.

Just then, the closet door opened, and the barking of the dog shattered the fantasy he'd conjured up in his mind, replacing it was a grim memory of the kind of damage a rifle could do to the human body. He held Riley close, hoping to shield her with his body.

"Quiet, Baby! Quiet, I say!"

Baby barked one more time and then whimpered.

"There's no one in this closet. Where would they fit? There's nothing in here but some old clothes and the letters Rocky sent me from prison. See! You can't even find a way in. Come on."

Baby whimpered again.

"Stop crying, and come back to bed. I need my sleep. Even on a good day, I'm starting to forget my own name. Pretty soon I'll be forgetting yours."

The closet door clicked shut.

It was only as he took a breath that Jack realized he'd been holding it. He thought he could hear the thump of the cane growing fainter, but he counted to ten before he moved.

"Come on," he whispered as he drew Riley with him. As quietly as they could, they made their way out of the closet. The hall was deserted, but they could hear the Chihuahua's nails scratching for traction on the wooden floor. The instant Baby started barking, Jack jerked open the apartment door, dragged Riley out and shut it firmly behind him.

Neither of them spoke until they'd reached the safety of the elevator and he'd pressed the button. What could he say? Jack thought as the car descended. For a few minutes, he'd forgotten everything. He'd very nearly taken her in a closet. Hell, he'd lost his mind! When he heard Riley's gurgle of laughter, he turned to stare at her.

"I'm sorry. I…just couldn't hold it in one second longer." Then she doubled over as a fresh wave of mirth overtook her.

His eyes narrowed. What was the matter with her? She'd been as involved in that kiss as he had. "You think it's funny?"

"I forgot she had a shotgun."

"You *knew* she had one?"

Riley took a deep breath and leaned against the wall for support. "She hangs it over the bed, but she doesn't keep any ammunition. She's a pacifist."

"She could have fooled me." But as he watched her clamp a hand over her mouth to smother a laugh, he couldn't prevent his own lips from curving. "That explains why you didn't take her out with your water pistol."

The moment their eyes met, Jack couldn't prevent the chuckle from escaping. An instant later their laughter filled the elevator. They were still struggling for control when they arrived in the lobby. Waving helplessly at Tommy, they hurried to the door and let themselves out onto the sidewalk.

"It's kind of sweet that Rocky's been writing to her from prison all these—" Suddenly, Riley stopped short.

"What is it?" Jack asked.

"The brooch. We didn't… We have to go back."

"No way," Jack said, taking her arm and urging her up the street. "Even if the gun is a sham, the teeth on that Chihuahua are very real!"

5
―――――

IT WAS BARELY DAWN. But through the kitchen window, Jack could see that the sky was going to be clear. Hopefully, he could get his mind to follow suit. He'd spent a restless night, drifting in and out of dreams. His nightmare hadn't returned. Instead, he'd been plagued with fantasies of how he'd like to finish what he and Riley had begun in Hattie Silverman's hall closet.

Frowning, Jack pushed the thought out of his mind just as he had countless times during the night. He hadn't mentioned it when they'd returned to the apartment, and neither had Riley. She'd merely wished him a good night and hurried off to her room. Finally, at three, he'd given up on sleep altogether and done what he should have been doing instead of breaking into that apartment—his job. He'd searched as much as he could of Riley Foster's apartment.

He'd found no sign of any more jewels, but he'd learned quite a bit about the Fosters. Avery Foster was a pack rat. He saved everything from old playbills, fan mail, and reviews to love letters from his various conquests over the years.

Ben was a movie buff. He had an enviable videotape collection. And scribbled on bits and pieces of paper taped to the walls and shoved into drawers were notes that resembled a screenplay in progress.

Yawning, Jack watched the first rays of sunlight sneak their way above the horizon. Normally, this was his favorite time of the day. But he needed caffeine. Shifting his gaze, he shot the coffeemaker an annoyed look as it continued to drip a little too lazily for his liking. He needed a lot of caffeine.

Nothing he'd learned about Riley had surprised him. She was scrupulously organized about her business. A map above her desk in the library had the locations of her clients circled in red and various routes for walking dogs traced in blue. Two duffel bags lined up next to the desk each contained identical items: clients' addresses, plastic bags filled with pet food, sets of keys and water pistols. Even her ledger was organized, and, from what he could tell, they were living on what she brought in with her pet-care service. Aside from Ben's college fund, there was no indication that any of them had any savings or any investments.

With a sigh, Jack leaned against the counter as the coffeepot sputtered and spit the last drops into the pot. The night had been a complete bust. He hadn't found any jewels, and he hadn't been successful in figuring out what he was going to do about the attraction he felt for Riley Foster.

It was different from anything he'd ever felt before. Hell, *she* was different. He'd never before come so close to losing control as he had in that closet. Grabbing a mug from a nearby hook, Jack filled it. The first sip scalded his tongue, and he welcomed the pain. He had to start thinking rationally again.

He could not afford to make love with Riley Foster. In his mind, he replayed the reasons. First of all, he had to focus on the job. Secondly, she just wasn't the kind of woman a man could have a romantic fling with. She would want more than that. She deserved more.

And he wasn't the kind of man who could give it to her. People who'd depended on him in the past had met with incredibly bad luck. He felt a sudden pressure on his ankle and winced. Glancing down, he pinned the culprit with a stern look. "Careful, Abra. That's where Baby sank his teeth into me."

And Hattie and her Chihuahua were another problem. He didn't have a chance of searching that apartment as long as Baby was guarding it. And until he could do that, he wasn't sure just how much credence he should give to the possibility that Hattie Silverman or her old boyfriend Rocky were involved in the burglaries. He made a mental note to stop by the precinct and see what he could find out about Louie "the Rock" Mancuso.

Just then, Abra rubbed against his ankle again.

"Ouch, I told you my ankle's sore."

"You should…see a doctor," Riley mumbled, squinting at him, as she made her way into the kitchen. "Get it…ouch," she muttered as she stumbled into the table, "…checked."

"I told you last night, it's fine. I had a tetanus shot two months ago, and I doused it with antiseptic." She was fully dressed in her usual uniform of jeans, T-shirt and denim jacket. But her eyes were barely open, and she was weaving a little as she made her way toward him.

"Coffee," she murmured, stretching out her arms and patting her hands along the counter in search of the pot.

Jack snagged a mug, filled it and wrapped her fingers around it. "You're not a morning person, I take it."

"No." After taking a sip of her coffee, she looked up at him through one eye. "But you are."

At their feet, Abra screeched.

Jack glanced down at the kitten. "Why is she lying there like that with her paws up in the air?"

Riley squinted down at the kitten. "She wants you to scratch her. When they roll over that way, it's a sign of trust. And the way she was rubbing up against you before, means that she's marked you as hers."

"No way," Jack said, but he crouched down and began to rub the kitten's belly. "Cats must be really dumb."

"No," Riley said as she aimed herself at the refrigerator.

"They actually have an IQ surpassed only by monkeys and chimpanzees." Opening the freezer, she extracted an ice cube and dropped it into her mug. Coffee sloshed on her hand. "Ouch."

"Why don't you go back to bed?"

"Can't." She swallowed more coffee and managed to get the other eye open. "Saturday mornings are busy. I have five dogs to walk, and...," she made her way to a chair, sank into it, and sighed, "an appointment with a contractor at ten."

"A contractor?"

"He's going to take a look at the space I've rented for the Foster Care Pet Center and give me an estimate."

"What happens then?" Jack asked.

"I read it and weep," Riley said, making a face. "When I'm through crying, I'll sit down and figure out how many more clients I need to take on in order to sign the papers and get started."

"Couldn't you borrow the money to start up with?"

"I tried. Banks frown on lending money to a person who is one year out of college with no background in business."

"What about your clients?"

"No," Riley said firmly. "If my business goes under, I'm the only person who is going to lose her life savings."

He studied her as she drained her mug, then turned to face him. She still had to make an effort to focus.

"Do you want breakfast? Eggs...or something?"

His brows rose. "Not if you're cooking."

"Funny," she said as she rose and moved toward him, extending the mug for a refill.

As he poured, he noticed how the first slant of morning sunshine lightened the tips of her hair. It was sticking out every which way as if some man had just run his hands through it—the way he wanted to right now. Setting the pot down, he shoved his hands in his pockets. Maybe it was time he settled the matter.

"I've been thinking about what happened last night," he said.

She blinked and when she met his eyes, he could see that she was still struggling to focus. "Last night…? That's right. I forgot. We have to get that brooch back to Hattie."

"No," Jack began.

"Oh, you don't have to come. In fact, I don't think you should. I couldn't guarantee that Baby wouldn't bite you again. He's usually so well behaved."

"That's not what I was talking about," Jack said. "I was referring to what happened in Hattie's closet."

"Oh," Riley said.

Jack frowned. Looking into her eyes had the strangest effect on him. "I don't want you to get the wrong idea."

"About what?"

"I shouldn't have kissed you."

As her eyes cleared, she shifted them to his mouth. His own gaze slid to her lips. They were parted, still damp from the coffee she'd just sipped. If he kissed her now, he would taste it, and her. Desire crawled through him as he realized just how much he wanted to kiss her again right now. She was sleepy enough, he was skilled enough, that he could have her out of those clothes and make love to her before either of them could think of all the reasons not to. His mind filled with the image of taking her right in the splash of sunlight on the kitchen floor. Even as the fantasy played out in his mind, she moved closer and put a hand on his chest.

The kitten let out a screech, and he stepped back against the counter. "No."

He saw the pain that one word brought to her eyes before she dropped them. It was for the best, he told himself. It would be better for them both if he hurt her. Because he wanted more than anything to touch her, instead he leaned down to pick up Abra.

"Look, I have a job to do. I want to get it over with as quickly as possible so that I can get back to work. And you have a job, too. It would be better for both of us if we straightened out this matter with the jewels as quickly as possible without any added complications."

"Yes, of course." This time she backed up a step. "You're right."

Damn! He was almost sure he saw her lower lip tremble. And her hand was shaking as she set her mug down. He felt as if he'd just kicked a small, defenseless animal. Abra's tongue moved against his wrist, but it gave him small comfort.

"There's cereal in the pantry," Riley said as she walked away.

It was best to let her go. Even as he thought it, he was halfway across the kitchen with his hand on her arm. "Riley, that didn't come out the way I wanted it to."

She faced him then, her chin lifted, her eyes clear. "It came out fine. But it would be better if you didn't touch me anymore. Every rational thought goes out of my mind when you do."

A buzzer sounded, and someone began to pound on the apartment door.

Riley started down the hall. "Who could that be?"

The buzzer sounded again, and the pounding paused. "Open up. It's the police."

Pushing his way past Riley, Jack strode to the door, opened it and found himself facing Alexandra Markham, Detective Carmichael and two uniformed cops.

Alexandra looked him over, raising her brows when she noticed his feet were bare. Then she gave Riley the same thorough inspection. "Did we wake you?"

"You've got a warrant." It wasn't a question. Jack could

see by the look in Alexandra's eyes that they did. Carmichael pulled it out of his pocket and handed it over with a flourish.

Jack didn't move. Instead, he opened the warrant and looked it over. "Does Captain Duffy know about this?"

"He got it for us," Alexandra said. "And now we have a search to make."

He stepped back then, drawing Riley with him as the little parade filed past them. Then he spoke very softly. "Where's Hattie's diamond pin?"

She patted the pocket of her denim jacket. "Right where I put it last night."

He slipped his hand into the jacket and removed the brooch. Then he unzipped the front of his jeans and slipped it inside.

"What are you doing?" Riley whispered.

"I'm putting it where none of those cops will be patting me down."

"But why?" she asked. "If they find it, your job here will be over. You can go back to work. That's what you want, isn't it?"

He met her eyes then. "Yeah. But I don't like their timing."

She gripped her hands tightly together. "I should be at the Zimmermans' right now. How long do you think they'll be?"

"It's going to take them an hour or two." Steering her back into the kitchen, he picked up her mug and handed it to her. It was only then that he noticed how pale she looked. Quickly, he urged her into a chair. "Don't you dare pass out on me again."

She took a sip of her coffee. "I won't. It's just that if they arrest me, what's going to happen to Ben and Uncle Avery? Who's going to take care of all the pets?"

He took her free hand and squeezed it. "You don't have anything to worry about. They're not going to find anything."

"You seem pretty sure of that," Alexandra said as she entered the kitchen.

"I am," Jack said, dropping Riley's hand and turning to the detective. "I've searched the place. And I'd like to know what the hell is going on."

Her brows rose. "It's pretty straightforward. We're executing a search warrant."

"Ms. Foster agreed to let me work undercover with the understanding that she wouldn't be harassed. She had Duffy's word on that."

"There was another robbery last night," Alexandra said.

"Where?" Riley asked.

"In this building, two floors down." Taking a notebook out of her purse, she flipped it open. "Mr. and Mrs. Abernathy were at the theater. They left at seven-thirty and returned shortly before midnight."

Jack studied Riley. Her knuckles were white where they were gripping the mug.

"The Abernathys claim that you regularly let yourself in and out of their apartment to care for their dog when they're out. Is that right?" Alexandra asked.

"Yes," Riley said.

"Were you in their apartment last night?"

"No."

Alexandra moved closer, pulling out a chair and sitting so that she was facing Riley. "Can you account for your time between seven-thirty and midnight?"

"I was here in the apartment until about ten when I went out for a while." Riley's hand shook as she set the mug on the table.

Alexandra scribbled in her notebook. "Where did you go?"

"I…" She paused to glance at Jack, then continued. "Detective DeRosa and I went out for about an hour."

Alexandra glanced at Jack, her brows raised. "You went out with her?"

"That's right," Jack said. "I'm Ms. Foster's assistant, and we paid a visit to a client in Ms. Cantrell's apartment building. You can verify that with the doorman who signed us in and out. After that, we came back here at around midnight and Ms. Foster retired."

"What about earlier? Can you account for every minute of her time?"

Jack frowned. "All of it except for about a half hour when I fell asleep."

Turning to Riley, the detective said, "That would have given you time to go down to the Abernathys and take the jewels."

"I didn't go down there."

"What jewels were stolen?" Jack asked.

Alexandra shot Jack an annoyed glance. "A diamond pendant and earrings. Mrs. Abernathy had decided not to wear them at the last minute because the catch was loose. She claims she left them on the dresser. It would have taken only a few seconds to pocket them and leave."

"I didn't steal anything," Riley said.

Alexandra turned to her. "We've dusted the bedroom for prints, and we'd like to get a set of yours. If there's no match, we can eliminate you."

"You don't have to agree to do it, Riley," Jack said.

Furious, Alexandra whirled to face him. "I want to talk to you in private."

"Fine," he said, leading the way into the hall.

Struggling to pitch her voice low, Alexandra said, "You're interfering in my investigation, Jack. What the hell are you thinking?"

"I'm just trying to save you some time. There are all kinds of reasons why her prints might be in that apartment. A smart lawyer will get any match you might find thrown out at a pretrial hearing.''

''Not all attorneys are smart. Just whose side are you on, Jack?''

''I want to find out who the thief is just as much as you do, Alexandra. I just don't think that all the facts are in, and if you arrest Ms. Foster too soon, the real thief may get away with it.''

''You want to know what I think?'' She raked him up and down with a glance. ''I think you've gotten too close to this case.''

A dog began to bark. Footsteps pounded down the hallway as a uniformed policeman raced toward them. ''Detective Markham, there's a problem. We opened one of the bedroom doors and something flew at Detective Carmichael.''

''The dog...did he attack Carmichael?'' Alex asked.

''Beowulf would never hurt anyone,'' Riley said, as she joined them.

''No,'' the officer explained. ''The hound came running out afterward. I think it was some kind of bird, and it was yelling at Carmichael to get out.''

Riley led the way down the hall with the policeman behind her. Just outside her bedroom door, Beowulf, barking at the top of his lungs, had two men cowering against the wall.

''Beowulf,'' Riley called softly. Immediately, the dog quieted and moved meekly to her side.

''Out, out, damned spot!'' The Bard's voice bellowed from the bedroom. ''Out, out, damn spot!''

''See?'' the officer said. ''Whatever it is, it talks.''

Detective Carmichael eased himself away from the wall. ''Damn thing flew right at my face.''

Jack struggled to suppress a laugh. Across from him, he saw Riley draw in a shaky breath. He quickly looked away.

Abra chose that moment to screech.

Beowulf whined and sank to the floor.

"Out, out, damned spot!" the Bard bellowed.

"What on earth is that?" Alexandra asked. But she didn't step closer to the door.

"It's a parrot," Carmichael muttered in disgust. "This place is a zoo. That damn bird wouldn't let me in the room."

Still careful to keep his eyes from meeting hers, Jack said, "Riley, why don't I give you a hand moving the animals into the kitchen? Then," he turned to Alexandra, "I'll help you with the search."

A HALF HOUR LATER, Riley was in the kitchen pacing back and forth. The three animals tracked her progress with their eyes. The police weren't going to find anything, she told herself. But no matter how many times she said it, she couldn't seem to stop worrying. For the first half hour, she'd called her clients and explained that she was running late. Then she'd washed the coffee mugs, cleaned the sink and polished the faucets. Finally, she'd made a fresh pot of coffee. It was only then that she'd allowed herself to pace. As she had the last three times that she'd passed it, she stopped and looked at the phone. She wanted very badly to call Jeff's house and talk to Ben. But what she wanted to ask him couldn't be said over the phone. What she wanted to ask shouldn't be said at all!

How could she possibly ask her brother if he'd been in the Abernathys' apartment last night?

Pausing, she lifted her hand to rub at her temple where a headache had started to pound. But try as she might, she couldn't get rid of the image of Ben leaving to go to Jeff's with one of the duffel bags that he regularly used to carry his books.

When the phone rang, she jumped. After drawing a steadying breath, she reached for the receiver. "Hello?"

"Are you all right?" Winnie asked.

"I'm fine. But the police are here. They're executing a search warrant."

"I know. The police commissioner just called me to let me know. We're on our way over in a taxi right now."

"Who's we?" Riley asked.

"Hattie, Gert, Prue and myself."

"Winnie, I don't think it's a good idea," Riley began.

"My godchild said there'd been another robbery. Where?"

"At the Abernathys'. They live two floors down from me. They were robbed some time between seven-thirty and eleven-thirty last night."

"When did you take care of that little errand we talked about?" Winnie asked.

"Errand?" Riley asked.

"I told you we're *all* here in the taxi and we'll *all* be there in a few minutes. Remember the errand we talked about in the kitchen yesterday?"

It finally dawned on her that Winnie was asking if she'd returned Hattie's brooch. "We didn't get to leave it there," Riley explained.

"We?" Winnie asked.

"Jack came with me. He...I..." Riley frantically searched her mind for some way to explain the fact that she'd told Jack about the brooch. She couldn't tell Winnie that he was working undercover. She had to think of something.

"I'm so glad you confided in him, my dear. He seems like just the kind of man you can depend on."

He was, Riley realized. Though she'd known him for less than twenty-four hours, she was coming to trust him and to rely on him.

"So the errand was unsuccessful?" Winnie asked.

"Yes. Jack and I tried, but Baby bit him, and...it's a long story."

"Is he all right? Tell me everything."

Riley glanced at her watch. The last time she'd checked,

the two uniformed men had been in her uncle's room, Detective Carmichael had been in Ben's, and Detective Markham and Jack had both been in the library, going through every single book. It wasn't as though she didn't have some time to kill. Sinking into a chair, she began to recap the series of mishaps that had occurred in Hattie Silverman's apartment. She'd just gotten to the part where Hattie had cocked the gun when she sensed that someone had come into the room. Jack. She knew it even before she turned around. There was something in the air that seemed to change whenever he was near, and it made every pore in her body sensitive to him. Standing there, leaning against the curve of the archway, he looked so big, so male.

"When we heard her cock the rifle, we hid in the closet," she said to Winnie. Quickly, she deleted what had gone on while they'd been in it. But she couldn't seem to erase it from her mind. Just mentioning the closet brought every sensation back. She recalled exactly how it had felt to have his mouth pressed against hers, softly at first, testing, then the pleasure that had streamed through her when his tongue had flicked over her lips, between them and touched hers. Even more clearly, she remembered the astonishing greed that had sprung up in her to demand more, to take more. Lust. That's what it must have been. And it had been about to consume her.

It would consume her again right now if he walked toward her. And she wanted him to. It didn't seem to matter that the police were searching her apartment. It didn't even seem to matter that he wasn't walking toward her, and that he didn't seem to be as...consumed as she was.

What in the world was wrong with her?

"Listen, Winnie, I have to go," she said.

"But where is it right now? Are the police going to find it?"

"No. We hid it in..." Her voice trailed off as her gaze

drifted to the place where the diamond brooch was. *Oh my heavens,* she thought as she struggled to find words. There was a lot more there than Hattie's jewelry. "It's so…" Blinking, she tried to focus on what she'd been saying to Winnie. "…that is to say, Jack hid them in…he put them…" Her throat was so dry, her skin felt hot and cold at the same time, she couldn't tear her gaze away from that particular portion of Jack's anatomy.

He was moving closer. She could hear Winnie saying something. She just couldn't separate the sounds into words. Jack's fingers brushed against hers when he took the receiver out of her hand, and she felt a ribbon of heat uncurl itself right down to her toes. With every bit of energy she possessed, she wrenched her gaze away from Jack's *oh my heavens* and stared at the floor instead. Gradually, she could distinguish between the black and white diamond-shaped tiles. Any second now, she'd be able to think again.

Suddenly, Jack's laughter filled the kitchen. "Yeah, you're right. That's where I've got it all right," he was saying into the receiver.

Great, Riley thought. Winnie and Jack were highly amused, and she was practically paralyzed. She had to get a grip. But before she could muster up the courage to actually look at Jack again, there were voices, surprised and annoyed. Her uncle's projected clearly above the others.

"Just who are you, madam, and why are you searching my library?"

Either Alexandra's reply didn't carry quite as well, or Avery couldn't be bothered waiting for it because the next sound was that of footsteps thundering down the hall. It was Ben who burst through the archway first. "What's going on?" he asked breezily as he tossed his duffel bag on the table and made a beeline for the refrigerator. "Hi, Jack," he said on his way.

"The police are here to search the place," Riley explained.

"Really?" Ben paused in his search through the freezer. "That's cool. Do you think they'd mind if I watched?"

"You can ask," Riley said.

Avery was the next to arrive. Pausing dramatically in the archway, he pointed a finger at Riley. "If you'd heeded my advice and hired an attorney, this wouldn't be happening."

"They had a search warrant, Uncle Avery. I don't think a lawyer can do anything about that."

"We're out of frozen pizza," Ben complained. "I'm starving."

Riley turned to her brother with a frown. "Didn't Jeff's mother feed you?"

"What? Oh, sure. But that was hours ago."

It was only as Avery left his dramatic position in the archway and swept into the kitchen that Riley saw that Winnie, Gert, Prue and Hattie were standing behind him.

"We brought cookies," Winnie said, raising the basket she was carrying.

"Great!" Ben said moving toward her.

"I have to sit down," Hattie said, using her cane to clear a path toward the table. She made it to Jack's side before she sagged. Catching her, Jack eased her into a chair.

"Policemen make me so nervous," she said in a weak voice.

"Never mind the police," Prue said, taking Ben's arm and giving him one of her brightest smiles. "I don't need them as long as I have someone like you around, Mr. DeRosa."

"I'm sorry," Ben said. "I'm not Mr. DeRosa. I'm Ben."

Gert elbowed Prue. "And he's a tad young for you. I told you to wear your glasses!"

Prue shot a dimmer version of her smile at her sister. "Men don't make passes at girls who wear glasses."

"Right," Gert chortled. "Well, if you squint real hard about three feet to your left, you'll see that Hattie stole Mr. DeRosa right out from under your nose."

"Ladies," Winnie said, "let's remember we came to offer support to Riley in her time of need."

It was only as Winnie moved through the archway that Riley saw Charles Cantrell. She moved toward him. "Charles, what are you doing here?"

"I was at my aunt's apartment when she got the call from the commissioner. The moment I heard your place was being searched, I insisted we come right over. Have they arrested you?"

"No." Glancing at the startled expressions on her uncle's and brother's faces, she repeated, "No. I'm not under arrest. And I won't be. They're not going to find anything."

"I'm ready to search this room now," Detective Carmichael said as he stepped through the archway.

"Out, out, damned spot," squawked the Bard.

"Ditto," said Avery.

"Can I watch?" asked Ben.

"I think I'm going to faint," murmured Hattie as she closed her eyes.

As if on cue, Beowulf lumbered to his feet and began to bark.

"That's it," Carmichael said. "The zoo has to go and so does everyone else. Ms. Foster, I'll give you five minutes to clear this room."

"By what right do you order a man out of his kitchen before he's even had his coffee?" Avery asked to Carmichael's departing back.

Riley tucked her hand in his arm and led him into the hall. "If you'll go quietly and wait in the living room, I'll bring the coffee in there. Okay?"

Avery sighed. "If you insist."

"I do," she said, planting a kiss on his cheek. Turning back into the kitchen, she saw that Jack and Charles were helping Hattie out of her chair. "Winnie, why don't you take the cookies right into the living room? Gert and Prue, you can get the Bard's cage, and Ben, you're in charge of mobilizing Beowulf.''

"Sure thing," Ben said, bending over the dog. "C'mon, boy. There's food."

Ten minutes of absolute chaos and several trips later, Riley stepped into the kitchen to find Ben with his back to her, talking on the phone.

"Yeah, last night was great, wasn't it? I know. A few more nights' work and we'll be all set."

He turned toward her, and for a moment their eyes met and held. Riley was almost sure she saw a flash of guilt before Ben glanced away.

"I gotta go," Ben said before he hung up the receiver.

"Who was that?" Riley asked. "And what night's work were you talking about?"

The guilt was gone when Ben met her eyes. "I was talking about math. The studying is going very well. I think I'll do fine on the exam."

Why didn't she believe him? Riley asked herself as she watched him walk away. But it wasn't the time to confront him. Maybe she was afraid to confront him, she thought as she picked up the coffee tray. When she turned, she nearly collided with Jack.

"You forgot something," he said as he took the tray from her and set it on the table. "You like to dilute yours with ice." He reached into the freezer, but when he removed his hand a second later, instead of an ice cube, he held a small plastic bag.

Several thoughts raced through Riley's mind as Jack opened it. It was the same kind she used to wrap Ben's sandwiches. It hadn't been in the freezer when she'd opened it earlier. And it didn't contain ice cubes. Her heart had already been dropping with each thought and it landed with a resounding thud when she saw the little waterfall of diamonds spill into Jack's hand.

6

"RILEY?" She'd gone so pale that he was afraid she was going to faint again. Taking two quick steps, he gripped her shoulder with his free hand and urged her toward a chair. "Sit."

She stiffened immediately and drew in a deep breath. "I'm okay."

She wasn't. She was staring at his other hand, the one that was still holding the plastic bag and the diamonds. "How did they get in the freezer?" she asked.

"You don't know?"

"No. I don't."

The fear in her voice was echoed in her eyes. He could have sworn she was telling the truth. Just not all of it. She knew or suspected something that she wasn't telling him. "You're...." out of the corner of his eye, he saw Alexandra step through the archway "...right. The ice cubes will make less mess if we put them in this plastic bag." Switching the bag to his free hand, he straightened and turned toward the detective at the same time he casually slipped the diamonds into his back pocket.

"Alexandra," he said as he met her eyes, "why don't you tell Carmichael that the coast is clear. All the ferocious and dangerous animals have been removed."

"What do you need ice cubes for?" the detective asked.

"Riley likes her coffee on the rocks." Turning, he walked toward the refrigerator, opened the freezer and emptied a tray of cubes into the bag.

"Mind if I check it?" Alex asked.

"Alexandra, Alexandra." Shaking his head, he smiled as she held the bag up to the light and inspected it. "Whatever differences in opinion we may have, you can't possibly think I'd be involved in hiding evidence."

She handed him the bag. "What I think is that you're acting strangely. And I said the same thing to Captain Duffy a few minutes ago when he called me on my cell phone. He wants to talk to you now." She handed him the phone. "He's number two on the speed dial."

"Right," Jack said, taking the phone. When he turned, he found Riley was standing with the tray in hand. Moving toward her, he placed the bag of ice on it.

"I'll have a look at that tray before you go," Alexandra said, then proceeded to lift each mug and stir a spoon around in the coffeepot, the creamer and the sugar bowl. "Okay. You can serve the coffee."

"Happy hunting," Jack said as he followed Riley down the hall. It was empty, and when they reached the door to the living room, she turned to him and spoke softly. "What are you going to do?"

"Call my captain."

"And what will you tell him?"

"I don't know," he said as he opened the door to the living room. As soon as she walked past him, he shut it behind her and moved across the foyer to the library.

What in hell *was* he going to tell Captain Duffy? he wondered. *Sir, I just happen to be wearing all the evidence we need to make an arrest?*

Pacing the length of the room, he tried to clear his mind. Explaining everything to Duffy was the smart thing to do. As much as he hated to admit it, he *was* way too involved in this case. Kissing the suspect was not standard operating procedure. Especially when he wanted to do more than kiss her. A lot more.

It was time to put a stop to it. If he simply pressed 2 on the cell phone and then told Duffy everything, he could hold the captain to his word and be back at his desk by Monday morning. That's what he wanted.

So why was he hesitating?

Riley'd had a golden opportunity to steal the pendant and earrings from the Abernathys last night right after she'd drugged him. In fact, she could have just been returning from that little endeavor when she'd stepped out of the bathroom and caught him holding Hattie's brooch. The late-night excursion to Hattie's apartment to return it could have been a spur-of-the-moment ploy she'd invented to throw him off.

And she'd succeeded. He couldn't have been more thrown off than he'd been in that closet. Hell, he was thrown off now!

Never had the evidence of a case clashed so strongly with his instincts.

Turning, he paced back to the door. His gut was telling him Riley hadn't hidden the diamonds in the freezer.

Sinking down on the couch, he stared at Alexandra's cell phone.

Right or wrong, he had to trust his instincts. And he had to try to be objective. She wasn't the only one who could have planted the diamonds in the freezer. And he'd bet the jewels he was currently wearing that she suspected Ben or Avery and that she'd do anything to protect them.

Flipping open the cell phone, he pressed 2.

"Duffy here."

"Captain, Detective Markham told me you wanted a call."

"She says you're interfering in her search of the apartment. What the hell are you thinking?" roared Duffy.

"I'm thinking I should do the job you assigned me to do," Jack said, keeping his voice very calm.

"Your job is to get this case off my desk ASAP. Finding

the Abernathys' diamond pendant and earrings would do that.''

"Riley Foster didn't steal the diamonds. But I may have a lead on who did. That would get the case off your desk, too.''

"Who?'' Duffy snapped.

"I don't want to say until I have some evidence,'' Jack said. "I'm more likely to get it if they don't know they're under suspicion.''

There was a short span of silence, broken only by the sound of a match being struck. Duffy was lighting up one of his cigars. It could be a good sign, or it could merely mean that his boss was getting out his big ammunition.

"Alexandra says you're involved with Ms. Foster,'' Duffy finally said.

"She's upset that you assigned me to work undercover on her case,'' Jack said.

There was another longer silence on the other end. Finally, the captain said, "I'll give you twenty-four hours to come up with something solid.''

"Fine,'' Jack said, then listened to Duffy break the connection.

He glanced at his watch. Ten o'clock. Twenty-four hours wasn't a lot of time, but it was something. And it meant he'd have to keep his mind focused on the case. He'd just stepped into the hallway when he heard the voices. The door of the apartment was ajar, and as he drew closer, he heard Charles Cantrell say, "I understand why you hired an assistant, but why is he living with you?''

"He doesn't have anywhere else to stay.''

"He's homeless, and you've taken him in? What were you thinking?''

"Jack's not homeless. He just hadn't found an apartment yet. If he had, I wouldn't have been able to hire him. The only way I could afford him was to offer him room and board as part of his pay.''

"I don't like the way he looks at you," Charles said. "I've half a mind to hire a security man I know to check into his background. You say his father and Captain Duffy were friends?''

"Charles, I would appreciate it very much if you would leave Jack alone. He's not looking at me in any special way that I can tell.''

"He looks at you the way a man looks at a woman he wants. The way I look at you.''

Jack moved closer to the door, his hand poised to grip the handle. If Charles made a move...

"Charles, I don't want you to look at me that way. I want us to be friends. That's all.''

"Then there *is* something between the two of you?''

"Jack?" Riley laughed. "No. You couldn't be more wrong. In fact, I wouldn't be surprised if he was gay.''

"You've got to be kidding.''

"No. He and Uncle Avery have really hit it off.''

"Well, I'll be," Charles said.

Ditto, Jack thought, fighting the urge to open the door and set both of them straight on his sexual orientation. He had stepped into the hall when the parade came pouring out of the living room.

"Oh, there you are, Mr. DeRosa," Prue said, beaming a smile at the air above his head.

"C'mon, Prue," Gert said, urging her toward the door. "We have to leave now.''

Prue batted her eyes in his general direction. "Perhaps, we'll see you later?''

Gert shot him a nod. "Only one of us will actually see you later.''

"Are the police gone?" Hattie asked, clinging to Winnie's arm as they stepped into the foyer.

"They're still here," Jack said.

The sound of footsteps bearing down on them sent Winnie and Hattie hurrying after Gert and Prue. Turning, Jack saw Alexandra leading the way. He pulled the door open for her just in time to see Cantrell following the bridge-club ladies into the elevator. Riley stepped back into the foyer.

"You called the captain?" Alexandra asked as she reached them.

Jack deposited her cell phone in her outstretched palm. "I did."

"What did he say?"

"You can ask him."

"Is the search over?" Riley asked.

"For the time being," Alexandra said, as she walked through the door. In the hall, she paused, waiting for Carmichael and the two other men to pass her and head for the elevator. "You're going to make a mistake, Ms. Foster, and then we're going to get you."

THE MOMENT the elevator doors slid shut, Riley let out the breath she was holding and turned to Jack. "Thank you."

"We have to talk."

She glanced at her watch. "I'm three hours behind, and I have to meet with that contractor in thirty minutes."

Avery stepped into the foyer carrying the tray. "You know, Harold has a friend who's a lawyer. He doesn't do defense work, but he could refer you."

"Uncle Avery, we've discussed this…" Riley began, and the moment she did, she could see it was a mistake. Her tone of voice was all it took to thrust Avery into a full-blown speech. Since there was no possibility of stopping him once he was on a roll, she tuned him out and focused her attention on her biggest problem: Jack. He was standing right next to her, and she had to get rid of him for a while. At least until she could talk to both Ben and her uncle in private. She had no idea how those diamonds had gotten into her freezer. But she could count on two hands the people who could have stashed them there. And she was sure that Jack was just as good at counting on his fingers as she was.

He was a cop. He was the enemy. And if he'd hidden the jewels on his person and saved her from being arrested, she was sure he had a cop's reason for doing it. She had to distance herself from him until she could talk to Ben and Avery, until she could figure out who had put those diamonds in her freezer.

"Let's take a vote on it, shall we?" Avery asked. "Shall I ask Harold to have his friend call us? All in favor, say aye."

"Aye," Ben said. "Everyone has an attorney these days. Once, when my friend Jeff got in trouble at school, his mom took a lawyer with her when she came in to talk to the principal."

Riley looked from her brother to her uncle. "I smell a conspiracy here."

Avery arched a brow. "I'd say you have a good nose. I vote aye also, and we're prepared to stand firm on this. What do you think, Jack?"

"Talking to an attorney wouldn't hurt."

"I'll take that as an aye. Three against one. You're outvoted, my dear. I'll give Harold a ring a little later when I'm sure he'll be up. Right now, I'm going to take a little nap."

"Me, too." Ben followed his uncle a few steps down the hall, then turned. "Jack, you're doing spaghetti tonight, right?"

"Sure," Jack said.

"Cool."

"Let's make it an early dinner. Harold and I are planning to work on the third act tonight," Avery said as he followed Ben down the hall.

"I think they're conspiring against you, too," Riley said.

"Do they do that often?" Jack asked.

"More than I like," she said, glancing at her watch again. "I'm going to be late."

"Riley, you and I have to—"

"Talk. Yes, I know. But that contractor isn't going to wait. We'll talk later."

"We can talk on the way."

"No! I mean, that won't be possible. You're going to have to handle my morning clients." Hurrying into the library, she grabbed the first duffel bag and pulled out a notebook. "This is my Saturday morning schedule—clients, pets' names, addresses, phone numbers and the times I'm supposed to be there." She ran a finger down half of the page. "I've already called these people to tell them I would be running late. I can't call them again. If you could just handle them, then I'll take care of the afternoon schedule as soon as I'm done with the contractor."

Jack studied the list for a minute. "They're all in one building—the one where Winnie Cantrell lives, right?"

"Yes. The park is right across the street."

"There's just one thing."

"What?" When she turned to hand him the duffel, he was closer than she thought. They were so close she could see his eyes weren't really black, but the color of smoke. The thick, dark kind that spewed up from a fire just before the flames shot up. And there she was—she could see herself right in the middle of all that swirling heat. A part of her wanted to move forward. But she couldn't. He was the enemy. Until she figured out what was going on, she had to remember that.

He put a finger under her chin. "I'm not gay."

She felt the heat flood her face. "You eavesdropped."

"Sooner or later, you're going to have to tell Charles the truth."

He was touching her with only one finger beneath her chin,

but she could feel it right down to her toes. Slowly, carefully, she drew back. "I know."

"There's another thing."

"What?"

"Baby. She doesn't seem to like me."

Riley frowned. "Skip her. I'll call Hattie."

"Or you could offer me battle pay to face her again."

He was joking. She could see the glint of humor in his eyes. "How about a good bottle of Chianti to go with the spaghetti?"

"Sold," Jack said.

But when she turned to leave, he caught her hand. "Sooner or later, you're going to have to tell me the truth, too."

IN THE LOBBY of the Carleton Arms, Riley took count of the dogs. Before she left, she wanted to make sure she had them all. Her head had been spinning ever since she'd parted company with Jack. She'd been so distracted during her appointment with the contractor that he'd had to repeat several questions for her. It would put the final cap on her day if she left for the park minus one of the dogs and had to return for it.

Roscoe the Doberman and Gigi the toy poodle strained at the leashes she held in her right hand, their noses leaving little clouds of steam on the glass doors that opened onto Park Avenue. Behind her, George and Gracie, the two golden retrievers, nudged each other aside and pushed against her in their quest to win her undivided attention.

"Problem, Ms. Foster?" asked the uniformed man behind the reception desk.

"I'm just making sure I've got them all, Mr. Gaffney."

"Looks to me like they've got you," he said, his deep laugh filling the small entrance hall.

Riley laughed too as George pushed her a step forward and Gracie nudged her from the side.

"Yes, you're beautiful. Both of you," she assured them, patting each of their heads in turn.

Roscoe growled deep in his throat as a woman inserted her key and pushed through the glass doors. Glancing up, Riley recognized the mother of Ben's friend Jeff.

"Did they get any sleep at all last night?" she asked, smiling the moment she saw Riley.

"Sleep?" Riley asked.

"Foolish question, I know," the woman said, laughing. "I knew the moment Jeff got home this morning that they'd been up all night. He hit the refrigerator and went right to bed. Was it another Hitchcock marathon or were they doing a Francis Ford Coppola retrospective this time?"

"I...I'm not sure," Riley said.

"I know the feeling," Jeff's mom said as she moved toward the elevators. "Next time they can come here."

Frowning, Riley stared through the glass front of the building. If Ben hadn't been at Jeff's, where had he been? She recalled the conversation she'd heard him having on the kitchen phone.

A few more nights' work and we'll be all set.

Her stomach sank. Could he be stealing from her clients to finance his filmmaking dreams?

The Doberman growled at a man passing by on the street.

"Roscoe, that's enough," she said.

Gigi whined.

"All right, you win. We're going," she said as she switched the leashes to one hand and opened the door with the other. She'd been looking forward to walking the dogs in the park, knowing that it would give her a chance to think. But right now, she didn't like the thoughts that were swirling around in her head. Was it really possible that he and Jeff had robbed the Abernathys? No. That just couldn't be. Ben would have a perfectly logical explanation for not spending the night at Jeff's and for lying about it. Wouldn't he?

Ahead of her, the light turned yellow, and she pulled the
dogs to a halt a few feet short of the curb. George and Gracie
nudged against her and she patted their heads absently. One
thing was certain. She had to talk to Ben alone. That meant
she had to walk the dogs and beat Jack back to the apartment.

Just then she spotted him. He was standing across the street
at the entrance to the park that she usually used, watching
her and waiting. She felt something knot in her stomach.
Fear, she told herself. But it was the first time that fear had
sent hot prickles of sensation moving along her nerve endings. The man had some kind of hold on her. And it wasn't
just physical. Because more than anything she wanted to
walk across the street and ask him to help her figure everything out.

She had to be crazy.

It was just as the light changed and she allowed the dogs
to move forward that it happened. Someone plowed into her
from behind, sending her stumbling forward off the curb and
into the street. Then before she could recover her balance, a
kid shoved her again from the side, pushing her out of the
way as he stooped to pick up Gigi. Frantically, she tried to
tighten her grip on the end of the leash, but she'd slackened
her hold and she felt the burn of leather against her skin as
it slid from her hand. He was halfway across the street before
she yelled, "Stop thief!"

JACK SWORE under his breath as he tried to shorten the distance between himself and the punk who'd snatched the poodle from Riley. The heavy traffic pouring through the park
entrance had separated them at first. And Jack had been
slowed some by traffic again when he'd had to run into the
street against the light. A taxi had missed hitting him by a
hair, and now he was being slowed even further by the weak-
ness in his leg. As the twinges became a dull, steady throb,
he had no choice but to favor it. As a result, he was running

like a gimp, and it was wreaking havoc with his good leg. Already he could feel the strain in his shin. Fifty paces in front of him, the punk shoved aside some walkers and began to widen the distance between them.

Just keep him in sight, Jack told himself as he took deep breaths and struggled to find a rhythm. Just keep him in sight. The day was sunny with a slight, steady breeze pushing at him. Inhaling air in slow steady doses helped to cool the fire that had started burning in his lungs. His bad leg was holding its own, but two months of sick leave had taken its toll on his stamina. He was losing ground when his quarry took a sharp right onto the bridle path that wound its way through Central Park.

It was a bad move on the kid's part. Now all Jack needed was a little luck. Increasing his pace as much as he dared, he shifted to the grass to soften the pounding on his bad leg. Then he frowned. He thought he heard the barking of dogs behind him. As he veered onto the bridle path, he allowed himself a quick look back and confirmed his suspicion. Riley and the three dogs were in hot pursuit.

Ruthlessly, he turned his attention back to his quarry and spotted the kid hotfooting it along about sixty paces ahead. On a sunny Saturday afternoon, the path was far from deserted. Jack passed by two people out for a morning walk and a power walker, but it wasn't until he made it around the first curve that he saw what he'd been looking for—two horseback riders about the length of a football field away. Focusing on his new goal, he tried to ignore the steady throbbing in his thigh.

His lungs were nearly bursting when he finally reached the riders. "Police," he managed as he pulled his badge out his pocket. "I need your horse."

It was the woman who dismounted and turned over the reins. The man didn't look too happy and was saying something, but Jack paid him no heed. Instead, he placed his good foot in the stirrup and hoped that his equestrian rotation in his Police Academy days would finally pay off. His leg protested loudly when he swung it over the saddle and then he was urging the horse into a canter.

"Police. Out of the way," he shouted to the people walking who scattered as he rode past. At last he was closing the distance. But somehow he didn't think jumping off a moving horse was going to go as smoothly as it did on TV. The moment he drew even with the dog snatcher, he freed his feet from the stirrups, took a deep breath, and dove for his quarry. Together, they pitched to the ground. The impact stole his breath and wrenched his shoulder. The kid was flattened beneath him, not going anywhere. And the poodle was racing around, barking, and trying to lick his face.

RILEY THOUGHT her lungs must be on fire. She wasn't even sure that she was getting breath into them anymore. But she couldn't slow down—not with the three dogs pulling her along at top speed. There was no way that she could stop them, no way to set them free. She'd wound the leashes tightly around her wrists the moment she'd realized Gigi had been snatched, and they'd taken off, dragging her with them. Heaven help her if she stumbled. She could picture herself being dragged along face down through the dirt, and just the image of it was enough to keep her going. That and the fact that she had to get Gigi back. Ahead of her, pedestrians parted, giving her and the dogs a wide berth.

Rounding the curve, she was just in time to see Jack mount the horse and canter off. He was magnificent. But he was going to kill himself! As the fear arrowed through her, she gathered up all her strength and began to gain on the dogs. Ahead of her Jack drew even with the dog snatcher. Her heart flew to her throat as she saw him dive from the horse and fall on the kid. She was sure her heart stopped. She heard nothing but the sound of her feet pounding the path until she reached his side.

"Jack? Are you all right?"

He raised his head. But whatever he said was drowned out by the din the dogs were making.

"George, Gracie, hush," she tried. But they paid her no heed. When Jack carefully levered himself up, the relief that washed through her weakened her so that she almost had to sit down. She might have if the dog snatcher hadn't chosen that moment to stir. The anger surging through her gave her the strength to pull her gun out of her duffel. Then squatting down next to Jack, she pressed the weapon into his hand. "Use this if you have to."

Finally, she unsnapped Roscoe from his leash. "Guard them," she shouted. The dog immediately snarled and bared his teeth. Gathering up the leashes of the other dogs, she mouthed the words carefully for Jack. "I'm going to get a cop. Keep them covered."

"I DON'T HAVE TIME for more than coffee," Riley said as she slid into a booth in the small delicatessen. "Ben and Uncle Avery are probably up by now. I have to grocery shop. And then—"

"I'll help you. I'm cooking, remember?"

"Oh, right." She shot a look at him before she became absorbed in settling her duffel next to her.

"We need to talk. You need to eat," he said, easing himself into the seat across from her. She fidgeted with her napkin for a moment, picking it up by the corner and rubbing it between her thumb and forefinger, then lining it up with the edge of the table. Nerves, Jack thought. She'd been jumpy ever since Alexandra had arrived with the search warrant this morning. Funny, she hadn't shown any sign of anxiety when she'd been dealing with those two thugs in the alley yesterday. And she'd been as cool and determined as Joan of Arc when she'd been dealing with Duffy yesterday and with the police in the park just a short time ago. She could be absolutely fearless when it came to herself, but she was nervous as a kitten when it came to her family. An abrupt movement of her hand sent a spoon clattering to the floor.

Clearly, she didn't want to talk to him. If she could have thought of a way out of it, she wouldn't have come into the restaurant with him. Jack let the silence spin out between them. It was one of the best tools he knew of for handling a reluctant suspect. He watched her glance around the small room that had begun to clear at two in the afternoon. A waitress was at the cash register, taking money from a departing customer.

Finally he said, "You're going to be here the same amount of time whether you eat or not."

Riley studied him a moment. "I bet you're very good at interrogating criminals."

Jack grinned at her. "I'm the best. But I usually don't bring them here to do it."

She sighed. "All right. What are you having?"

"I can recommend the pastrami on rye."

She looked at him then and frowned. "It's bad for you."

He shrugged. "A lot of things are." And one of them was sitting right across the table from him. All he had to do was look into those deep-as-the-sea blue eyes of hers to be reminded of that. He had to remember that he had an agenda. "The turkey's good, too."

"You come in here a lot?"

"Yeah." At least he used to come in here, he thought as he glanced around. But not since he'd lost his... It occurred to him that he'd been purposely avoiding the place since the night Billy died. And yet when the police had finally taken the dog snatcher away, he'd brought Riley here almost automatically.

"Good to see you, Jack. Heard you were hurt," the waitress said as she reached the table. "The leg, wasn't it?"

"Yeah, Maggie. But I should be back to work soon."

She hesitated for a second, then said, "I was sorry to hear about Billy. He was a good kid."

"Yeah." The pain, a sharp arrow of it, sliced through him. Then he felt a hand close over his. Riley's. He glanced down and, beneath the spread of her fingers, he could see the whiteness of his knuckles. Slowly, he relaxed his clenched fist.

"Shall I fix your usual?" Maggie asked. At his nod, she turned to Riley and gave her an appraising look. "Shall I make it two?"

"Yes," Riley said.

The waitress smiled at her then. "Good choice. I'll bring the drafts right over."

"Drafts?" Riley said in a low voice as soon as the waitress was out of earshot. "I didn't think cops drank on duty."

She wasn't going to ask about Billy, he realized. He wasn't going to have to talk about it. Suddenly, the pain inside him became more bearable. "I'm not on duty."

She tilted her head to one side and studied him for a minute. "I could have sworn you were when you brought me here. You had your cop's face on from the moment I led those two patrolmen over to arrest that dog thief."

Jack stiffened. "I like to have my cop's face on when I'm dealing with other cops. Especially when they find me pinned to the ground by a Doberman. Didn't it occur to you to tell that dog who the bad guy was?"

"You're annoyed about that? Roscoe wouldn't have bitten you."

"He could have fooled me. His teeth are a lot bigger than Baby's. I got a good look at them when he snapped them about two inches away from my face."

"Okay." She raised both hands, palms out. "Maybe I should have helped you to your feet before I left you there.

But I thought your leg needed a rest. I didn't know what kind of shape you were in after you fell off the horse.''

"Fell off the horse? I jumped off the horse to tackle your dog snatcher. And my leg held up pretty good. I got your poodle back.''

Maggie slapped two draft beers down and said, "Why don't the two of you go to your respective corners and cool down?''

Jack took a long swallow of his beer and watched Riley sip hers. He'd brought her in here so that he could get information. Why was it that every time he thought he'd come up with a plan to handle this woman, it went up in smoke? He took another swallow of beer. It was time for a new approach. "Look," he said, setting down his glass. "How about we call a truce?''

"Meaning?''

The suspicion in her eyes nearly made him grin. "Let's say for the length of time it takes us to eat, I'm not a cop, and you're not a suspect.''

Her eyes narrowed. "You're not going to grill me about those diamonds you found in the freezer?''

"As long as you don't ask me what I plan to do about them.''

She frowned then. "But I—''

"No *buts.* If you're not a suspect, you shouldn't be worried about that.''

Riley considered it for the amount of time it took the waitress to serve their pastrami sandwiches.

"Here's mustard and extra Russian dressing," Maggie said before she hurried away.

Riley's hand beat his to the Russian dressing, and he watched her lavishly slather it on to her sandwich.

"This stuff's bad for you, too," he pointed out as he added a more moderate amount to his.

She licked some off her finger. "When you're going to indulge in bad stuff, I believe in going all the way."

"I'll keep that in mind."

She picked up her sandwich. "Okay, the truce starts when I take the first bite."

He watched as she bit into the rye bread. "How in the world did a nice girl like you ever get into the pet-care business?"

"That's a question," she pointed out. "You're not supposed to grill me."

"I'm not asking you something that's related to the case. I'm just curious. Did you always know that you wanted to spend your life caring for animals?"

"Yes," she said, setting her sandwich down and adding more dressing. "My big dream was to become a vet."

"Why didn't you do that?" he asked.

"I'm still going to. I just have to postpone it for a while. After my dad died," her face clouded for a second, "there wasn't enough money for me to keep going to school."

"That must have been hard—losing your parents and at the same time having to adjust to a different lifestyle."

Her eyes narrowed. "We're not supposed to talk about the case."

"I didn't think we were."

"Detectives Markham and Carmichael are sure that the sudden change in fortune I faced after my father's death gives me a perfect motive for stealing from my clients. And they think I started Foster Care as a front to get into wealthy people's apartments."

Jack met her eyes steadily. "One thing I've learned as a cop. There's always more than one way to view the evidence, and tunnel vision can lead to disaster. Why don't you tell me why you really started your business?"

"I needed a way to make money and at the same time establish a clientele so that I could open the Foster Care Pet

Center. I know there's a need for it. Do you know how many people there are in Manhattan who want to have pets but don't because they just don't have the time to devote to them?''

''I never thought about it,'' Jack said.

''Well, you're going to have to. What are you going to do with Abra once you go back to work full-time?''

''Now wait a minute. I can't take responsibility for that kitten.''

''The first time she rubbed against your leg, she marked you as hers. It's going to be tough to walk away.''

Frowning, Jack leaned against the back of the booth. Why was it that every time he talked with her, the conversation had a way of veering off on tangents? ''Okay. Say I decide to keep Abra. What would the Foster Care Pet Center offer me?''

''Everything you need so that you can enjoy your pet without feeling guilty that you live in New York and don't have enough time to spend with her. You can drop her off on your way to work, knowing that she'll get all the food and exercise she needs.''

As she continued to talk, her face became more animated, her gestures, too. There wasn't a doubt in his mind that her enthusiasm was genuine. And it was becoming equally clear to him that, while she might be impulsive when it came to rescuing strays, she had a very well thought-out plan for establishing her business. She would hardly jeopardize something this important to her by stealing from her clients. And she definitely wouldn't be careless about hiding the evidence.

Something was *definitely* rotten in Denmark, Jack thought. When she finally paused to take a sip of her beer, he asked, ''So you've decided to give up veterinary practice for pet day-care?''

''No.'' She picked up her sandwich and pulled a piece of pastrami free. ''I've simply put vet school on hold. Once I build the business to the point where it would make an attractive franchise, I'm going to sell it. By that time, Ben should be out of college and..." Pausing, she put the sandwich back on her plate.

"What is it?" he asked.

"Nothing," she said. "But I must be boring you with all this talk about my plans." Lifting the top slice of bread off her sandwich, she reached for the dressing again. "What about you? Did you always dream of being a cop?"

He stared fascinated as she began to layer the Russian dressing between the thin slices of pastrami. But he didn't miss that her knuckles were white where they gripped the knife. The nerves were back in full force. "Why do you even bother with the meat? You might as well just eat that dressing with a spoon."

"You're avoiding my question," she said, licking her fingers.

She was right. He was. "Yeah, I always wanted to be a cop. My aunt insisted I go to college first." And where had that come from? he wondered. He never spoke about his aunt to anyone. She'd gotten him off on a tangent once again. Reaching for his beer, he took a long swallow.

"Did you go to college?" she asked.

"No."

Riley set her sandwich down. "It was still good advice. Your aunt is a smart woman. Maybe she could talk some sense into Ben."

He shook his head and carefully set his glass down. "She died two years ago."

"I'm sorry." She covered his hand with hers again. He turned his over and linked his fingers with hers. "I don't see that you can do much if Ben decides against college and wants to try his luck at this filmmaking thing first."

"But he...I..." This time it was a knife she knocked to the floor.

Maggie scooped it up as she neared the table. "How are the sandwiches?"

"Great," Riley said. "But before I finish it, I have to visit the ladies' room."

"It's at the back, the door on the right."

Jack frowned as Riley slid out of the booth. It was the mention of Ben that had brought her nerves back in full force. It only confirmed what he already knew. She knew something about her brother that he didn't.

7

As SHE MADE HERSELF walk to the back of the restaurant, Riley's mind was racing. What had she been thinking of—sitting there, stuffing herself with pastrami and pouring out her hopes and dreams to Jack DeRosa? Why couldn't she be in his presence for more than three minutes without forgetting who he was or what he wanted? Thank heavens, Ben's name had come up, or she'd be sitting there now.

Opening the bathroom door, she slipped inside and locked it behind her. The room was small, holding just a toilet and a sink. In the narrow space between, she began to pace. She needed ten minutes alone with her brother. Just enough time to find out where he'd been last night. But how was she supposed to get it with a cop as her shadow?

A glance at her watch told her it was two-thirty. Jack was going to grocery shop with her, and once they got back to the apartment, she couldn't see shaking him long enough to talk to Ben. Plus, the truce they'd agreed to was nearly over. When she went back to that table, the inquisition would begin. Pausing, Riley glanced at her reflection in the mirror. She'd never been good at lying. And Jack DeRosa was very good at his job. Ten minutes alone with him and she'd be spilling everything she knew.

And she couldn't. Not until she discovered where Ben and Jeff had been last night and if her brother knew anything about how Hattie's brooch had gotten in the duffel with his decaying bologna sandwich. She had to find out so that she could protect him. How? She could try calling him on her cell phone...if she hadn't left it back at the table in her duffel.

Clearly, she was not cut out for covert activity.

It was then that she spotted it behind her on the wall above the toilet. A narrow window up near the ceiling, tilted outward to let in fresh air.

Shoving the toilet seat down, she stood on it. The window was level with her chin, about three feet long, but there was only about a foot of squeezing room between the sill and the slanted pane. It would be a tight fit, but she could manage it. What worried her more was the drop to the ground. Standing on her toes, she gauged the distance at a good ten feet. That meant going feet first through the window.

Taking a deep breath, she gripped the sill with both hands, then levered herself up so that she could get one knee on the ledge. Then she twisted and wiggled until she was lying along the length of the ledge, straddling it. Pausing only for another breath, she twisted again, shifting her shoulders and upper body back into the bathroom for balance while she swung her other leg outside. She tried not to imagine how she looked, teetering half in and half out of the window. But somehow that image was more appealing than the one where she was dropping to the alley below. Or, worse still, lying there smashed and broken on the concrete.

There was a knock on the bathroom door. "Are you all right?"

It was the waitress's voice. But with the windowsill pressing hard against her stomach, she couldn't find the breath to speak.

"Honey, are you all right? Jack's worried."

Jack was worried! *She* was terrified. And she had to get out fast.

Don't think about it, she told herself as she grunted, wiggled and muscled her way backward. Thinking was what had gotten her into the mess. Getting a death grip on the ledge, she lowered herself slowly until she felt the inexorable pull of gravity. Bricks scraped her cheek. It was too late for second thoughts now. All she had to do was relax her fingers and drop. Squeezing her eyes shut, she clung fiercely to the ledge.

JACK SPOTTED HER the moment he turned into the alley and his heart nearly stopped. She was hanging from the window ledge, and the floor of the alley was a good eight feet below her. Ignoring the protest the muscles in his leg made, he raced forward. The hunch had come the moment Maggie had told him there was a window in the bathroom. But he never would have asked her to check on Riley if it hadn't been for the call on her cell phone. Damn it, why hadn't he anticipated that she'd panic? Why couldn't he ever predict what she'd do? Skidding to a stop directly beneath her, he said, "Riley, let go. I'll catch you."

"I can't."

"Sure you can." Reaching up, he wrapped his hands around the calves of her legs. "See how close I am? All you have to do is let loose. I'm right here." He tugged on her legs to encourage her, and the next moment she dropped. He caught her tight against him, then setting her down, he turned her so that he could see her face. Now that she was safe, he wanted to shake her.

"Are you going to arrest me now?"

"No. But I'm thinking of arresting your brother or your uncle once I—damn it!" He didn't think it was possible for her to turn any whiter. Ignoring the skip of panic that raced up his spine, he gripped her shoulders and urged her down until she was sitting with her back against the wall. Then he shoved her head to her knees. "Take deep breaths."

She drew one in and let it out. "They wouldn't steal from my clients."

He squatted down beside her. "Yeah. That's what I figure, too."

Her head came up at that, and she met his eyes. "You do? Then you think Hattie and her boyfriend could be the burglars."

"Not exactly. Hattie seems to be petrified of cops. I don't think she was faking when she nearly fainted in the kitchen this morning. I can't imagine she'd want to risk going back to jail at her age. And if Louie 'the Rock' Mancuso is involved, why isn't he going after what's inside the safes? I'm not saying I've eliminated them."

"But my brother and my uncle are higher up on your list of suspects?"

"They're the obvious ones, after you. But they'd have to know it would ruin your business. I can't see them doing that."

She let out a relieved sigh. "Exactly. You do understand."

Wincing, he rubbed his thigh, then sat down beside her and stretched his leg out. "Yeah. But understanding and hunches aren't proof. A good cop investigates each suspect thoroughly before he eliminates him or her. And he doesn't play favorites. So why don't you tell me what you know? What were you so afraid to tell me that you had to drop out of that damn window?"

Shaking her head, she sighed. "See, this is exactly why I had to do it."

"I don't see at all."

"I knew if I stayed, I'd tell you everything. I have no will power at all when it comes to you."

Jack stared at her as feelings streamed through him. He couldn't recognize them all. He didn't want to sort them out. All he wanted was to— "Riley, do you have any idea what saying that does to a man?"

"No, I—" It was her turn to stare at him as understanding flooded through her. "I didn't mean…"

"Shut up." Cupping her chin in his hand, he covered her mouth with his.

Each time it was different, Jack thought. Was that why he couldn't resist her? This time there was a flavor deep within her mouth that he couldn't quite identify. Something about her scent had changed, too. He nipped at her bottom lip and knew that he'd never heard her breath hitch quite that way before. And the desire twisting through him was different—hotter, riper, more desperate. Murmuring her name, he pulled her closer until her arms were locked around him and her fingers were in his hair.

Needs sprang up with a sharpness he'd never felt before, and the low, deep sound of approval he heard drove him further. He had to touch her, to feel her skin heat and grow moist beneath his hands, and then to taste and taste. His fingers moved to pull at the snaps on her jacket. There was so much he had to explore, so much he needed.

Each time it seemed to get better. That was the thought that streamed through her mind before it spun away in a flood of sensations. She could feel everything. The hard line of his body, the heat of his lips. Everywhere he touched and pressed, dozens of little explosions sprang to life along her skin. His hands weren't gentle; his mouth wasn't tender. It moved over hers with a desperation that only fueled her own. And his taste…it poured through her like the darkest, sweetest chocolate, melting everything in its path. She wanted more. She had to have more. Moaning in protest, she tightened her grip when she felt him start to pull away.

"Don't stop," she said.

"I have to. We have to."

A truck sounded its horn twice, then began to roll down the alley.

Jack drew her with him as he scrambled to his feet. Then he shifted her against the wall of the building, using his body to shield her as he refastened the snaps of her jacket. As soon as the truck lumbered past, she slipped her arms around him and laid her head on his chest. The sweetness of the gesture flooded him with a new set of emotions and, for a moment, all he could do was simply hold her.

She wasn't like any woman he'd ever met. She stirred up feelings that no one else ever had.

"What are we going to do?" she murmured as she raised her head to look at him.

It was the same question that was on his mind. And if she were any other woman, the answer would be easy—simple, in fact. But Riley was different. He'd come very near to taking her without any regard for the fact that they were in a public place. An alley. It struck him then that, from the moment he'd seen her hanging from the window ledge, he'd never once thought of that other alley where Billy had been killed. He hadn't thought of anything but her.

The question she'd posed had only one answer. Gripping her shoulders, he set her away from him. "We're not going to let it happen again."

"Why not?" Riley asked.

"Because I have a job to do, and you're interfering with it." He saw the hurt flash into her eyes, and he wanted to soothe it. But if he touched her... Stuffing his hands into his pockets, he said, "Riley, I'm no good for you. Anyone who gets close to me gets hurt. And we both need to concentrate on clearing you and your brother."

Immediately, she frowned. "You said you agreed with me—that he couldn't have done it."

"It would help if we had some hard evidence. He didn't spend the night with his friend Jeff, did he?"

She stared at him. "How did you know?"

"Something had you worried enough to wiggle out that window. So I used an old cop trick of theorizing out loud. Suspects usually fall for it and believe I know a lot more than I do. Plus, I've had all morning to think about it. I also know he had a set of keys with him because he took the duffel bag with him last night."

"You're really good, aren't you?"

He gave her a wry look. The surprise in her voice did not soothe his ego. Then again, a limping cop she was making a habit of rescuing with a water pistol had a long way to go. "I know I haven't made much of an impression so far."

She patted his arm. "You're still recovering. You did a very good job on that horse. And you did catch me when I let go of the window ledge."

"Thanks."

Her eyes narrowed. "You're laughing."

"Me?"

"With your eyes. What's the joke?"

He drew her close then and kissed just the tip of her nose. It was all he could allow himself. "I'll explain later. Right now we're talking about your brother's possible nocturnal activities."

Riley frowned. "I know there has to be some explanation."

"If it makes you feel any better, I can think of a few reasons why two teenage boys might stay out all night. None of them have to do with burglary."

She shot him a look. "But you still need evidence, right? Before you can eliminate him."

"You got it."

"How do you plan to get it?"

"You can have a talk with him after dinner. If that doesn't work, I'll have one—man to man."

"That might work."

"Thanks." Privately he wondered if the Bard knew the quote about damning a man with faint praise.

She grabbed his arm and started pulling him along toward the mouth of the alley. "But you don't have to wait until after dinner. You could talk to him right now. That's what I was planning to do.''

He stopped at the corner and whistled for a taxi. ''We can't go back to the apartment right now.''

''Why not?''

As the taxi squealed to the curb, he said, ''Winnie called while you were making your great escape. She wants to see you ASAP. Some kind of emergency that she didn't want to talk about on a cell phone.''

THE MOMENT they arrived, Winnie drew them into the living room.

''What is it?'' asked Riley as she glanced hurriedly around the room. On the way to the apartment, she'd imagined all sorts of horrors. But she couldn't see any signs of a crisis. Prue and Gert, the dogs at their feet, were sitting on the sofa sipping tea. Chopin flowed softly from a speaker. Barking in sharp, staccato bursts, Baby scooted out from beneath a chair and raced toward them.

''What's the matter, boy?'' Riley asked, dropping to her knees when the Chihuahua skidded to a halt in front of Jack and continued to bark fiercely. ''He's a friend.'' In an undertone, she said to Jack, ''Kneel down and let him sniff your hand.''

''I like my fingers,'' Jack said. But he squatted down.

''Let me show you,'' Riley said. Slipping her free hand into Jack's, she drew Baby's attention to their joined hands. ''Now, while he's smelling you, scratch behind his ears.''

''You're right to be wary, Mr. DeRosa. That dog never did care much for men,'' Prue observed, fluttering her lashes at Jack and patting the cushion beside her. ''Why don't you come over here? Frack and I promise not to bite you.''

''You've got to be able to see someone to bite them,'' Gert muttered under her breath.

Having assured herself that Baby wasn't going to attack

Jack, Riley glanced around the room again. It was only then that she noticed who was missing. "Where's Hattie?"

"Let me just pour you some tea, and I'll explain," Winnie said.

Gert snorted. "What's to explain? Hattie's in the library monopolizing the time of that gorgeous P.I."

"Yes," Prue said, her smile fading a little. "He only spent a few minutes with Gert and me. We weren't married to a mobster!"

"Now, she wasn't married to Rocky," Winnie said.

Riley stared at Winnie. "Hattie's talking to a P.I.?"

"There's no guarantee she's just talking to him," Gert grumbled.

Winnie beamed a smile at Riley. "Since the police can't seem to clear up the burglaries, I've hired a private investigator. Sam Romano. He works for a big security firm. It was Charles who gave me the idea to call them. He says that the police are bungling the case. He was so afraid that they were going to arrest you this morning."

As if on cue, the library door opened, and Hattie appeared, her hand on the arm of a lean, dark-haired man in a well-tailored suit. Smiling, she glanced up at him. "What did you say your name was again?"

"Sam. Sam Romano."

"And you think you can track down my Rocky for me?"

"I can't see that it will be a problem."

Turning, Hattie shot a triumphant look at Gert and Prue as Sam eased her into a chair. "Mr. Romano has agreed to take my case."

Prue patted the seat next to her, beaming a smile at the library door. "I have a case I'd like to talk to you about, too, Mr. Romano."

"He's over to your left," Gert said. "You don't need a P.I. You need a Seeing Eye dog."

"Ladies, Mr. Romano's primary job here is to find out

who is burglarizing us. And he hasn't yet talked to Riley and Mr. DeRosa.''

"Sam has been telling me about all his high-tech equipment. That's why he won't have any trouble finding Rocky,'' Hattie said.

"He told me that his last case took him less then twenty-four hours to solve,'' Prue added.

"Hmmph,'' Gert said. "He told *me* he solved one in ten minutes flat!''

Riley's stomach sank lower with each revelation. Not only did she have a cop shadowing her, but now a super-sleuth was going to spy on her as well. Images flashed into her mind—mug shots of her Uncle Avery, Ben and herself, all lined up in a row.

"Mr. Romano,'' Jack said with a nod.

"Mr. DeRosa. Why don't I start with you?''

Riley let out a breath she hadn't been aware she was holding. This was her chance. While the super-sleuth was talking to Jack, she would slip away and talk to Ben. The thought had no sooner entered her mind when Jack's hand clamped around her wrist.

"I think it would be better if you talked to both of us at the same time,'' he said, as he followed Sam Romano into the library.

THE MOMENT he shut the door, Sam gestured them toward a leather sofa. "Why don't you begin, Mr. DeRosa? I understand you were hired yesterday.''

"We don't have to put on an act in here, Romano. Riley knows I'm a cop.''

Riley glanced from one to the other. "You two know each other?''

"Yeah,'' Jack said.

"My brother A.J. and Jack worked in the same precinct for a while,'' Sam explained. Then he turned to Jack. "I thought when I saw you out there that you must be working undercover.''

"I am," Jack said. "The ladies believe that I'm Riley's new assistant.''

Sam's brows shot up. "But the prime suspect knows you're a cop?''

"It's a long story. The short version is Winnie Cantrell's godson is the police commissioner. He called my captain, and Duffy convinced Ms. Foster to set up my cover. How did you get roped into this? I thought your specialty was corporate espionage.''

Sam grinned. "Winnie Cantrell has another godson—my boss. She called him because the police are bungling the job. That's a direct quote. Although he didn't say it in so many words, my boss would be very pleased if I could exonerate Ms. Foster here." Sinking into the chair across from them, he asked, "I take it you've already done that?''

"No," Jack said.

Sam raised his brows. "You still suspect her?''

"No. But I haven't found any evidence that eliminates her.''

Sam shook his head, then turned the full force of his smile on Riley. "Police work is so shoddy these days. It brings me more business than I can handle.''

Jack's derisive snort told Riley that this was a conversation the two men had had before. Sam was chuckling, but Jack was frowning.

"Stick to business, Sam," he said.

Sam shot Jack a speculative look. "You posting signs?''

"Posting signs?" Riley asked.

"Yeah," Jack said, ignoring her.

"Would the two of you stop talking as if I'm not in the room? And what do you mean by *posting signs?*''

"We're being rude," Sam said shaking his head again,

"very rude. My apologies, Ms. Foster. Whenever I associate with a cop, my manners go to pieces."

"That's not the only thing that's going to be in pieces," Jack warned.

With a grin, Sam raised both hands, palms out. "Truce. I'll stick to business." But the smile he turned on Riley hadn't lost any of its charm. "I'm thinking I could use a refill on my tea. Would you mind?"

"Sure," Riley said as she rose.

She was at the door when Jack said, "Don't even think of running."

He waited until the door closed behind Riley to say, "You don't want any tea."

Sam's expression grew serious. "No. I wanted a moment alone with you. I'm detecting a certain lack of objectivity on your part."

Jack's gaze narrowed. "It won't interfere with my job."

Sam studied him for a moment. "What makes you think she didn't do it?"

"Instinct," Jack said.

"How about the brother or the uncle?"

"I don't think they're involved."

"That leaves the ladies in the other room or Louie 'the Rock' Mancuso. What's your take on any of them?"

Jack sighed. "About the same as yours, I imagine."

"The brother or the uncle are much more viable suspects."

Jack nodded.

"What happens if I find solid evidence that one of them did it?"

Jack thought of Hattie's brooch and the Abernathy's diamonds, solid evidence that he was carrying around right now on his person. "I'll arrest him or her."

Sam leaned back in his chair. "Want to know what my instinct is telling me?"

"I'm sure you're going to tell me."

The smile that spread across Sam's face was cocky, confident. How many times had he seen that same smile on the basketball court over the years when he'd played hoops with the Romano brothers? Sam, younger and smaller than his brothers, had always been the most competitive.

"My instinct tells me you're holding something back. I'll just have to find out what."

PUSHING THE DOOR OPEN, Riley paused before she reentered the library. She still sensed tension between the two men.

"What did I miss?" she asked as she carried the tray to the table between them.

Immediately, the two men relaxed slightly. Sam smiled and Jack made an effort to do the same.

"Sam here thinks I'm holding back evidence," Jack said.

It was only by concentrating very carefully that she was able to set the tray down without spilling it.

"But I'm surprised that the super-sleuth we were hearing about from the ladies hasn't solved the case already," Jack continued as he picked up a teacup.

"Ouch." Wincing, Sam fisted a hand at his chest, then drew it away as if he were removing an arrow. Then he picked up his pen and notebook from the table. "I think that's my cue to get busy. I'll check with Rocky's parole officer for a current address and I'll run a check on the cab company records to see if the any of the ladies paid a nocturnal visit to the Abernathys'. But that still leaves Riley here, the uncle and the brother."

"They didn't do it," Riley said. "They wouldn't want to hurt me."

"Neither one has an alibi for last night," Jack said.

"That's not true," Riley objected. "Uncle Avery spent the night at his friend Harold's."

"I haven't had a chance yet to verify that with Harold," Jack said. "And I imagine he would lie to cover for Avery.

Ben claims he spent the night at his friend Jeff's, but neither one of them were at Jeff's house.''

"But we haven't had a chance to ask Ben what happened," Riley said.

Sam tapped a pencil on his notebook. "And each would probably lie for the other. What about you, Ms. Foster?''

"I was at my apartment last night," she said. "Except for the time when Mr. DeRosa and I went out to—''

"We paid a visit to Hattie Silverman," Jack said. "Riley wanted to check on Baby, and she didn't want to disturb Hattie. She used her key.''

Sam glanced at Jack. "You went with her?''

"Yes.''

"Were you with her all evening?''

Jack met Sam's eyes. "This stays in this room.''

Sam nodded. "Agreed.''

"I can testify that she was in the apartment the rest of the night except for the hour that I fell asleep.''

When Sam's eyebrows shot up, Riley said, "It wasn't his fault. I put one of his pain pills in his soup.''

"You drugged him?" Sam turned to Jack. "She drugged you.''

"Yeah," Jack said.

"His leg was bothering him because he tried to come to my rescue. He thought I was being mugged, but they were only kids, and—''

Jack held up a hand. "As fascinating as Sam finds this story, I'm sure he wants us to stick to the facts.'' Turning to Sam, he said, "I fell asleep on the job, and so I can't testify to the fact that she didn't go down to the Abernathys' and steal their diamonds.''

Setting his notebook and pen on the table, Sam leaned back in his chair. "One solution is to assign a tail to each of the suspects until the next robbery takes place.''

"Have you got that kind of manpower?" Jack asked.

Sam glanced at his watch. "I can get it by tomorrow."

"Now, wait just a minute. You're talking about tailing Ben and Uncle Avery?" Riley asked.

"Along with the ladies, too, of course. That way we'll have hard evidence they're in the clear the next time a robbery occurs," Sam explained.

Or evidence to convict, Riley thought as she rose from the sofa. "No. I won't have it. I don't want my family treated as if they're common criminals."

Jack rose, too, and his hands were hard when they gripped her shoulders. "Think."

Riley met his eyes. They were hard, expressionless, the eyes of a cop. Why couldn't she remember that's what he was?

"This isn't some kind of game," he said. "Someone is stealing from your clients. If it isn't your uncle or your brother, then you have nothing to worry about. If it is one of them, it's better that Sam or I find out than the police. Unless you think they're guilty?"

"No." Of course, she didn't. But Ben was keeping secrets from her. Just as her father had. If he hadn't... When she realized Sam was talking to her, she tried to focus on what he was saying.

"...anyone else we should add to the list of suspects," Sam said. Then he turned to Jack. "You got any favorites?"

Jack shook his head. "No one specific. Unless..."

"What?" Sam and Riley asked in unison.

"What if we're coming at this from the wrong angle? What if the motive is more complicated than simple burglary? What if someone is trying to put Riley out of business?"

"A business rival?" Sam asked. Then turning to Riley, he handed her his notebook and pen. "Why don't you make a list?"

She stared down at the pad, then back at Sam. "I don't know of anyone."

"Who were your clients using before you took them on?" Sam asked. "Is there anyone else who wanted that space you rented for your pet day-care business? Start with them. And while you're doing that, Jack can fill me in on what the police have so far."

Riley frowned as she settled Sam's notebook on her lap. There had been a man who'd come into the store that day, just moments after she'd signed the lease. He'd been very annoyed that the deal had been closed. A real estate agent who'd just lost a commission, she'd supposed. But the space had been on the market for over six months. And she certainly didn't know the man's name. But her agent might. She jotted the possibility down on the pad and then frowned. The whole idea was ridiculous. Why would someone, anyone, go to such lengths to get a store space? It wasn't as though real estate was at a premium in Manhattan. Riley looked up from her task, intending to tell the two men just that. But they were deep in conversation, both leaning forward, their arms resting on their knees.

The camaraderie of a few minutes ago had disappeared. Now both men were intent, focused on what they were discussing. In profile, the differences between them struck her. Everything about Sam was smooth and polished from his neatly trimmed hair and manicured nails to his designer suit and shoes. He gestured frequently with his hands, and he was doing most of the talking. It was easy to picture him tracking criminals at his desk or charming clients in a boardroom. Sitting across from him, Jack's rougher edges were even more apparent. He gestured so rarely, as if he was determined to give nothing of himself away. He was even frugal with his words. But it was more than just the difference in wardrobe or manners. There was a toughness about Jack DeRosa that went to his core. He was the man she would want beside her in an alley.

He was the man she wanted period. He was listening to Sam now, and she could feel a sharp, aching desire fill her just as it had when he'd kissed her earlier in the alley. She could smell him. Above the scent of leather-bound books and lemon wax, even above the faint scent of Sam's aftershave. It occurred to her that she would know he was in the room even if she were blind. And just looking at him, she could remember what it was like to taste him, to feel the press of his...

"Riley?"

Riley blinked, then reined in her wandering thoughts. The two men were looking at her curiously. "Sorry. What?"

"Have you finished that list?" Sam asked.

Riley glanced down at the notebook, then handed it over as she explained about the real estate agent who'd seemed so upset when she'd signed the lease. "It probably doesn't mean anything."

"I'll check it out," Sam said. "I also need to know who besides you might have access to your clients' apartments. Jack tells me there's more than one set of keys."

"I had three sets made up for the times when both Avery and Ben are working with me. That way we can split the workload and each take a separate building."

"Did Ben ever take his friend Jeff along while he was working?" Jack asked.

Riley frowned. "Sure. But you're not suggesting that—"

"I'm not suggesting anything. But it's important that we know exactly who might have had access to both the keys and the apartments," Jack said. "I'm going to assume Avery's friend Harold might have also been invited along."

"I suppose," Riley said.

"Do the police know all this?" Sam asked.

"They never asked," Riley said.

"There was no mention of any other leads being pursued in the files I read," Jack said. "How much manpower can you put on this?"

Sam smiled. "It depends on how quickly my boss wants this case to go away. Another call from his godmother wouldn't hurt. I'll mention it before I leave. But I won't be able to put tails on everyone until sometime tomorrow."

"We need to cover at least Ben and Avery tonight." Turning to Riley, Jack said, "Can we make sure Ben stays in tonight?"

"Absolutely," she said. "You're cooking spaghetti." And she intended to have a long talk with Ben—in private.

Sam sighed. "That leaves me with Avery, right?"

"Absolutely," Jack said.

8

"WHAT'S ALL THAT green stuff?" Ben asked.

"This is fresh basil." Jack pointed to the bunch he'd just set on the kitchen counter. "The other one's parsley."

Ben wrinkled his nose. "I thought you were cooking spaghetti with meatballs."

"Ben hates anything that resembles a vegetable," Riley explained as she burrowed her way into a cupboard next to the stove.

"The basil and parsley will flavor the sauce," Jack began, but the Bard interrupted him.

"Double, double, toil and trouble."

"Does that bird have a line for every occasion?" Jack turned to find that in the length of time it had taken him to empty the grocery bags, the kitchen had become crowded. Ben had jumped off the couch in the library and followed them into the kitchen the moment they'd arrived. Now Beowulf was pressing against the back of his leg, Abra had leapt onto the counter to inspect the parsley, and Avery, wearing a red velvet lounging robe, had assumed a pose in the archway.

"Marvelous bird. He received his early training at the Old Vic," Avery explained.

Moving closer to Jack, Ben spoke in an undertone. "The Bard says that line whenever we start to cook anything."

Abra switched her attention from the parsley to the package of ground beef.

Grabbing it, Jack passed it to Ben. "Your job is to protect the meatballs."

Riley held up a pot. "It's not a cauldron, but it's the biggest thing we've got."

"It's fine," Jack said.

"Okay. C'mon, Ben," Riley said, wiping her hands against her jeans as she rose to her feet. "While Jack fixes dinner, you and I can talk."

"Can't we talk after dinner?" Ben asked. "I want to watch Jack make the sauce."

"We really need to—" Riley began.

"Oh, let the boy watch." Pulling a notepad out of his pocket, Avery settled himself at the table. "I'm going to take notes."

"Notes?" Jack asked.

"Absolutely. Never know when it will come in handy. I always used to watch my cooks. Picked up several pointers. One time I played a chef in a major film. I was murdered in the middle of making a soufflé." Whipping out a pen, he glanced up at Jack expectantly. "Proceed. You won't even know I'm here."

"Ben, I think it would be better if we talked now," Riley said.

"Aw, c'mon, Sis." Then he turned to Jack. "Actually, I was wondering... Would you mind, I mean...would it be all right if I filmed you?"

"Filmed me?" Glancing around the kitchen, Jack saw six pairs of eyes trained on him.

"It's an assignment for my film class," Ben explained. "I have to practice taking close-ups, camera angles. That kind of stuff."

Jack tried to rid himself of the feeling that he'd just become a smear on a microscope slide. "I've never cooked in front of an audience before." The fact was he hadn't cooked at all in quite a while. Not since he'd hurt his leg.

"You won't even know I'm here," Ben said.

"Ben, Jack is being kind enough to make dinner—" Riley began.

"Please."

It was the pleading look in the boy's eyes that did Jack in. "On one condition."

"What?" Ben asked eagerly.

"First, you have to help me do some of the prep work."

"Me?" Ben asked. "I don't know how to cook."

"It's not rocket science," Jack said. "My aunt started teaching me when I was your age."

"Really?" Ben asked, the hesitation still clear in his voice. "I always thought cooking was for girls."

"Nonsense," Avery said. "The famous chefs are always men."

"You're forgetting Julia Child," Riley pointed out.

"Why didn't *you* ever learn to cook, Uncle Avery?" Ben asked.

"Never had the time," Avery said.

"There's no time like the present," Jack said. "If we all pitch in, we'll eat that much sooner."

Ten minutes later, Jack leaned back against a counter and watched his budding chefs at work. The air was filled with the scent of fresh basil, garlic and onions.

Whack! Ben brought a cleaver down on a clove of garlic with all the force of a samurai warrior going in for the kill. "This is great! Bet I'm done before you are, Uncle Avery."

"This isn't a race, my boy," Avery said as he sliced slowly into the onion with a concentration that bore testimony to all of his years as a method actor. "Every work of art requires precision. Each part makes a contribution to the whole."

"Double, double, toil and trouble—" began the Bard.

"Yeah, yeah. Whatever," Ben said, drowning out the rest of the bird's speech with three quick whacks on the board.

"I have no talent for this," Riley said, setting her knife down with a sigh.

"Nonsense," Jack said, moving toward her. "If you're going to be a vet, you'll have to do surgery, and that means you'll have to learn to handle a knife."

Riley glanced up at him. "You must be really good at handling suspects," she said so only he could hear.

"Why do you say that?"

"You know exactly which psychological buttons to push," she complained.

He felt the corners of his mouth twitch. "Whatever works. You hold the knife like this." He placed it in her hand, then kept his over hers, guiding her as she drew it slowly through the folded basil leaves. "You want to be gentle so that you don't crush the leaves. It makes all the difference in the flavor."

Even as he said the words, the memory slipped into his mind. His aunt had said the same words to him when she'd first taught him to work with basil. Too much pressure on the knife would cause the leaves to turn brown, subtly changing the flavor. How many times had she repeated the words as she'd worked patiently with him in the tiny kitchen of her apartment until he'd mastered the technique? As if it were yesterday, he could recall the pungent aroma of sauce in the air, the warmth of her arms around him as she guided each stroke of the knife in his hands.

He could hear the sound of her voice in his ear, as he said, "You have to feel it. Just the right amount of pressure." Later, when the sauce was done and the spaghetti was boiling, they would sit at the tiny table to eat. It would be a Sunday, the only day the restaurant where she worked was closed. After he finished telling her what had happened at school during the week, she would entertain him with stories about the restaurant.

"There. That's it," Riley said.

"What?" Jack asked.

"The basil's done." She turned to study him for a minute. "You look as though you're hundreds of miles away."

No, he wanted to say. *Just about fifty blocks.* That was how far it was to the tiny, cold-water flat in the Village that he and his aunt had shared. He hadn't thought of his life there, hadn't allowed himself to think of their hand-to-mouth existence, for years. It occurred to him then that this was the first time a memory of his aunt hadn't brought pain. Instead, it had brought a feeling of…home. As the realization flooded through him, he quickly pushed the emotions down. Hadn't he learned yet not to wish for what he couldn't have?

"I'm back now." He made a conscious effort to focus on Riley. Drawing in a steadying breath, he caught her scent above the basil. This time it reminded him of spring rain. And he was suddenly and totally aware of how close they were standing. His arms still caged her against the counter. One step and their bodies would brush. Just imagining the contact had his body tightening, and a quick, hot spiral of desire moved through him. As his gaze remained steady on hers, the curiosity he saw darkened into something else, something that pulled at him. His gaze dropped to her mouth. Her lips were parted, moist, offering a feast that had nothing to do with the meal they were preparing. Did she have any idea what she did to him? He wanted to taste her. To touch her. He wanted to lose himself in her, to forget about what he couldn't have.

"I'm done," Avery announced.

The moment the words penetrated, Jack dropped his hands to his sides and stepped back from Riley, stunned by the realization that he'd forgotten for a moment that they weren't alone.

"You said you weren't racing," Ben said.

"I wasn't. I just finished first." Avery raised his hands

like a surgeon who'd just finished a particularly difficult operation and strode to the sink. "I need to scrub now. Water."

Reaching over, Jack twisted the faucet.

"I'm done, too," Ben said, moving in beside his uncle at the sink. "Actually, I was done three garlic cloves ago. I just like smashing them with that cleaver."

"A likely story," Avery said.

"How about a rematch?" Jack suggested as he opened the package of ground beef. If he kept his mind on the meal, he just might be able to keep his hands off Riley. "We'll see who finishes shaping their meatballs first."

RILEY LEANED BACK in her chair and pressed a hand to her stomach. The platters that had seemed heaped with food when they'd carried them to the table were almost empty. She should get up, clear the table, but she wasn't sure she could move. And she still had to have that talk with Ben, she reminded herself. But she quite simply didn't want the meal to end. Not yet.

For now, she just wanted to enjoy the moment and the scene before her. Jack was the one who'd suggested using the dining room. Avery had produced candles and insisted on using the best china. Ben had transported the Bard's perch from the kitchen and selected the music. The low sound of saxophones could be heard beneath the spirited conversation that had been going on for some time.

She couldn't recall the last time she and Ben had shared a family meal. Her father had rarely been home for any kind of a family gathering. And since they'd moved in with Uncle Avery and she'd started her business, mealtimes had been haphazard at best. Usually, they all grabbed something on the run.

"I still say that *Psycho* is the film that best portrays Hitchcock's genius as a filmmaker," Avery said, poking at the air with a fork to emphasize his point.

"I vote for *Vertigo*. It's a masterpiece of psychological drama." Ben leaned forward. One of his hands was fisted on the table, the knuckles white, as he proceeded to enumerate the reasons for his stand.

Clearly, film was her brother's passion. Riley wished, not for the first time, that he could be this intent on something more practical. It was a bone of contention between them, but she was beginning to believe that she was losing the battle. Perhaps, it wasn't even worth the fight. It had been a long time since she'd seen Ben as happy and as animated as he was tonight.

And the person she had to thank for that was sitting in the chair next to hers, petting the kitten on his lap.

"Which Hitchcock film gets your vote?" Jack asked.

Suddenly realizing that she was the focus of everyone's gaze, Riley said, "Me?"

"You must have an opinion," Jack said.

"She doesn't like films," Ben said.

"Yes, I do. I just…" Catching herself on the verge of launching into a lecture she'd given to Ben before, she cut herself off and said, "I just don't feel like an authority."

"Which of his films did you like the best?" Jack asked.

Riley thought for a moment. *"North by Northwest."*

"The crop-dusting scene is one of his best," Ben said, nodding his head in approval.

"No, no, no," Avery said, pounding his fist on the table and rattling the china. "That movie is so obvious compared to the subtleties of *Psycho!* There's no comparison. Surely, you agree with me, Jack."

"Sorry. I have to go with *Vertigo*." His announcement won a whoop of triumph from Ben and a glare from Avery.

"I demand a vote on his best scene," Avery said. "You'll all have to agree that the shower scene from *Psycho* is by far the best. The sound effects he used when that knife slashed down again and again and…"

"Is this a dagger I see before me?" the Bard intoned from his perch.

"Right you are," Avery beamed a smile at the bird. "At least someone agrees with me!"

"I don't," Ben said.

"You can disagree all you want, but you're wrong," Avery said.

"No way. Listen," Ben began.

As the debate increased in intensity, Riley watched Jack lean back in his chair. In spite of the fact that he might not talk as long or as loudly as Ben or her uncle, when he did say something, they both listened. His detailed knowledge of film had surprised her. In fact, Jack DeRosa had been surprising her from their first meeting.

It had never occurred to her until tonight that cooking could be fun. But he'd made it seem that way. Studying him in profile, what she saw wasn't the competent cop she'd seen earlier in Winnie Cantrell's library, nor was it the rather frightening warrior who'd charged into the alley to save her the first time they'd met. Instead, she saw a kind man who, in spite of his discomfort, had allowed Ben to take movies of him. She watched as he nodded at something Avery was saying, then dropped his hand to his lap to run it over the sleeping Abra again. The sweetness of the gesture melted something within her. And when she raised her eyes to his face, she found that he was watching her, too. Once again, the intensity of his gaze held her and pulled at her. He'd looked at her that same way in the kitchen when she'd finished chopping the basil. As if he wanted to eat her alive. And she'd wanted him to do just that. But now she could see beneath the hunger to the need. It matched perfectly what she was feeling herself.

This might be the first and last time Jack DeRosa might share a meal with her. Just thinking about that twisted a little band of pain around her heart. It wouldn't be long before they found out who was stealing the jewels, and then she wouldn't have any need for an undercover cop as her assistant. She could concentrate on opening her pet day-care business. After all, that was what she wanted. Raising her hand, she rubbed the spot on her chest to ease the tightening sensation.

"No, no, no!" Avery pounded his fist on the table. "The true mark of Hitchcock's genius was the shower scene. The restraint he showed left the horror to the imagination of the viewer. I couldn't take a shower in a motel room for years after I saw that film."

"Is this a dagger I see before me?" the Bard asked.

"I've got two votes," Avery said.

"He's a bird. He can't vote," Ben said. "And I'm still voting for *Vertigo* when James Stewart is climbing those stairs to the bell tower. What do you think, Jack?"

"I'm voting for *Psycho*."

At Avery's whoop of triumph, Jack raised a hand. "But not the shower scene. I like the overhead shot of the P.I. climbing the stairs. And all the while the audience knows what's up there waiting."

"That is a great scene," Ben said, nodding.

The P.I. The words brought reality flooding back into Riley's mind as the discussion continued. She couldn't help but think of Sam Romano and the fact that he was sitting outside in his car, waiting to tail her uncle if he left the apartment. And she had to have a talk with Ben and find out where he'd been last night. She'd procrastinated long enough. Standing, she lifted her plate and reached for Ben's.

"We're never going to agree on which scene," Avery said as he rose from his chair. "Let's just call it a draw."

"Please sit down, Uncle Avery. I didn't mean to put an end to the discussion," Riley said. "I'm just going to clear the table."

"I have to get dressed anyway," he said as he moved

toward the door. "Sorry to eat and run, but I promised Harold I'd come over so we could run lines again."

"I have to get going, too," Ben said as he stood up and followed his uncle.

"Wait." Riley had to hurry into the hallway to stop him. "Ben, you're not going out tonight."

He turned back, his expression puzzled. "It's Saturday night. I've made plans."

"You're not going out again until we have a talk."

"Not going out *again?*" Ben stared at her, the color rising in his cheeks. "Are you grounding me? For what?"

Riley drew in a deep breath and tried to ignore the sickening feeling in the pit of her stomach. "I'm not grounding you. You agreed we could talk after we finished eating."

He glanced at his watch. "Can't it wait? Jeff's waiting for me."

"That's what we need to talk about. You weren't at Jeff's house last night."

"Were you spying on me?" Ben asked.

"No." But she would be, starting tomorrow. The thought had the knot in her stomach tightening. "I ran into Jeff's mother. She thought that Jeff spent the night here. I want to know where you were."

The color rose in Ben's face. "You're not my parent, you know. You don't have any right to tell me what to do."

"You're right." She wasn't his parent. In another year, he'd be eighteen and he could do anything he wanted. He could do that now, and yelling at him wasn't going to do her any good. She took another deep breath as she reached out to place a hand on his arm. "But the police believe one of us, me or Uncle Avery or you, might be stealing from my clients. They're not going to stop with that search warrant this morning. It's important that we each have an alibi that will hold up."

Ben jerked his arm away. "Do you think I'm robbing your clients?"

"No, of course not. But I need to know where you were last night. You said you were going to Jeff's."

"At the last moment, we decided to go to Henry's. Satisfied?"

Riley's heart sank. He was lying. She was almost sure of it. "No. I think it would be better if you stayed in."

"I'm not going to take orders from—"

Even before Ben's sentence trailed off, Riley could sense that Jack had appeared behind her. Her tension began to ease even before he spoke.

"Why don't you take Beowulf for a walk, Ben?" he asked. "While you're doing that, Riley and I will clean up the kitchen. By the time you finish, perhaps both of you could come up with a compromise."

After a moment's hesitation, Ben said, "Fine." Then whistling for Beowulf to follow him, he turned and walked down the hall to the foyer.

Riley waited until she heard the apartment door close before she turned to Jack. "Thank you for suggesting that. I hope you have a plan for keeping him in the apartment when he gets back."

"I think you should let him go to Jeff's and study his math," Jack said as he stacked the rest of the dishes and headed for the kitchen.

"But I'm not sure he's telling the truth. I know this Henry. His parents are never home. If I call him, I'm sure he'll cover for both Ben and Jeff."

"It may not be a cover."

"You think they were really studying at Henry's?" Riley asked as she took the dishes from Jack and began to scrape them and load them into the dishwasher.

"Maybe."

"But what if they weren't?"

"There's one sure way to find out if Ben's lying to you. We could follow him tonight when he leaves."

She looked at him then. If she did, she would be guilty of doing exactly what he'd accused her of—spying on him. If she didn't...

"Is someone going to take that dog for a walk?" Avery asked as he paused in the archway.

"Beowulf?" Riley asked, stiffening.

"He wandered into my room a few minutes ago and he's looking at me as though I'm his last hope." He glanced at his watch. "I still need to shave and I'm running late as it is."

"We'll take care of it," Jack said.

Riley turned to him the moment she heard her uncle's footsteps fade. "But Ben said... I thought I heard the door close."

"Yeah," Jack agreed as he moved toward the hall. "You whistle for the dog. I'll check Ben's room."

As she watched him stride away, thoughts swirled through her head, adding impetus to the panic skipping up her spine. Two things were clear. The cop was back, and Ben was up to something. He never would have sneaked out to study math.

"Something is rotten in Denmark."

Riley turned to stare at the bird. He had an uncanny knack of getting it just right.

ONCE THEY WERE out of the building, Jack glanced up and down the street. On the corner, the lights of a car blinked on and then off. "That's Sam," he said, drawing Riley with him as he hurried toward the car. Beowulf stopped pulling on his leash and trotted happily along behind them. Sam had the window down when they reached him.

"Did you see a young man come out? About five foot ten, thin—" Jack began.

"Wearing a Mets cap and carrying a duffel," Sam finished. "He walked across the street and headed south. I lost him when he turned right on 85th St."

"That's the way he would go to Jeff's," Riley said.

Sam shifted his gaze to her. "Your brother? I thought he was going to be in for the evening."

"Change of plan," Jack said. "I need to borrow your car."

"That's a pretty big change," Sam said.

"I'll owe you one," Jack replied. "The uncle is shaving. He's going uptown to his friend Harold's. You'll be able to follow him on foot."

Opening the door, Sam slid out from behind the wheel, and Jack quickly took his place. Shaking his head, Sam took Riley's arm and escorted her to the passenger side. "These cops. They have no manners." But when she opened the door and Beowulf bounded into the back seat, his grin changed to a frown. "The dog's going with you?"

It was Jack's turn to shake his head. "These P.I.'s. They're so slow."

"You owe me two," Sam called as Jack peeled away from the curb.

The speed with which he turned the corner had her reaching for her seat belt. When he floored the gas pedal and cut across three lanes, she said a silent prayer of thanks that traffic was light. Then, before she could take a breath, she tensed, bracing both hands on the dashboard as he made a right on two wheels.

"Does my driving make you nervous?" he asked as he sped down the street.

"No," she managed. "I was just wondering if you moonlighted as a taxi driver."

His laugh was quick and charming. And then suddenly, the smile faded and he slowed, moving into the right lane. "There he is."

Riley glanced quickly in the direction of his gaze. She spotted Ben immediately, striding along at a clipped pace, his duffel slung over his shoulder. She was reaching to roll down her window when Jack grabbed her hand. "No."

"I want to talk to him. Don't you?"

"Not yet," Jack said as he slowed the car even further. "He'll only evade our questions. If we follow him, we'll find out a lot more."

He was right. They would find out a lot more. But what?

"We have to find out the truth," Jack said. "Facing your fears is the only way to get past them."

"Okay," she said. "We'll follow him."

He was good at tailing, Riley discovered in the twenty minutes it took to reach Jeff's apartment building. Twice, he turned down a side street, made a U-turn and then followed at a greater distance for a while. On the other hand, Ben didn't seem in the least worried that he was being followed. No doubt he thought he'd made a perfect getaway. And if it hadn't been for Beowulf, he would have.

"Jeff's building is right there," Riley said, pointing.

"Yeah," Jack said. "And this is the corner where that goon snatched the poodle."

"Right," Riley said, and then she frowned. Instead of pressing the buzzer and getting admitted to the building, Ben was walking toward a black stretch limousine parked by the curb. To her astonishment, the door opened and he got in. The moment he was inside, the limo pulled away from the curb.

"Who does he know who drives a limo?" Jack asked as he cut in front of a car and edged into the lane the limousine had taken.

"I don't know," Riley said, her mind racing. "I don't think any of my clients are that rich."

"Winnie Cantrell is. But I wasn't thinking of your clients."

"Who then?" Riley asked.

"We'll know soon," he said as he flew through a light that was no longer amber. A horn blasted and Riley grabbed for the dashboard again.

"You're going to kill us."

"Relax," Jack said. "I drove a patrol car for three years before I became a detective, and I never lost a passenger."

He took the next corner sharply. Pressing a hand to her throat in an effort to force out her voice, Riley said, "There's always a first time. You could be out of practice."

His laugh was cut short when he swore. "I don't see it. Check the next cross street."

Her teeth snapped together when he slammed on the brakes, but she spotted the limo. "There. To the right."

Her shoulder slammed into the door as he jerked the car into the turn. When the car shot forward, she was pitched against the back of her seat.

They were heading north toward Harlem. As the blocks sped by, one thought was uppermost in her mind. "Where is he going?"

"Or being taken," Jack said.

Being taken? A whole set of new worries suddenly replaced the others that were swirling around in her mind. Was Ben being kidnapped? Was he the victim of some kind of white slavery ring?

"Can't you go any faster?" she asked.

He shot her an amused glance. "I thought you were worried about the safety of pedestrians."

"That was before I thought someone might be kidnapping my brother."

"I don't think it's a kidnapping."

"What then?"

"I was thinking more along the lines of a party. One of those exclusive after-hours gatherings. Certain designer drugs are available."

Turning, she stared at him. "You can't be serious."

He shrugged. "There's a lot of that going on in the city right now, especially with kids Ben's age."

"No." Riley shook her head. "Absolutely not. Ben wouldn't."

Jack slammed on the brakes and pulled the car to the curb. Looking through the windshield, Riley saw that the limousine had stopped, too. She recognized both Jeff and Ben when they climbed out of the back seat. The street ahead had been blocked off. Huge, portable stadium-strength lights illuminated the area beyond the barricade, making it seem like daylight. "What is going on?" she asked.

"My guess is someone's shooting a movie," Jack said as he opened his door and slid out.

"Stay, Beowulf," Riley said as she scrambled out her side of the car.

Sawhorses had been spread across the width of the street. By the time they reached them, Riley had lost sight of Ben. Several trucks blocked her view, but in the narrow space between two of them, she spotted a camera on a dolly, and some men drinking coffee from foam cups.

"Sorry, we can't let anyone through," a heavyset security guard said as Jack began to push aside one of the sawhorses.

"McClusky, is that you?" Jack asked.

"Detective DeRosa." A smile blossomed on the older man's face. "Good to see you."

Jack turned to her. "Riley, Sergeant McClusky was the desk sergeant at the precinct before he retired."

"Pleased, ma'am," McClusky said with a nod. But when Jack put his hand on the sawhorse again, the sergeant said, "Sir, it'll mean my job if I let anyone through."

"You let my brother through," Riley said as Jack's hand dropped to his side. "He just got out of that black limousine."

McClusky frowned. "The assistant director was waiting for him. That means he was on the VIP list."

"I want to know what he's doing here," Riley said.

McClusky turned to Jack. "I can check for you. If you'll wait right here...?"

Jack nodded. "We'll wait."

Riley waited for the man to walk away before she said, "I thought a detective could flash his badge and get in anywhere."

"I can. And I will if we don't like what McClusky finds out."

He didn't want his old desk sergeant to be fired. Riley studied him in the dim light. Why did his sweetness always surprise her? Perhaps it was because he projected an aura of toughness even when he wasn't trying, even when he was making spaghetti sauce or petting a kitten. One of the other security guards had moved closer the minute McClusky walked away. But he was keeping his distance.

"You wouldn't even need your badge to get past these guards."

Jack turned to meet her eyes. "I don't think Ben is in any trouble."

And neither did she, Riley suddenly realized. When had the knot in her stomach melted? She suspected it was at about the same moment that Jack had decided Ben wasn't in trouble. Were they that much in tune? The intense way he looked at her told her they were. It was the same way he'd looked at her in the kitchen earlier. And once again, it was if he touched her in every way—mind, heart and body. She could feel something dissolving inside of her, something she'd been careful to build up. It was frightening to feel it slip so easily away.

"Your brother and his friend are special guests of the director."

They turned in unison to face the sergeant. She hadn't even heard him approach.

"He met up with them at their school where he gave a talk to a film class and invited them to the shoots. They've been here the last two nights."

Jack's gaze narrowed. "Someone could testify to that?"

"Sure. According to the assistant director I spoke with, the producers weren't all that happy about having a couple of kids on the set. Worried about liability. So they hired a bodyguard to watch out for them. He's the guy that brought them here in the limousine. He'll bring them home, too."

"Once a good cop, always a good cop," Jack said. "Thanks."

A smile spread slowly over McClusky's face. "They should be home by dawn. If you like, I'll personally keep my eye on them. Make sure they get loaded into the limo."

"I'd appreciate it," Jack said. As he drew her with him toward the car, feelings warred within her. She felt relief that her brother was not involved in the robberies. But it wasn't strong enough to push aside what she'd been feeling just before the sergeant had approached them.

She was almost sure that she'd fallen in love with Jack DeRosa—a man who'd come running into her life only a day ago. A man who'd walk out of it just as soon as they figured out who was stealing from her clients.

A man who drove like he was possessed and kissed like—

No, she wasn't going to think about Jack DeRosa kissing her. If she did, she'd lose what little grip she had left on her sanity. And she had to think. What in the world was she going to do now?

9

In the well-lit coffee shop, Jack chose a table where they could be seen from the street. He'd driven twice around the area without spotting Sam, so they would wait for him to spot them. "You're sure this is where Harold lives?" he asked as Riley sat in the chair across from his.

"The Vincent Building on Fifty-seventh and Third. I wrote it down when Uncle Avery mentioned giving Harold some of my business cards. We don't have any clients in this area yet. I intended to get some flyers printed up so that they could put them in mailboxes, but I…"

Her sentence trailed off when a waitress breezed up to the table. The plastic badge on her apron declared her name to be Bridget. Jack ordered coffee, then waited for Riley to make a selection from the herbal teas that the young woman was rattling off. One explanation for the fact that he hadn't spotted Sam would be that Harold and Avery had gone out and Sam had followed them. And the fact that two men had decided to go out together on a Saturday night didn't mean that they were burglarizing anyone, he reminded himself. It occurred to him then that he wanted Riley's brother and uncle to be innocent of the thefts just as much as she did.

Studying her in the bright light, he could see that she was tired.

"I'll try the spearmint ginseng," she said when Bridget finally came to the end of her list. With a smile and a nod, the waitress hurried away. Riley lifted a hand to rub her temple.

"Headache?" he asked.

She dropped her hand. "The tea will help."

Jack pushed back his chair. "I'll take you home. You don't have to wait for me to give Sam his car keys."

"If you take me home, who's going to be my alibi?"

He settled back into his chair. She was right. It was altogether too easy for him to forget that she was part of a job.

"At least Ben has one now. If he was with that film crew last night, he couldn't possibly have robbed the Abernathys. I should feel relieved." Pausing, she frowned. "I should be happy that he has this opportunity to see a film being made. But mostly, I feel hurt that he lied to me."

Jack said nothing, merely watching as she picked up the napkin the waitress had left and began to fold it into a narrow strip.

"I know why he lied. He was afraid that if he asked me for permission to stay out all night to watch a film being made, I would say no." Glancing up, she met his eyes. "And I would have. So I suppose in a way I forced him to lie. And I'm not sure that I wouldn't have done the same thing in his position. But I...I hate being lied to."

"Everyone hates it," Jack said, reaching for her hand. Her fingers immediately wrapped around his and held on.

"Ben was right earlier. I do act like a parent. I can see why he resents that."

"How long have you had the responsibility for raising him?" Jack asked.

"My mother died when he was five and I was twelve."

"What about your father?"

Her shoulders moved in a slight shrug. And when she spoke, her voice had tightened. "He was never around. And his business made it necessary for us to move around a lot. There were nannies, a whole string of them. Just about the time we got used to a new one, we would move again. Ben came to depend on me."

"What kind of business was your father in?" He knew. He'd read it in her file. But he sensed that she needed to talk about it.

"Investments. He provided clients with high-risk, high-reward opportunities. We always had lots of money...until he lost his touch." Her lips curved slightly, but the smile didn't quite reach her eyes. "When I was a little girl, he always used to tell me that he had the Midas touch, like in the fairy tale. Every investment he came in contact with turned golden."

Jack nodded.

"Then he lost it." Even as she said the words, her voice went flat. "After he died, I learned from his attorneys that when things started going bad, he began putting money into even riskier ventures, and things got worse and worse. Then he started taking on new clients, and instead of investing their money, he would use it to pay dividends to other clients until he could recoup his losses, which was illegal. He even started gambling. When I would see him, I could tell that something was wrong, but he always denied it. If he'd just told me the truth..."

"You wouldn't have been able to stop him." He kept his fingers linked with hers as she drew in a breath and let it out. Then Bridget was serving their drinks, and she slipped her hand from his to stir her tea.

"Thanks," she said, glancing up at him with a smile.

"For what?" he asked.

"For not telling me that I shouldn't be blaming Ben because I'm still angry at my father."

His brows rose. "I'm a cop, not a psychologist."

After taking a sip, she set her tea down. "I know that Ben's lie can't be compared to my father's. And I know that I'm not being entirely fair to him about this film business."

"It's his dream, so it means a lot to him," Jack said simply.

She met his eyes then. "I know. It's just that he's been so used to having money. I wanted him to study something else in college, something more practical than filmmaking."

"You can't change somebody's dream."

"You're right." She tilted her head to one side, studying him. "You sound as if you're speaking from experience. Did your mom or dad give you a hard time about following your dream?"

"No." The moment he saw the hurt flash into her eyes, he deliberately shifted his gaze out the window. "I can't imagine what's keeping Sam, unless Avery and Howard have gone out."

His change of topic had been meant to distract her. He didn't want to talk about following his dream and what it had cost him. But when he turned back and saw that worry had replaced the hurt, he could have kicked himself.

"You don't think…no," she said. "Uncle Avery wouldn't be involved in the thefts. I know he wouldn't. It's bad enough that I let myself suspect Ben. I…" She raised her hands and dropped them. "I hate this. I want to find out who's doing this."

"We're going to do that," Jack said. "The first step is to have absolute proof we can take to the police that you and your family are not involved. We may have that by morning. And I don't believe that Avery is involved. It's a Saturday night. He and Harold probably finished running their lines and decided to go out."

"Right," she said and managed to summon up a smile. "It is Saturday. I forget sometimes what day of the week it is."

Was it any wonder, he thought. With the kind of schedule she kept, the week must fade into a blur.

"Don't you ever do something fun on the weekend?" he asked.

"You're beginning to sound like Winnie. She thinks I

ought to get out more. That's why she set me up with Charles.''

The stab of jealousy he felt at the mention of the man's name surprised him. Telling himself that he had no right, certainly no cause, to feel it didn't seem to make it diminish. He watched her closely in the harsh overhead light as she began to pleat her napkin again, and he had to fight down the urge to take her hand. No, he wanted to do more than hold her hand. He wanted her to himself in a very small space. Whatever he told himself or her, it was clear to him that the woman sitting across from him had gotten under his skin. ''Things didn't go well with Charles, I take it?''

Riley set her napkin down and picked up her cup. ''He's a very nice man. It's just that a date on the weekend wasn't enough. He wanted more. He wanted to get serious. He even offered me the money to hire an assistant. And then he was annoyed when I wouldn't accept it.''

''He didn't seem pleased that you'd hired me,'' Jack said.

She looked at him then, a smile curving her lips. ''I don't think you were the kind of assistant he had in mind.''

He took her hand again, but this time she didn't link her fingers with his. ''I'm sorry.''

''For what? It has nothing to do with you that Winnie's little plot to bring Charles and me together didn't work.''

''Not for that. I'm sorry for earlier, when I changed the subject. I didn't mean to hurt you. It's hard for me to talk about my family.''

''It's okay.''

The memory moved through him then. His aunt had said the same thing to him when she'd held him that last time in the hospital. He hadn't believed her then, and her words hadn't eased the terrible ache in his chest. But deep inside of him, he felt something ease now. He let out a breath he hadn't realized he was holding.

''I don't remember my mother,'' he said. ''And my dad

spent most of his life in and out of jail. My aunt said he'd started stealing just to keep food on the table. She was the kind of woman who gave everyone the benefit of the doubt.''

Riley covered the top of his hand with hers.

"It was my aunt who raised me. She worked as a chef in a small restaurant close to her apartment. I would go there after school and do my homework in the kitchen while she prepared the customers' food. She was always finding the bright side of things, always finding something to laugh about.''

"She loved you," Riley said.

"Yes. When I told her that I wanted to become a cop, it was the first time I'd ever seen her really angry. She wanted me to go to college, and she'd worked hard to put aside the money to send me. I wouldn't listen. We argued for months. I wanted her to take the money and open her own restaurant. She said there'd be plenty of time for that after I had my degree. It was a real bone of contention between us, and when I started at the academy, I moved out." Pausing, he drew in a deep breath and let it out.

"You don't have to tell me," Riley said.

"I want to finish. I didn't know when I moved out that she'd already been diagnosed with cancer. If I'd known…"

She went to him, sliding into the booth beside him and putting her arms around him.

"Six months later, she died." He'd never talked about it to anyone. Not even to the police shrink they'd been forcing him to see.

Riley said nothing. She just continued to hold him. He couldn't have said how long they remained like that or what it meant to him. But he knew that he felt whole in a way that he hadn't in a very long time.

Finally, he said, "I'm going to take you home. Sam will know where to find us."

RILEY LAY on her side, staring out the window at the lights of the city. Usually, the sight cheered her up in much the same way staring at a lit-up Christmas tree always did. But tonight… Frowning, she glanced at the illuminated dial of her watch. One-fifteen. Correction, *this morning,* it depressed her.

With a sigh, she turned over on her back. Immediately, she felt Beowulf stir at the foot of her bed. Then came a flapping noise from the cage in the corner. The Bard was awake, too. This was ridiculous. As long as she was tossing and turning, the animals weren't going to get any sleep, either.

Sitting up, she switched on the lamp. "Sorry, guys."

Two pairs of eyes stared back at her. Beowulf settled his head on his paws, a woeful expression on his face. She reached out to run a hand over his head. "I know. You need your beauty sleep."

"Out, out, damned spot," the Bard said.

She looked at the bird. "My problem is a little different from Lady Macbeth's. If it were just a nightmare keeping me awake, I'd fix some warm milk."

Beowulf raised his head and whined.

"Out, I say!" said the Bard.

"Forget it. You two have had more than enough to eat today." Although perhaps the warm milk wasn't such a bad idea. It never failed to put her to sleep. She glanced toward the door. If she went to the kitchen, it was only a few steps farther to the library, and that was where Jack had decided to sleep.

With a sigh, she pulled up her knees and wrapped her arms around them. When they'd gotten back to the apartment and found it empty, she'd expected some kind of fairy-tale ending to the fantasy she'd been building in her mind. Not even the jarring ride in the car had been able to shake it loose. In that coffee shop, she'd felt so close to Jack. And she was sure that he'd felt it, too. Once they'd reached the foyer and locked the door, she'd expected him to take her in his arms and forget everything he'd said when he'd kissed her in the alley.

But he hadn't. When he'd turned back to her after throwing the dead bolt, he'd looked every bit as remote as he had the very first time she'd met him. Slowly, she replayed the scene in her mind.

"You go ahead. I'm going to sleep in the library. That way I'll hear them the moment they come in."

When he turned and walked away from her, she stood there as if she'd been turned to stone. How many times had her father done the same thing? Then she'd watched Abra march right into the library with Jack. Why hadn't she just followed the kitten? Instead, she'd gone meekly to her room just like a good little girl.

"I'm a coward," she said aloud.

Beowulf blinked at her, and the Bard said, "Cowards die many times before their deaths."

"I'm not a coward all the time," she said. Just when it came to Jack.

"Frailty, thy name is woman," said the Bard.

Narrowing her gaze, she stared at him. "I'd like a little support here, if you don't mind."

And then suddenly, it struck her. Maybe she wanted too much support. Perhaps she was asking too much of Jack to sweep her off her feet and take the choice away from her. It wasn't so hard to understand where he was coming from. They'd both lost people they'd loved. Fear was paralyzing both of them. Maybe it was up to her to make the first move. Throwing off the covers, she got out of bed. At the door, she turned back to the animals. "Frailty is not my name."

"Out! Out, I say!" said the Bard.

Taking it as a vote of approval, Riley opened the door and

stepped out into the hall. The first thing she saw was Abra running toward her.

"What?" she asked, leaning down to pet the kitten.

Abra immediately slipped out from beneath her hand, then raced toward the end of the hall and careened around the corner. Something was wrong. Riley hurried after the kitten. The door to the apartment was still locked, the dead bolt in place, and when she stepped into the library, she found a light on and Jack, stretched out on the couch, fast asleep.

The rush of relief was mixed with annoyance. How could he sleep when she couldn't? But as she drew closer to the couch, she could hear that his breathing was uneven, and there was sweat pearled on his forehead.

"Billy…"

The word came out on a breath. But it was enough for her to hear the fear and to understand what was happening. Billy had been the name of his partner, the name that had made him freeze up in the deli when the waitress had mentioned it. He was having a nightmare. Ben had had them frequently after their mother had died. She knew what to do. When she touched his shoulder to shake him, she had just enough time to register how cold his skin felt, before he rose up to grip her shoulders hard. Then in a move that reminded her how quick he could be, he pulled her across him and pinned her between his body and the back of the couch.

As she watched, the fear in his eyes faded slowly to awareness, then alertness, and his grip on her tightened even further. "What are you doing here?"

"You had a nightmare."

It wasn't until he loosened his hold on her slightly that she realized just how tight it had been. "Are you all right?" she asked.

"I'm fine. You should go." But he didn't move, didn't remove his hands from her.

Riley met his eyes steadily. "I'm not going anywhere."

AND HE WASN'T going to let her, Jack realized. He couldn't. She felt too damn good pressed close against him like this. Too right. Raising a hand, he rubbed his thumb over her bottom lip. The tremor was still moving through her, through him when he covered her mouth with his.

Her taste, the sweet-tart flavor, was everything he remembered. Even as her lips parted beneath his and her tongue sought his, he knew he had to have more. How long had it been since he'd touched her? Hours? Forever? Through the thin fabric of her nightshirt, his hand sought her breast. Soft and small, it fit perfectly into his palm. Then he moved his hand lower to explore the strong, narrow rib cage, the slender waist. And, all the while, her flavor poured into him, and her scent moved like a mist through his brain. Still it wasn't enough. Suddenly impatient, he drew back.

"Don't go."

The sound of her words shot through him, the pleasure, sharp and sweet.

"I'm not going anywhere," he said as he lifted her nightshirt over her head and tossed it away. Then, for a moment, he didn't allow himself to touch her. Meeting her eyes, he said, "If you want to stop this, it had better be now."

Riley framed his face with her hands. "I don't want to stop this. I want you to make love to me. Now."

When his fingers streaked into her hair and fisted there, delight streamed through her. His mouth wasn't gentle this time when it crushed hers, nor were his hands as they moved over her, molding and pressing. She barely had time to absorb each new sensation before another, even sharper, pierced her. And each one had such clarity. The scratch of his chin on her cheek, the scrape of his teeth on her earlobe. Then the heat of his mouth as it moved down her throat, over her shoulder, and finally to her breast. The flames he ignited seared right through her skin into her bones.

And through it all was the pleasure that filled her heart.

How long had she waited to be wanted like this? To be needed? Dragging his mouth back to hers, she poured herself into the kiss.

As her mouth moved on his, avid, hungry, Jack knew that he was losing himself to her, bit by bit, piece by piece. She was so hot, almost liquid wherever he touched. And so generous. So giving. Each sigh, each tremor that moved through her, had his own needs, ones he'd buried long ago, springing to the surface. He could no more stop them than he could prevent himself from breathing. They burned through his blood to his heart. Dragging his hand lower, he touched her and watched her arch her back and cry his name. He had to have her. With an oath, he sat up and dragged her with him to the floor.

"Clothes…help me." Together they struggled with his jeans, pulling at the snap, pushing and dragging them down his legs. The press of her fingers on his hips, his thighs…was going to drive him crazy.

Desperate, his control slipping, he pulled her beneath him, as one sane thought forced its way to the surface. Rising above her, he paused, trying to capture it.

"Protection…" he finally managed, looking down at her. Her breathing was as ragged as his. "Do you…?"

"In my bag. Let me…"

"No." Levering himself off of her, he moved quickly into the foyer.

Riley lay on the floor, just trying to breathe. She'd been so filled with him, so focused on the moment, she'd completely forgotten. He hadn't. If she hadn't already tumbled into love with him, she'd be falling now.

"Out you go, kitty." Jack spoke in a low tone as he shut the library door. Then he was above her again, his eyes searching hers.

"The box wasn't in your bag earlier."

"I know," she said, feeling the heat rise in her cheeks. It

was hard to keep secrets from a cop. "I bought them this morning after I left the contractor. I thought…"

He leaned toward her then, and she felt his lips curve in a smile against hers. "I'm glad you thought. Otherwise, we might have had to improvise a bit. As it is," pausing, he laced his fingers with hers and drew both their hands out to the side, "just look at me."

She did as he made a place for himself between her legs. She felt a huge pressure, then he entered her slowly, carefully.

"You feel so good." His face was inches above hers, his eyes focused totally on her. She knew she would never forget the intensity of his look, not as long as she lived.

"Tell me you want me," he said.

"I want you," she said as he began to move in a slow, steady rhythm. "Only you."

The words had the thin control he'd managed to drag into place slipping. Any thought he'd had of taking it slow and easy vanished the moment she wrapped herself around him and drew him closer. They moved together then, faster and faster. He couldn't think; he didn't want to. All he wanted was Riley. Her heat searing through him, her voice in his ear, saying his name over and over again like a chant. He was losing himself. It was the only thought that seemed to penetrate the pleasure that beckoned to him, trapped him. Helpless, all he knew was her, as he pushed them both to the finish.

WHEN SHE finally surfaced, Riley found herself lying on top of Jack with his arms holding her tight. She must have slept, she thought. That was why she felt so full of…energy.

A loud screech pierced the air.

When she started, he ran a hand over her hair. "It's just Abra. She's annoyed that I shut her out."

The kitten started scratching at the door.

"Are you all right?" Jack asked.

"I think so." When she raised her head, she found him studying her.

"I was pretty rough on you," he said.

She grinned at him. "Were you? Maybe you should try again and remind me."

The slow smile that spread over his face changed suddenly to alarm when they heard the sound of the apartment door being opened.

"Thanks for the ride, Ben."

Riley stared into Jack's eyes, totally paralyzed, as her uncle Avery's voice carried quite clearly into the room.

"No problem. The limo driver had to drop me off anyway. He's one of Mr. Weller's bodyguards."

Her uncle and her brother were standing on the other side of the library door, not fifteen feet away from where she and Jack lay naked on the floor!

"Being chauffeured around Manhattan in a limo brings back memories of my more illustrious youth," Avery said.

"It could be just a hint of things to come," Ben said. "Mr. Weller really liked your performance. He was impressed last night, but tonight he said—"

The rest of Ben's sentence was drowned out by Abra's screech. Then she began to scratch at the door again.

"What's that kitten doing here?" Avery asked.

"She's probably looking for Jack," Ben said. "She's gotten very attached to him."

Drawing Riley's head down, Jack whispered. "Get behind the couch."

She wasn't sure she could have moved if he hadn't levered her off of him. As she crawled over her nightshirt, she grabbed it and took it along.

"After Mr. Weller finishes the New York scenes for this film, he's going right into production on another one. And he said he might have another job for you."

"Let's wait until we see the dailies tomorrow, my boy. You can never tell how well a scene has gone until you watch it on the big screen. And, remember, not a word of this to Riley. I want to surprise her. The money for this film will cover the cost of that contractor she wants to hire."

"Are you kidding? If I said anything to her, she'd know that I haven't been studying math for the last few nights."

Riley had just managed to wedge herself between the wall and the couch when Avery continued. "In the meantime, we both need to get some sleep."

"I don't think I can. I feel wired."

"You need a nice boring book," Avery said.

Riley felt the couch move, then suddenly Jack, jeans in hand, was lowering himself over the back, and she was pinned beneath him.

"What subject bores you most in school, my boy?" Avery's voice grew louder as the library door swung open.

"Math," Ben replied.

Don't move. Riley saw Jack's mouth form the words. With his body pressed along every inch of hers, movement wasn't an option. She could barely breathe.

"Besides that?" Avery asked.

"History," Ben said.

"It's easy enough to find a boring book on that subject," Avery said.

Riley could hear Avery's footsteps as he strode across the room. And then a scratching sound on the other side of the sofa distracted her. She glanced up in time to see Abra poised above them. She barely had time to mouth the name to Jack before the kitten dropped to the top of his head. She felt his quick intake of breath and the tensing of each one of his muscles. But he didn't make a sound.

"*The Decline and Fall of the Roman Empire*. If that doesn't put you to sleep, I don't know what will," Avery said. "C'mon, my boy. We have a big day tomorrow."

The footsteps were retreating. Jack's body was crushing hers. Surely that would be enough to contain the laugh she felt bubbling up inside of her. But he had a kitten on his head, and they were lying naked behind the couch! Just the thought was… Pressing her lips together, she bit down hard on the inside of her cheeks. It might have worked if she hadn't looked into his eyes. They were filled with the same amusement that was threatening to burst out of her.

"Shhhh." The word was barely a breath, but it was enough to tickle her skin. A giggle bubbled out of her on a gasp. Jack's hand clamped down on her mouth at the same moment that they heard the library door click shut. After a count of five, he said, "At least they didn't have a shotgun!" Holding each other tightly, they laughed as silently as they could until they were completely spent.

Finally, he got to his knees and said, "Could you get the kitten off my head?"

Sitting up, Riley tried to lift Abra, but the kitten hissed at her.

"Ouch!" Jack said. "She sank her claws into my scalp."

Riley grinned at him. "It's a sign of affection."

Jack reached for the kitten and, lifting it carefully, set it on the floor. This time Abra made no objection.

Riley's brows shot up. "You've got yourself a pet."

"Nonsense," Jack said as he backed out from behind the couch and began to pull on his clothes. "I've explained to her and to you that I don't do pets."

"I don't think she's getting it."

Jack strode toward the door, and Abra followed close at his heels.

"Where are you going?" Riley asked as she wiggled into her nightshirt.

"I'm going to go down and get Sam. I'm assuming he followed Avery and Ben back here. From what we just heard,

your uncle and your brother have an alibi for last night, and
it's time we started thinking of other suspects.''

When he opened the library door, Abra scooted out with
him. Stooping down, he picked her up and held her so he
could look her in the eye. ''Get this straight, kiddo. I never
wanted a pet. I don't want one now.''

Life was funny that way, Riley thought as she heard Jack
let himself out of the apartment. *Sometimes we get exactly
what we don't want.*

10

SAM TUCKED his cell phone into his pocket and leaned back in his chair. "Sometime today I should have a current address on Louie 'the Rock' Mancuso, and we should also know if any of the bridge-club ladies took a cab to the Abernathys' the night before last." He checked his watch. "Ms. Cantrell has promised to get Hattie and Baby out of their apartment by ten so that I can search it." Glancing up at Riley, he paused and then said, "Why so glum? At least we've eliminated your uncle and your brother from the suspect list."

"I don't want Hattie or the other ladies to be involved in this, either," Riley said.

"I don't think they are," Jack said as rose from the couch and began to pace.

"Thinking and knowing are two different things," Sam said.

"Yeah." The problem was the case just didn't make any sense. And the fact that he couldn't get a handle on it—or even form a theory about it—had a tight ball of fear lodged in his stomach. He'd purposely steered them all into the library when he'd brought Sam up to the apartment. The noise of their voices would be less likely to disturb Ben and Avery, and he wanted to look at the map. There had to be something there. She'd drawn red circles around the four buildings that Foster Care serviced. Blue lines traced the routes between them.

"What happens after we eliminate everyone?" Riley asked.

"We have to think harder and come up with more suspects," Jack said. "Who would benefit if Foster Care went under?"

Riley thought for a minute, then shook her head. "No one. I started my business with referrals that other pet-care services couldn't or didn't want to handle. Some of my clients need a lot of personal attention. That takes time that wasn't translating into money for them."

"Maybe they don't want you to open the Foster Care Pet Center," Sam said. "I still have the real estate agent on my list."

"Someone is going to a lot of trouble to get you thrown in jail," Jack said. And it was about time he started thinking like a cop and figured out who. It was the only chance he had of controlling the fear he was feeling. If Riley's relatives weren't the thieves, and it wasn't Hattie or Rocky, then something in his gut was telling him that she might be in real danger.

Tearing his gaze away from the map, Jack turned to face them. "Let's make a chronological list of all the burglaries."

Sam flipped through his notebook. "I already did. The robberies started with Winnie and over a period of three weeks spread to members of her bridge club. But it wasn't until the thefts spread out of the building that the police targeted Riley as the prime suspect and began to question her. Since then, the thief has begun to move more quickly. Hattie Silverman was robbed two days ago, the Abernathys were robbed the night before last, right here in this building."

"And yesterday, someone tried to snatch a poodle she was walking in the park," Jack said.

Sam glanced at him. "That's not a burglary."

"It's a theft. And if it had been successful, it could have cost her clients."

"Gotcha," Sam said as he jotted it down.

"And twice, someone has planted jewels on her."

Sam glanced up, his eyes narrowed. "I knew there was something you were holding back."

"I thought it might have been counterproductive to mention it earlier," Jack said.

"The police didn't find the planted jewels, I take it?" Sam asked.

"Nope," Jack replied. "Riley, we could use some more coffee."

"Too bad," she said. "I'm not leaving the room. But feel free to talk about me as if I'm not here."

Sam studied Jack for a minute. "I guess you're pretty sure she didn't do it."

"Yep."

Sam nodded. "Anything else you haven't told me?"

"Nope. I'm telling you all this now because when you consider everything that's happened in the past forty-eight hours, it looks like whoever's behind this is starting to get desperate."

Sam nodded. "Looks that way to me, too. What can I do?"

"Just what you're doing." Then Jack turned to look at the map again and frowned. There was definitely something that he was missing. He could feel it in his gut. "And put a man in the four buildings she services. Whoever is pulling off the thefts not only has copies of her keys, but can also get past the doormen." He stared at the four red circles. "Who could get into all four of those buildings?"

"Have all four been robbed?" Sam asked.

"No." Staring at the four red circles, Jack's frown deepened. "If someone is trying to frame Riley, why wouldn't they rob all four?"

Before anyone could answer, the phone on the desk rang. Lifting the receiver, Jack said, "Hello?"

There was a pause. "I want to speak to Riley."

Jack recognized Charles Cantrell's voice immediately. "She's still asleep. What can I do for you?"

"I'd like you to wake her up. My aunt has been robbed again, and I'm sure she could use Riley's support."

"I'll let her know," Jack said, then cut off whatever else the man was saying by setting the receiver back in its cradle.

"Who was it?" Riley asked.

"Charles Cantrell. He had good news and bad news. There was another robbery last night, so you're definitely in the clear. It will be my pleasure to inform Duffy of that."

"And the bad news?" Riley asked.

"Winnie was robbed again."

"ANYONE FOR fresh tea?" Winnie sailed into her living room, carrying a tray and set it down on the coffee table.

Riley glanced up. For a woman who'd been robbed for the second time in a month, Winnie looked very cheerful. And when she saw Hattie, Prue, and even Gert were all grinning at her, she attempted a smile.

Earlier when she had arrived with Jack and Sam, the bridge-club ladies had all looked as though they were in mourning. But they'd perked up quickly enough when Jack had explained to them that he'd been working undercover to find their jewels. Of course, the news that he was really a policeman sent Hattie right into a fit of the vapors, but she recovered miraculously when Sam carried her to the couch and assured her that they hoped to locate her Rocky momentarily.

And then Jack and Sam had left.

Riley struggled to make her smile more genuine. It was silly to feel so abandoned simply because Jack hadn't wanted to take her along. She was being a baby about it. If only he hadn't looked so cool and distant when he left. And he hadn't kissed her. He hadn't touched her since they crawled out from behind the couch in the library. All she had to do was to think of the couch to have the heat moving through her again.

"I'm sure that Jack and Sam are going to find the real thief in no time at all," Winnie said, refilling her cup.

"I'm betting on the P.I. to solve it first," Hattie announced.

"Now which one is he?" Prue asked. "I'm having a little trouble keeping them straight."

Gert leaned toward her twin. "Do the words *blind as a bat* mean anything to you?"

"The cop has muscles, just like Rocky," Hattie said. "The P.I. has the brains."

"Humph," Gert said. "It wasn't just his brains you were admiring when you attached yourself to his arm yesterday."

"I needed support. I didn't have my cane with me."

"Only because you stashed it in the hall closet the moment you saw him," Gert said.

"I prefer a man with muscles, so I'm putting five dollars on the cop to solve the case," Prue said, digging into her purse. "Anyone else care to wager?"

"Gambling's illegal. Your cop might have to arrest you," Hattie pointed out.

Prue's smile shot up several watts. "Exactly."

"Ladies," Winnie said in an admonishing tone. "The most important thing is that Riley will soon be cleared."

Riley sighed. "I'm already cleared. I couldn't have robbed you last night because I was with Jack."

"Made a move on my cop, did you?" Prue asked.

"No...well, yes. I mean..." Riley's voice trailed off when she realized that the four women were all gazing at her expectantly.

"Don't leave us hanging. Tell us what happened," Winnie said. "Inquiring minds want to know."

Riley drew in a deep breath. "I'm in love with Jack." The sentence ended on a gasp when she realized what she'd just said. It certainly wasn't what she'd intended to say. She hadn't even fully articulated the thought in her mind when the words just…popped out!

Winnie patted her hand. "We were wondering how long it would take you to figure it out."

Riley stared at her, surprise and panic still warring within her. "You knew? How? I've barely figured it out myself."

"I knew it the minute the two of you walked in here the first day." Prue glanced around the room, her hand stretched out, palm upward. "I put five bucks on it and today I'm collecting my winnings."

"Not from me," Winnie said. "I didn't take the bet because I knew it, too." At Riley's questioning look, she continued, "There was something in the way you looked at him, my dear. And I think it's wonderful."

"It's terrible." But even as Riley spoke the thought that was in her mind, she couldn't deny the bubble of joy that had begun to grow within her from the moment she'd spoken the words. "I didn't want to fall in love with anyone. I don't have the time. I have my business to open."

"With the right man, you'll find a way to make the time."

"That's just it. Jack isn't the right man. And he doesn't want anyone in his life, not even a kitten. He's going to find out who's behind the robberies and then I'll never see him again."

"Not if you stop him," Winnie said,

Riley blinked. "And how do you propose I do that?"

"The right clothes work wonders," Prue said, smoothing her dress.

Gert snorted. "That was back in the days when you could see what you were putting on in the morning! My advice is to forget clothes. Everyone knows that the way to a man's heart is through his stomach. Good food's the answer."

"He doesn't trust my cooking," Riley said.

Hattie cleared her throat. "I've always found that wearing no clothes at all works wonders."

The four women stared at her.

"It always worked with my Rocky. He took a picture of me once, wearing nothing but my shotgun."

Riley blinked and stared.

"You're a smart girl," Winnie said, patting her hand again. "I'm sure you'll think of something."

Riley turned to Winnie. "I thought you wanted... I mean, you introduced me to Charles, and you seemed so happy when I went out with him."

"I was happy. I thought someone like you would ground him." A line of worry formed on Winnie's brow. "He and Christina haven't seemed to find any purpose in life yet. That's why I wanted both of them to meet you. I thought you might rub off on them. But the moment I saw you and Jack together, it just seemed perfect to me."

Perfect? Riley couldn't think of two people who seemed less perfect for one another. The man didn't even want a pet.

But he had one. As she thought of Abra, a little spurt of hope joined the bubble of joy deep within her. The kitten had made her way into Jack's life because she never took no for an answer.

Just then the phone rang, and Winnie lifted the receiver. "Hello? Oh, I'm fine, Charles. Yes, she's still here." Passing the phone to Riley, she said, "He wants to talk to you."

"Riley, I need to talk to you. Alone. Your new assistant seems to have appointed himself your bodyguard. Could you meet me in the coffee shop right next to my aunt's apartment?"

Riley hesitated for a moment. She'd promised Jack that she wouldn't leave Winnie's until he got back. But Charles was right. They did have to talk. "I'll meet you there in a few minutes."

"YOU DON'T SAY? Thanks." After tucking his cell phone into his pocket, Sam used both hands to steer as he wedged his car between two taxis, then shot through an intersection. "We can eliminate Rocky Mancuso. He's been laid up in the hospital with a broken hip the past four weeks. His story is that he hasn't called Hattie because he was too ashamed to let her see him while he was flat on his back in the hospital."

"I was ready to eliminate him when I discovered that every one of those boxes in Hattie's closet was filled with letters he wrote her from prison."

Sam glanced at him. "You checked them all?"

"Enough to come to the conclusion that he wasn't trying to drag her back into a life of crime."

Twisting the steering wheel, Sam pulled his car into the curb. "This is as close as I can get to the building. You want to tell me why we're stopping here?"

Jack glanced across the street at the one apartment building serviced by Foster Care that hadn't been robbed. "I've been thinking about how the thief is getting into these buildings. I figure the safest time to burglarize a place is at night—especially when you're dealing with people who are at home all day. And it occurred to me that the thief is probably impersonating Riley or Ben or Avery. All he or she needs is a duffel bag with the Foster Care logo on the side and a set of keys. Riley does almost all of her business by day, so the doormen on the night shift wouldn't necessarily recognize her or her brother or uncle on sight."

"Okay, I'm following you. But why are we stopping at this particular building? This is the one that hasn't been robbed, right?"

"Yeah. I'm figuring it would be too dangerous to try to pull off that kind of masquerade in a building where you might be easily recognized as a tenant."

"Got it," Sam said, a slow smile spreading across his face.

"Let's go have a look at the list of those tenants," Jack said, climbing out of his side of the car.

"Right. And you can tell me why it took you so long to figure it out."

"Me?" Jack said. "I'm just an underpaid cop. You're the super-sleuth."

"Hi, Tommy," Riley said with a smile as she headed out of Winnie's building.

"Two visits on a Sunday morning. That's a record even for you, Ms. Riley."

With her hand on the door, Riley paused a turned back. "Two visits?"

Tommy nodded. "I had to check the sign-in book when the police were here. The new night man signed you in at three-fifteen. He put down that Ms. Silverman's dog was ill. How's little Baby doing?"

"Fine," Riley said, crossing to the desk. "Could I see the sign-in book?"

"Sure thing."

Riley stared down at the signature. It certainly looked like hers. But as far as she could remember, she'd never made a visit to any of her clients at three-fifteen in the morning. So the new night man wouldn't have any idea if it was the real Riley Foster or an impostor who'd signed in. She had to call Jack. She had her cell phone out when she remembered that she didn't know his number. And she didn't know Sam's number, either.

The moment she stepped out on the sidewalk, she spotted Charles walking toward her. When he reached her, he took her hands. "I've been so worried. How are you?"

"I'm angry. Not at you," she hastened to assure him as he linked her arm through his and they started walking. "I'm furious at whoever is robbing my clients and trying to blame it on me."

"You must let me hire you a lawyer this time. When Winnie told me about the latest burglary, I was so afraid for you. The police will have to make an arrest now even if she calls the commissioner again. I want you to have the best representation possible until this mess is straightened out."

"I appreciate your offer. But I don't need an attorney. They're not going to arrest me. Not for a while anyway. I have an alibi for last night. I was with Jack."

"You were with Jack?"

"Yes." They'd stopped walking and he'd turned to face her. Under his suddenly narrowed gaze, Riley felt the heat rise to her cheeks. Charles had no reason to be jealous, but it was clearly anger that she saw in his eyes.

"Surely, you don't expect the police to give much credence to the word of some man you ran into on the street and hired on a whim. Believe me, this time they're going to have to arrest you," he said.

Riley blinked and stared at him. "You sound like you want them to."

Charles drew in a deep breath. "Nonsense. I'm trying to help you."

But it wasn't a friendly offer of help she saw in his eyes. Nor was it jealousy. The man hated her. The moment she realized it and took a quick step away, his grip tightened on her arm.

"This is all your fault," he said, pulling her with him. But it wasn't until he turned into the alley that panic skipped up her spine.

"The coffee shop is two doors up," she said, digging in her heels.

"And that's exactly where we'd be going if you didn't have nine lives," Charles said as he drew a gun out of his pocket. "Instead, we're going into this alley to wait for Christina. And if you scream or try to run, I'll have to use this."

"SHE'S NOT AT Winnie's apartment." Fighting down a wave of fear, Jack tossed down Sam's car phone. "She left a few minutes ago to meet Cantrell at the coffee shop a few doors down. Step on it." But even as he said the words, Sam had the speedometer climbing.

"The coffee shop's a public place. He can't do anything to her there," Sam said. "And we don't know for sure yet that Cantrell is behind the robberies. All we know is that his apartment building hasn't been robbed yet."

"Yeah," Jack said, "but I've got a feeling." It was the same feeling that he'd had the night he'd visited his aunt in the hospital and found that she'd passed away. And it was the same feeling that he'd had that night he'd followed Billy into that alley.

Three blocks later when Sam slowed for a red light, he said. "Run it. If you get a ticket, I'll fix it."

Tires squealed and two cars nearly collided as Sam ran the light. "My boss isn't going to like it if I wreck this car."

Jack's feeling grew stronger. It wasn't going to happen again. He couldn't lose Riley.

"Much as I hate to admit it, I've got a feeling, too," Sam said as he swerved around a taxi, then slowed fractionally before sailing through the next intersection. "It's only two more blocks."

Tires were squealing again behind them as Sam rammed the car into the curb in front of Winnie Cantrell's apartment building.

"CHRISTINA?" Riley said, fighting down the panic. She wanted very much to scream, to run. But the man who'd just drawn the gun out of his pocket wasn't the mild-mannered man who'd taken her out to dinner and danced with her. The only resemblance between this angry stranger and the man she'd dated was that the hand holding the gun was shaking a little. She concentrated on that.

"She was waiting for us in the coffee shop. When she sees us turn into the alley, she'll follow. This is the way she wanted to handle it all along."

As they moved farther into the alley, Riley tried to focus her mind on details. It was the only way she knew of keeping the fear at bay. And she had to keep Charles talking.

"I don't know what you're talking about, Charles. What did Christina want to handle?"

"You," Charles said as he urged her deeper into the dimness of the alley. "When we found out what Aunt Winnie had done, she said we had to do something. It was Christina's idea to burglarize the old ladies. She made wax impressions of your key ring one day when you were busy having tea with them. Once she had the duffel made up with the Foster Care logo, the doormen on the night shifts never gave her a second glance. She figured the police would suspect you right away, but she was wrong. That's when she came up with the idea of planting the jewels on you."

"She put Hattie's brooch in Ben's duffel bag?" Riley asked.

"She wasn't happy about the fact that Ben showed up that day instead of you. But I told her that the bags were always getting mixed up."

Riley stopped short and turned to Charles. "But she didn't put the Abernathys' diamonds in my freezer. You did."

"How did you—?" Charles's eyes narrowed. "The police didn't find them."

"No. Jack did." Riley dug in her heels when Charles pulled at her again. "Just whose idea was it to snatch Gigi the poodle?"

Tightening his grip on her arm, Charles shoved her forward. "Christina's. She was furious with me when the police didn't find the diamonds or Hattie's brooch when they searched your apartment. She was so sure they would. I told her that kidnapping a dog wouldn't work, but she was getting desperate, and she was determined to discredit you in Aunt Winnie's eyes. Christina gets very frustrated when her plans don't work. Here, this is far enough. We'll wait for her here.''

Riley glanced quickly around in the gloom. They were standing in a small cul de sac formed by a circle of Dumpsters. She had to get clear of them if she wanted to make a run for it. ''Do you always go along with Christina's plans, Charles?''

''No. This time I had a plan of my own. I wanted to marry you. That way we could keep the money in the family. But she said it wouldn't work.''

''What money are you talking about?''

He shoved her again, and she stumbled backward, reaching out to steady herself on a Dumpster. ''Don't pretend you don't know.''

''Know what?'' Riley asked. The hand holding the gun was shaking even more now. She moved away from the Dumpster. ''I don't have any money. I told you about my father the first time we went out.''

''I'm talking about Aunt Winnie's money. When she changed her will, she left part of it to you.''

Riley stared at him. ''You must be mistaken.''

''He's not mistaken,'' Christina said, her high heels clicking on the cement as she joined them. ''Shoot her, Charles.''

SHOOT HER, CHARLES.

The words had a ball of fear tightening in Jack's chest. He was edging his way carefully along one side of the alley and Sam was moving along the other. They'd ruled out running in with their weapons drawn. They couldn't afford the risk. Not while there was a chance that one or the other of the two Cantrells had a weapon. Christina's words had confirmed that there was a gun. As he ducked behind a Dumpster and flattened himself against it, the stench filled his nostrils. He felt the familiar wave of fear from his nightmare. He even felt the icy paralysis begin to move through him. Neither compared to the terror that had filled him the moment he'd realized that Riley was in the alley with Charles Cantrell. Pushing all feelings aside, Jack gripped his weapon in both hands and glanced out from behind the Dumpster.

"You're the one who wanted to shoot her. Here, you take the gun," Charles said.

Jack swore to himself. Riley was blocking any clean shot he had of Charles. And Sam's path was blocked by another Dumpster.

"I'm not going to shoot her," Christina said. "You were supposed to seduce her and you failed. I pulled off all the burglaries. The least you can do is shoot her."

"It's your gun."

"I don't know how to shoot it," Christina said.

Jeez, Jack thought. Amateur shooters were more dangerous than professional ones. One false move on his or Sam's part and the gun could go off and kill Riley by accident. His view of her was still blocked by a Dumpster that jutted out from the wall. Crouching low, he risked a quick look. Riley stood between him and Charles, and fear hit him in a fresh wave when he saw her hand slip into the duffel bag. She was going to use the water pistol.

He stepped out from behind his Dumpster just as Sam stepped out from behind his. But it was Riley who raised her gun and shot first.

Charles's scream filled the air as his gun fell to the ground. Jack was moving forward, his gun trained on Christina when he heard the shot and felt a burning sensation in his upper arm.

Then Riley was running toward him, but it was hard to make out what she was saying. Charles's howling was too loud.

"You're hurt," Riley said. "There's blood on your arm."

It was only as he grabbed her and held her to him that he felt the pain.

"I STILL THINK you ought to go to the hospital and have them check out your wound," Riley said as the patrol car holding both the Cantrells pulled out of the alley. Sam was deep in conversation with an officer in the remaining car.

"It's not a wound." Jack had no desire to move. It didn't matter that he was seated on the concrete, leaning back against a Dumpster. All that mattered was that he was holding Riley safe in his arms. He couldn't let her go. Not yet. "It's just a scratch."

"It was bleeding like more than a scratch."

"I'm fine," Jack said as he ran a finger down the worry line that had formed on her brow. And he would be, he suddenly realized. Not once had his leg bothered him during that long walk down the alley.

"When I saw that gun go off, and I knew that he'd hit you, I...I can't get the image out of my mind."

Jack watched in horror as the tears filled her eyes. He'd never seen her cry before. "Riley, don't. I..." Feeling helpless, he laid a hand on her cheek and drew her closer. "I felt the same way when I heard Christina say *shoot her*. But it didn't happen. We're both fine."

And they were. He had to concentrate on that, and not on the image that filled his mind whenever he let himself think....

She pressed her cheek against his. "I thought I might lose you."

He tightened his hold on her. "No. You're not going to."

For a moment, neither once of them spoke.

Finally, Riley sniffed. "It's a good thing I saved us with my water pistol."

Jack felt the corners of his mouth twitch. "Why is it that

whenever I try to rescue you, you always think you're rescuing me?"

"At least I wasn't afraid to use *my* gun."

"No." Jack sighed. "That's the problem."

"You need a hand?" Sam asked as he walked over to them. "They want us to come down to the precinct and sign a statement."

"Why don't you go ahead and start without us?" Jack asked.

"Gotcha," Sam said with a wink before he turned and walked away.

"We should get out of this alley," Riley said.

"No." Jack tightened his grip to keep her at his side. "I've got something to say first."

Riley studied him. The frown was back on his face. And there was something in his eyes that reminded her of the man who'd followed her into the alley three days ago. She felt the skip of panic. He was going to say goodbye. "I don't think this is the place. Why don't we go back to the apartment?"

"No, this isn't the place," Jack said, "but it's going to have to do. There's something that we've got to settle."

Riley's mind was racing. He couldn't dump her now. "You've just been shot. You're not thinking clearly."

He gripped her shoulders hard. "I told you. I'm fine." Pausing, he drew in a deep breath. "Marry me."

Riley stared at him.

"Well?"

A bubble of laughter pushed against the fear that had lodged hard in her throat. "Marry you?"

His frown deepened. "That's what I said."

Riley felt the laugh escape and fill the air.

Jack's gaze narrowed. "I'm not joking."

She pressed a hand against her stomach and tried to catch a breath. "Hattie thought I might need a shotgun."

"What?"

She managed to stifle a giggle and continued, "Gert thought I should feed you, Prue thought I ought to buy some new clothes, but Hattie was voting for no clothes at all." When the giggle escaped, she felt his fingers under her chin tilting it up so that she had to meet his eyes.

"What are you talking about?"

"The bridge ladies gave me lots of advice on how to catch you."

His eyes narrowed into slits, but she could see the amusement fill them. Along with something else that made her heart start to pound.

"Do you know how much courage it takes for a man to propose? Or how he feels when the only response is laughter?"

"And you did it so romantically. In an alley! To my dying day, the stench of garbage will make my heart beat faster. And it will make such a funny story to tell our grandchildren!"

Jack drew her closer until she could barely breathe. "Is that a yes?"

"Yes." It didn't take much breath to say it. And it filled her with such joy.

"I love you, Riley Foster," Jack said as he lowered his mouth toward hers.

"I love you, too," she whispered against his lips. And then she forgot about breathing at all.

Epilogue

"TOSS IT RIGHT HERE!" Squatting in the traditional position of the catcher at home plate, Gert pounded a fist into her hand. "Come to Mama!"

"No, over here," Prue called, waving her hands in wide circles.

"Don't you listen to them," Hattie chirped and brandished her cane. "Those flowers have my name on them!"

The tall, distinguished man behind her plucked a piece of lint from his sleeve. "Not unless you spell your name *H-A-R-O-L-D*, they don't."

"Rubbish! *G-E-R* and *T* are the only letters on that bouquet. Toss them right here, Riley!"

Tightening her grip on her flowers, Riley stared at the group of waving, screaming fanatics standing in her uncle's library and murmured under her breath, "All I wanted was a small, quiet wedding."

Jack chuckled and gave her hand a comforting squeeze. "Well, it's small. One out of two's not bad."

Up until now her wedding day had been perfect. She had exchanged her vows with Jack in the library of her uncle's apartment in full view of the couch where Jack had first made love to her. Ben had been Jack's best man, the bridge-club ladies had been her bridesmaids, and Abra had been the ring bearer. Her Uncle Avery had not only given her away, but he had also insisted on paying for everything. Thanks to his appearance in Mr. Weller's film, he had been rehired as a regular on his old soap. And thanks to Jack, Ben had recently announced that he was looking into the possibility of majoring in film at NYU. As if her cup hadn't already been overflowing, she was going to open the Foster Care Pet Center in two weeks with a full set of clients. Everything was perfect—except for this. She glanced down at her flowers.

Jack leaned close and whispered in her ear, "Toss the thing, Riley. As soon as you do, we can be alone. I've been waiting all day to get you alone on that couch."

Even as the image filled her mind, she focused on the bouquet. "Everyone here wants it." She scanned the eager faces. Hattie and Gert and Prue had formed a neat circle about ten feet away. Behind them Winnie stood between Harold and her uncle. To their right, the Bard stood watch on his cage, and to their left Louie "the Rock" Mancuso leaned against his walker.

"Not everyone," Jack pointed out. "Sam and Ben have clearly taken themselves out of the competition. In fact, they each slipped me a twenty to toss the garter as far away from them as possible. I'm beginning to think they came strictly for the food. That's definitely all Beowulf came for."

"True," Riley said with a frown. The three males in question were hovering over the buffet table. Beowulf had just pulled himself up to inspect the wedding cake, but Ben quickly shoved him away.

"Stop stalling, Riley," Gert said, pounding her fist into her palm. "Put it right here!"

"Frailty, thy name is woman!" the Bard intoned.

"That's it," Riley said. "I'm going to toss it." Turning her back on the fanatics, she took a deep breath and shot it over her head. "Tell me who got it."

"See for yourself." Gripping her shoulders, Jack turned her around so that she had to watch the bouquet shoot straight into the ceiling, then split apart and fall in a shower of flowers. Hands waved at the ceiling. Winnie grabbed a rose, Gert and Harold each snagged an orchid, and Prue snatched a spray of daisies from the top of her head. In the midst of the commotion, Hattie's cane connected with the ribbons and smacked what was left of the falling bouquet right into her Rocky's chest.

"We got it, Rocky," she crowed. "That means we're next!"

"That was perfect," Jack said, drawing her into his arms as cheers filled the library.

"Now everyone can be just as happy as we are," she managed just before his lips closed over hers.

Naked in New England

Jacquie D'Alessandro

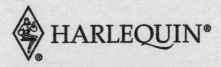

HARLEQUIN®

TORONTO • NEW YORK • LONDON
AMSTERDAM • PARIS • SYDNEY • HAMBURG
STOCKHOLM • ATHENS • TOKYO • MILAN • MADRID
PRAGUE • WARSAW • BUDAPEST • AUCKLAND

Dear Reader,

Ever have one of *those* days—you know, the kind where everything goes wrong, and just when you think it can't get any worse, it does? Well, if you're anything like me, those days happen routinely. When I finally realized I couldn't stop life's everyday disasters from occurring, I decided to make the most of them and use them in my stories!

In my house we have a saying—"It's going in a book." Every time something unusual happens—the sort of thing that usually requires a plumber, electrician or the fire department to stop by—I jot it down on my trusty notepad. In fact, there's one scene in *Naked in New England* that comes directly from my life. No, I won't tell you which one now, but if you drop me a letter or e-mail, I'll let you know. You can contact me at 875 Lawrenceville-Suwanee Road, Suite 310-PMB 131, Lawrenceville, GA 30043, or e-mail me through my Web site at www.JacquieD.com, where you can enter my monthly contest and find out all my latest news.

Enjoy,

Jacquie D'Alessandro

This book is lovingly dedicated to the memory of a beautiful young woman who loved to laugh, Miechelle "Kelli" Bourgeois, and her incredible mother, Deborah Dahlmann, whose strength and courage I admire more than words can say.

And, as always, to Joe and Christopher, for filling my life with love and laughter.

Acknowledgments

I would like to thank the following people for their assistance and expertise in areas I knew little or nothing about—namely raccoons, interior design, architecture and the city of Boston. Blame me for any mistakes—they tried their best to save me: Tami McGraw, Denise Welmering, Serena Fogelberg, Sherri Browning, Jeanette Carter, Kristin Henck and Melissa Browne. A huge thank you to my critique partners, Donna Fejes, Susan Goggins and Carina Rock, and also to Jenni Grizzle and Wendy Etherington. Lastly, I want to thank the following people for their incredible support— an army of cheerleaders has nothing on you guys: Damaris Rowland, Brenda Chin, the members of Georgia Romance Writers, Kay and Jim Johnson, Lea and Art D'Alessandro, Kathy Guse, the ladies of RBL Romantica, Denise Forbes and the terrific staff at Jackson Elementary, Steve and Michelle Grossman, Nancy Krava, Julie Teasley, Jeannie Pierannunzi, Jo Beth Beard and all the romance lovers who live in my neighborhood. And a special thank-you to all the wonderful readers who have taken the time to write to me.

1

GRIPPING HIS GYM BAG IN one hand and his laptop case in the other, Ryan Monroe walked up the narrow dirt path to the cabin he'd be calling home for the next two weeks. He looked around and shook his head.

Man, talk about being out in the middle of *nowhere*. Nothing here but a bunch of trees and an eerie lack of noise, except for the pine needles and fall leaves crunching beneath his Italian loafers. His nose twitched as he breathed in a pungent, damp, earthy scent he could only describe as "foresty." Definitely not like what he was used to in Boston. Maybe coming to this desolate spot wasn't such a smart idea—

He sliced off his niggling doubts. Sure, it was quiet and peaceful here—that was the whole point.

Craning his neck, he caught a glimpse of the shimmering lake between the trees. The sun was just setting, and bright orange and gold ribbons flitted over the water. Clouds, however, loomed over the mountains, and he congratulated himself on arriving at his destination before the forecasted rainshower broke loose.

Struggling to withdraw the key from the pocket of his khakis, he surveyed the cabin with an architectural eye. Clean lines, two chimneys, sturdy construction. His buddy Dave had purchased the place last year as a weekend getaway, but he'd been happy to loan the place to Ryan while he was away on his honeymoon. Dave had assured him that in spite of the rustic setting, he'd enjoy every comfort.

And, God knows, he needed it. Needed the time and relaxation not only to physically remove himself from the recent upheavals in his personal life, but for his work. The opportunity to design an estate for one of the world's most eccentric and reclusive authors came along once in a life-time—and he wasn't about to blow it. But with his creativity hitting a brick wall, drastic measures were needed. Hopefully, this complete change of scenery would open his mind and focus his thoughts in new directions.

Yup, there was no havoc here. Just him. And all this peace, fresh air, and quiet. *Goodbye city-induced stress, hello idea-inspiring…desolation.*

Juggling his cases, he slipped the key from his pocket and opened the door to paradise.

Or maybe not.

The gym bag slipped from his fingers and slapped against the wood floor—or was that his jaw hitting the ground?

Every comfort? For whom? A person accustomed to living in a cave?

The large, rectangular-shaped room was completely empty. Not a sign of the cozy armchairs, or overstuffed sofa Dave had raved about. No welcoming logs set in the grate, no homey doodads decorating the mantle. Nothing but a few clumps of dust and several pine needles scattered across the dark oak floor.

In a daze, he turned and looked at what he supposed was the eat-in kitchen, but it was hard to tell since there was no table or chairs. The green-tiled countertops were completely bare, and based on what he'd seen so far, he guessed the stained oak cupboards were in the same condition.

Lowering his laptop to the bare floor, he raked his hand through his hair. This was definitely the right cabin. Dave had written out detailed directions and the key fit the lock. What the hell could have happened? Had the place been robbed? Maybe, but according to Dave, there wasn't anything worth stealing—no VCR, or stereo, and the TV had been an old portable. And after living with Dave for four years during college, Ryan knew his best friend's decorating taste. He couldn't imagine anyone wanting to steal Dave's beat-up sofa and garage-sale chairs.

Huffing out a frustrated breath, Ryan looked up and noticed that one item remained. A huge moose head hung at a drunken angle on the far wall, its horns adorned with something. Ryan walked slowly across the room, fighting off the uneasy sensation that the moose's glass-eyed gaze followed his every move. Animal heads hanging on the walls. Sheesh. Give him a city landscape any day.

Standing in front of the mounted head, he peered upward and realized that the something hanging from its horns was a wisp of fabric. A wisp of fabric that looked suspiciously like a pair of panties. Black, lacy panties.

Great. Several local colleges were within easy driving distance. Probably a bunch of college kids had staged a frat party/panty raid here and had carted off the furniture. A mental image of muscular fraternity boys hoisting Dave's sofa and chairs and parading them out of the cabin and into their cars filled his mind.

Clearly a trip back to town was going to be necessary, a prospect that filled him with annoyance. The nearest town was a good twenty miles away, and the first fifteen of that consisted of nothing more than a wide dirt path that had already no doubt done considerable damage to his Lexus's suspension. He didn't even want to contemplate the possible scratches marring the car's glossy black paint. He'd brought along enough food to last him for the duration of his stay, but he certainly hadn't brought any chairs, blankets or pillows.

Blankets and pillows. Jeez, was there even a bed here to use them on, or was that gone, too? He dragged his hands down his face and shook his head. While he hadn't expected the cabin to be a suite at the Ritz, he definitely hadn't planned on two weeks of what was rapidly promising to be something along the lines of survivalist training.

But returning to his condo was simply not an option— not if he hoped to get any work done. Marcie and her belongings had all but taken over his home and he still hadn't completely exorcised his ex-girlfriend's presence from the rooms. And reminders of ex-girlfriends were not conducive to a healthy work environment. With only two weeks to design the house of his life and his creative juices bone dry, he desperately needed unencumbered, distraction-free time.

Maybe he'd be better off just checking into a hotel, but damn it, he *hated* hotels. He spent so much time in them as it was, and they were full of distractions—noise, restaurants, bars, clubs…*people*. He really needed this time alone to focus on his project. Perhaps the rest of the cabin wasn't so bad. So bare.

Determined to find out, Ryan turned to stride down the hallway he assumed led to the bedrooms. Before he'd even taken a step, the most god-awful groaning he'd ever heard in his life came from behind one of the closed doors off the hall.

His entire body froze, except the hairs on the back of his neck; they stood straight up. The muffled sound echoed again. What the hell was that? It didn't sound human. It sounded like some poor creature in horrible pain. He hoped it was a relatively *small* creature and not a large, hungry bear who liked to snack on architects.

Another inhuman moan came from down the hall.

So much for quiet, stress-free country life.

Moving cautiously across the room, he looked around for a possible weapon and spied a plastic fork in the sink. It wasn't much, but these were desperate times. A further look yielded a woman's spiky-heeled shoe propped in the corner. Probably belonged to Dave's bride, Carmen. He briefly considered grabbing the panties, but decided they wouldn't do him much good. What was he going to do— *strangle* a bear with them? Gripping his makeshift weapons, Ryan crept down the hall.

When he reached the first door, he flattened himself against the wall and drew a deep, steadying breath. Damn it, what did he know about wild animals? Did he look like a show host for *Creatures of the Wild and Their Habitats?* The closest he'd ever come to large, man-eating beasts was at the zoo, and his last trip there had been way back in tenth grade on a science/zoology field trip. And even then he'd been more focused on Shari Watson's short skirt and long legs than lions and tigers.

And bears.

Oh, my.

Sweat popped out on his forehead. Jeez, did bears make those awful groaning noises? He blew out a long breath. All right. Maybe he wasn't a forest ranger, but he certainly knew what to do if there was a bear in that room.

Remain calm, and don't panic.

Then slam the door and run like hell.

After offering up a quick prayer to whichever saint or angel was in charge of looking after about-to-become-hors-d'oeuvres architects, he gently pushed open the door. Peering around the corner, he saw no one, but noted that the bedroom—which at least had furniture in it—was a complete shambles. Every dresser drawer yawned open, decorated with an assortment of T-shirts he surmised belonged to Dave hanging over the edges. The sheets and bedspread were pulled off the twin bed, and pillow feathers covered every surface, including a pile of clothes in the corner.

Frustration welled up inside him. Damn it, if college kids had indeed done this and he caught them, he was going to make the pranksters clean up this mess. Of course, if the culprit was a crazed cabin-dwelling architect-eating bear, Ryan figured he'd cut the bear a break and clean up the mess himself. But if it was anyone else, he was going to make them set this place back to rights. And he had the plastic fork and high-heeled shoe to make them do it.

He suspected that the half-opened door in the corner led to a bathroom and possibly hid his culprit. Tightening his grip on the fork and shoe, he crept closer.

Through the ajar door he caught sight of a towel rack. Yup, it was a bathroom all right. He paused when he heard a ripping sound. Uh-oh. Ripping *and* groaning? Was there more than one thief or *whatever* lurking in there? The ripping sound continued. Deciding the element of surprise was his best bet, he approached the door on silent feet. Yes, definitely the best thief was a surprised thief. Same thing applied to bears.

Probably.

He slowly pushed the door open several more inches and peeked around it, ready to heave the shoe. And for the second time in minutes, his jaw dropped.

The bathroom looked like junior high school students had toilet-papered it. Long streamers of white toilet tissue littered the floor and hung from the towel rack and curtain rod. The medicine cabinet gaped open. An assortment of medicine bottles and tubes lay on their sides, most having spilled over onto the white marble vanity. And the destructive culprit sat in the porcelain sink.

A small, fuzzy brown raccoon.

Its body not much bigger than a football, the raccoon nestled in the bathroom sink, tearing pages from a magazine, a long ribbon of toilet paper draped about its body like an old-fashioned feather boa. Ryan stared, dumbfounded, as the animal tore out a glossy page and tossed it. It seesawed back and forth in the air then glided to a halt at Ryan's feet. Glancing down, he read the bold, black headline: Put More Sizzle in Your Kiss—Mastering Man-Melting Mouth-to-Mouth Techniques.

A glugging sound came from the sink and Ryan's gaze snapped back to the raccoon who was now drinking from a plastic bottle. Ryan peered at the label. Maalox.

The furry animal caught sight of him and slowly lowered the bottle from its mouth. Clutching the Maalox container between its tiny paws, the raccoon stared at him through small, bright, curious eyes, then twitched its whiskers.

Ryan huffed out a relieved breath. There was no reason to be nervous about a raccoon. Was there? Nah. Especially a raccoon who appeared to be *smiling* at him.

Or was it just showing its teeth? It's rabid, sharp, make-you-bleed-to-death-if-it-bites-you teeth. He knew zip about raccoons—except that they apparently liked to read women's magazines and swill antacid.

The raccoon flicked its bushy tail. With remarkable dexterity, the animal set the Maalox bottle on the vanity, then agilely jumped to the floor and dashed through the doorway into the hall. Ryan wasn't sure where the creature was going, but he had bigger problems at the moment. Like that god-awful groaning, which—suddenly stopped.

His gaze was drawn to a half-open door in the corner. Another sound filled the air, coming from beyond that door. Running water. Like the shower was on.

Shower? Could that awful noise have been caused by the

shower pipes? Possibly. The plumbing in his old apartment had moaned and groaned like someone with a semi-truck rolling over their toe.

Hmm. This put a whole new complexion on things. He didn't know much about bears, but he doubted they took *showers*. So that meant he was either dealing with a human—probably the thief who'd made off with Dave's stuff—or the damn smartest bear in the world.

Neither thought was particularly comforting.

Maybe the raccoon had turned on the shower? No, Ryan decided. The animal hadn't been wet, and as agile as he appeared, it didn't seem likely the beast could have turned on the water and gotten away dry.

Moving cautiously, Ryan crept closer to the door until a vinyl shower curtain came into view. Obviously the tub was fitted against the right side wall. A towel rack with two neatly folded white towels hung on the left wall of the narrow room. The toilet faced him.

Billows of steam rose from the top of the curtain and Ryan sniffed the moist air. A hint of citrusy spice. Very…unbearlike. That was good. Possibly thieflike, however. That was bad.

At that instant, the groaning started up again, nearly stopping his heart. Another sound joined the groaning—a sound Ryan immediately recognized as human.

Unless a bear could whistle a classic Rolling Stones' tune.

While he didn't have to face a bear, a relief to be sure, he *was* faced with the unpleasant prospect of dealing with the person most likely responsible for the cabin's condition. It struck him as odd that a thief would take the time to shower, but hey, at least the guy wouldn't be able to conceal a weapon. And while he wasn't Muhammad Ali, Ryan was confident he stood a pretty good chance against whomever was in the shower. Most likely it was just some hung-over college kid he could reason with and convince to bring back Dave's stuff and clean up the mess.

Yup, most likely.

The shower abruptly stopped, and the groaning noise faded to silence, confirming that the pipes were probably the source. The whistling also tapered off, replaced by soft, melodic humming.

He frowned. Wait a second. That didn't sound like a guy. It sounded like a—

The curtain was pushed aside with a metal scrape of rings against the pole. A long, slim, unmistakably feminine leg stepped sideways from the tub. A matching leg appeared, and he found himself staring at what had to be the finest backside in the free world.

Holy naked lady.

She stood with her back to him, which was just as well because he suspected his eyeballs had sprung two feet out of his head. She pulled a towel from the rack and used it to vigorously rub her long, dark hair that in spite of being flattened from the shower, still showed signs of curling.

He tried, *really* tried to look away, but, well, she had appeared so *suddenly*. And the view was so…fine. It was as if his gaze was Crazy Glued to her butt.

She bent over from the waist, drying her legs with the towel, affording him an X-rated view that made him forget how to breathe. *In with the good air, out with the bad air.* Wow. This girl could start a fire in a fish tank. Every cell in his body tensed until he couldn't move a muscle.

Maybe his muscles were frozen in place, but there was nothing wrong with his vision. Hey, if she *was* the thief who'd emptied the place of all its belongings, he'd need to give a detailed description of her to the cops, wouldn't he? His gaze slid over her. Not a single identifying scar or tattoo anywhere. Only lots of creamy, moist, soft-looking, incredible-smelling flesh. Long, long legs, slim ankles, narrow feet with nails painted flamingo pink.

His stupefied brain cells roused themselves and tapped on his forehead. *Helloooo…earth to Ryan, you're staring at a naked stranger who is most likely a thief. And even if she isn't, she doesn't know you're looking at her. That borders on being a pervert.*

He jolted back to reality. Damn! He wasn't a pervert. He was just…surprised. He hadn't had time to…react. But now that his mind was once again functioning, sort of, he needed to stop looking at—okay, *ogling*—all that gorgeous, creamy, damp, female flesh. And he *would* have stopped, except at that instant she wrapped the towel around herself and turned around.

A breath he hadn't even realized he held *whooshed* from his lungs like a popped balloon.

Her hair stuck up in odd punk-rocker type spikes from the towel-drying. Big blue eyes stared at him. She looked like a sea goddess, rising from a billowing mist of steam.

And boy, could she scream.

She let loose an ear-splitting howl that no Hollywood actress could beat. It echoed in the small room like a sonic boom. Clapping a palm over one aching ear, nearly stabbing himself in the head with the plastic fork, he said, "Whoa, lady, relax. I'm not—"

Her mouth opened wider and her scream increased to a volume that would surely shatter the windows. Jeez, didn't she need to stop to *breathe* or something? Apparently not, because the scream continued unabated as she scrambled back, away from him. If she wasn't careful, she was going to—

Slip on the wet floor.

Before he could make a move to save her, her feet slid

out from under her. She frantically grabbed on to the shower curtain, but the clear-and-white stripped vinyl couldn't support her weight. The metal rings broke off one by one, with a rapid succession of *ching-boing* sounds, like shrapnel bouncing off a Sherman tank. With the curtain clutched in her hands, still screaming loud enough to wake the dead, she fell backward into the tub.

Ryan dropped his fork and shoe and rushed forward to help her. "Are you hurt?" he asked, skidding to a halt beside the tub.

The shower curtain engulfed her like mummy rags, covering her from her waist up, head and all. Clearly she wasn't unconscious because her muffled yells were audible and her arms were flapping around, trying to free herself from her vinyl prison. Her legs, hanging over the edge of the tub, kicked fiercely. Looking down, he noticed that her towel had apparently gotten lost in the shuffle. She kicked her legs open and he quickly averted his gaze, knowing that in her fright, she would have inadvertently afforded him a view of womanly flesh he bet only gynecologists normally got to see.

Jeez, thief or not, he hadn't meant to terrorize her, and she was clearly scared out of her wits. Trying to avoid her thrashing limbs, he leaned over and untangled the shower curtain, pulling it back away from her head. When her flushed and panic-stricken face appeared, he offered her what he hoped was a reassuring I'm-not-a-pervert-or-murderer smile.

"Are you all right?" he asked.

Her arm whipped out from beneath the curtain and she squirted him right in the eyes with some sort of gel. He jolted upright and staggered backward, his shoulders hitting the tile wall.

"Ouch! That stings like hell!" He swiped at his eyes to

wipe away the gel, but the instant he touched it, it turned into a floral-scented foam. Probably that same sort of feminine shaving cream stuff Marcie had used. "What did you do that for?"

Squeezing his burning eyes shut, he felt along the wall for the towel rack. He heard her grunting and thrashing around in the tub. Good God, the woman was a menace. He'd lived in the city of Boston for six years without incident, but five minutes in the damn country and he'd been assaulted by a screaming, naked, shaving cream-tossing madwoman. If she'd just hold still and be quiet for a second, he'd be happy to tell her he wasn't Norman Bates and this was not a reenactment of the shower scene from *Psycho.* He hoped he survived—with his vision intact—long enough to tell her.

His fingers encountered the cool metal of the towel rack and he gratefully snatched the towel and scrubbed at his stinging, watering eyes. Cracking open his lids, an effort that burned like the fires of Hades, he saw she was frantically trying to step out of the tub while securing the shower curtain around her body.

Blinking rapidly against the fierce stinging, he said, "Look, I think—"

Another blob of gel landed on cheek. He wiped it off and barely dodged two more missiles. She had aim like a major league pitcher.

"All right, that's enough," he said when a third gel-bomb whizzed by his ear, missing him by a hair. Dropping his towel, he forced his eyes open and grabbed a pale green can from her hand. He tossed it on the floor then held up his palms so she could see he was unarmed.

Forcing his voice to remain calm, he looked at her through his sore, watery eyes. "Please, calm down. I'm not going to hurt you. My name is Ryan Monroe. My friend Dave Newbury owns this cabin and he gave me the key.''

For an answer, she snatched a pink, girly-looking safety razor from the edge of the tub and brandished it at him like a sword. ''If you come near me, I'll cut you to shreds,'' she said in a fierce voice.

''Not coming nearer,'' he assured her, blinking rapidly to clear his vision. Damn it all, his eyes really *hurt*. He didn't dare bend down to retrieve the towel to wipe his eyes again. She'd probably take that razor to him and whack off his ears.

Damn crazy woman. After several seconds, the burning subsided enough so that he didn't feel like clawing his eyeballs out. He looked at her, one white-knuckled hand holding the pink razor, the other clutching the shower curtain around her. Clearly unbeknownst to her, one of the curtain's wide clear stripes ran across her bosom which rose and fell with her hard, rapid breathing.

Her breasts were as centerfold-worthy as her butt.

Forcing his gaze back to her face, sympathy for her nudged his annoyance aside. In spite of her militant stance with the razor, she was obviously very frightened. She was also wet, almost naked and...he squinted at her...and, somehow, *familiar?*

In spite of the shaving cream residue clouding his vision, he realized he'd seen her somewhere before. And recently. He prided himself on never forgetting a face. Hmm. Better keep things friendly just in case he'd seen it in the post office on the FBI's Most Wanted poster.

Clearing his throat, he said, ''Please, accept my apology. I swear I didn't mean to startle you.''

Her gaze darted to the back of the door. He turned and spied a ratty-looking purple robe hanging from a hook. ''Would you like your robe?'' he asked.

She swallowed once then nodded.

Moving slowly, not making any moves that could be interpreted as threatening, he pulled down the robe then tossed it to her.

"Turn around," she ordered.

"Okay. But you put down the razor."

When she narrowed her eyes at him, he huffed out a breath. "Look, I'm not a weirdo, a rapist, or an ax murderer. I'm an architect, for crying out loud. With soapy eyes. I'm Dave Newbury's friend—he owns this cabin."

His words must have at least partially convinced her he wasn't going to kill her and bury her in the New Hampshire woods because she slowly lowered the razor then set it on the edge of the tub, still easily within her reach. Under the circumstances, with her obviously believing him to be a homicidal maniac and all, it was the best he could hope for.

"All right," she said. "Now turn around. And don't try any funny stuff. I'm...I'm a black belt."

"Fine." Turning his back to her, he stared at the white, tiled wall and watched three gobs of shaving gel trail slowly downward, like sudsy snails. He could hear her struggling to unwrap herself from the shower curtain, but he didn't dare offer to help her. Her halting speech and frightened eyes led him to doubt her claims of karate expertise, but he didn't care to test her knowledge in case she really was an expert. He already knew she was lethal with shaving cream.

"You say you're Dave Newbury's friend?" she asked from behind him.

"That's right. Known him since high school. We're like brothers."

"Are you normally in the habit of sneaking up on women? What are you—some kind of voyeur?"

He hadn't meant to sneak, and he wasn't a voyeur. At least he never had been until he'd stepped into this bathroom and seen her. He'd always considered himself a basically upstanding, well-mannered guy. At least that's what his mother had always told him.

Realizing Miss Shower had a point, he said, "I'm sorry. I didn't mean to sneak up on you, or to frighten you. I unlocked the door with the key Dave gave me. I heard a god-awful groaning and wasn't sure what it was."

"You've never heard old pipes acting up before?" she asked, her tone ripe with suspicion.

"Well, yes, but I wasn't expecting anyone to be in the shower. Believe me, I was as surprised to see you as you were to see me."

"How do I know you're telling the truth about Dave letting you stay here? This cabin is supposed to be empty."

Her speaking voice, much calmer now, reminded him of a hot, buttered rum—with a whiskey chaser. "Yes, it is, which, um, makes me wonder, who are *you* and how did *you* get in?"

"I'm a friend of *Mrs*. Newbury's, and I'm here at her invitation."

A friend of Carmen's? Is *that* why she seemed familiar? Maybe, but Carmen had introduced him to most of her friends and he knew he'd never formally met this woman. Yes, she was familiar, but in a much more fleeting way. Like he'd seen her in line at the movies, or in the produce aisle at the supermarket, or on an elevator.

Or on one of those true-crime cop shows.

"May I turn around now?" he asked.

"I suppose but, remember, no funny stuff."

Ryan wasn't sure what funny stuff was, but he knew he definitely didn't want to do it. God knew he didn't want her screaming, or shooting shaving cream at him again.

Facing her once more, he studied her carefully while she watched him through wide-spaced, startlingly blue eyes still lingering with suspicion. Wrapped in her ratty purple robe, she certainly didn't *look* like a thief, but hey, what did he know? He didn't think *he* looked like a crazed killer, so clearly he wasn't a good judge.

She was undeniably pretty, in an understated sort of way—a fact he could ascertain now that her mouth wasn't stretched around a scream. Pale freckles scattered across her small nose. Although her lips were pressed tightly together, her mouth appeared luscious. Yes, he'd definitely seen her before.

"If you're Carmen's friend, why weren't you at the wedding?" he asked, but the instant the words left his mouth, the imaginary light bulb above his head clicked on.

"I *was* at the wedding." Although she didn't add the words *you doofus,* they were clearly understood. Relaxing her militant posture a bit, she leaned forward and peered at him through the dissipating steam. He knew the instant she recognized him. Her eyes widened and a deep flush rushed into her cheeks.

"Ohmigod, it's you," they said in unison.

Images flashed through Ryan's mind. The reception. Squeezing his way through the throng of milling guests to get to the podium to make the toast, his cuff link had gotten tangled in the bow on the back of her dress. Not wanting to rip the material, he'd stopped in his tracks.

"Don't move," he'd warned her.

She'd looked at him over her shoulder and asked, "Is this a stickup?"

He vividly recalled thinking *wow* at the punch-in-the-gut impact of those big blue eyes. But he'd shoved the feeling firmly aside. Relationships were off his list for the foreseeable future—maybe for, like, the next fifty years. Forcing himself to concentrate, he'd performed several contortionist-like moves and freed his sleeve without damaging her dress, all the while ignoring her spicy, flowery scent.

Her hair had been pulled back in a severe style, and she'd worn a modest, navy dress with a high neckline—very much in contrast to the glittery, sexy outfits many of the other female guests wore. Prim, proper, and neat were the words he'd have used to describe her. It was difficult to equate her to this tousle-haired woman with the sinful body he'd accidentally viewed, but they were definitely one and the same.

He hadn't seen her again after his toast, and he'd forced himself not to look for her—or to ask Carmen or Dave about her. No point since he was through with relationships.

Realizing the silence was stretching into the uncomfortable zone, he held out his hand. "Ryan Monroe."

She hesitated, then offered her own. Her skin was warm and silky. "Lynne Waterford."

"I know all Dave's and Carmen's friends. Why haven't we ever met before?"

"Carmen and I were good friends in high school, but we'd lost touch. We only met up with each other again a few months ago." She eyed the plastic fork he'd dropped. "So...were you going to stab me with that or did you stop by hoping for some lunch?"

He indicated the razor on the tub's edge with a jerk of his head. "That depends on your plans for that thing. I can't say I relish being shaved to death."

She drew a deep breath. "I, uh, suppose I'll let you live. Would you mind explaining what you're doing here? Besides scaring me to death?"

"Dave told me I could use the cabin while he's on his honeymoon."

"I see." Her gaze drifted to the high-heeled shoe lying on the tile floor. "And you had my shoe because…?"

"When I heard those groaning pipes, I thought it might be…a bear."

Her eyes widened. "A *bear?* What were you planning to do—ask a grizzly to play Cinderella?"

"Ha-ha. There wasn't exactly a huge assortment of weapons lying around here. Which reminds me…where's all the furniture?"

"Gone."

"I can see that. Was the cabin robbed?"

"Robbed? No. I'm an interior designer. Carmen hired me to decorate the cabin while she's honeymooning. It's a surprise wedding gift for Dave."

Uh-oh. This did not sound good. He braced himself for what he feared was coming next. "And the furniture?"

"The local salvage yard picked it up first thing this morning," she said. "Everything except the moose head and a bearskin rug stored in the closet. They'll be back for those tomorrow."

Good grief, Dave was going to blow a gasket. If he came home from his honeymoon and found his comfy bachelor pad filled with girly geegaws, he'd hit the roof.

Man, what was Carmen *thinking?* She was a great gal, but why did women always find it necessary to mess with a guy's stuff? *Good thing I'm here to avert this redecorating fiasco before it goes any further.*

His duty was clear. He needed to get in touch with Dave. While he hated to interrupt his friend's honeymoon, this situation definitely fell into the realm of "emergency." Dave would undoubtedly tell this decorator chick to hit the road.

But just in case he couldn't reach Dave, he'd have to tell her himself. She probably wouldn't be pleased about packing up her fabric samples and toddling on home, but she could reschedule after Dave returned and was apprised of Carmen's "gift." In the meantime, he'd see to it that Miss Lynne Waterford arranged for the salvage yard to bring back Dave's furniture.

He couldn't help but feel sorry for her. No doubt this would screw up her work schedule, but better to have a screwed-up schedule than be responsible for Dave and Carmen's divorce.

"If you don't mind, Mr. Monroe, I'd appreciate it if we could continue this conversation after I've put on some clothes. I'm not exactly dressed for guests."

Her words inadvertently drew his gaze back to her robe-clad body. Even that ragtag robe couldn't hide the fact that the woman had more curves than a mountain road. An image of her, naked, bending over, flashed in his mind. Gritting his teeth, he firmly filed the image in his mental "forget about it" file, right next to Marcie. The last thing he needed was a distraction—like a woman who looked like damp sin and sounded like hot sex.

"No problem," he said. "But I think I should warn you." He lowered his voice and jerked his head toward the other room. "There's a raccoon out there. It seems friendly enough, but—"

"Oh, you mean Waldo."

"Waldo?" Jeez, was that varmint a *pet?*

"Yes. Did he frighten you?"

Hell, yes. "Heck, no. But—"

"Oh, no. Don't tell me he's been in the *bathroom.*"

"All right, I won't tell you that."

She winced. "Did he get into the bandages and tooth-paste again?"

"Nope."

"Well, that's good."

"But I think he's put a serious dent in your Maalox supply and your *Cosmo* magazine has seen better days."

"Oh, boy. That's bad." She eased past him, and a hint of citrusy scent wafted behind her, reminding him of steamy, tropical beaches, palm trees swaying, and steel drums playing. His mind filled with a picture of her, emerging from the ocean, naked, wet, beckoning him—

"Oh, Waldo!" she wailed from the other room. "What on earth have you done?"

Ryan mentally shook himself. Damn. It wasn't fair that he'd seen her naked. Bending over. Shrink-wrapped in a peekaboo shower curtain. He'd never be able to erase that image from his memory, and women were supposed to be the *last* thing on his mind—especially *this* woman who was a major pain in the butt, or at least the eyeball. Why couldn't Carmen's decorator have been a hundred and three years old? And fully clothed?

"Don't think about it," he muttered. "Think raccoon, think raccoon."

Thinking raccoon, he walked back into the room Waldo had "decorated." The beast was nowhere to be seen, but the open Maalox bottle still sat on the vanity and glossy magazine pages littered the floor. Ryan raised his brows at the magazine cover blurb adorning the countertop: How to Touch a Naked Man—Caress His Secret Hot Spots and Drive Him Wild.

A tingle zipped through him. He glanced at Miss Lynne Waterford. In spite of her hair, which looked like someone had stuck a mop on her head, and her very *un*sexy robe, he found himself wondering if she'd read the article.

He mentally thunked himself on the forehead. He had to get a grip. What difference did it make if she'd read it or not? He didn't want this woman, or any woman—at least not now. He had work to do—important work that required his undivided attention. And because of her, the furniture was missing in action. And besides, he needed quiet and she was easily the *noisiest* female he'd ever met.

She stood with her hands planted on her hips, shaking her head. "It's going to take me hours to clean up this mess."

She turned to face Ryan and he found himself staring into those big, baby-blue eyes. While her expression didn't indicate that she was thrilled with his presence, at least she no longer appeared to think he was the Boston Strangler.

"Waldo's very sweet," she said, "but, as you can see, very mischievous. He's not really destructive, just insatiably curious."

"How did you end up with a raccoon for a pet? You know, most people have dogs. Or cats. A gerbil, maybe."

"I found him five years ago in a hollow tree stump near my parents' cabin, which is only about five miles from here. The poor baby was around a month old and he'd apparently been abandoned by his mother. I brought him home, and he's sort of belonged to my family ever since. Even though he's a devil, Mom and Dad love having him around."

"What's he doing *here?*"

"I hiked to my folks' cabin yesterday morning and he followed me back here. He comes and goes through the pet door which the cabin's previous owners must have installed. I'll need to drive Waldo back tomorrow before the workers arrive so he doesn't cause any more trouble."

"I see." Ryan glanced at the Maalox bottle. "Will that stuff hurt him?"

"No, thank goodness." She picked up the bottle and tossed it into the trash can. "I thought I'd tightened the cap sufficiently, but raccoons are remarkably dexterous."

"Obviously." Ryan plucked the torn magazine cover

from the vanity and handed it to her. "And their choice of reading material is, er, interesting, to say the least."

She glanced at the headline and a bright blush suffused her face. Thrusting the paper behind her, she said, "Oh! He, uh, usually prefers *Field and Stream*, but, uh..." She cleared her throat, then stared at the door in a pointed fashion. "If you don't mind, I really need to get dressed."

"Sure," Ryan said. "But prepare yourself. If you think Waldo made a mess in *here*, wait 'til you see the bedroom."

He'd expected she'd be angry—God knows he'd be pissed by the disaster awaiting her in the next room—but she just blew out a resigned breath.

"Don't tell me," she said. "The pillows?"

"'Fraid so. You might want to invest in polyfilled instead of feathers. And your clothes..." He shook his head sadly.

"All over the place?"

"Lady, you've got panties hanging from the moose head."

Her blush deepened, and he had to force his gaze away from that utterly beguiling color. When was the last time he'd seen a woman blush? *Sixth grade.*

No, actually, it had been at Dave and Carmen's wedding—and it had been this woman.

Inching his way toward the door, he said, "Well, I'll just wait in the living room until you're dressed." Taking pity on her and the mess she faced, he added, "Then, if you like, I'll help you straighten up."

"Um, thanks, but I can manage." She didn't add *as if I'd want* your *help, you sneak-up-on-women-when-they're-showering pervert, you,* but she might as well have. She caught her lower lip between even white teeth, drawing his gaze to her mouth. So what if she had gorgeous lips? Full, pouty, pink, and moist. And big deal that the creamy skin showing above the ratty robe's neckline looked good enough to lick. He backed out of the room. "I'll be in the living room. Me and the moose."

"Okay."

Turning, he swiftly crossed the messy bedroom, closing the door behind him and made a beeline for the living area. Once there, he raked his fingers through his hair and huffed out a frustrated breath.

Just his luck. He'd left the comfort of Boston and his Back Bay condo to tramp into the New Hampshire wilderness to get away from everything, women included, and what does he find? A screaming female, with *the* finest ass he's ever seen, invading his space. Well, as soon as she got some clothes on—and the sooner the better—he'd just send her and her pesky raccoon friend on their merry way. Then he'd settle down to work.

Restless, he opened the fridge and was gratified to see it well stocked. He helped himself to a canned soft drink, making a mental note to replace it from the supply in his car, then popped the lid. Leaning his hips against the counter, he enjoyed a long, icy swallow. Muffled noises came from behind the closed bedroom door, and he imagined her digging through the mess to find something to wear.

Something to cover those enticing curves.

Even as he tried to force his thoughts in another direction, he recalled his instant attraction to her at the wedding—an attraction he'd squashed like a bug. Women were nothing but trouble. His disastrous relationship with Marcie had simply capped off a recent series of harrowing dating experiences.

There'd been Delia, the woman he'd dubbed Miss Corporate. She'd dumped him when she'd started an affair with her company's CEO.

Then came Jayne, aka Miss Jock. The woman lived and breathed sports—but nothing as tame as football, basketball, or hockey. No, she loved bone-breaking stuff like cliff diving and rock climbing. She'd dumped him when he'd turned down the once-in-a-lifetime "opportunity" to join her on a thousand mile trek across the frozen Alaskan tundra.

And he'd never forget Rachel, Miss Hot-to-Trot. He shook his head, still amazed by her. She'd wanted to have sex *everywhere*. He didn't consider himself a prude, but sex in the frozen food aisle of the grocery store just wasn't his cup of tea.

Then came Miss Life Sucks, Miss We've-Gone-on-Three-Dates-Let's-Get-Engaged, Miss You-Don't-Earn-Enough-Money, followed by Miss Three-Ex-husbands, Miss Pathological Liar, and Miss I-Wasn't-Convicted-And-It-Was-Only-Embezzlement-Anyway.

Then he'd met Marcie and for a while things had been great. Then she'd accepted a job in Chicago. Ryan knew it would be difficult to maintain a long-distance relationship, but he was willing to try—until he'd visited Marcie and discovered another guy's briefs under her bed. Marcie had morphed into Miss You-Don't-Mind-If-I-Sleep-Around-Right?

Wrong. He minded. Maybe he was old-fashioned, but he didn't warm more than one bed at a time, and he'd expected the same courtesy from her. Although their parting was a mutual decision, and he was more annoyed than heartbroken, he resented the way she'd tied him up in knots. The time and energy he'd spent on her had exhausted him and dried up his creativity. Relationships. Phooey. Who needed them?

His gaze wandered over to the moose head and riveted on the black lace panties hanging from the horns. The mere thought of that wisp of lace filled with Lynne Waterford's curvy derriere clenched his fingers around the soda can. Any woman who looked like that would be nothing but a distraction, and distractions were exactly what he didn't need.

Good thing she'd be leaving.

LYNNE PUSHED HER DAMP HAIR from her eyes and scavenged through the clothing littering the bedroom floor. Spying a pair of panties in the pile, she quickly slipped them on and continued searching. Next she snatched a bra from the floor, setting up a whirl of pillow feathers. An oversized T-shirt and baggy jeans, both hopelessly wrinkled, followed.

A long sigh of relief escaped her. Okay, she was dressed. And in control. Certainly much more so than she'd been when she'd turned around in the bathroom and found herself face-to-face with a stranger...or at least a man she'd *thought* was a stranger.

Her initial fright had been so intense, she'd actually feared she might faint. She absolutely hadn't recognized him, no doubt because her brain had frozen with fear. She was alone in the mountains... A shudder ran through her, followed by a grunt of disgust when she recalled falling backward into the tub, trapped by the shower curtain. She was lucky he hadn't been a serial killer. He could have carved her up like a Thanksgiving turkey while she flailed about, trussed up in vinyl.

Upon reflection, she realized he hadn't *looked* especially threatening, in spite of the plastic fork and high-heeled shoe he held, but with so many whackos running around, you never could tell. And while she'd lied about being a black belt, she *had* taken a self-defense course several years ago. Surely that made her something—like a beige belt, maybe.

Recognition had hit her like a bucket of icy water. He was none other than the best man from Carmen's wedding—the gorgeous guy with the killer smile and bow-entangling cuff links.

During the ceremony, she'd noted that the tuxedo-clad best man appeared incomparably attractive, but she'd shrugged it off. What man didn't look good from a distance, especially in a tux?

But when he'd become attached to her dress at the reception, she'd discovered that even up close, he was, for lack of a better word, lovely. Thick, ebony hair that begged for female fingers to ruffle through it; intelligent, warm, brown eyes with intriguing gold flecks; and an arrestingly attractive—yet not model-perfect—face. They'd laughed over the incident, and he'd disentangled himself. After making sure he hadn't damaged her dress, he'd apologized, flashed her a heart-stopping grin, then continued on his way. She'd pegged him as friendly and thoughtful, even if he was kind of a klutz.

And he'd smelled great. Clean, with just a hint of woodsy spice—like he'd just stepped from the shower. During that brief moment when he'd stood behind her, her pulse had zoomed. Good thing she wasn't prone to heaving gushing, feminine sighs, or she would have heaved and gushed all over him.

She'd considered asking Carmen about him, but had firmly discarded the idea. She needed a man like a hole in the head. Besides, he was probably married. Or gay. Or out on parole. She'd left the reception soon after their brief encounter, anxious to get home and finish packing for her stay at the Newbury cabin. She certainly hadn't expected to see Mr. Ryan Monroe again.

Especially when she was naked.

A groan escaped her. Figures that the first guy she'd found attractive in months had to discover her in such an awkward situation.

Her fear now gone, embarrassment—with a hefty dose of suspicion—moved right in and took up residence. Good Lord, how long had he been standing there? She recalled bending over to dry her legs. Had he seen *that?* She hoped not, but she suspected he had. Anger joined embarrassment and suspicion. If he was any kind of a gentleman, he would have immediately spoken up, or coughed, or *something* to let her know he was there.

Of course, he *had* handed her her robe, and he *hadn't* hurt her—except for the coronary his presence had nearly brought on. And he *was* Dave and Carmen's friend. So maybe he wasn't a *complete* pervert. But even so, she'd be glad to see him go.

Moving to the mirror, she suppressed a groan at the image staring back at her. Her crinkled clothes looked like an elephant had sat on them, and her hair, the bane of her life, surrounded her head like a nuclear explosion. Good grief, why in the world did women spend hundreds of dollars on perms to make their hair *curly?* As far as she was concerned, the only good thing about the bazillion corkscrew curls covering her head was that they prevented her from being bald. Still, at least once a week she considered shaving her head and wearing a wig. And the only reason she kept her hair long was because the one time she'd cut it short, in high school, the damn hair had stuck straight out from the sides. She'd gone to the prom looking like a brunette Bozo the Clown.

Snatching a hot pink scrunchy from the vanity top, she pulled the mass of curls back with impatient fingers, secured it into a tight ponytail, then twirled it into a snug bun at her nape. There. Now she looked presentable. Wrinkled and makeup-free, but presentable.

Translation: not naked.

Hot chagrin again suffused her at the thought that the very attractive Ryan Monroe might have been standing behind her while she *bent over*. She flatly refused to think about how long it had been since she'd been naked in front of a man. *Okay, nineteen months, three weeks and five days, but who's counting?* It didn't matter anyway. She was through with men.

Especially yuppie city slickers—or ''yucs'' as she called them. Boston was crawling with the breed and she'd suffered through enough dates and fix-ups to know the type. Good-looking, Italian loafer-wearing smooth talkers, every one of them. Definitely not to be trusted.

Just like every other yuc she'd met, Ryan Monroe wore expensive shoes and sported a hundred-dollar haircut, and she'd bet her bottom dollar that some fancy, sleek foreign car was parked outside the cabin. Unlike every other yuc she'd met, however, Ryan Monroe had—most likely—seen her bare-assed. Up close. Good Lord, sheer embarrassment was going to make her move to another state.

Yes, indeedy, she could name every one of those yucs— she'd dated them all. Mr. I-Can't-Commit, Mr. Don't-Touch-My-Porsche!, Mr. Hey-Where's-the-Remote?, Mr. I-Bought-You-Dinner-So-Let's-Have-Sex, Mr. Can't-Talk-'Til-Halftime, and the last in her miserable string of disasters—Mr. You'd-Be-Real-Cute-If-You'd-Lose-Ten-Pounds.

After she'd slammed the door in *his* face, she'd sworn off relationships and concentrated on herself and her career. The last thing she wanted was to bounce into some rebound-type situation with another yuc. And she hadn't felt so much as a tingle until Ryan Monroe attached himself to her dress. He'd sent not only a tingle, but a whole battalion of goose bumps marching down her spine—and he'd barely touched her.

But no matter. It didn't make any difference how tingle inducing he was. Oh, no. Stick a fork in her, she was done with men like him.

Grabbing two white socks from a pile of feathers, she slipped them on. Thunder boomed, followed seconds later by a flash of lightning. She quickly hunted down her Keds. She needed to get the yuc on his way home before the storm struck. These mountain roads quickly grew treacherous with heavy rain, and the last forecast she'd heard hadn't sounded promising.

An image of Ryan Monroe sneaked into her mind and she firmly pushed it away. Any man who looked like him, with those soulful yet teasing brown eyes, would be nothing but a distraction, and distractions were exactly what she didn't want. He definitely had to go, and the sooner the better.

But he'd be easy to get rid of. Experience had taught her men were dogs. If she threw a stick, he'd leave.

2

RYAN STARED AT THE composed, severely coiffed woman wearing baggy clothes who emerged from the bedroom. She wore loose-fitting jeans and a yellow T-shirt that proclaimed If They Don't Have Chocolate in Heaven, I Ain't Going. She bore little resemblance to the towel-clad, steamy goddess from the shower.

Except for those big blue eyes.

And that lovely, full mouth.

This was more of what his first impression of her had been—prim and proper, yet very attractive. No wild curls, or curves that had "sin" tattooed on them. If he hadn't seen her undressed with his own eyes, he never would have guessed at the eye-popping delights her loose clothing hid.

He wished he didn't know.

"I helped myself to a Coke," he said. "I hope you don't mind."

"Of course not. In fact—" A distant thunderclap cut off her words. Frowning, she walked to the window and peered outside.

"Rain will be here soon," she remarked, and Ryan suddenly realized that the room had grown noticeably darker in the last few minutes. She was going to have to hustle to gather up her things if she had any hope of leaving before the forecasted shower struck.

She touched a switch next to the door and the gloomy room flooded with light from an overhead fixture. "Listen," she said, turning to face him, "I don't mean to rush you, but you'd better get going before the rain starts."

He froze with the cola can halfway to his lips. "Excuse me?"

"The rain really slicks up these dirt roads. If you don't leave now, you might get stuck."

"What makes you think *I'm* leaving? Dave loaned me this cabin for the next two weeks. I'm staying."

She stared at him as if his elevator didn't quite reach the top floor. "I've explained that I'm redecorating the cabin at Carmen's request—"

"Well, Carmen shouldn't have made such a crazy request. Dave liked this place fine just the way it was."

"And he'll like it even better once I'm finished with it."

"I don't want to insult you, but *are you nuts?* If Dave comes back and finds all his stuff gone, he'll probably call 1-800-DIVORCE and name *you* as some sort of co-conspirator." She opened her mouth to speak, but he plunged on, "Look, I'm sure Carmen meant well, but she should have checked with Dave before she hired you. Moving out all his things, well, that just has 'bad idea' written all over it. Believe me, the best thing would be for you to leave, arrange to have the furniture brought back, then wait until Dave gets home before you do anything."

She mumbled something under her breath that sounded suspiciously like *where's a stick? I need to throw a stick.*

A stick? Jeez. What was she planning to do? Whack him with it?

Offering him a patently false smile, she said, "While I appreciate your suggestion, I'm afraid my leaving is not an option. Carmen and I have an agreement and I won't cancel it."

"Fine. Just postpone it until they return from their honeymoon and Dave can okay all these plans."

"That's impossible. Arrangements are already in place."

"Anything can be *un*-arranged with a simple phone call." Ryan set his soda can on the counter and drew a deep breath. "I need this place for the next two weeks to get some work done in peace and quiet—"

"Then you'll definitely want to leave because starting bright and early tomorrow morning I have contractors, plumbers, roofers and landscapers all scheduled to arrive. I'm afraid they'll be very noisy, Mr. Monroe."

"Not if you pick up the phone and tell them not to come." He tunneled his hands through his hair. "Look, Lynne—may I call you Lynne?" At her nod, he continued, "Trust me when I tell you that Dave will *not* appreciate this redecorating scheme."

"His wife disagrees. And *she* hired me." She crossed her arms over her chest and pursed her lips. "So, Ryan— may I call you Ryan?" Before he could answer, she said, "The bottom line here is, *one* of us has to leave, and it's not going to be me. I am *not* going to cancel my workers, and I *am* going to redecorate this cabin as per my agreement with Carmen."

Darn stubborn woman. Unless he planned to pick her up and physically remove her, she clearly wasn't budging. And while he grudgingly admitted that he didn't really have any right to disrupt Carmen's crazy idea of a wedding gift, he *knew* Dave was going to be royally ticked off. *And he'll never forgive me if I don't halt this feminine takeover of his space.* Yes, it was clearly his duty to save Dave's cabin from Carmen's misguided good intentions.

"Obviously there's one only way to settle this," he said. Walking into the kitchen, he lifted the receiver from the wall-mounted phone.

Amusement flickered in her eyes. "Who are you going to call? The 'Interior Decorator Removal Service'?"

Actually, he thought "Pest Control" was more apt, but he didn't voice his opinion. "No, I'm going to call Dave," he said, pressing numbers.

"On the cruise to nowhere? How do you propose to reach him?" She pointed to his laptop case. "What's in there, your trusty ship-to-shore radio?"

Man, if there was one thing he didn't like, it was a smart-ass. He nearly smiled in relief. This was good. He didn't like her. Surely he couldn't find a woman he didn't *like* attractive.

He glanced at his watch. "They're probably on board the ship, but they don't set sail for another hour. Dave's a stockbroker. His cell phone is permanently attached to him."

"Even on his *honeymoon?*"

"I'd be willing to lay odds."

She shook her head. "Unbelievable. Whatever happened to romance?" Without waiting for an answer, she continued, "You realize you're ruining Carmen's surprise."

"Can't be helped."

"She's going to be very upset."

"Probably. But I'm sure she'd rather be upset than divorced."

The phone rang twelve times before Dave answered. "Hello?" he said, sounding distinctly out of breath.

Uh-oh. Definitely sounded like he'd called at an inopportune moment. "Dave, it's Ryan. Is this a, uh, bad time?"

Dave blew out a long breath. "No. Hearing from you five minutes ago would have seriously strained our friendship, but now is fine. Is everything okay?"

"Yeah, but we need to talk."

"Sure. Just make it quick. Carm's freshening up, but when she's done we're going to explore the ship. So far all we've seen is the stateroom." Dave chuckled. "Gotta tell ya, buddy, this being a married man is fiiiiiine."

"That's great, Dave. Now listen."

Ryan quickly filled him in on the situation at the cabin.

"Holy hell," Dave said. "*All* my stuff?"

"Except a bed, dresser, a moose head and a bearskin rug she says is in the closet."

Dave emitted a tortured moan. "This is unbelievable. The sofa and chairs are from our *frat house!* And me and my dad made that table together. Listen," he said in an urgent whisper. "I don't want to screw up my honeymoon by getting Carmen angry with me. You know how women are. Once they're mad, they stay mad, for like *weeks,* but I've gotta have my stuff back." Desperation crept into his voice. "You gotta help me, man!"

"The salvage guy only came this morning. Your furniture's probably still on his truck. I'll head to his place as soon as we get off the phone."

"Thanks," Dave said. "I owe you, man. Big time."

"No problem." Ryan glanced at Lynne who was trying to reach her panties hanging from the moose's horns. Lowering his voice he asked, "What should I do about the decorator?"

"Hell, if I cancel the whole thing, Carmen'll be hurt and no doubt royally pissed since Lynne is one of her good friends. No way I'm going to start off married life sleeping on the sofa. But if Carmen finds out I know about her 'surprise' she'll be totally bummed." Dave huffed out a breath. "Okay, here's the plan. I won't let on I know about the decorating scheme. I guess the rooms could stand a coat of paint and maybe some curtains or something, but..." His voice dropped even lower. "I know this is a favor of biblical proportions, but you can't let her turn my cabin into 'Camp Girly-Girl'. I'm counting on you to—"

A deafening clap of thunder rattled the windows, followed by a fierce slash of lightning. "What did you say, Dave?" Ryan asked into the receiver. "Dave?"

Silence.

"Damn." They'd been cut off. Stupid cell phones. He immediately redialed Dave's number, but after three unsuccessful attempts, he realized it wasn't Dave's stupid cell phone causing the problem.

The phone in the cabin was dead.

"WHAT'S WRONG?" LYNNE ASKED, tucking the panties she'd retrieved from the moose head into her jeans pocket. Darn that mischievous Waldo.

"The phone's dead."

She inwardly groaned. Now she had no way to talk to Carmen to insure that Dave and Mr. Yuc didn't screw up the decorating plans. "Must be from the storm. I'm afraid it happens frequently up here."

"No problem. I'll just get my cell phone from the car. Be right back." He walked toward the door.

"I wouldn't bother...unless you want to climb a tree."

He halted and looked at her as if she'd sprouted a second head. "Climb a tree?"

"It's the only way to get reception."

"You're joking."

"'Fraid not. And I'd advise against it—unless you want to get crispy fried by a lightning bolt."

He dragged his hands down his face. "I don't even want to know how you figured out you need to climb a tree to use a cell phone."

"That's probably for the best. So tell me, what did Dave say?"

"Well, I hate to say I told you so, but he was pretty steamed about his stuff being gone. He wants it back. As for the decorating, he said some *minor* improvements were okay—like freshening up the paint, but nothing too girly.''

''*Girly?* What does he think I'm planning to do? Paint the place pink and decorate it with dolls and ruffled doilies?'' One look at his face told her that, yes, that's exactly what Dave thought. Drawing a deep breath, she fought to control her temper. Men. Sheesh. *Can't live with 'em, can't kill 'em.*

Well, she'd show Dave, and Ryan Monroe, too. She'd worked hard on her ideas and plans for this cabin and they were damn good. This job was too important to let slip through her fingers. A successful redecoration of the Newbury cabin was the first—and, therefore, the most crucial—step in her plan to free herself from the constraints of her present position at the design firm in Boston. Between the existing homes and new construction in this area, there were enough potential customers here to allow her to fulfill her dream of starting her own decorating business.

The best advertising was word of mouth from pleased customers, and Lynne had every intention of using this job as her long-awaited opportunity to jump-start her dreams. She wanted her own business, away from the city, far from the rat race, noise, traffic and pollution. Her gaze settled on Ryan Monroe.

Away from men like him. *Give me a pig farmer any day.*

Well, Mr. Gorgeous-City-Slicker was *not* going to disrupt her dream. She was *not* leaving. He could just pick up his gym bag and hike on out to whatever fancy-schmancy car he'd driven up here in and scram. If he refused to leave, she'd just whack him with the moose head. In fact—

''Well, I'd better get going before the weather turns worse,'' he said.

The fine temper she'd been working herself into deflated like a popped balloon. ''Huh?''

Another flash of lightning filled the room with slashes of light, followed by a boom of thunder that shook the windows. "I passed several inns on my way up here. I need to drive back to town and find a place to stay."

"Oh." Relief swept through her. He obviously wasn't going to cause any problems. He'd delivered his "no girly stuff" message and was going to leave her in peace. Dave hadn't wanted her tossed out on her ear. She'd won, he'd lost. She resisted the urge to stick out her tongue and chant, *Nah, nah.*

Knowing she'd emerged the victor in their skirmish, however, she couldn't help feel a bit sorry for him, especially given how graciously he was accepting defeat. Feeling generous, she said, "I'd suggest the Shady Tree Inn. It's small, but well run, and they serve a wonderful breakfast."

"Thanks." Crossing the room, he picked up his laptop case and adjusted the strap on his shoulder.

For some reason she couldn't explain, guilt washed over her. Darn it, it was just like when she was a kid—she'd always beaten her brother at Monopoly and then felt *bad* about winning. She had no reason to feel guilty.

But she did.

Maybe because he'd spent several hours driving up here and now had to leave. Maybe because he'd probably only get halfway down the mountain before the rain struck. Maybe because the annual Fall Foliage Festival was this week and there probably wasn't a room available at the Shady Tree Inn or anywhere else in the area and he'd have to drive a long way for a room.

Before she could say anything, however, he said, "Dave wants to keep his moose head and bear rug. Since the phone's out, I'll try to contact the salvage yard from my cell phone in my car and tell them to hold Dave's things.

But just in case I can't reach them, don't let them take the Bullwinkle or the rug.''

Lynne nodded. ''All right.'' She could live with that. Of course there was no need to tell him that Bullwinkle would have to join the rug in the closet.

Another bolt of lightning flashed. She caught a glimpse of the tall trees tipped with red and gold leaves swaying in the wind.

''I need to go,'' he said.

She crossed the room and extended her hand. ''Sorry about this mix-up.''

He clasped her hand in a warm, firm, long-fingered grip. A tingle zoomed up her arm like a mini bolt of electricity.

A slow, sheepish smile curved his lips. ''Sorry about scaring you.''

Whew. There was no denying this was one genetically blessed guy—especially when he smiled. Too bad he wasn't a pig farmer. ''That's okay. For your sake, I'm glad I wasn't a bear.''

He laughed and she absolutely did *not* notice how attractive he was when he did. ''Me, too.'' He released her hand and opened the door, letting in a swirl of leaves and wind. ''Bye.''

''Bye. Drive carefully.''

He flashed her a heart-stopping grin. ''Okay, Mom.''

She watched him walk down the short path, fighting the gusting wind. He opened the trunk to a sleek black Lexus and placed his laptop and gym bag inside while she mentally awarded herself a high five for correctly guessing the sort of car he'd drive. If he ran true to yuc form—and she was certain he did—he also preferred expensive wines, trendy restaurants and sleek model-type blondes.

The wind whipped around her and a raindrop splashed on her arm. He slid into the driver's seat, started the ignition, then opened his window halfway. Waving at her, he called, "See you tomorrow." The window closed and he drove slowly away.

Lynne closed the door and frowned. Tomorrow? Locking the door, she shrugged.

She must have misunderstood him.

AS HE DROVE AWAY FROM the cabin, Ryan turned on his cell phone, but as Lynne had warned, he couldn't even get a dial tone. Jeez, how did people *live* in godforsaken, dead-airspace places like this? Concrete, skyscrapers, crowds, even the Big Dig—bring them on! He'd try to call again once he reached the main road. Hopefully the salvage yard would still be open. Turning off the phone, he concentrated on his driving.

He hadn't even navigated a quarter mile down the winding dirt road before all hell broke loose. The sky darkened to midnight and the heavens opened, dumping sheets of rain that instantly defeated the Lexus's windshield wipers. Unable to see the road, he stopped and shifted the car into park.

Irritation rippled through him, but rain this intense couldn't last long. He'd just wait for it to taper off then he'd continue on. He glanced at his watch and frowned. He hoped he wouldn't be delayed too long. He had to get to the salvage yard and rescue Dave's furniture, then check into an inn.

While staying at an inn wasn't what he'd call ideal for working on his project, he'd manage and still be able to enjoy the country surroundings. Sure, he'd have to check up on the Martha Stewart wanna-be for Dave, but that shouldn't take up much time. Of course, in the interests of keeping his concentration intact, he'd have to be careful not to surprise her in the shower anymore.

After ten minutes, the rain showed no signs of abating. In fact, the storm worsened with each passing moment. The wind howled, buffeting the car, driving the rain against the windows in violent splashes. At this rate, he wouldn't make it to town until midnight.

Deciding to try the cell phone again, he pressed the phone's power button and waited for the familiar beep signaling the instrument's readiness. Instead, the digital display flashed "low battery."

"Damn!" And naturally the plug-in adapter was in his laptop case which he'd just stored in the trunk. Pinching the bridge of his nose, he shook his head. Less than two hours ago, all had been right with his world. Then he'd entered Dave's cabin and everything had gone to hell.

Words to a children's song popped into his mind and he chanted, "Rain, rain, go away. Come again some other day."

Didn't work. If anything, the volume of water pounding on the car increased.

Another fifteen minutes passed, with the rain still showing no signs of lessening. He tried to tune in a weather report on the radio, but nothing came through the speakers except static. What if the storm didn't let up? There was no way he could drive down the mountain. He could barely see two feet in front of him.

Huffing out a frustrated breath, he decided he'd better get the cell phone adapter. Maybe with a full charge he could get a call through—a call he suspected he was going to need. Given the way his luck was running, he'd need to call a helicopter to rescue him.

Lifting the lever next to his seat that unlocked the trunk, he braced himself, then opened the car door. A barrage of cold rain pelted him in the face. Sucking in a deep breath, he stepped from the car and closed the door.

And immediately sank ankle deep in thick, oozy mud.

Cursing, he held on to the car roof to balance himself and struggled to lift his foot. A hideous sucking sound reached his ears and his foot came free. His *bare* foot.

Damn it, this situation just went from bad to worse. Bending down, he stuck his hand into the hole that had eaten his Italian loafer. Mud oozed between his fingers and he grimaced. He shook his head to clear the rain from his eyes and realized his bumper rested nearly on the ground.

He froze, rain streaming over him like a waterfall. Either someone had stolen his tires out from underneath him, or…

Squinting through the driving rain toward the front of the car, he confirmed his suspicions.

His tires, like his loafer, had been completely swallowed by mud.

With the Lexus not going anywhere anytime soon, his choices had just narrowed down to staying in the car for God knows how long…or trudging through the storm back to the cabin.

He thunked his forehead against the cold car door.

What the hell else could go wrong?

Thunder crashed with a deafening boom, and he quickly withdrew the question.

He had a sinking-in-the-mud feeling he didn't want to know the answer.

3

LYNNE PACED THE EMPTY living room, pausing every few seconds to peer out the window. The rain fell like a blanket of water and showed no signs of letting up. She'd moved her clock radio from the bedroom into the kitchen and listened with growing alarm to severe thunderstorm and flash-flood warnings.

Good Lord, Ryan was stuck out there in the middle of this mess. She offered up a quick prayer that he was only stuck—and hadn't careened into a tree. Or driven off the mountain. A chill passed through her, and she cursed herself for not suggesting he stay and wait out the rain, but she hadn't anticipated such a violent storm.

He couldn't have traveled very far. The skies had opened up within minutes of his departure. Surely he had stopped and was just sitting in his car, waiting for the weather to clear.

But even if he was, there was no way he'd make it down the mountain tonight. Even if the rained stopped right now, the road would be too slick and dangerous. And if he wasn't all right...

She simply couldn't sit here in the cabin while he might be hurt. Or worse. At the very least, he was stranded. Even though he was a yuc and an ogler, she didn't want anything to happen to the guy. She had to try to help him.

Walking swiftly to the closet, she pulled out her slicker

and shiny red rubber rainboots. She'd need the flashlight from the top kitchen drawer and—

The front doorknob rattled. "Lynne," a deep voice called. "It's me, Ryan. Let me in."

Thank God. Whooshing out a relieved breath, she dropped her boots and ran to the door.

The man standing on the porch looked nothing like the smooth, urban professional who'd left less than an hour ago. *This* man looked like something that had been dragged from the lake. Rain dripped from his laptop case hanging over his shoulder. In one hand he clutched his gym bag, in the other a black umbrella that had been blown inside out from the wind, its silver spokes flapping loosely.

His dark hair was plastered against his head, except for one errant piece on the top that stuck straight up like a rooster's tail—sort of like Alfalfa from the *Little Rascals.*

Her gaze wandered downward. His polo shirt adhered to his obviously nicely muscled chest and abdomen like a second skin. And the way his mud-splattered, soaked khakis molded to his strong male legs and his…well, *that*…had to be illegal. In spite of the fact that he was barefoot, it certainly appeared that his body was in fine form—er, un-injured.

"Are you going to invite me in?" he asked in a decidedly testy tone. "Or should I just stay outside and begin building an ark?"

Lynne pulled her gaze away from his wet pants. "Sorry. Please come in." Stepping aside, she held the door wide open. He stomped in, splattering wet, muddy footprints in his wake. While he dumped his belongings in the corner, she dashed into the bathroom and returned with a large towel.

"Thanks," he said, wiping his face.

"Are you hurt?" she asked. "Where's your car? And your shoes?"

"Not hurt. Mud ate my tires and my shoes." He looked down at his filthy pants and feet and grimaced. "I need to clean up then change into some dry clothes. Do you mind if I use the shower?"

"Help yourself."

"Thanks." Slinging the towel over his shoulder, he knelt next to his gym bag. Lynne watched his profile as he struggled with the wet zipper and tried to convince herself that he was gross. But even with the Alfalfa hair, he was incredibly attractive.

How come *he* looked so good all wet while *she'd* looked like something Waldo unearthed in the backyard? It just wasn't fair. On the "men versus women" scorecard, men definitely had an unfair edge. Not only did they look good all wet and disheveled, they never had to wear panty hose, mascara, or high heels, and they could eat chocolate without it permanently adhering to their thighs. *In my next life, I wanna be a man.*

Ryan finally won the battle with the zipper. Separating the canvas sides to reveal his clothes, he groaned.

"What's wrong?" she asked, peering over his shoulder.

"Look at this." He held up a yellow polo shirt and wrung a good cup of water from it. "Jeez, no wonder this bag weighed a ton." He pawed through his clothes, down to the bottom. "Everything's soaked."

"Well, that flimsy bag isn't exactly a suitcase."

He shot her a potent glare. "I didn't need a big suitcase. I only brought a few clothes." Shifting his glare back to the bag, he said, "You can be damn sure I'm going to write a strongly worded letter to the manufacturer about this."

She pressed her lips together to keep from laughing at his grumpy expression. "Why don't you put your clothes into the dryer?'' she suggested. "The laundry room is at the end of the hallway. While you're doing that, I'll put on some coffee.''

"Great. But what am I supposed to wear in the meantime?''

"You can borrow my robe if you'd like.''

He stared at her. "You mean that ratty purple thing? I don't think so.''

"Listen, Barefoot-Boy. I don't need your critique of my 'ratty' lingerie. You want to stay in those wet things for a few more hours, maybe 'til mold grows on you, suit yourself. Just clean up any puddles you drip on the floor.''

"Do you at least have some sweatpants I can borrow?''

"If you can find a pair under the pile of feathers, help yourself.'' Her gaze involuntarily wandered down his masculine form. "But I somehow doubt my sweats would fit you.'' Forcing herself to look away from him, she walked to the kitchen and busied herself making coffee.

Humph. Ratty bathrobe indeed. What a lot of nerve. She loved that robe. It was warm and soft and snuggly. All right, so it wasn't something out of a slinky lingerie catalog, but she wasn't the slinky lingerie type. She'd tried a pair of thong underpants once at the insistence of a boyfriend. Never again. It had felt like she'd had an atomic wedgie the entire day. Nope, she was definitely a ratty robe sort of girl. And darn proud of it, too.

Casting a surreptitious glance at Ryan while she mentally counted coffee scoops, she observed him grumbling to himself as he hauled his wet clothes into his arms. He stalked down the hall, and she absolutely did *not* notice what great buns he had. She did, however, somehow lose track of how many coffee scoops she'd added to the filter and had to start all over again.

Ryan entered the laundry room and dropped his pile of

clothes on the floor with a splat. Damn it, he was wet and cold, tired and hungry. Thirsty. Grumpy. This entire episode reminded him of some sort of boy scout camp from hell.

He flung his clothes into the dryer and shrugged out of his sopping shirt, adding it to the pile. After a moment's hesitation, he pulled down his dripping Dockers and tossed them in as well. As uncomfortable as his wet boxers were, he'd have to make do. He wasn't about to run around bare-assed. Looking down at himself, he realized he might as well be bare-assed. The wet boxers clung to him like paint and they were all but see-through. The mere thought of Lynne seeing him like this shot a hot tingle through his groin.

Squeezing his eyes shut, he sighed. Great. That was just what he needed. An erection. Looks like he'd have to borrow her robe after all.

He turned the knob to maximum dry and pushed the start button.

Nothing happened.

Frowning, he pushed the button again.

This time, something happened.

All the lights went out.

THE KITCHEN PLUNGED INTO inky darkness and Lynne groaned. Thunder boomed and lightning flashed. She tried flicking the light switch off and on with no results. The storm must have knocked out the electricity.

"The power's out," she called.

Ryan said something she couldn't quite hear, but there was no mistaking the loud "Ouch!" that followed.

"What happened?" she hollered.

"I stubbed my damn toe. Do you have a flashlight?"

"Yes. Just stay put. I'll be right there." Feeling her way

across the counter, she opened a drawer and groped among the contents until her fingers closed over the flashlight. She flicked it on, relieved that it worked, then headed down the hall.

The beam of light landed on Ryan standing in the laundry room. Ryan, wearing nothing but wet boxers. Wet boxers that covered him about as well as cellophane.

She halted like she'd walked into a wall of glass. And she stared.

Whooooaaa baby. Like every other woman in America, she recognized that body—it was the one they used in all those men's underwear ads. Broad chest covered with a dusting of dark hair, washboard abs, and the rest of the picture...

Holy cow.

She'd always thought cold water caused *shrinkage* in men.

Apparently not.

She swallowed, and it was a good thing she did, because until then her mouth had obviously been hanging open. Jerking the light up, away from *that,* she shined it directly in his eyes.

"Hey!" He shielded his face. "I can't see."

Don't worry about it. I saw plenty for the both of us. "Sorry." Pointing the beam at her feet, she walked slowly down the hall, keeping her gaze carefully trained on the floor.

So what if he was built like a Greek god? Lots of men were. She saw their pictures in magazines all the time. The world was littered with them. Overflowing.

And who cared what he looked like anyway? This guy was nothing but a pest. A pest who'd ogled her while she was naked. Of course the DNA fairy had blessed him—he had to have *something* going for him, and it certainly wasn't his personality or character.

Halting outside the small laundry room, she asked, "So, are your clothes dry yet?"

"Oh, you're a riot. You should give up this decorator gig and go on the comedy circuit."

"You know, you're a real grouch."

"Noooo, I'm not," he said in a tone one might use with a two-year-old. "What I *am* is wet, cold, hungry, thirsty, sore, and my toe hurts like hell."

"I see. But other than that you're fine?"

"Physically, yes."

She had to agree with *that*. "Terrific. Don't move." Marching into her bedroom, she grabbed her robe and a towel. "Here," she said handing him the towel. "Take off that sopping underwear and dry off. Then put this on." She tossed him her robe and it hit him in the chest. "Once you're dressed, I'd suggest you take your clothes out of the dryer, wring them out, and lay them flat to dry. Who knows how long the power will be out? And if you leave them in a lump, they'll stay wet, grow moldy, and smell bad.

"While you're doing that," she continued, "I'll make us something to eat and drink, then see if I can find a bandage for your toe. Waldo used most of them when he indulged in his bandage party, but there's probably one left." Raising her brows, she stared at him through the flashlight's glare. "Does that solve all your immediate problems?"

"Uh, yeah."

"Good. Here." She handed him the flashlight and headed back toward the kitchen.

"Except one."

She turned. He stood in a pool of light that accentuated

things she did *not* want to see. Fastening her gaze on his face, she asked, "Which problem did I miss?"

"I'll still be sore. Too bad you're not a chiropractor instead of a decorator. I could really use a shoulder massage."

An inelegant snort escaped her. "Massage? Forget about it, Bathrobe-Boy. I'm more likely to smack you with the moose head."

A slow grin eased across his face. "And you call *me* a grouch?"

Tearing her gaze away from that beautiful, devilish smile, Lynne walked back to the kitchen. Aided by the flashing lightning, she located a box of matches and two candles. She lit them, casting the cabin in a warm, cozy glow. She could hear Ryan down the hall, opening the dryer.

Against her will, she visualized him peeling off his leave-nothing-to-the-imagination boxers. Heat scissored through her. How would his skin feel under her hands if she massaged his shoulders? Her eyes drifted closed. Hmm…warm, taut, muscular. Heavenly.

Her lids popped open. Good grief, she was losing her mind, fantasizing like that. She didn't even *like* him! Good thing, too, because if she *did* like him, she suspected she'd be in big headed-for-heartache trouble.

Nope, she didn't like him.

Not one bit.

RYAN FELT LIKE AN ABSOLUTE idiot.

The ratty purple robe only covered him to his calves, the sleeves only to his elbows. And no matter how hard he tried to pull the sides together, a big V-shaped portion of his chest lay exposed.

The good news was he was warm, dry, his privates were covered, and his budding erection had subsided.

The bad news was that until his clothes dried, the ratty robe was the only thing standing between him and indecent exposure. And the damn garment bore that sexy, citrusy fragrance that clung to Lynne's skin. Wearing her robe, her scent teasing his senses every time he inhaled, was like having *her* wrapped around him—

He tried to slice off *that* disturbing thought before Mr. Happy started acting up again, but it was too late. His groin tightened and, looking down, he watched the purple terry cloth form a tent.

Dragging his hands down his face, he huffed out a breath. Jeez, what the hell was wrong with him? He hadn't suffered such trouble controlling his body's responses since high school. Granted, he hadn't slept with anyone since he and Marcie had broken up almost two months ago, but he hadn't experienced any trouble with his hormones until he'd seen *her*—the schoolmarm/sea goddess.

It's only because I saw her naked. Yeah, that was it. Nothing more than a law of nature—see a naked woman bending over, have fantasies, get an erection. Simple as that.

Because it wasn't as if he *liked* her or anything. Hell no. She was a major pain in the privates. Literally.

Nope, he didn't like her one bit. And he bet that the longer he was stuck in this cabin with her, the less he'd like her.

Mr. Happy, unfortunately, didn't agree.

4

RYAN ENTERED THE LIVING area and breathed a mental sigh of relief. Lynne was busy near the sink, her back turned toward him. He made a beeline for the snack bar, strategically positioning himself so the lower half of his body was obscured. In spite of the discomfort, he'd slipped on his damp boxers. With the way his body was misbehaving, there was no way he was going "commando" around the woman.

She glanced at him over her shoulder. "Feeling better?"

"As well as a guy can feel wearing a girl's bathrobe." Realizing he sounded ungrateful, he added, "Uh, thanks for the loan."

"No problem." Turning, she walked toward him holding a tray filled with cheese, crackers and grapes which she placed on the snack bar. Her gaze wandered over his exposed chest, and she clearly fought to suppress a smile.

"Don't even think about laughing," he said, snagging a piece of cheese.

"I wouldn't dream of it." She popped a grape in her mouth and studied him with a serious expression. "You know, I do believe ratty purple is your color."

He sent her a fulminating glare and grabbed a cracker.

In response, she smiled sweetly and held out a bright yellow plastic cup adorned with cartoon characters. "Drink?"

He cast the kiddie cup a dubious glance. "What is it? Arsenic and Kool-Aid?"

"Chardonnay. Tell me, are you always this grumpy?"

He took the glass and surreptitiously sniffed the contents. Smelled like wine. "I'm not grumpy."

"Like hell. I bet if I looked up grumpy in the dictionary, your picture would be right there." She picked up a plastic cup that matched his and held it aloft. "How about a truce? Unfortunately, we're stuck here for a while, so why don't we just try to make the best of the situation and get along? I won't make fun of your girly attire if you'll try to recall that the storm that's stranded you here isn't my fault."

He looked into her eyes and heaved a mental sigh. "To a truce," he said, touching his cup to hers. He sipped and raised his brows at the surprisingly good Chardonnay.

Helping himself to another cracker, he noted the glowing candles that cast the room with soft shadows and scented the air with a delicate hint of vanilla. Rain slashed against the windows, and intermittent rumblings of thunder and flashes of lightning marked the ongoing storm. It occurred to him that this setup had "seduction" written all over it. Cabin in the woods, wine, food, candlelight, stormy outside, cozy inside…a beautiful woman. The only thing missing was a fire in the grate.

Hmm. In his mind's eye he pictured Lynne, reclining on a bearskin rug before a low-burning fire. She wore nothing but black lace panties and a wicked smile. Her lush body glistened in the muted glow, a tempting banquet of delights—and him a starving man. Crooking her finger at him, she whispered, *Come here, Ryan.* As in all good fantasies, he magically appeared next to her, naked. He leaned forward to kiss her. To taste that magical mouth. To run his hands over those incredible curves. To—

"I'm a little chilly," Lynne said, jerking him from his sensual reverie. "I'm going to make a fire."

"No!" The word burst from his lips like a gunshot. Heat crept up his neck when she looked at him with a questioning expression that clearly indicated she thought he was a few eggs short of a dozen. Feeling like an idiot, he said, "Uh, I mean *I'll* light the fire."

The instant the words left him he wanted to snatch them back. Just what he needed—more freakin' heat. It was already three hundred degrees inside the cabin. Coupled with his fantasy problem, a fire was the last thing he wanted. He somehow resisted the urge to wipe his brow. How the heck could she be chilly? He felt like a blowtorch was flaming under his robe, igniting him in places that...well, shouldn't be ignited.

"Great," she said, handing him a box of matches. "We can roast some hot dogs once the fire's going. I'll set up the bearskin rug by the hearth and we'll have an indoor picnic. How does that sound?"

"That sounds...great."

That sounded like pure torture.

RYAN STARED AT THE STACKED logs next to the fireplace and frowned. Uh-oh. Not a pre-packaged Duraflame log in the bunch. A brief examination of the fireplace confirmed that there was no gas key, either. Great. At least he had the box of matches. He definitely wasn't in the mood to rub two sticks together.

"There're more logs and loads of kindling outside on the porch," Lynne said from the kitchen. When he hesitated, she asked, "Do you know how to lay a fire? Because if you don't, I could—"

"Of course I know how," he said, biting down on his irritation. He stomped toward the front door, the ratty robe flapping around his calves. Sure, he'd only ever used Duraflame logs, but he'd seen plenty of people light fires on television—in those old westerns where pioneers lived in the wilds. How the hell hard could it be to light a fire? He was an intelligent man. He had a college degree. All he had to do was toss some dry twigs on a bunch of logs, throw in a match, and *voilà!* No problem.

TEN MINUTES LATER, Ryan stepped back to view his architectural masterpiece. A trio of logs sat in the grate, arranged in a perfect pyramid, surrounded by symmetrical tufts of kindling. Resisting the urge to pat himself on the back, he knelt on the hearth, struck a match, and watched with satisfaction as several dry pine needles flared to life. He lit a second match, touching the burning tip to the strategically placed kindling. As the flame caught, he couldn't hide the smug smile tugging at his lips. Who needed Duraflame logs? Not him. No sir. Why, he was a regular kick-ass, log-and-kindling Boy Scout. In fact—

"It smells sort of smoky in here, Ryan," came Lynne's voice from the kitchen. "Did you open the flue?"

Flue? Uh-oh. "Um, of course," he lied. "But, uh, maybe I didn't get it open all the way."

"You check it—I'll open the door and some windows."

The fire was barely burning, but he took care not to set the ratty robe—or himself—on fire. Leaning forward, he reached up, and pushed the metal flue lever upward. The chimney immediately sucked up a plume of smoke.

And spewed out a torrent of soot.

Black ash showered over him, covering his head and arm with the gunk from God knows how many previous fires. "Damn!" He jumped up, shaking himself like a dog after a bath, an effort that he quickly realized only spread the soot over more of him.

Lynne ran across the room, skidding to a halt in front of him, and simply stared, round-eyed, for several seconds. Then her lips twitched.

"Don't say it," he warned, glaring at her through soot-laden eyelashes.

"What? That you look like a crispy-fried forest ranger?" She pursed her lips and cocked her head, examining him as one would a painting in a gallery. "Actually, you look like a bathrobe-wearing Santa who got caught in the chimney. Throw a red suit on you, give you a bag of toys, and we've got Christmas."

He blew a puff of soot from his lips. "Yeah. Ho, ho, freakin' ho."

"Oh, dear, Santa's grumpy. Probably a shower would make him feel better. Leave the robe on the back of the door. I'll shake the ashes from it while you clean up."

Through gritted teeth he forced out, "Great." Mustering as much dignity as he could, he walked toward the bathroom, blinking soot from his eyes.

A shower? Ha! The only thing that would make him feel better would be to wake up from this damn country nightmare and find himself back in the city where he belonged.

LYNNE SPEARED a hot dog on a long stick she'd found on the cabin's porch, then handed it to a soot-free Ryan who held it as if she'd given him a snake.

"I know it's not exactly the Ritz," she said, spearing a hot dog for herself then leaning forward to cook her dinner over the log burning in the fireplace, "but it's not that bad. I'm a terrible cook and even *I* can do this. Didn't you ever go camping?"

"Yeah," he said, scooting forward on the bearskin rug and gingerly poking his hot-dog-laden stick into the flame.

"Computer camp. Every summer. We slept in dorms. *Furnished* dorms. And all the meals were catered."

"I hate to tell you this, but that's not camping."

"Compared to this, I guess not, but it's my only frame of reference."

She cast him a sideways glance and drew a deep breath. He should look ridiculous, sitting cross-legged in her too-small robe, his hair rumpled, five-o'clock shadow shading his jaw, awkwardly rotating his hot dog stick.

Instead he looked like a female fantasy come true. Good enough to eat. The fire's glow cast his handsome face in an intriguing array of dancing shadows. She tried to focus her attention on her dinner, but she couldn't seem to pull her gaze away from him. The firelight danced over him, affording her teasing glimpses of his chest. The muscles in his forearms flexed as he turned his stick and she suppressed a sigh. Her gaze wandered down to his legs…his very fine legs…and she bit her lip. For a guy who'd spent his summers tapping on computer keys, he had great legs. And great arms. And a great chest.

He might be a pest, but boy, oh boy, he was, by far, the yummiest pest she'd ever seen.

Hmm. What was he wearing under her robe? Anything besides naked flesh? Her eyeballs seemed to have grown a mind of their own because she couldn't stop them from trying to sneak a peek. Darn, she couldn't tell.

I mean, good! Good thing I can't tell. She'd already seen more of him than she'd wanted to. Absolutely.

A long sigh she couldn't contain eased past her lips. Forcing her gaze away from *that,* she looked at his face and nearly swallowed her tongue.

Ohmigod. He was watching her! Watching her watch him. With a very speculative expression that conveyed he knew he'd just been on the receiving end of an extended ogle.

Heat rushed through her like a brushfire, and she knew without checking a mirror that her chest and neck had turned blotchy from embarrassment.

"They're damp, but they're on," he said.

"Huh?"

"My boxers. I'm wearing them."

"Oh. Uh, good." And she vividly recalled how incredible he looked in them. Why was there never a hole to bury yourself in when you truly needed one? Determined to regain her dignity, she returned her attention to the fireplace.

"Umm, Ryan...your wienie's on fire."

"Can't argue with that."

When he made no move to pull his hot dog from the fireplace, she grabbed his stick from his hand and blew out the flames engulfing his dinner. Shaking her head, she handed the charred mess back to him. "You're a worse cook than I am. Lucky for you we have plenty of mustard."

He shot the dog a dubious look. "I don't think there's enough mustard in the free world to help this."

Removing her own well-done dog from the flame she nodded her agreement. "Don't throw it away. Waldo likes his wienies like that."

"Nuclear fried?"

She laughed. "It's his favorite. You'll be his new best friend."

"Uh, great. Where is he?"

"I'd lay odds he's napping under the porch. He'll be back soon, I'm sure."

Since he didn't appear to know what to do with the hot dog remains, she took the stick from him and set it down on the hearth. Pulling a bun from the bag next to her, she wrapped it around her dog then passed it to him with a flourish. "Have mine," she said. "It's a little overdone, but not like your towering inferno. I'll make another one for myself."

"Thanks." He accepted her offering and their fingers brushed. Feeling like she'd been zapped by lightning, she snatched away her hand. After passing him the mustard, she busied herself spearing another hot dog onto her stick, berating herself all the while for her ridiculous reactions to this man. Good grief, she was acting like she'd never seen a guy before. Like a man had never touched her. What was wrong with her? Must be some sort of stress-related problem. Or post-traumatic syndrome. Yeah, that was it. He'd scared the willies out of her in the bathroom earlier and now her nerve endings weren't firing on all cylinders. No doubt after she ate and replenished her system she'd be fine. She just had a few synapses out of whack from the adrenaline rush.

Yup. That was her story, and she was stickin' to it.

RYAN BIT INTO HIS mustard-laden hot dog and nearly groaned with pleasure. He hadn't realized how hungry he was until that first tangy bite. Probably because he'd been in some sort of hormonal rage since he first encountered Lynne in the shower. Once he fortified himself with some much-needed nutrition, he'd be fine.

He cast a sideways glance at her. She had a lovely profile, and the tendrils of shiny chestnut hair springing loose from her severe hairdo intrigued him. He was a sucker for long, curly hair. An overwhelming urge to undo her bun washed over him and he forced his attention back to his meal.

She's the enemy. Decorator public enemy number one. A pest. An intruder on my solitude. A despoiler of Dave's country haven.

Yeah, that put things back into perspective. *I don't like her, she doesn't like me.*

Then how come she'd been looking at him like she was a mouse and he was a piece of cheddar? Could she be afflicted by the same strange attraction he felt? Must be something in all this smog-free air. Or maybe he was just losing his mind. Either way, it was no big deal. So perhaps they found each other mildly attractive. So what? They certainly weren't about to *act* on that attraction.

What he should be concentrating on was finding out exactly what her ideas were for the cabin so he could strategize which ones he'd need to circumvent for Dave.

He finished his last bite of dinner, then turned to her. "So what are your decorating plans for this place?"

Pulling her hot dog from the fire, she said, "I'm redoing every room. It's going to be fabulous."

Ryan inwardly groaned. He could just picture "fabulous." He watched her maneuver her dog onto a bun and take a dainty bite, proud that he didn't notice how erotic her lips looked wrapped around that hot dog. "Give me some specifics."

She swallowed then shifted to face him. He absolutely didn't notice how the firelight played over her delicate features, accentuating her wide-set eyes. "Ninety percent of the changes are simple and cosmetic."

"Such as?"

"Well, the hardwood floors need redoing."

Ryan cringed. She probably planned to lay some fancy, feminine, fringy Oriental rug.

"The hardwood is oak and in good condition," she continued, "but it needs sanding and refinishing. I'll strip the kitchen cabinets and restain them in a pale oak. Paint all the rooms, replace the old window blinds with natural wood shutters, and update the kitchen and bathroom fixtures."

"What about furniture?"

She leaned forward, her face animated. "Oh, the new furniture is wonderful. A sectional sofa, a chair-and-a-half with an ottoman, this great redwood coffee table I found at an estate sale—all very functional, but cozy and comfortable."

Ryan frowned. That all sounded…really good.

"Had you seen this place lately?" she asked.

"No. I've never been here. Dave only bought it about a year ago, and with my crazy work schedule, I just haven't had a chance to visit."

"No offense to Dave, but this cabin looked like something out of *Animal House*. The furniture was old, beat-up and musty."

"Maybe because it was a bachelor pad."

"*Was* is the operative word. When I'm finished here, you won't recognize this cabin."

"I think that's what Dave's afraid of."

"Change is good."

"Not always."

"Believe me," she said. "In this case, it is. I take my work very seriously. Making my clients happy is my first priority and I'm very good at my job."

While it didn't sound like she was going to turn the cabin into Camp Girly-Girl, he still intended to make sure she didn't. And even though the new furniture sounded nice, he would still rescue Dave's stuff.

I'm very good at my job. He had to admit that there was something incredibly attractive about a confident woman, one who believed in herself and her abilities. It was refreshing to hear after dating so many women who seemed to require constant compliments, bolstering and ego stroking.

She closed the package of rolls and wrapped the remaining hot dogs in foil. "I'm going to put these in the fridge, but since there's no telling how long the power will be off, I don't want to keep the door open for long. Do you want anything? A soda maybe?''

"No, thanks." He nodded toward the bottle of Chardonnay next to her. "I'm enjoying the wine."

After putting away the food, she rejoined him by the fire and accepted her refreshed cup of wine.

"So, what do you do for a living?" she asked, stretching out her legs.

"I'm an architect. Actually, I think I mentioned that earlier, in the bathroom, but since you were threatening my life with your safety razor at the time, it probably slipped your mind."

She sent him a potent look over the rim of her cartoon cup. "I guess so. Do you work on your own or for a firm?"

"I'm with Taft, Hobson and Brown."

Her eyes widened. "They're one of the best architectural firms in the country."

"Indeed we are."

"Have you worked on any projects I'd recognize?"

He named several buildings in the Seaport, Fenway, Back Bay, and downtown sections of Boston. She smiled at the last address he mentioned.

"My company rents space in that building," she said. "It's beautiful. You did a terrific job."

Pride filled him and he returned her smile. "Thanks, but I can't take the credit. It was a group effort."

"Still, it must give you a great sense of accomplishment every time you see it."

"It does."

"You mentioned you came up here to get some work done. Is it a new project?"

Ryan sipped his wine before answering. "Only the most important project of my career. It's a once-in-a-lifetime opportunity—different from anything I've ever designed before. And just when I need it most, my creativity has hit a brick wall. I was hoping some peace and quiet would help. No offense, but between you being here and this storm, things haven't exactly gone as I'd planned."

"Well, if it's any consolation to you, this cabin project is vitally important to *my* career. You and this storm aren't helping me much, either. I only have two weeks to finish, and if my workers can't get up here, I'm sunk."

"Success on this project puts you in line for a promotion?"

"No. Just the opposite. This is a freelance job that I'm hoping will jump-start other opportunities in this area so I can leave my firm. There are existing cabins that need renovations and a large number of lots available for building. I want to move up here—away from the rat race of Boston—and start my own interior design business."

For some reason he couldn't understand, Ryan felt let down at the thought of her moving away from the city—a ridiculous reaction. He didn't care if she relocated to Timbuktu.

"So what's the prize for you?" she asked. "A partnership?"

"Possibly. This project has the power to cement my reputation, which would be great. But it's the huge bonus that's the main attraction. It will give me the freedom to fulfill some of my dreams."

A cynical sound erupted from her. "Like what? Buy a new sports car? Frolic in the Caribbean?"

Her dismissive tone irked him. "No, although I can't deny a vacation would be nice. I want to design and build a theatre and arts center in my mother's memory. Because this is a high-profile project, it could help me attract financial backing. The bonus, along with what I've set aside over the years, would provide the kickoff.''

Pure chagrin washed over her face. ''Oh. I'm sorry. For my snarky comment and for the loss of your mother.'' She reached out and touched his hand, a soft, tentative gesture that he found sweet and comforting. ''She liked the theatre?''

''Loved it. Ballet, the symphony, and especially opera. She instilled a love and appreciation for them in me.''

Lynne flashed him a smile. Damn it, on top of everything else, she had dimples. Not fair. How much was a guy supposed to take?

''That's great,'' she said. ''I thought most men thought opera was Latin for 'death by music.'''

''Yeah,'' he said with a chuckle. ''That pretty much describes most of my friends.''

''Did your mom die recently?''

He shook his head. ''Eight years ago. And I've been planning her arts center ever since.'' Raising his cup he said, ''Here's to the success of our projects.''

She tapped her cup to his. ''To success.''

Lightning flashed and she turned toward the window. ''I guess you realize you're spending the night.''

''Well, I was hoping you wouldn't want me to trek back to my car.''

''Of course not. No doubt this rain will stop soon and the power and phone will be restored by morning.'' She hesitated, then added, ''But there's only one bed, and I've got dibs.''

A picture of her lying in bed, surrounded by a cloud of curly hair popped into his mind, but he banished the image like it harbored the plague. Reaching out, he patted the bear rug's head. ''No problem. Me and Smokey here will do fine. Do you have an extra pillow and blanket?''

"Thanks to Waldo we're pillow-less, but I do have a blanket." She drained her wine cup, then stood. "I'll go get it."

She walked toward the bedroom, and just as he hadn't noticed all evening, he didn't notice the sway of her hips beneath her baggy clothes. Good thing she didn't seem to prefer halter tops and short-shorts, because then he'd never be able to ignore her. And he was doing a great job of ignoring her. Yup, he sure was.

She returned several minutes later and handed him a pale-pink blanket made of some soft, velvety-like material. "Do you need anything else?"

"I think that's it," he said, looking up at her.

"In that case, I think I'm going to hit the sack. It's been a long day and…"

Her voice trailed off, her gaze riveted on his face. The look she gave him was so intense, his breath caught.

"Don't move, Ryan," she whispered. Slowly, she dropped to her knees in front of him.

He sat perfectly still, mesmerized by her expression. No doubt about it, she was going to jump him. Kiss him with that plump, luscious mouth. It was a bad idea. Really bad. God help him, he couldn't wait. His heart thumped like a jackhammer, shooting blood straight to his groin.

Leaning closer, she reached out one hand and he tensed, anticipating her touch.

She swatted the side of his head with her palm then jumped to her feet.

"Hey!" he yelped, holding his ringing ear. "What the hell did you do that for?"

"Wolf spider," she said. "Didn't think you'd want it crawling on you." She stomped her foot on the floor near the hearth. "Got it!"

Ryan stared at the squashed insect and actually felt the

blood drain from his head. It looked like a hairy brown golf ball with legs. "That...*thing* was *on* me?"

She nodded. "On your hair, by your ear. We should check you over. They sometimes travel in pairs."

He jumped to his feet and proceeded to smack his hands over his entire head. "Augh!" *Pairs?* Damn! What the hell kind of place *was* this? But that's exactly what it was—hell. He continued beating on his head until she grabbed his hands.

"Relax," she said, grabbing his flailing hands. "It was only a baby. Wolf spiders look worse than they are. They won't hurt you." A smile tugged at her lips. "But that head smacking you gave yourself might result in a concussion."

He stood still, breathing hard from the exertion of nearly beating himself unconscious. Her smile deepened and he glared at her. "What the hell is so funny?"

A giggle escaped her. "You. Dancing around in my robe, whacking yourself in the head." She waggled her brows at him. "Nice moves. Very smooth."

"Gee, thanks. It was my fondest wish to entertain you."

"There you go, getting grumpy again." Before he could reply, she added, "I suppose I should have told you what I was going to do, but I didn't want to freak you out by saying 'oh, there's a spider in your hair.'"

"I did *not* 'freak out.'"

"Okay, whatever you say."

"Normal, everyday spiders I can deal with." He risked another look at the squashed, hairy brown golf ball. Cripes, it looked like the damn thing had eyeballs. "*That* is not a normal, everyday spider."

"Certainly not for a city boy."

He narrowed his eyes to slits. "I guess I owe you my thanks."

She chuckled. "Wow. Don't strain yourself with gratitude."

In spite of his best efforts to remain fierce, her smile was somehow contagious, and a sheepish grin pulled at him. "I'm sorry. Thank you." Grudging admiration filled him at her calmness. "Obviously you aren't afraid of spiders."

"That little thing? Nah. I grew up in the country. You should see those suckers when they're full grown. They're almost the size of a baseball."

Thank God I live in the city. Only his male pride—dented though it was—kept him from dropping to his knees in thanks that he'd only had a baby on him. "How did it get in my hair?"

"It probably was on one of the logs you carried in from outside."

"Swell." He ran his gaze over the extra logs he'd stacked by the hearth, but didn't see anything suspicious. Looking back at her, he realized she was still clasping his hands. And they were standing less than a foot apart.

Her hands were warm, and incredibly soft. He inhaled and her citrusy, spicy scent filled his head. He must have drunk too much wine because he suddenly felt intoxicated. Their eyes met and that same gut-punch sensation he'd experienced when he'd seen her at the wedding hit him. Her face was devoid of makeup, her hair was pulled back like a schoolmarm's, and her clothes completely camouflaged her body.

Still, all he could think was *wow.*

His gaze settled on her lips. *Double wow.* That pouty, lipstick-free mouth beckoned him with a siren's call. Some force he couldn't explain seemed to have taken over his common sense. His intelligent brain yelled, *You're through with relationships! And even if you weren't, this gal is not for you. She's taken over the cabin, disposed of Dave's*

*furniture which you're now in charge of getting back—like
you have nothing else to do—and she has jeopardized your
chances of finishing your project on time. As if that's not
all bad enough, she wants to move…out here…to the bug-
infested ends of the earth. You already know all about long-
distance relationships.*

Yet all the while his intelligent brain spouted those intelligent things, his unruly hormones chanted *Kiss her. Kiss
her now.*

His unruly hormones won.

He raised his gaze to hers. Their eyes met and there was
no mistaking the electric spark that sizzled between them.
Whatever this insane thing was, she clearly felt it, too. He
leaned forward and her breath caught, a tiny sound of anticipation that tensed every muscle in his body.

He brushed his mouth lightly over hers, inhaling her sigh.
Drawing her closer, he deepened the kiss, his tongue glid-
ing into the velvety warmth of her mouth.

Triple wow.

Her feminine curves pressed against him in a perfect fit,
touching him everywhere, spiking his already rapid pulse
into overdrive. She tasted like smooth wine and soft
woman—a heady combination that shot blood straight to
his groin. He heard a low groan, but wasn't sure if it came
from him or her.

She felt so damn *good* in his arms. Tasted so
incredible…like spicy, velvet heat. Her scent wrapped
around him, a silken web of feminine fragrance that made
him want to bury his face in the curve of her neck and just
breathe her in.

When his hands skimmed down her spine, she eased her
head back several inches, ending their intimate kiss. Everything inside him moaned in protest. She gazed at him with
the same dazed, confused expression he was certain had to

be on his face. And like him, her chest rapidly rose and fell.

"Ryan, I—"

A deafening clap of thunder sounded, startling them both. Lightning flashed. Ryan's gaze was drawn to the window, and his heart almost stopped.

A man stood at the window, staring in at them.

Every slasher movie he'd ever seen about psycho killers who stalked their victims in the woods flashed through his mind. All his protective instincts kicked in.

"I want you to go into the bedroom," he whispered, squeezing Lynne's hands.

Her eyes widened, then narrowed. "Well, now, isn't that special? Listen, just because I might have lost my mind for a second and kissed you, doesn't mean—"

"It means there's someone outside, looking in the window. Go in the bedroom and lock the door behind you." Lightning flashed again.

The face was gone.

Lock the door behind you. Ryan's gaze flew to the door and his stomach dropped to his feet. It wasn't locked.

Before his brain could even tell his feet to move, the door burst open. A swirl of leaves and damp, chilly, autumn-scented air rushed into the room.

Lightning flashed, illuminating the silhouette of a huge man in the doorway.

He held an ax in his right hand.

Slick fear oozed down Ryan's spine. Shoving Lynne behind him, he whispered, "I'll distract him. Get to the bedroom, lock the door and crawl out the window. Then run like hell."

Lightning flashed again, this time clearly illuminating the

man's face. Rain poured from his long beard and hair, plastering his dark clothes against his huge body.

Behind him, Lynne gasped. "Oh, my God," she said. "That's Killer Claymore!"

5

RYAN PRAYED THEY WEREN'T about to die.

He watched in horror as Lynne dashed forward, running directly toward Killer Claymore. What the hell was she doing?

"Stop!" he yelled, going after her.

Before he could stop her, she launched herself at Killer. The ax clattered to the floor. Killer's arms encircled her, hauling her off her feet. Then he planted a resounding kiss on her lips.

Ryan skidded to a halt, his breath panting from his burning lungs like a bellows.

"Killer!" Lynne exclaimed, wrapping her arms around the huge man's neck. "How wonderful to see you! It's been over a year!"

"Lynne, luv! How absolutely grand!" Killer turned her around in circles while her feet dangled two feet from the floor. "You look positively cracking!"

It took Ryan a good twenty seconds to find his voice. Lynne and Killer droned on, blah, blah, blah, happy as clams at high tide, while *he'd* practically suffered a coronary.

He coughed to dislodge his heart from his throat and resettle it back in his chest where it belonged. They continued to ignore him. Now that it was clear they weren't about to be murdered, irritation prickled his skin. Who the hell was this guy—and why the hell was the woman who'd just been wrapped around *him* now wrapped around this big goon?

"I take it you two know each other?" he finally asked, his tone reflecting his annoyance.

Lynne turned toward him, her feet still dangling above the floor, her arms still wrapped around the giant's neck. "Oh, Ryan! Goodness, I forgot all about you."

Not the sentence a guy wants to hear seconds after his life just flashed before his eyes. And especially not from the woman whom he'd just been kissing. His mood disintegrated from annoyed to downright grumpy.

The giant set Lynne down, but Ryan noticed that he kept a hand resting on her shoulder.

"Ryan, this is Killer Claymore. He's a dear friend who owns a cabin not far from here. Killer, meet Ryan Monroe, an architect from Boston."

Even though he knew it was unreasonable, the impersonal description of him as "an architect from Boston" irked Ryan.

Killer stepped into the room and the firelight illuminated him. It was difficult to distinguish his features beneath his wild hair, dark mustache and overgrown beard. He looked like a cross between something out of the movies *Deliverance* and *Grizzly Adams,* and it was impossible to tell if the man was thirty or sixty. Reaching out a hand the size of a ham, Killer said in a cultured voice, complete with English accent, "Chuffed to bits, mate."

Ryan stared. The guy looked like an ax murderer and sounded like Prince Charles. Ryan extended his hand. "Ah, yeah. Chuffed…Killer," he said, not sure he meant it.

"Actually, my Christian name is Michael. But call me Killer. All you Yanks do." His sharp eyes assessed Ryan from head to toe. "Don't believe I've ever met a bloke who dresses quite like you."

Ryan resisted the urge to tug on his ratty robe. Instead, his gaze slid to the ax on the floor. "Don't believe I've ever met a guy who peeps in windows and carries an ax."

"Just trying to see if anyone was about. As for the ax, well, you never know when you might need it to chop up some firewood. Or a Yank." He guffawed at his own joke. Looking at Ryan's expression, he quickly added, "I say, Yank, you look positively gobsmacked. Didn't mean to put the scare on you. I'm only pulling your plonker."

Ryan silently vowed that if Killer tried to pull his plonker, things would definitely take a nasty turn.

"Killer means you look stunned, and that he's just kidding," Lynne said, joining them near the fire. Ryan noted that Killer again placed his hand on her shoulder.

"I, uh, knew that." *Whew.* "So why are you called Killer?"

"Seems I've got a handy knack for the stock market."

Ryan had to admit he was glad it wasn't because Killer chopped Yanks into little pieces with his ax.

Lynne reached up and tugged on Killer's beard. "Thanks for the offer to chop wood, but we have a half cord of nice dry logs stacked on the porch. How are you enjoying retirement?"

Killer sent her a slow smile. "It's absolutely the dog's bollocks, luv."

Based on Killer's smile, Ryan guessed the dog's bollocks was good even though it sounded really bad. He watched their affectionate byplay and his mood shifted from grumpy to grumpier. "So what brings you out on a night like this…Killer?" he asked.

"I'd called on Lynne's mum earlier today and she told me Lynne was putting up at the Newbury cabin. When the storm made a dog's dinner of the roads, I wanted to make certain she was all right." He turned to Lynne then jerked his head toward Ryan. "Didn't mean to interrupt. Your mum didn't tell me you were here for a bit of a dirty weekend." He threw her a wink. "Not something a mum should know, eh?"

Ryan watched Lynne's face bloom like crimson rose. "It's nothing like that. Ryan is Dave Newbury's best friend," she explained. "He was on his way back to town when the storm stranded him."

Killer raised his brows, but didn't comment. Turning to Ryan, he asked, "Is that your Lexus stuck down the lane?" When Ryan nodded, Killer said, "When the rain stops, I'll help you pop it out."

Ryan wasn't sure he particularly cared for this dude who'd frightened ten years off his life, but since Killer looked like he could lift the Lexus with one arm, he decided he'd let bygones be bygones—except for the fact that he'd kissed Lynne *and* the guy's pawlike hand still encircled her shoulders. That decidedly set his teeth on edge.

"Let me get you a towel," Lynne said.

"Don't bother, luv. I'm going to clear off."

"You can't possibly go back outside," Lynne protested. "You can spend the night here."

"Thanks, pet, but the rain's tapered off a bit and I'll be fine. Besides, I've a guest of my own waiting for me." His eyes narrowed on Ryan with a look that could curdle milk. "Unless you need me to stay?"

Lynne shook her head. "We'll be fine."

He sizzled another look at Ryan that clearly said *she'd better be right or your Yank ass is grass*. "Then I'm off. You know where I am if you need me, luv." He nodded toward Ryan. "See you when the storm's over. Keep your pecker up."

Lynne walked him to the door, shutting it behind him.

She faced him with a broad grin. "That means keep your chin up."

"That's…a relief."

"It was thoughtful of Killer to stop over, don't you think?"

I think the ax-giant almost put me into cardiac arrest. And clearly his "mum" never taught him to keep his hands to himself. "Yeah, he's a helluva guy. Is he a boyfriend?" Ryan mentally thunked himself on the head. What the hell did he care?

"No," she said, joining him in front of the fire. "Strictly platonic." For reasons he didn't care to examine, relief washed over him.

"Seems like you've known him a while."

"About four years. He made a killing in the stock market and built a place near the lake. After years of the stress of Wall Street, he loves the peace and quiet here."

Peace and quiet? Ryan shook his head. The next time he experienced peace and quiet in this godforsaken forest would be the *first* time. Between the rain, mud, raccoon, soot, hairy spiders, ax-wielding neighbors and Miss Lynne Waterford, he was one step away from certifiable.

She bent down to retrieve the blanket she'd brought him before the spider and ax-killer fiascos. "Here you go. If you don't mind, I think I'll turn in now. There's a flashlight on the counter if you need it."

He took the blanket. "Thanks."

She cleared her throat. "Ah, about that kiss…"

Heat rushed through him at the thought of that mind-blowing kiss that might have led who-knows-where if Killer hadn't shown up. He didn't know whether to thank the guy—or punch his lights out. "What about it?"

"Nice as it was, it wasn't a great idea."

"Nice?" Hot and steaming were more like it.

He took one step forward and she immediately moved back two paces. Good. She wasn't as unaffected as she'd like to appear.

"Okay, better than nice," she amended. "But still a bad idea. You're leaving in the morning, and…"

Her voice trailed off, and his common sense knocked on his forehead, telling him she was right. He had no time for women right now. And even if he did, he'd have to be an idiot to start up something with *her*. She wanted to move to the baseball-sized spider, dead-airspace *woods*. He wasn't about to waste his time on a woman who would only turn into Miss Long-Distance-Part-Two.

"A bad idea," his common sense murmured in agreement.

She breathed an unmistakable sign of relief. "Glad we agree. Well, good night, Ryan."

"'Night."

She pulled a slim penlight from her pocket and headed down the hall. When the bedroom door clicked shut behind her, he huffed out a breath he hadn't realized he'd held.

Dropping the blanket onto the bearskin rug he raked his hands through his hair.

Damn. What a day.

Almost blinded by shaving cream, his car and his favorite shoes swallowed by mud, forced to wear a girly bathrobe, covered with soot, nearly beating himself unconscious after a spider nested in his hair, then ten years scared off his life by an ax-carrying Brit named Killer. Anyone who thought living in the city was dangerous had obviously never spent any time in the friggin' country.

And then there was *her*: the craziest, scariest part of this entire ordeal. He'd known her for less than a day, yet in that short time she'd somehow wreaked havoc with his emotions. He couldn't deny he'd enjoyed her company at dinner. She was intelligent, amusing, had kindly given him her hot dog, and possessed an air of confidence he liked and admired. And she sent his libido into a tailspin. Yeah, kissing her had definitely been a mistake—because instead of satisfying him, that brief taste of her had only whetted his appetite.

What the hell was he thinking? He obviously wasn't thinking. That was the problem. Why was he so drawn to her? There were hundreds, thousands, of attractive women in Boston. He should know—it seemed like he'd dated half of them. But none of them had affected him like this one.

The only logical explanation was that he was sex starved. Yeah, that was it. *Any* woman would look good after enduring celibacy since Marcie's exit. That's all this was—a simple case of horniness. Just abstinence having an adverse affect on him. A small voice inside his head piped up and said, *abstinence never affected you like this before. And why hasn't any other woman grabbed your attention?*

A frown pinched his brow. Well, there was a logical explanation…and he'd figure out what it was when he wasn't so tired.

As of now, his common sense was firmly anchored back in place. He'd concentrate all his energies on his project. There would be no women, no more kissing, and especially no Lynne. She was nothing but another Miss Long Distance wrapped up in a pretty pouty-lipped, blue-eyed, dimply-smiled package. *Been there, done that, bought the T-shirt.*

Removing Lynne's robe, he bunched it up for a pillow. Then he settled down on the bearskin rug, pulling the blanket over him. Both the robe and the blanket smelled citrusy and sexy and female. Like her. Mr. Happy, damn him, noticed—making it impossible to get comfortable. Like Mr. Happy, the floor was hard as hell, and even with the addition of the robe, the bear's head made a lousy pillow. He did a visual scan of the room to double-check that no more spiders lurked nearby.

Thank God this day was over. By tomorrow, the storm would be over and his clothes would be dry. He'd dig out his car, retrieve Dave's furniture from the salvage yard, then get busy on his project.

Yes, tomorrow would definitely be a better day.

Because it sure as hell couldn't be any worse.

LYNNE ROLLED OVER, COUNTED sheep, but sleep simply would not come. Her mind was too full—of *him.*

Good grief, it was bad enough when she'd only thought he was beautiful on the outside. But now...

Her heart pinched when she recalled how he'd spoken about his mother. Had he realized how wistful his voice had sounded? Or how lovely his determination to honor her was? And the fact that a big, strong guy like him was afraid of spiders—how cute was *that?* Of course, she couldn't really blame him. Those wolf spiders *were* scary looking.

He might not like spiders, but clearly he didn't lack courage. She recalled the way he'd tried to protect her from what he'd thought was an intruder. He'd turned into a knight in shining armor right before her eyes.

And that kiss.

Whoa, baby.

He'd made her feel like steam sizzled from every pore in her body. From a *kiss!* Whew. If they ever made love, she'd probably go up in smoke. A dreamy sigh escaped her and she mentally slapped herself. Smoke was bad. Very bad.

Get a grip, Lynne. There was no way he could be so attractive *and...* well, nice. There had to be something wrong with him. After all, if he was so terrific, why hadn't some girl already snatched him up?

Maybe some girl already had. Maybe he had a woman. Or a dozen women. Men who looked like him didn't lack for female companionship. She'd make it a point to ask him in the morning.

She clapped her hand to her forehead. Good grief, what was she thinking? Who cared if he had a girlfriend? And if he did, it just proved what a creep he was—kissing her socks off up until he'd seen Killer at the window.

A long sigh escaped her. What would have happened if Killer hadn't come by? *Smoke. And lots of it.*

Nothing, she amended fiercely. She would have come to her senses and given him a shove. *Liar, liar, pants on fire,* her pesky inner voice taunted. *You wouldn't have stopped him and you would have received another mind-blowing kiss...and another...and another. And then...*

She pressed her lips together and rolled over. So Ryan Monroe was an incredible kisser. So what? Most men were. Well, except Mr. Not-'Til-Halftime who'd slobbered all over her in his haste to get back to the third quarter.

She had to remember that Ryan was a pain in the neck and grumpy to boot. She had an important job to accomplish, and he was in the way. He'd be leaving in the morning and she'd never see him again. Good. She wasn't going to give him another thought.

Nope, not one.

RYAN AWOKE SLOWLY, his internal body clock indicating it was early morning. Slumber gradually drifted away, and he became aware of something warm and soft caressing his belly. He inhaled and his senses flooded with a sexy, citrusy scent.

Lynne.

Oh, boy. She must have come to him during the night. Fully awake, senses on red alert, he lay perfectly still, eyes shut, heart slapping against his ribs. Clearly she'd reconsidered her opinion about their kiss because this had "bad idea" tattooed all over it. But, damn, there was no way he could turn her away. He wouldn't have made the first move—definitely not—but as long as she had...

His body tightened, anticipating her lovely face flushed with desire, her big blue eyes warm with sexual want. He was more than ready to give her whatever she wanted.

He slowly opened his eyes.

And stared into Waldo's masked, whiskered face.

The animal sat on his haunches in the middle of Ryan's bare chest, his furry tail swishing back and forth over Ryan's abdomen. He held the nuclear-fried hot dog from dinner in his tiny paws, taking delicate nibbles while watching Ryan with bright curious eyes.

"Ackkkkkk!" Ryan rolled to his side, flipping Waldo onto the bearskin rug, then shot to his feet as if a rocket launcher was attached to his ass. Waldo sent him what appeared to be a reproving glance, then, with a flick of his tail, sauntered into the kitchen with his hot dog clenched between his teeth.

Raking his hands through his hair, Ryan drew a deep breath. Damn it! If he managed to get out of this place without needing the paramedics, it was going to be a miracle. In fact—

The bedroom door burst open and Lynne dashed into the room. She skidded to a halt in front of Ryan, her anxious gaze roaming his face.

"What's wrong? Did you hurt yourself? Did you see another spider?"

He opened his mouth to tell her that her damn raccoon had scratched another decade off his rapidly depleting life span, but the words froze in his throat.

She wore a faded blue T-shirt that ended mid-thigh and

bore the slogan Men Are Like a Box of Chocolates: You Can't Tell Which Ones Are the Nuts. His gaze skimmed down her long, bare legs to her pink-polished toes then back up again. Whew. He knew exactly what that T-shirt barely covered, and a thin layer of sweat popped out on his brow.

But it was her hair that rendered him speechless. A disarrayed mass of chestnut corkscrew curls tumbled over her shoulders and halfway down her back. It was the sort of incredible, sexy hair that every woman in every fantasy he'd ever indulged in possessed. His fingers twitched with the overwhelming urge to plunge into that glorious tangle of mess-with-me curls. The mere thought sent his hormones into overdrive. Mr. Happy nudged against his boxers, pulling him from his slack-jawed stupor.

Jeez. This was freakin' embarrassing. He and his suddenly uncontrollable penis were going to have to have a long chat. Clearly he needed several layers of clothes when this woman was around. Something in armored steel might help—like an erection-protection shield.

Lynne stood in front of him, trying to catch her breath. A trilling sound captured her attention and she turned toward the kitchen. Waldo sat on the counter observing her with his bright eyes. She assumed her furry friend had simply startled Ryan, as he appeared unharmed.

She returned her gaze to him and swallowed. No, he appeared…incredible. Rumpled. Unshaven. Masculine. Sexy as only a man can look first thing in the morning.

Her gaze wandered downward. His body was as sigh-inducing as she recalled from the night before. The crisp, dark hair covering his broad chest narrowed into a fascinating dark ribbon that bisected his abdomen then disappeared into his boxers.

Her gaze dipped lower and her lungs froze. Whoa, baby. He sure had great…legs.

At that instant, he grabbed her robe from the floor and held it in front of his *very* intriguing groin, thus thwarting her view. Darn. *I mean good! Good!* She had no desire to see *that*. Nope. None at all.

Drawing a deep breath, she focused her attention back on his face. "What happened?"

"I woke up and found Waldo sitting on my chest, eating that nuked hot dog."

She laughed. "I told you he liked them. And he wouldn't hurt you."

He sent her a baleful glare. "So maybe he wouldn't claw me to ribbons. He sure as hell startled me."

Arranging her face into what she hoped was a suitably serious expression, she said, "I'm sorry. I should have warned you that he might come in during the night. He likes sleeping next to people. He's very gentle, I promise. You probably scared him more than he scared you."

Some of the annoyance drained from his face. "I'm not sure about that, but no harm done, I guess."

His gaze wandered over her and embarrassed heat rushed through her. Yikes. She knew she had to look like a disaster area, her hair resembling a demolition site.

A low rumble of thunder drew their attention to the window. Rain fell in a steady stream, not wildly like last night, but in a silent, heavy curtain. The gray, stormy atmosphere even managed to dull the vibrant red and gold leaves.

"It's still raining," she said unnecessarily. "Looks like you're not going anywhere this morning."

"Apparently not."

Their eyes met and held for the space of several heartbeats. Lynne's pulse jumped and she mentally scolded herself. His expression was unreadable, but she suspected he wasn't any happier about their unwanted captivity than she was.

Backing up a step, she said, "I'm going to get dressed now."

"Good idea. I think I'll throw on some clothes then hike down to my car to rescue my cooler and drafting table. As long as this rain shows no signs of stopping anytime soon, we could use the food, and I could at least try to get some work done."

"Sounds good. Do you want some help?"

"Thanks, but there's no sense in both of us getting wet and muddy. Maybe while I'm gone you could work on breakfast?"

"You mean, 'man go scavenge food while woman cook with fire'?" She shook her head. "Why don't you just whack me over the head with your caveman club and drag me by the hair to the kitchen?"

"Sheesh. Now who's acting grumpy?"

"Sorry. It's just that I'm no Julia Child even under the best of circumstances. Without the use of the stove, you're really taking your chances."

"Beggars can't be choosers. Besides, I'm not a fussy eater. The only thing I really don't like are lima beans, and I'd eat them if I had to."

She laughed. "Okay, no lima bean omelettes. Promise."

"Great." His gaze settled on her hair and she inwardly cringed. He was probably comparing her to the Bride of Frankenstein—and the Bride was the winner.

"I'll see you when you get back," she said, resisting the urge to cover her head with her arms. "Don't slip in the mud, city boy." She turned and walked back to the bedroom with as much dignity as she could muster under the circumstances—which wasn't much.

Closing the bedroom door behind her, she closed her

eyes, pressed her lips together, and again recited all the reasons she could not, would not find Ryan Monroe attractive. When she finished, she realized with a sinking heart that she had only one hope.

Pray for all she was worth that the rain would stop today.

6

CARMEN NEWBURY LOUNGED on a padded recliner by the *Seafarer*'s pool and blew a kiss to her new husband as he headed off toward the bar to fetch them each a morning mimosa. The instant he was out of sight, she reached into her straw bag and pulled out her cell phone.

Dialing the cabin, she prayed Lynne would answer. She hadn't had a moment's privacy to check on the redecorating, and she was anxious to know how things were progressing.

A satisfied smile tugged her lips. Not that she was complaining about spending every minute with Dave. No indeed. But now that she had a free moment, she wanted to see how her surprise wedding gift was shaping up. She couldn't wait to see Dave's face when he saw the metamorphosis of his grungy cabin into a romantic getaway.

A recorded message sounded in her ear, advising her of problems on the line. She hung up with an impatient huff. No doubt the phone in the cabin was dead again. The darn thing was out of commission more than it worked. Muttering an oath that consigned the phone company to Hades, she dialed Lynne's cell phone number, keeping one eye alert for Dave. The call went through and she heaved a sigh of relief. *Come on, Lynne. Answer your phone.*

DAVE NEWBURY BLEW A KISS to Carmen, then trotted toward the bar. The instant his wife couldn't see him, he whipped out his cell phone. Rapidly dialing the cabin, he muttered, "Come on, Ryan. Be there, man."

A mechanical voice informed him there was trouble on the line and he groaned. The cabin's phone was dead more than it was alive. He quickly dialed Ryan's cell phone, but another mechanical voice informed him that the person he was trying to reach was unavailable at this time. Damn. Ryan's phone wasn't on.

He snapped his phone closed, slipped it into his pocket, then ordered himself to relax. There was no need to worry. Ryan had promised to save his stuff and his best friend wouldn't let him down.

While waiting for the mimosas, he idly wondered what Ryan had thought of Carmen's friend Lynne. Dave had only met her twice before the wedding, but he'd liked her warm smile and sense of humor. Carmen had mentioned several times that she thought Lynne and Ryan would be perfect for each other, but Dave had put the kibosh on the matchmaking—at least for now. He knew Ryan was not only still smarting over his bust-up with Marcie, but he had to concentrate on his project. Women were not a priority at the moment. Still, both he and Carmen had noticed the unmistakable spark that had flared between their friends at the wedding when Ryan's cuff link had ensnared Lynne's bow.

Maybe it wouldn't hurt to go along with Carmen's suggestion and invite them both for dinner when they got back home. Who knows? Maybe they'd really like each other.

LYNNE HEARD THE FAINT ringing sound and frowned. Her gaze flew to the phone mounted on the wall, but that wasn't the source. It sounded like her cell phone.

Slapping her hand to her forehead, she groaned and sprinted toward the bedroom. Good grief, she must have

left it on! Entering the bedroom, she snatched up the ringing instrument from the dresser and punched the receive
button. "Hello?"

Carmen's voice came through loud and clear. "Hello,
Lynne? Are you there?"

"Carmen! I'm so glad—"

"Lynne, are you there? Hello?"

"Yes! I—"

"Hello? Hello?"

Lynne groaned. Clearly Carmen couldn't hear her.

"Listen, Lynne, I know how flaky the phones can be at
the cabin, so on the off chance that you can hear me, I'm
just calling to see how things are going with the redecorating. I had an awesome idea for the bedroom that I really
want to run by you, so if you can hear me, please call me
back, okay? We're having a terrific time and I highly recommend married life. Hey, since you caught the bouquet,
you're next! Ha, ha! Speaking of which, I saw those
fireworks sizzling between you and Ryan—you know, the
best man. He's a real honey, and cute, too! I'll be sure to
invite you both for dinner when we get back. Who knows?
You guys might like each other. Well, gotta go. Have fun
redecorating and call me if you can! Bye!"

The connection ended and Lynne huffed out a breath.
Carmen obviously wasn't aware that Dave knew about her
surprise. Or that Ryan was at the cabin.

Humph. What had her friend called him? *A real honey?*
Phooey. He was a real pest. *And cute, too!* Well, she supposed she couldn't argue with that. But who cared? Pest
outweighed cute every time.

She groaned at the prospect of calling Carmen back. She
really didn't want to climb a tree, especially when there
was no guarantee the call would even go through.

Heaving a resigned sigh, she slipped on her raincoat then headed toward the door.

A decorator's gotta do what a decorator's gotta do.

RYAN TRUDGED THROUGH THE mud and rain, lugging his heavy food-packed cooler. A half-dozen plastic grocery store bags containing bread, chips and other assorted necessities dangled from his arms. Cool rainwater sluiced down his skin, running off his chin as he squinted through the gray mist.

This was his second trip back from his car—his Lexus that was now sunken to the hubcaps in oozy mud. If this damn rain didn't stop soon, his entire car would disappear, sinking below the muddy horizon like it stood in quicksand. He wondered if he was insured against mud swallowing his car. The way his luck was running, the answer was undoubtedly no.

Well, he might lose his car, but at least they wouldn't starve. The food he'd packed on dry ice would surely keep until the electricity came back on, but even if it didn't, he'd brought a huge jar of peanut butter and several loaves of bread. Good thing, too because God knew how long he'd be stranded in the cabin from hell.

Stranded with *her.*

A strangled sound erupted from his throat. The damn woman was going to drive him nuts.

As soon as she'd entered the bedroom to dress, he'd sprinted down the hall to the laundry room. His clothes were still a bit damp, but he'd immediately felt more in control as soon as he shrugged into a pair of jeans and a polo shirt. He'd be soaked before he ever reached his car, but there was no way he could go around half-dressed with Lynne around. Something about her made him want to just peel off his clothes, then remove hers—with his teeth.

She'd emerged from the bedroom just as he was leaving the cabin. She'd changed into jeans and another faded T-shirt, this one adorned with a monster-like creature who warned, Just Give Me the Chocolate And No One Gets Hurt.

She'd tamed her hair into the same severe bun she'd worn the day before and he'd breathed a sigh of relief. Except his relief was short-lived when he realized that all he could think about was undoing her carefully arranged coiffure and running his hands through her luxuriant hair. Mumbling a quick goodbye, he'd left the cabin like he was shot from a catapult.

Now stomping back to the cabin, he shook his head. Damn it, what was *wrong* with him? He'd never acted like this…like some testosterone-inflated frat boy whose world revolved around sex—not even when he had been a frat boy. He was a mature, thirty-year-old man whose decision-making processes took place *above* his belt.

Or at least he had been until yesterday. One look at Lynne Waterford—and damn, what a look it had been— had turned him into a walking, talking hard-on.

Well, this trek in the rain had helped. Yup, sure had. He'd forgotten all about her during his quest to rescue his food and drafting table. Nothing like a good brisk walk in the mud and rain to cool a guy's ardor. And that's just what he was—cool. Nothing in the world he couldn't handle, including that woman. He'd just set up his table and work, work, work. No problem.

The cabin loomed ahead and he breathed a sigh of relief. His arms and shoulders ached with the strain of hauling the heavy cooler. He hoped Lynne would have breakfast ready because he was hungry enough to chew on the pine needles squishing under his soaked Nikes.

He climbed the steps to the porch, then peered in the screen door. "Lynne? Can you get the door?"

No answer. Probably in the shower. *Don't think about her in the shower.* Okay, probably in the bedroom. *Don't think of her in the bedroom. Damn it, just stop thinking about her!*

Struggling under his burden, he managed to open the door. Depositing the cooler on the floor, he crossed the living area to the kitchen and plopped the grocery bags on the counter.

The empty counter.

A frown pulled his brows. Empty counter, no signs of breakfast. He sniffed the air. No breakfast smells, either.

"Lynne?" When she didn't answer, he walked through the entire cabin, calling her name.

Where the hell was she? Maybe she'd walked over to Killer's place—a thought that knotted his shoulders with annoyance. He could just hear Killer now: *So glad you dropped by, luv, and without the Yank. Got my ax all ready. Shall I chop the bloke into pieces for you?* He raked his hands through his sopping hair. No doubt the guy's hands were all over her again and—

But wait. What if something had happened to her? Like maybe she got eaten by a bear. Dread crept down his spine. What if—

"Ryan? Are you there?"

Relief swept through him at the distant but unmistakable sound of her voice. It sounded like she was outside. Walking out onto the porch, he yelled, "Where are you?"

"Out back, behind the cabin."

Squishing through the ooze, Ryan walked around the cabin. And saw nothing but colorful leaves and forest. "I don't see you."

"I'm up here, in the tree to your right."

Looking up, he saw her, soaking wet, perched on a branch about twenty feet above his head. "What the hell are you doing?"

She lifted her chin. "I had to make a phone call."

He simply stared at her. "You have *got* to be kidding. Who was so important to speak to? The President?"

"Carmen called my cell phone which I'd accidentally left on. I could hear her, but she couldn't hear me."

"What did she want? Is everything okay with her and Dave?"

"Everything's fine, honeymoon's terrific. She wanted to tell me about an idea she had for the cabin, but she must have turned off her phone because I couldn't reach her. And now…uh, well, I seem to be sort of…stuck."

Planting his hands on his hips, he surveyed the tall pine. "How the hell did you get up there?"

She sizzled down a baleful glare. "By helicopter. Duh. I climbed up."

"So climb down the same way."

"I can't. The main branch I used to get up here broke off. There's a length of rope in the bottom left cupboard in the kitchen. If you could toss it up to me, I can get down."

"Bottom left cupboard. Got it." He squinted up at her. "Are you all right?"

"Fine. Just wet. And annoyed at myself."

"Well, hang tight. I'll be right back."

He ran back to the kitchen, returning with the rope. "The rope's only about twelve feet long," he said, rolling it up to toss to her. "I'll help you down the rest of the way. Here it comes."

She caught the rope with the skill of a major league outfielder. From the ground, Ryan watched her tie a sturdy knot around the tree branch she sat on. When she finished, he jumped up and grabbed the end, swinging on it with all his weight.

"Good job," he called. "That will hold you. Come on down."

With a smooth agility worthy of a gymnast, she eased herself off the branch and onto the rope. She slid slowly downward, her hands and legs wrapped around the rope.

"Okay," he said. "You're close to the end of the rope. Stay still and I'll get you."

"I can jump down the rest of the way."

"Not a good idea. The ground is slippery and you might hurt yourself." Reaching up, he grabbed her around her waist. "Okay, I've got you. Let go."

She released the rope then set her hands on his shoulders. Her wet body dragged slowly along his as he gently lowered her. When he set her on her feet, he still clutched her waist, her hands still rested on his shoulders, and a dime couldn't have squeezed between them.

They stood perfectly still, eyes locked, both breathing hard, rain dripping down on them. Damp chestnut tendrils that had escaped her bun surrounded her face like a curly halo. She looked like a wet, blue-eyed angel. Heat sizzled through him and his heart slapped against his ribs like he'd run a marathon.

"You okay?" he asked, his voice a husky rasp.

"I'm fine. You?"

"I'm..." *Majorly in lust with you. Dying to kiss you again. Losing my mind,* "...fine."

"My hero." A smile curved her lips and her dimples winked at him. "I didn't know architects could handle a rope like that."

"I didn't know decorators could climb trees like that."

"Only when we have to. Never let it be said I don't go that extra mile for my clients." Her gaze traveled down to where her palms still rested on his shoulders. Emitting a nervous-sounding laugh, she lowered her hands from his shoulders, then stepped back. "From what Carmen said, it's clear she isn't aware that Dave knows about her surprise."

"Dave told me he wasn't going to let on he knew. Glad to hear the honeymoon's going great. Did she say anything else?"

"Nope. Not a thing," she said in such an innocent voice, he was immediately suspicious.

"You sure?"

"Positive." Her gaze settled on his shoulder and her eyes widened slightly. "Don't move, Ryan."

Uh-oh. He recognized those words, that tone. A sick feeling settled in his midsection and he resisted the urgent need to slap his hands against his head.

"Another spider?" he asked, praying for all he was worth that it wasn't.

She shook her head and slowly approached him. "Praying mantis. Don't worry. It can't hurt you. Wow. It's a big one."

He'd always enjoyed hearing a woman say *Wow, it's a big one*—until now. Turning his head, he found himself face to face with what had to be the biggest damn bug in the world. It was green, it had long arms, and it was rubbing its hands—or whatever the hell they were—together, probably in preparation of making Ryan its next meal. It looked like it could eat the entire state of Massachusetts.

Before he could so much as move, Lynne's hand swished the thing off him.

"Holy hell," he yelped, jumping back a good three feet. The praying mantis landed on a mound of pine needles and continued on its way as if nothing out of the ordinary had just occurred.

A shudder ran through Ryan. "Damn. Look at that thing. It's big enough to throw a saddle on. I bet it could tow my car out of the mud."

Lynne chuckled and patted his shoulder. "C'mon, Davy Crockett. Let's head inside and rustle up some grub. I'll even let you shower first."

"All right." He immediately headed toward the cabin, anxious to wash any bug goop off him. He thought he heard her snickering behind him which really irked him. Damn it to hell, he just did not like bugs. So what? Was that so terrible? And for cryin' out loud, that praying mantis thing shouldn't even be classified as a bug. It was more like a small, green...horse.

Sheesh. A guy was entitled to not like *one* thing. Look at Indiana Jones—he didn't like snakes. *I don't like snakes, either.* Okay, bugs *and* snakes. A guy's entitled to not like *two* things.

"Ryan?"

Thoroughly irritated, he turned and met her serious blue gaze. All right, so maybe she wasn't laughing at him. *Now.* But he'd definitely heard at least one snicker.

"Thanks for your help," she said.

He recalled the exquisite feel of her in his arms and heat rushed through him, evaporating his annoyance. "My pleasure. Thanks for saving me from that man-eating insect."

A smile curved her lips. "All in a day's work. Enjoy your shower—but I have to warn you, there's no hot water."

"No problem," he said, heading once again toward the cabin, his wet, muddy Nikes squeaking against the wet, muddy ground.

A cold shower was exactly what he needed.

FRESHLY SHOWERED AND comfortably dressed in dry jeans and her There's No Such Thing As Too Much Chocolate

T-shirt, hair tamed into submission, Lynne opened the refrigerator and quickly pulled out breakfast items. The fridge's interior was still cool, but she wanted to use the things that could spoil lest they go to waste before the electricity returned.

She assembled eggs, bacon, milk, bread and orange juice on the counter while Ryan set a fire in the fireplace. She suppressed a chuckle when she observed him warily eyeing each log before adding it to the grate. Waldo scampered in from wherever he'd been hiding and trilled at her.

Crouching down, she scratched behind his ears in a way that delighted him. "How are you, little guy?" she asked, tickling his back. He enjoyed her attention for a full minute, then rolled over to present his tummy.

"You're shameless," she said with a laugh. Waldo cocked his head to one side and twitched his whiskers at her in a way that clearly said, "I know. Keep rubbing the belly."

She obliged him, tickling her fingers over his soft fur.

"He seems to like that."

She looked up at Ryan. He stood next to her, watching Waldo squirm with delight. "Yup. Loves to have his tummy rubbed."

His gaze slid to her and their eyes met. A devilish half grin touched his lips. "It's a guy thing."

Lynne's fingers faltered as a vivid image of herself running her hands over Ryan's abdomen filled her mind. She pulled her hand away, and Waldo immediately trilled in protest.

"I think he wants more," Ryan said, crouching down next to her.

"Why don't you take over?" she suggested. "And I'll start cooking." When he hesitated, she took his hand and placed it on Waldo's warm belly. "He won't hurt you," she said. "Just pet him, like you would a dog or cat."

She released his hand, then watched him tentatively stroke Waldo who immediately trilled and squirmed.

"I never had a dog or cat," he said, getting into the spirit of things, much to Waldo's delight.

"Really? Our house was always like a menagerie. Cats, dogs, frogs, birds, you name it."

"Must have been…interesting."

She laughed at his dry tone. "Never a dull moment around the Waterford house." Rising, she gathered the cooking supplies while Ryan and Waldo bonded over tummy rubbing—an activity that ended the instant the scent of bacon wafted through the air.

Waldo scampered to the fireplace with Ryan close behind. "What can I do?" he asked, sitting next to her.

"Keep your eye on the bacon. I'll see what I can do with the eggs." She handed him a pair of long handled tongs. "Use these to pull the pan from the fire."

Fifteen minutes later, they peered into their respective pans. "This bacon doesn't look so good," Ryan said, shaking his head. "Hard to believe, but I think it looks worse than last night's hot dog."

"I'm afraid the eggs didn't fare much better. They look like road tar. How on earth did pioneer women prepare a meal?"

"Beats me." He peeked into her pan and grimaced. "Man, you weren't kidding when you said you couldn't cook."

Her hackles immediately rose. "That sludge in *your* pan isn't exactly gourmet fare, either."

Reaching out, he tweaked a curl that had worked free of its restraint and shot her a crooked grin. "Lighten up, Blue Eyes. I was teasing." He jerked his head toward their matching culinary disasters. "I vote we ditch this before it hardens into cement. How do you feel about peanut butter sandwiches for breakfast?"

His handsome face was only a foot away from hers. He really had the most beautiful brown eyes...sort of a velvety, whiskey color. Very warm and inviting. And it really wasn't fair that a guy should have such long eyelashes. Her foolish heart skipped a beat and she mentally shook herself. *Get a grip, Lynne. The better looking they are, the worse they turn out to be.*

"Peanut butter works for me," she said, standing up to put some distance between herself and his potent magnetism. "But let's save the fire-crisped bacon for Waldo. He loves it."

TEN MINUTES LATER FOUND them sitting on the bearskin rug, with a platter of thick peanut butter sandwiches and plastic kiddie cups of orange juice. Waldo sat next to Lynne, a bowl of water and plate of cut-up bacon set in front of him.

Ryan watched, fascinated and amazed as Waldo carefully selected a small piece of bacon, then swished it back and forth in the bowl of water. After sloshing it around for almost a minute, the animal popped it into his mouth, then selected another piece and started the process all over again.

"I'm not so sure he likes the bacon," Ryan said, passing Lynne a sandwich. "Or maybe he thinks it's dirty."

"He loves bacon," she said with a laugh. "Raccoons dip their food before they eat it. I'm not sure why."

"Incredible." They polished off the entire plate of sandwiches, watching Waldo the entire time. After Lynne assured him it was okay to do so, Ryan offered the animal a bit of sandwich which Waldo eagerly accepted. As he had with the bacon, Waldo swished the treat around in his water. But he washed it a bit too long. When he lifted his paw from the bowl, the bread had disappeared and the peanut butter dripped off his little fingers like dew.

The look on Waldo's face was priceless. He cocked his head at Lynne and chirred, clearly asking, *Hey! Where's all my stuff?*

Laughing, Ryan offered him another small piece. "Might want to forgo the washing on this one, buddy."

Waldo seemed to understand the problem. He held the second treat in his paws, alternating his keen gaze between it and the water. After a few seconds, he settled himself on his square little bottom and ate the treat without washing it.

"That's amazing," Ryan said, shaking his head. "He's really smart."

"Raccoons are very intelligent," Lynne agreed. "He'll never forget that. If you give him that treat again tomorrow or next week or even next year, he'll remember not to wash it or it will disappear."

After polishing off his second sandwich and splitting a third with Lynne, Ryan wiped his mouth with a paper napkin. "That was the best breakfast I've ever had."

"Ha. That's only because you had one foot on starvation and the other on a banana peel."

He waved a negligent hand. "Whatever. All I know is that even filet mignon and Dom Pérignon never tasted so good." He glanced at Waldo who was kneading his paws into the bearskin rug, clearly making a comfortable napping spot for himself. His gaze then shifted to the windows where the rain still flowed down in a steady sheet.

Then his gaze wandered toward Lynne like a bee drawn to honey, even though his mind yelled *Don't look at her!* She knelt on the rug, gathering up the remains of their breakfast. As if she felt the weight of his stare, she looked over at him. She offered him a friendly smile, complete with those beguiling dimples, then rose.

"I brought some paint and supplies with me," she said, walking into the kitchen. "If you don't mind, I'll head into the bedroom and get started."

"Fine," Ryan said. "I'll set up my drafting table out here."

"Great. Then I'll see you later." She walked into the bedroom, closing the door behind her.

Ryan stared at that closed door, feeling oddly let down. They'd enjoyed an easy camaraderie over breakfast, laughing over Waldo's antics, and he'd been reluctant to see the meal end. He dragged his hands down his face. *Good God, man, get a hold of yourself. Set up your table and get to work.*

Yeah, that was it. Work. Jumping to his feet, he walked purposefully toward his drafting table. He was here to work. To design the house of his life. To earn the respect of his peers and capture the bonus that would enable him to realize his dreams.

Yes, this was the opportunity of a lifetime. All he had to do was design the house. No problem.

THREE HOURS LATER, RYAN crumpled up but yet another piece of drafting paper. Muttering an expletive, he tossed the lump into the corner where it joined its wadded-up comrades—all two dozen of them. A groan escaped him and he lowered his aching head into his hands.

Nothing. Absolutely nothing. Not one original idea, not a single fresh plan. It was as if some sort of long-fanged architectural vampire had sucked all the creative blood from his body.

The fact that he couldn't connect to the Internet because

of the downed phone lines screwed things up royally. He'd planned to spend at least a day or two surfing the Net, researching his famous client, reclusive novelist Leyton Dracmeyer. Not a big fan of the sort of gory, blood-and-guts, futuristic horror novels Dracmeyer penned, Ryan didn't read his books—a fact he now cursed. If he were at least familiar with Dracmeyer's work, he might have a clue what made the man tick, something that could give him an edge. If Dracmeyer liked his design, his career was set. If he didn't—

Ryan groaned. *If he didn't* just wasn't an option.

The problem was that the eccentric author hadn't given him any guidelines. His only instructions had been, "Price is no object. Just come up with something brilliant that I'll love."

Well, how the hell could he hope to design something "brilliant" if he knew nothing about his client? And how could he find out anything if he couldn't hook up to the Internet? And how was he supposed to access the Internet while he was stranded here in the electricity-free, dead-airspace, spider-ridden, gigantic bug-infested WOODS?

Another groan escaped him, and he fisted his hands in his hair, wondering when he might wake up from the nightmare his life was becoming—a nightmare about being stuck in the middle of nowhere, with his career headed down the toilet. *What the hell else could go wrong?*

He heard the bedroom door open and he gritted his teeth. Oh, yeah. *That's* what else could go wrong. The schoolmarm/sea goddess who had his libido in a frenzy could enter the room and liquify whatever few brain cells he still possessed.

He listened to the quiet patter of her sneakers crossing the room. She rested a hand on his shoulder.

"Are you all right, Ryan? I heard you groan."

Blowing out a long breath, he raised his head and looked into blue eyes filled with concern.

"Good grief," she said. "You look awful. Are you ill?" She pressed her hand to his forehead. "You don't feel feverish."

"I'm not sick." Rising from the small chair attached to his desk, he paced the floor. "I'm just…disgusted. With myself." He indicated the pile of crumpled papers littering the floor. "This is the most important project of my career, and I can't get even get to first base. Hell, I can't even get out of the batter's box. It's like I've fallen into a big, black creative abyss." Raking his hands through his hair, he continued to pace. "If I knew something about this client—his likes, dislikes—*anything*. But that's part of the challenge he presented to our firm. 'Come up with something I'll love,' he said. 'Use your imagination.'" A humorless laugh escaped him. "How can I design the perfect house with no direction from the client?"

"He sounds very…unusual," Lynne remarked. "Who is it?"

"Leyton Dracmeyer."

"*The* Leyton Dracmeyer? The author?"

He stopped pacing and looked at her. "Yeah. You read his stuff?"

A near reverence lit her face. "Ryan, you do not simply *read* a Dracmeyer. You savor it. Devour it. Stroke it like a lover."

"I…see." A tiny sliver of hope flickered on his dark horizon. "I don't suppose you know anything about the guy?"

"Actually, I know just about *everything* about him—or, at least, all that he's allowed anyone to know. He's very reclusive."

Ryan covered the distance between them in two long

strides. Grasping her shoulders, he said, "Tell me you're serious, that this isn't a joke. Good God, woman, don't toy with me here!"

"I'm perfectly serious. I'm a *huge* Dracmeyer fan. I've read all his books at least twice, kept every magazine article ever written about him, and I can recite, practically verbatim, the one and only television interview he's ever given. What exactly do you want to know?"

Mentally muttering *Thank you, God, thank you, God,* Ryan grabbed a legal pad and a fresh pencil. "Okay," he said, trying to contain his excitement. "You talk, I'll take notes. Just tell me everything you know about Leyton Dracmeyer."

"*Everything?* Do you have about five hours?"

A slow smile eased across Ryan's face and he drew his first easy breath in hours. "My darling, Lynne. I have all the time you need."

7

LYNNE TALKED FOR SEVERAL hours about Leyton Dracmeyer, answering Ryan's constant stream of questions. He alternately listened and jotted down notes, sometimes nodding with a serious expression, other times smiling.

He'd seemed so full of despair earlier, her heart had gone out to him. She well understood the frustration brought on when the creative muse decided to go on vacation. His current enthusiasm was gratifying, and it pleased her to think she might help him jump over the artistic hurdles blocking him.

Lunchtime approached and things were going along swimmingly...until Ryan slipped on a pair of wire-rimmed glasses. Lynne stumbled over her words and stared.

Oh, boy, this wasn't good. She had a "thing" for guys in glasses. She watched him, head bent over his legal pad, scribbling furiously, glasses on, and a tornado of heated lust whipped through her. An overwhelming desire to sit on his lap, slide those very serious spectacles off his gorgeous face, and kiss him 'til his eyes glazed over slapped her like a hot, wet towel.

Hmm. And while she was kissing him, why not get rid of his shirt and run her hands over all those lovely muscles? And his pants...yes, they needed to go, too. And his boxers—

"Something wrong, Lynne?"

His voice jerked her back with a start. "What?"

"You okay? You're a million miles away."

No, I'm actually right here. Sitting on your lap, stripping you bare. And boy, do you look good naked. "Sorry. Lost my train of thought for a minute." She swallowed, then wet her bone-dry lips. "I, uh, didn't know you wore glasses."

"Only when my eyes get tired. The light isn't very good in here." He slipped off the wire-rimmed fantasy-inducers, setting them on his drafting table. "And listen, *I'm* the one who should apologize. I've grilled you all this time without a break." He flipped his pad closed, setting it next to his glasses. "It's incredible how you remember all those little details about Dracmeyer. Thanks to the information you provided, a design is starting to take shape in my mind. I can't tell you how much I appreciate your help."

Pleasure rushed through her at his praise and the unmistakable warmth and admiration in his gaze. A tiny voice in her head warned *you're in big trouble here with this man,* but she mentally ordered her tiny voice to pipe down. She could handle that he wore glasses...especially now that they weren't on his face. And that crazy fantasy? Just an aberration.

Smiling, she said, "A break and something to eat sounds good. What do you propose we scorch for our next meal?"

He laughed. "I have a couple of steaks in my cooler. Why don't we try those?"

"I'm game if you are." She glanced out the window where the rain continued to pour down in an unrelenting torrent. "I can't believe this rain. How long do you suppose it can go on?"

"I don't know, but let's hope it stops by tonight. Then I can leave tomorrow."

She turned toward him. Their eyes met and her breath caught.

"It, uh, would be good if I left tomorrow," he said, watching her with an intense expression that hardened her nipples and whooshed heat directly into her womb.

She crossed her arms over her chest. "Yeah, that would be swell." With an effort she dragged a breath into her lungs and forced a smile. "Now, how about those steaks?"

RYAN LOOKED INTO HIS PAN. "My steak looks like a hockey puck. How about yours?"

"Mine looks like a piece of charcoal." She sighed. "Even Waldo wouldn't eat this."

"Good thing I bought the giant-size jar of peanut butter." Looking at the mess in his pan, he said, "I think we should file this mess under T.L."

"What's T.L.?"

"Total loss."

"Ah. I know that file well," she said, nodding. "My very first cooking attempt made it there. Of course, there is some debate whether setting a baloney sandwich on fire actually constitutes cooking, but I tried my best."

"Something we have in common. As much as I hate to admit it, I can barely boil water."

"Well, *that* I can do," she said. "It's what comes after boiling the water that I stink at."

"Lucky for us, I make great peanut butter sandwiches." He rose then walked into the kitchen. Slapping a dish towel over his forearm, he assumed his best French chef voice. "Tonight's selection ees made from zee finest selection of peanuts from zee bouillon section of France. Does mademoiselle prefer *pain du* whole wheat or white?"

She flashed him a dimpling smile that raised his temperature a few notches. Joining him in the kitchen, she said, "Whole wheat, *s'il vous plaît, monsieur.*"

"Hey, don't get all fancy on me. I don't actually speak French, you know."

"Don't worry. *S'il vous plaît* means 'please' and it's one of the very few French words I know."

"Ah. In zat case, which wine shall we have with zee dinner? Merlot? Or perhaps you prefer zee more delicate Chardonnay?"

"Oh, definitely the Merlot. Your masterpiece deserves a robust wine."

"Excellent choice."

Ryan prepared the sandwiches while Lynne poured the wine and washed a bowlful of grapes. His mind buzzed with dozens of ideas for Dracmeyer's house, and after their meal he intended to commit them to paper. His gaze slid to the fireplace where Lynne was setting down their plastic wine cups along with a bowl of food for Waldo. The raccoon had scampered off through the pet door soon after breakfast and hadn't reappeared.

He watched Lynne add another log to the fire. The flame's warm glow highlighted her ivory skin and ruthlessly pulled-back chestnut curls. Man, if she were his woman, he'd toss out every bobby pin and hair-confining thingamabob she owned. Then he'd explore every one of those gorgeous, sexy curls. Then he'd—

Whoa! Hold it right there, buddy. What the hell are you thinking? Your woman? He'd lost his mind for sure. He didn't want a woman. And even if he did, he most definitely did not want *this* woman. This curly-haired, blue-eyed goddess. His pain-in-the-ass inner voice snickered, *Ha! Don't want her, huh? Then how come you just smeared peanut butter all over your wrist?*

Muttering in disgust, he wiped off the peanut butter, then slapped the sandwiches onto a plate. The woman was a hazard. The instant he finished eating, he was going to glue his butt to his drafting table chair and forget all about her.

All he had to do was get through their meal. He could do that. Eat a sandwich, sip some wine, scarf down a couple of grapes, mumble a few pleasantries, then *poof!* He was a vapor trail. And she was forgotten. No problem.

As he headed into the living area with the sandwiches, a series of loud knocks sounded at the door.

"Lynne, are you about, luv?" came Killer's muffled voice.

Swell. The ax-wielding Brit. "I'll answer it," he said, handing Lynne the plate.

He opened the door. A soaking-wet Killer entered, his arms laden with a big box, leaving a trail of muddy footprints behind him.

"Blimey, this storm takes the biscuit," he said, lowering his burden on the kitchen counter. Lynne joined him and he tweaked her nose. "Thought you might be peckish, so I brought you and the architect Yank some grub. We've got bangers, neap and tatties, and mushy peas."

"Oh, wonderful!" Lynne said.

Gross. "Yeah, wonderful."

He smiled at Ryan. "I also threw in some toad in the hole for you, mate. Some spotted dick, too. Thought you might enjoy it."

"Killer, quit teasing Ryan. He's turning green."

"Aw, he knows I'm just pulling his plonker, don't you, mate?" Killer slapped him on the back with an enthusiasm that almost dislodged Ryan's eyeballs. "Toad in the hole's just batter with sausages embedded in it, and spotted dick is pudding with dried fruit. They're both totally scrummy."

"Scrummy?" he asked.

"Delicious."

"Will you stay and eat with us?" Lynne asked.

"Thanks, luv, but no. Just wanted to check on you." Reaching inside his raincoat, he pulled out a magazine. "Here's the latest issue of *Decorator's World*. I marked several pages you might find useful."

"Thank you, Killer. You have such a wonderful eye."

He waggled his brows at her. "Among other things."

Lynne laughed delightedly and annoyance trickled through Ryan. He didn't think that was all that funny.

She walked Killer to the door. The giant leaned down and planted a smacking kiss on Lynne's lips—a gesture that elevated Ryan's annoyance several points. Obviously kissing *Killer* didn't fall into the realm of "bad idea." After closing the door behind Killer, Lynne offered Ryan a smile.

"Ready for some bangers? Or would you rather have some spotted dick?"

"Ah, appetizing as that sounds, I think I'll stick to peanut butter."

"You should at least taste them. They're much better than they sound."

"Right. They're *scrummy*."

She laughed. "Yes, they are."

He eyed the plastic containers lined up on the counter. "Any lima beans in there?"

"Not a one."

"In that case, I suppose it couldn't hurt to try a little piece. A *very* little piece."

"Done. And don't worry if you don't like it. Waldo will eat yours. He loves toad in the hole."

"I just bet he does. I only hope none of my friends find out I've had spotted dick."

"Your secret's safe with me." She sent him a saucy wink that tightened his groin. "And I'm not pulling your plonker, mate."

That's what she thought.

LYNNE WASHED A BITE OF toad in the hole down with a sip of Merlot and watched Ryan share a piece of sausage with Waldo. Waldo trilled his thanks then commenced with the washing ceremony which brought a chuckle from Ryan. Those two were getting along like gangbusters.

Ryan turned toward her and smiled and her breath simply stalled. The firelight highlighted his handsome features and dark hair. A single lock fell over his forehead, begging her to brush it back in place. Laughter crinkled his warm eyes at the corners and his lips were…perfection. She'd thoroughly enjoyed their meal as well as their entire afternoon. He was easily the most attractive, intelligent, amusing man she'd met in a long time. Okay, ever.

Carmen's one-sided conversation had indicated that she wanted to set her and Ryan up. An unwanted *zing* shot through her and she pushed it aside. Tons of women had to find this man attractive. So why was he available? Or was he?

"Waldo's very entertaining," Ryan remarked. "He really—"

"Do you have a girlfriend?"

Lynne barely suppressed a horrified *ack! I didn't just ask that. I couldn't possibly be that much of a dork.* But she could tell by his speculative gaze that she indeed had blurted out the girlfriend question. Jeez! Why couldn't life be like a courtroom where you could jump up and say *I'd like my last statement to be stricken from the record, your honor.*

"No girlfriend. How about you?"

"Nope. No girlfriend for me, either."

A crooked half grin curved his lips. "I meant a boyfriend."

"None of those, either. I gave the last one his walking papers and haven't bothered to replace him."

"Why?"

"Because it's been my experience that men are more trouble than they're worth."

"I meant why did you break up with him."

"Oh." She shrugged. "We had a strong difference of opinion regarding monogamy in a relationship. I believe it's mandatory. He felt it was optional."

A humorless laugh pushed past his lips. "Sounds like my last girlfriend. She moved to Chicago and decided cheating didn't count as long as her affairs took place in a different state. Unfortunately, I didn't realize that until I visited her and found some other guy's underwear under her bed. Definitely cured me of long-distance relationships."

"Yikes. You're positive the underwear wasn't yours?"

"They were briefs. I'm strictly a boxer man."

An image of him wearing nothing but wet boxers flashed in her mind and her heart skipped a beat. She could only shake her head in amazement that some woman was foolish enough to cheat on this man. She laid a commiserating hand on his shoulder.

"I'm sorry, Ryan. I understand exactly how you feel. My ex adopted some newfangled definition of cheating. He thought it was perfectly acceptable to have another woman's lips wrapped around his private parts."

"Sounds like our exes were cut from the same cloth," he remarked.

"Yeah. Maybe we should introduce them," she agreed in a light tone, trying to ignore the little voice in her head that thumped out *he's available, he's available!* like some sort of jungle drum.

Their gazes held for a long moment and the air in the cabin suddenly felt thick. Heat suffused her as she realized that if she didn't stand up and break the spell, they were going to kiss. And that would only lead to all sorts of problems because she suspected that if they kissed again, they wouldn't be able to stop....

Forcing herself to look away from his compelling eyes, she stacked their empty plates. He rose, and together they cleaned up the mess. But for some reason their earlier ease with each other had vanished, leaving behind a charged tension. She cast a surreptitious glance at him. He was frowning and she wondered what he was thinking.

When they finished washing up, he slipped his hands in the pockets of his khakis. "I'd like to spend the rest of the afternoon sketching some ideas for Dracmeyer's house."

"Great. I want to continue with my spackling and painting in the bedroom. I'll need to use the sink, but I'll try not to disturb you."

"Thanks." He stepped toward his drafting table, then halted and turned to her, his brown eyes serious. "Lynne, I want you to know that..." He frowned, as if he couldn't find the right words for what he wanted to express, and she held her breath, waiting to hear what he'd say.

"Your boyfriend was a fool."

Air whooshed from between her lips, and warmth enveloped her as if he'd wrapped her in a velvet quilt. Before she could return the compliment, he went on, his voice low and husky, "And even though you didn't ask, I only share my private parts with one woman at a time."

His words rendered her dry mouthed and speechless. She watched him walk to his drafting table then sit on the small, attached leather seat.

The gentle warmth his unexpected compliment had induced surged to bonfire proportions at his provocative words...and at the images they provoked. Images of him. And her. Sharing their private parts.

And instead of being appalled by her thoughts, they

aroused her, spiking her curiosity about what it would be like to—

No! She cut that impossible, disturbing thought right off at the pass. *Remember, Lynne, curiosity killed the cat.*

She heaved a sigh.

Yeah. But what a way to go.

BY SIX THAT EVENING, Ryan had finished the first rough sketches of Leyton Dracmeyer's house. Setting aside his parallel rule, pencil and compass, he leaned back to examine his work—and reveled in the thrill that zipped through him.

It was good. He could *feel* the rightness of it…in the clean lines, high ceilings, arched breezeways and formal courtyard. From Lynne, he'd learned that Dracmeyer hated to feel closed in. He'd spent his boyhood living in a crowded inner-city orphanage. As a man, he demanded open spaces. Ryan could already envision the blueprint, the heart and soul of the house he'd designed.

He slipped off his glasses then rubbed his tired eyes. Yes, he'd designed it, but the ideas had been sparked as a result of his conversation with Lynne. Her knowledge of Dracmeyer had proven invaluable, and gratitude rushed through him. A perfectly acceptable reaction. But something else accompanied the gratitude, taking root in the region of his off-limits heart. Something warm and fuzzy that was unmistakably more than lust.

And that was not so acceptable.

Damn it, he *liked* her. Her laugh. Her smile. Her sense of humor and intelligence. She made him feel like…

He blew out a long breath and shook his head. Like he didn't know what. Like he'd never felt before.

As hard as he tried, he could no longer think of her as a pest who'd messed up his time at the cabin and interfered with his project—and he wanted, needed, to think of her in those terms. When the storm finally ended, as it had to eventually, he'd leave here and never see her again.

His throat tightened as he realized that *that* prospect was very unacceptable.

But for the sake of his sanity, it was unavoidable. Burned once by a Miss Long Distance, he was not about to jump back into the fire. And the mere thought of living in the country was enough to induce hives and a permanent eye twitch.

Turning around in his leather seat, he noticed a pot sat on the grate over a low burning fire. Hunger scraped at him and he smiled. Lynne must have put on something for dinner. A very thoughtful gesture, and just one more thing to like about her. He'd vaguely heard her at the sink several times, but he'd been so engrossed in his work, he hadn't turned around—hadn't wanted to risk interrupting his flow of ideas.

But now that he'd leaped over the first creative hurdle, he needed a break, and some food. As if on cue, his stomach let loose with a raucous growl. Rising, he stretched his stiff back muscles, then headed toward the fireplace.

A wooden spoon rested in a bowl on the hearth, and Ryan used it to stir the pot's contents. Looked like some sort of beans. He sniffed the air and frowned. Didn't smell like any beans he'd ever eaten, but they *were* operating under primitive culinary conditions.

He glanced toward the bedroom door and noted it was closed. Obviously Lynne was still painting. He briefly considered knocking on the door, but discarded the idea. She'd been so great about not disturbing him, and he well understood how difficult it was to resume working once you'd been interrupted.

He might not be a gourmet, but he could certainly try to

help the dinner preparations along. Rummaging through his cooler, which thanks to the dry ice was still frosty cold, he pulled out several items. Whistling softly, he added them to the beans and stirred.

Satisfied, he returned to the kitchen where he spied a bowl on the counter in the corner. He peeked inside, nodding in approval. Hummus. One of his favorites, and just what the doctor ordered to take the edge off his appetite. He resisted the urge to slip his finger into the bowl and sneak a taste. Better to find the package of crackers he'd brought. And maybe open a bottle of wine. Yes, indeed, he felt like celebrating.

He uncorked a bottle of Chardonnay and poured it in a plastic kiddie cup. The mellow flavor eased over his tongue, down his dry throat, and a satisfied *ahh* escaped him. An aroma wafted over from the bubbling pot on the fire. It wasn't quite enticing, but it was certainly…interesting.

Setting down his cup, he walked to the fireplace then knelt on the hearth. He gave the contents a brisk stir, then spooned up a sample, blowing on it several times to cool it down. His stomach rumbled in anticipation, and he brought the spoon to his mouth.

He chewed once, then his jaw froze while his lips puckered in protest. Good God, he hadn't tasted anything so awful since he and Joey Seever had sampled the mudpies they'd made in second grade. And in truth, the mudpies were better.

Resisting the overwhelming urge to immediately spew the entire foul affair out of his mouth like a geyser, he dashed to the sink.

"Patooey!" Man, the woman hadn't been kidding when she said she couldn't cook. Damn! The inside of his mouth tasted like…flowers? He was about to reach for his cup of wine to wash down the floral flavor when the bedroom door opened.

Her hair was pulled back, but dozens of reddish-brown curls had sprung free, surrounding her flushed face. A streak of cream-colored paint decorated the bridge of her nose. Her lips curved upward in a warm smile when she saw him, erasing all thoughts of the wine he'd been about to sip.

"How are the sketches going?" she asked, pushing a curl off her forehead with the back of a paint-splattered hand.

"Great. The light's going, so I thought I'd quit for today and get something to eat." His gaze wandered to the fireplace and a shudder ran through him.

She walked to the sink and worked on washing paint splotches from her fingers. "Perfect timing," she remarked. "Just let me clean up here and we'll see what we can crispy fry. Or do you just want to do the peanut butter thing again?"

"Peanut butter's fine." He raked his hands through his hair. He didn't want to insult her, but it had to be said. "Uh, Lynne...about those beans you're cooking..."

She briefly glanced away from her soapy hands and sent him a confused frown. "Beans? What beans?"

"Okay, the *soup*—or chili—or whatever it is in the pot on the fire. No offense, but it's the most godawful—"

"Potpourri."

He simply stared while she turned off the faucet and dried her hands. Finding his voice, he managed one word. "Huh?"

"Potpourri. I love making my own, but..." She sniffed the air, then wrinkled her nose. "You're right, it smells really odd. Serves me right for trying to make it when I didn't have all the ingredients."

First spotted dick, and now this. Jeez, he was going to end up with an ulcer—if he didn't die of potpourri poisoning first.

"So, um, is there anything like...*lethal* in that concoction of yours?"

"Oh, no. Just water and some dried flowers." She smiled at him, but something in his expression clearly gave him away because her eyes widened. "Don't tell me you *ate* the potpourri!"

"Okay, I won't tell you that."

Leaning closer to him, she flicked her finger over his bottom lip, then held the evidence aloft. "Good grief, you did! This piece of rose petal was stuck to your lip." She pressed her hands to her stomach and laughed until tears rolled down her cheeks.

Ryan wiped his mouth with the back of his hand. "Well, how was I supposed to know it was some girly stuff in the pot? If I'd known *that,* I wouldn't have added the hot dogs to it."

Her laughter cut off like he'd chopped it with a machete. "You put hot dogs in my potpourri?"

Considerably cheered by her horrified expression, he offered her a smug smile. "Yup. A couple of sausages, too."

They stared at each other for several seconds, then she chuckled. "Just like grandma used to make, I bet."

His lips twitched. "Grandma Monroe never tried to poison me." His gaze strayed to the bowl in the corner and he offered up a silent prayer of thanks he hadn't tasted the contents. "About your hummus—"

"Hummus? What hummus?"

Uh-oh. "In the bowl."

Her eyes bulged. "That's spackle! Don't tell me you ate that, too!"

Even if he had, wild horses wouldn't have dragged the

admission from him. And if he lived to a hundred—which didn't look good at the moment—he'd never admit how close he'd come to smearing her spackle on a cracker. "Of course not," he said with a dismissive gesture. "Just teasing you. I'm an architect—I know spackle when I see it." Usually.

She leaned her hips against the counter. With mischief dancing in her eyes, she waggled her brows at him. "Good thing you didn't eat the spackle. If you had, I'd have to Heimlich you."

Damn if she wasn't adorable with that paint on her nose and that teasing gleam in her eye. Unexpected amusement, accompanied by a healthy dose of heat, rippled through him. Unable to stop himself, he moved to stand directly in front of her. Leaning forward, he braced his arms on the counter on either side of her, bracketing her in.

"Heimlich me," he repeated softly. "Now that sounds very…intriguing. I propose we forget about the 'Heim' part and move right on to the 'lick.'" He leaned forward to demonstrate, but she clapped her palms on his chest.

"Hold it right there."

"Ah, c'mon. Give us a kiss. Just a little one." He pursed his lips and made exaggerated smooching noises.

"Impossible." Clearly holding back a laugh, she lifted her chin. "I made it a rule long ago—lips that touch potpourri shall never touch mine."

He looked down into her laughing eyes, her full lips curved in a teasing smile, her body only inches from his, and desire slammed into him like a hammer to his midsection. She must have seen it flare in his eyes because her breath suddenly caught, and her pupils dilated.

"All right. I won't kiss your lips." Even as the warning bells clanged in his head, he leaned forward and brushed his lips over her smooth cheek.

A sigh escaped her, and he kissed his way along her jaw, then down her slender neck. Although his arms still bracketed her, he only touched her with his mouth, carefully holding his body away from hers.

When he touched his tongue to the rapidly beating pulse at the base of her throat, she moaned. Lifting his head, he gazed into her slumberous blue eyes. Damn, he'd barely touched her and already his skin was on fire. What had started only a moment ago with teasing and laughter suddenly wasn't so funny anymore.

He wanted her. Under him. Over him. Wrapped all around him. This was undeniably lust…but different. *This* had a fierceness and heat that was totally unfamiliar to him…an intensity that overrode his common sense. Damn, what was wrong with him? The mess with Marcie had been bad enough, but at least their breakup had been *unexpected.* Why the hell was he even considering involving himself with a woman who he knew *going in* would only embroil him in another dead-end, long-distance relationship?

Clearly he'd gone around the bend. Fallen under some sort of spell. Aliens had abducted his better judgement.

On the other hand, she was gazing up at him with unmistakable desire shimmering in her eyes. Whatever spell was possessing him had her, too. Since this situation was the hand he'd been dealt, and he'd never been one to simply fold his cards, he cupped her face between his palms and lowered his mouth toward hers.

"This is a bad idea," she whispered.

"Very bad," he whispered back.

"Well, as long as we agree…"

"Oh, I definitely agree."

The instant Ryan's lips touched hers, the dam of anticipation that had built inside Lynne burst like detonated dynamite. Had she ever wanted a man to kiss her so much she actually ached?

Rising onto her toes, she pressed herself against him. A moan of pure, female satisfaction growled in her throat at the unmistakable—not to mention impressive—evidence of his arousal. His arms wrapped around her like bands of steel, and she reveled in the sensation of being surrounded by his strength, breathing in his masculine, woodsy scent, feeling the hot hunger in his kiss as his tongue explored her mouth.

She lost all track of time. He kissed her senseless, his mouth coaxing and teasing one minute, then fierce and demanding the next. Without breaking their kiss, he turned them until his hips leaned against the counter. His hands skimmed down her back to cup her bottom, pressing her more tightly against his rigid arousal.

Fire erupted under her skin, stinging her, pulsing need and want through her veins. God, it had been so long since a man had touched her. She wanted, *needed,* to feel him...his skin beneath her fingers, his flesh against her own. In a heated daze, she pulled his shirt from the waistband of his pants and laid her palms on the warm, firm skin of his abdomen. He broke off their kiss and sucked in a breath.

They stood perfectly still, breathing hard, his hands cupping her bottom, hers splayed on his stomach. His gaze pierced hers, a golden-brown storm of desire. He swallowed once, hard.

"You know where this is going," he said, his voice a husky rasp that sent a tingle down her spine.

God, yes, she knew. And, as ill-advised as it was, she couldn't wait to get there. Yet even as she managed a jerky nod, her common sense roused itself from its dormant state and tapped her on the shoulder.

Um, excuse me, Common Sense said, *but you're staring right down the barrel of a shotgun full of heartache here. This guy is nothing but a yuc. Granted, he's sexy, intelligent, amusing, kind, utterly likable, and belongs in the Guinness Book of Records under the heading World's Best Damn Kisser, but underneath, he's just like all those other career-first smooth talkers who've made your dating life miserable.*

And, Common Sense continued, *don't forget he said he's done with the long-distance dating game—and you're moving to the country. Ryan and the country mix like oil and water. Don't start something you can't finish.*

She drew a deep breath. Okay. Even though her screaming hormones wanted to kick her ass black and blue, Common Sense won out. She opened her mouth to tell Ryan they needed to stop, but before she could utter a word, her hormones tossed a grenade into her emotional mine field.

You know, Hormones said in a sly tone, *nothing says you have to fall madly in love with the guy—or even see him again once he leaves here. Why do you have to take everything so seriously? Why can't this just be sex? Indulge yourself in a quick fling with a man you find majorly attractive.*

Her breath stalled at the very thought of making love with Ryan. But how could she indulge in sex with a man she barely knew, with whom there was no chance of anything developing? She'd never done anything like that before.

"Not to rush your apparent decision-making processes," Ryan's voice broke into her reverie, "but I'm dying here." He withdrew his hands from her butt, then raked unsteady fingers through his hair. "There can't be any doubt in your mind what I feel like doing."

"Uh, no. I can feel it...pressing against me." Her brain

told her feet to move away from him and his hard arousal. Her feet told her brain to piss off.

With his serious gaze steady on hers, he reached out and slowly removed the bobby pins taming her hair. They *pinged* as they landed on the wood floor, a gentle sound that contrasted sharply with the heavy thump of her heart.

He eased the scrunchy from her hair, spreading her out-of-control curls around her shoulders. She stifled a groan, knowing she had to look like something along the lines of Godzilla.

But apparently he liked Godzilla, because he sifted his fingers through her hair, then buried his face in a handful of curls. And with a sexy, husky groan, he whispered a single, warm word against her ear.

"Wow."

Desire gushed through her like a geyser and she squeezed her eyes shut.

"I want to get naked. With you." His words brushed through her hair, and a battalion of goose bumps marched down her spine.

"Don't say the word 'naked.' Please."

With his fingers continuing their sensual perusal through her hair, he leaned back to look at her. The desire burning in his eyes melted her insides to goo.

"Okay, no 'naked.' I guess that means you don't want to hear the 's' word, either."

"Supper?"

"Sex."

That single syllable, spoken in that husky timbre, made her mouth go dry. "I would rather we concentrate on something to eat."

"Sounds...delicious."

Oh, boy. Didn't sound like they were on the same page. "I meant like something we could spread mustard on."

"Sounds...adventurous."

"I meant like a ham sandwich."

His heated gaze bore into hers for several heartbeats. "Liar."

Yes, she was. A big, fat liar. Thank goodness she wasn't Pinocchio or her nose would have grown two feet and poked him right in the eye. She wanted him and he knew it. But she'd been down romance's rocky road enough times to know you can't always get what you want. Yet that didn't stop her from wanting...

"There're at least a dozen good reasons why we shouldn't do this," she forced herself to say.

"I know. I can ignore them if you can."

"As much as I'm tempted, I'm afraid there's one problem we can't ignore."

"You don't engage in casual affairs."

"No, I don't."

"Actually, neither do I." He gently tucked a curl behind her ear. "But nothing feels casual about this, Lynne."

He might as well have hit her with a sledgehammer. Oh, boy, this was big trouble. He was *not* supposed to say stuff like that! Where was that "my-long-term-is-three-hours" yucs philosophy? Why wasn't he running true to form?

And God, he was right. Nothing felt casual about this. It felt serious and...right. And that scared the bejesus out of her.

She drew a deep, steadying breath. "You're leaving when the rain stops. 'Casual' is all we could have."

He studied her for several seconds, his expression impossible to read. "Agreed."

He agreed—and wanted to forge ahead. She stood alone on the precipice of indecision. Time to take the plunge— or retreat.

Lifting her chin a notch, she said, "I'm afraid there's another reason we can't do this."

"Can't? Or shouldn't?"

"Can't. We don't have any condoms."

His fingers stilled in her hair. "And if we did?"

All the air seemed to leave the room. Pushing Common Sense aside, she threw herself over the edge and prayed she'd land safely. "Then I think we'd be in for a hell of a night."

He nodded slowly. "Well, I have some good news and some bad news."

"Good news first."

"I have condoms."

Thank God. "Bad news?"

"They're in the glove compartment of my car."

"How fast can you run?"

Tangling his fingers deeper into her hair, he dropped a hard kiss on her mouth. "Fast. Really, really fast."

She wound her arms around his neck and ran her tongue over his bottom lip. "Show me how fast."

A slow, wicked smile curved his lips, igniting her pulse.

Yes, indeed, they were in for a hell of night.

8

HE HAD THREE CONDOMS.

He wished he had four dozen.

Ryan slipped the trio of foil packets into his wet pants pocket, then locked and slammed his car door. He jogged through the rain back to the cabin as fast as the slippery ground and fading light permitted. His heart pounded from far more than the exertion of his sprint to the Lexus, and he silently gave himself a stern, precoital pep talk.

This was nothing more than a quick, no-strings-attached, casual affair. They'd enjoy each other until the condoms ran out, then they'd each go their separate ways. Nice, neat, tidy. Uncomplicated. No messy feelings getting in the way. It was the perfect setup for a guy in his position—a guy whose mind said "no more relationships" but whose body, unfortunately, had different ideas. Yup, it was perfect.

So why the hell was he so…unsettled? He should be as happy as a pig rolling in mud. And he was, except for the niggling little voice in his head that kept saying, *You think this is nuthin' but sex? You really believe this woman is a one-nighter? Ha! You're an idiot.*

He forcibly silenced his niggling little voice and when he arrived at the path leading to the cabin, he doubled his pace. The woman who launched a thousand fantasies waited for him. She was his until the storm stopped and the real world started again. So he did something he hadn't thought he'd ever do again.

He looked up at the sky and prayed for more rain.

RYAN ENTERED THE CABIN, closing and locking the door behind him. A low fire burned in the grate, lighting the living area with a warm, inviting, golden glow. The bedroom door stood ajar, and he walked toward it like a man in a trance, leaving a trail of wet footprints on the wood floor.

Glancing around the bedroom, he saw that she'd set several candles on the dresser, their dancing flames casting long shadows on the pale walls. The maroon and navy comforter was turned down on the bed, and their plastic wine cups sat side by side on the nightstand. The faint smell of fresh paint hung in the air, a fact he noted, then instantly forgot as she emerged from the adjoining bathroom.

Her fabulous hair lay in wild disarray around her shoulders. Wrapped in her ratty purple robe, her eyes shining with a half-innocent, half-I-want-to-eat-you-alive expression, she looked like a wicked angel. Hot desire arrowed straight to his groin.

As she walked slowly toward him, he forced himself to remain still, wanting to see what she'd do, wondering if she'd changed her mind while he was gone, praying for all he was worth that she hadn't. She stopped several feet away from him, and his muscles clenched in anticipation. She ran her gaze slowly down, then back up his body until their eyes met.

Reaching out, she brushed a single fingertip down his soaked polo shirt. "You're all wet," she observed in a smoky voice.

A relieved breath pushed past his lips. She hadn't changed her mind.

"It's raining pretty hard." His gaze settled on her full

lips, and his pulse kicked up another notch with the need to taste her. Snagging her hand, he drew her into his arms, brushing his mouth over hers while his hands drifted up and down her back. He deepened the kiss, his tongue slipping into the heated satin of her mouth. God, she tasted like no other woman.

She sighed, then seemed to simply melt into him like warm wax, her body fitting to his from chest to knee. Her arms encircled his waist, and her palms ran up his back, urging him closer. A groan rumbled in his throat, and he slipped one hand up her nape, into her hair, holding her head immobile while he explored all the fascinating intricacies of her luscious mouth. He ran his lips along her jaw, then gently bit her earlobe.

She gasped, then went utterly still.

He immediately leaned back to look at her. "Did I hurt you?"

She shook her head. "Um, Ryan, I feel a bulge."

"That can't be a surprise."

"On your back. Under your shirt. Don't move."

Uh-oh. *Don't move.* Damn, he hated those two words. "How, um, *big* is the bulge?"

"Just stand still." She stepped behind him, then pulled his shirt from his waistband, easing the material up to his shoulders. He felt her hand brush over him just below his shoulder blade.

"Okay," she said. "It's gone."

He turned around, his gaze darting across the floor. "What was it this time? A tarantula?"

"Caterpillar." She opened her loosely fisted fingers to display a fuzzy, black, two-inch bug. "Perfectly harmless. Insects just seem to have a thing for you."

"Lucky me."

"I'll just deposit our friend on the porch."

The instant she left the room, he yanked off his wet shirt in case any other creepy crawlers had decided to nest in it. At least a caterpillar wasn't so bad. Not like the spider with the hairy legs or that green giant thing with the long arms.

"I hope that didn't kill the mood," she said from the doorway.

He walked toward her, stopping when only several inches separated them. Reaching out, he captured her hand, brought it to his chest, and pressed her palm over his rapidly beating heart. "Honey, *nothing* could kill the mood." With his free hand, he fingered the lapels of her ratty robe. "What are you wearing under this?"

"Skin."

Air rushed from his lungs, and he had to remind himself to take another breath. He lowered his hands to the tie at her waist and loosened it with fingers that weren't quite steady. Slowly parting the material, he eased the robe down her arms then let it slip to the floor.

Wow, wow, *wow.*

She was incredible. Curvy, utterly feminine. His avid gaze slowly roamed over her full breasts, round hips, down to the triangle of dark curls nestled between her shapely legs. His mouth went dry and he raised his gaze to hers.

Lynne looked at the man who was about to become her lover and simply forgot how to breathe. The way he was looking at her…with all that focused, intense heat…as if she were the only woman in the world. As if nothing mattered except her.

Placing his hands on her shoulders, he slowly ran his hands down her arms, then entwined their fingers.

"Beautiful," he said, softly, his gaze touching her everywhere. "Absolutely perfect."

Raising their joined hands to his lips, he pressed a warm kiss in her palm. Her body tingled in anticipation of his touch, but instead of obliging her, he stepped back and removed his wet pants and boxers in one fluid motion.

All the spit in her mouth dried up. Clamping her lips together so her jaw didn't swing open, she indulged in an unhurried, heart-stopping perusal of what his wet clothes had hinted at but hadn't done justice to.

Her gaze fastened on his broad chest, then drifted lower, along the narrow ribbon of dark hair bisecting his toned abdomen, then lower, to his arousal.

Whew! He sure was…aroused.

Even while desire all but strangled her, sudden doubts assailed her. It had been so long since she'd done this…what if she'd forgotten how? Her concern must have shown on her face, or in her eyes, because he asked, "Nervous?"

"Sort of." *Very.* "It's been a while for me."

"For me, too. So, let's just take it nice and slow."

Nice and slow sounded lovely. He drew her into his arms until her breasts brushed his bare chest and his erection pressed against her stomach. Lowering his head, he laid a long, hot, deep, toe-curling, mind-boggling kiss on her that drained every thought from her head. While he kissed her senseless, his hands worked magic, smoothing over her back, then skimming up her front to cup her breasts. He teased her nipples into sensitive, aching points with his fingertips, then bathed them with his mouth and tongue.

She tipped back her head and reveled in the sensations shooting through her body like exploding stars. Her restless hands ruffled through his hair, over his shoulders, touching him everywhere she could reach. But when her fingers encircled his erection, he gently grasped her wrist.

"Not yet," he murmured against her mouth. "I want to touch you, taste you, first. Let me…"

He swept her up in his strong arms and carried her to the bed and laid her gently in the center.

Any initial awkwardness she may have felt vanished as he simply took over her body, slowly, thoroughly, with an exquisite care that left her skin tingling, her insides humming. He left no part of her untouched, lavishing her with licks and kisses and heated caresses from her hair to her toes. It was the most exquisite torture she'd ever endured. Her body arched beneath his clever hands, aching for release.

"Ryan..." His name ended on a desperate moan.

He left the bed and she fought the urge to scream. Propping up on her elbows, she watched him rummage through his pants pockets. Returning to the bed, he held a trio of condoms aloft. "Sorry. Didn't mean to leave you high and dry."

Holding his face between her hands, she impatiently pulled his mouth to hers. "High and dry?" she breathed against his lips. "You've got to be kidding. I've never been lower or wetter." She bit the side of his neck. "Or hotter. God, hurry."

In the several seconds it took him to roll on the condom, she thought she'd burst into flames. But then he loomed over her, slipping inside her with one smooth, deep thrust that dragged a ragged moan from her throat, and she realized she hadn't begun to feel the fire.

His movements were maddeningly slow and deliberate as he withdrew nearly all the way from her, only to glide deep again. She raised her hands over her head and he clasped them tightly, his eyes burning into hers, his face dark, intense. Her heart rapped against her ribs and her choppy breathing burned her lungs.

"Come for me," he whispered, increasing his tempo. "Come for me, now. Together."

His husky voice, his deep thrusts, pushed her over the edge. Release gushed through her, a torrent of pleasure, leaving her breathless, weak, deliciously languid. Tiny aftershocks rippled through her and a vaporous sigh escaped her. They were still intimately joined, his weight holding her to the mattress with a heavenly, decadent pressure. As soon as she was capable of moving, she'd stretch like a satisfied cat.

Prying open her heavy eyelids, she found herself staring up into his beautiful, very serious face.

Her heart performed a crazy roll. He looked as bamboozled and blown away as she felt.

Managing a weak smile, she said, "Holy cow."

"Yeah. That was..."

"Utterly marvelous. Completely..."

"Wow." A grin tipped one corner of his mouth. "Between us, we can finish a sentence."

"I'm afraid that's about all I'm capable of." She hummed out a long *mmmmmmmm*. "That was better than a five-pound box of Godiva chocolates...and that's a sentence I never thought I'd say."

He rolled them onto their sides. "I'm flattered. And in total agreement." Brushing a tangle of curls behind her ear, he said, "You have the most unbelievable hair."

"Ugh, I know. It's a horror."

"Are you nuts?" He drew a long spiral to his lips. "It's gorgeous. Soft. Sexy." His eyes met hers. "Very...you."

If she hadn't been lying down, she would have slithered to the floor. Gathering her scattered wits, she said, "You're not so bad in the gorgeous and sexy departments yourself." Her pelvis nudged him a bit. "But as for soft, well, absolutely not."

"Should we take that to the complaint department?"

"No way."

Rising up on her elbow, she gently pushed him onto his back, then ran her gaze down the length of him. Even in a relaxed state, he was impressive. And she intended to see that he didn't remain relaxed for long.

Reaching over him, she plucked the two remaining foil packets from the comforter. "Is this all we have left?"

"'Fraid so."

"Then we're going to have to make them last because I have plans for you."

Heat flared in his eyes. Raising his arms, he cushioned his head on his linked hands. "What sort of plans?"

She ran a single fingertip down the center of his chest. His muscles jumped under the feathery touch and pure feminine satisfaction surged through her. While her finger drew lazy circles around his navel, she leaned down and whispered in his ear exactly what she intended to do to him.

When she finished her sensual recitation, she leaned back to look at his face. Heat all but smoked from his eyes.

"Any objections?" she asked.

"You've got to be kidding." Reaching up, he fisted his hand in her hair and dragged her down for a long, hot, openmouthed kiss.

And she knew without a doubt that she'd enjoy condom number two as much as he would.

RYAN LAY ON HIS SIDE ON the bearskin rug, his head propped on one hand while the other fed the last of their grapes to Lynne. The firelight coaxed red highlights from her mass of hair and danced shadows across her naked body. Her lips were moist from the grapes and swollen from his ardent kisses.

They'd made mind-blowing use of condom number two nearly two hours ago, and he'd curbed his impatience to embark on activities that would make him want to rip into number three too quickly. Since their second bout of love-making had left them both ravenous, they'd raided the cooler, preparing a feast of ham and cheese sandwiches. But now their meal was finished, and sensual hunger nipped at him again.

She lay on her back on the rug, her eyes shining in the firelight, laughing when he teasingly pulled the last grape just out of reach of her lips. With a mischievous grin, she grabbed his wrist, pulled down his hand, then slowly sucked the grape and two of his fingers into her warm mouth.

Desire knifed through him, and he alternately thanked God he had another condom, then cursed that he didn't have an additional four dozen. Condom number three sat in its foil package on the floor within easy reach. *This is it. The last time...the last time...* The words beat through his head like a drum.

He planned to make the most of it.

Slipping his fingers from her mouth, he leaned down to kiss her. A soft chirring noise caught his attention, and he looked up.

Waldo sat on his bottom next to the bear's head, his masked face the picture of curiosity. His whiskers quivered and his bright eyes clearly asked *whatcha doin'?*

Ryan couldn't stifle a chuckle. "We have company."

Lynne twisted her head around and laughed. "He looks very intrigued."

"Can't blame him. You're very intriguing. But, well, he's not going to stay and *watch,* is he?"

"Not if we ask him to leave." She rolled over onto her stomach, then made gentle shooing motions with her hands. "Time for you to go outside Waldo. Go on."

Appearing more than a little insulted, but clearly taking the hint that his presence wasn't welcome, Waldo flipped his tail, then turned to leave. He'd taken several steps, when he paused, whiskers twitching, eyes zeroing in on something. Ryan followed the animal's gaze and his heart skipped a beat.

Before Ryan could move, Waldo shot across the room, vanishing through the pet door—with condom number three clenched between his teeth.

RYAN RAN OUTSIDE, BARE-ASSED, clutching Lynne's penlight. A stream of very inventive curses fell from his lips as he peered into the darkness that had swallowed Waldo.

Even though Lynne was just as frustrated and disappointed as Ryan, she had to laugh at the picture he made, lowering himself onto his hands and knees in the mud, rain dripping off him as he peered into Waldo's lair beneath the porch.

"C'mon, Waldo," he coaxed, training the flashlight into the small space. "Where are you? I'll give you a thousand bucks. Or how about a year's supply of peanut butter?"

Lynne stood behind him, enjoying the view of what had to be the best male butt in the universe. And all bent-over, too. My, my. She cocked her head to the side to catch the display from a different angle. Yes, indeed, this exhibition was full vindication for the peep show she suspected she'd given him when he'd surprised her coming out of the shower.

"He's gone," Ryan said, standing up.

Rain dripped off his face, down his body. Mud covered his hands and his legs from the knees down, and he looked steamed enough to chew glass. No doubt about it, he was one pissed-off architect.

The penlight flashed several times, then blinked out.

"Perfect," he all but snarled.

She watched him, expecting him to fling the dead flashlight into the mud and stomp off, but instead he looked at her and shook his head in clear amazement. "Can you *believe* this?"

She struggled to contain her amusement. "Actually, I can. Waldo loves shiny things. That foil packet is right up his alley."

"That's great."

A giggle bubbled up her throat at his grumpy tone, and she coughed to cover it up.

His eyes narrowed and he stepped closer to her. "Are you laughing?"

"Who? Me?"

"Yeah, you." He stepped closer, until they almost touched. The heat emanating from his body enveloped her like a hug. "Because if you are, I won't invite you to take a shower with me."

"*I* don't need a shower. I'm not all dirty."

He lifted his hand and covered her breast with his muddy palm. "Wanna bet?"

Fire shot straight to her womb. "Hey, touch my other breast and you're in big trouble."

He immediately dropped the dead penlight and palmed her other breast, teasing her nipple. "I think I'll risk it."

A groan passed her lips. The man had magic fingers. Sliding her arms around his waist, she said, "I was very impressed with your rescue efforts. You dropped to your knees in the mud, completely heedless of any creepy crawlers that might have lurked. Very heroic."

"I'm just sorry I wasn't successful." His fingers drew drugging circles around her nipples. "Sorry and incredibly disappointed. I was nowhere near done with you."

She squeezed her eyes shut. She would never forgive Waldo.

He lowered his lips to her ear. "Let's go take a shower,

then we'll see how many ways we can figure out *not* to use a condom. I can think of five without even trying.''

Five? Whoa, baby. It just proved that old adage, she decided as they entered the cabin hand in hand: when life tossed you lemons, you really could make lemonade.

RYAN AWOKE SLOWLY, HIS senses coming to life one at a time. The first thing he noticed was the texture of her skin. She slept next to him in the bed, on her side, one arm thrown across his bare chest, her thigh resting across his. Man, she was so *soft*. Like if satin hadn't been invented, they'd have to say ''soft as Lynne.''

He breathed deeply, inhaling her scent. That spicy, citrusy fragrance teased him, mingling now with the intimate musk of their lovemaking. He knew it was a smell he would never forget.

The sweet, exotic tastes of her lips and body lingered on his tongue, and his ears rang with the music of her low moans, breathy sighs and cries of release.

It had been an incredible night. One he hadn't wanted to end. Opening his eyes, he stared up at the ceiling, his mind reliving their time together in a series of flashing images. He'd enjoyed what had been, without a doubt, terrific sex. Lynne was an inventive, considerate, stimulating bed partner. But somehow—and he couldn't figure out how—a hell of a lot more than just sex had happened.

They'd enjoyed the intimacy of a long shower, their soapy hands touching, exploring, learning. Then they'd continued their explorations in bed, using their mouths and hands to pleasure each other. They'd laughed and talked, teased and shared, until they'd finally fallen asleep just before dawn.

Yes, it had been a hell of a night.

And now it was over.

A frown pinched his brow and his insides cramped in protest. *It's over,* his inner voice repeated, and again his insides pinched, annoying him.

Damn it, what was wrong with him? But even as he asked himself the question, he knew the answer.

He wanted another night like that. Wanted dozens of them. Nights filled with warm laughter, easy camaraderie and white hot passion. Nights with this woman. And days, too.

He blew out a frustrated breath. She made him feel things that he didn't want to feel, especially not now when his career had to take priority. The timing reeked like week-old fish.

Yet meeting her at *any* time would've been equally bad. Her goal was to move away from Boston, up here to the bug-infested country, and that alone made her totally wrong for him. He gazed down at her sleeping form and his throat tightened. But damn, she felt so totally right in a way that no other woman ever had.

He had to accept that their night was over. As soon as the rain stopped, he had to dig out his car, rescue Dave's furniture, then return to civilization to finish his project. There was no room for Lynne Waterford in that equation. But right now, this minute, she was snuggled in his arms like she belonged there. And until the rain stopped, she did.

He turned toward the window, and his heart nearly stuttered to a stall. Streaks of muted sunlight filtered through the sheer curtain.

The sun was shining.

The rain had stopped.

LYNNE WOKE UP ALONE.

Well, not exactly alone. Waldo sat on the end of the bed, nibbling on a cracker. Pushing her tangled hair from her face, she sat up and frowned at her pet. Waldo immediately chirred and sent her his best repentant blink.

"Humph. Just because you're cute doesn't mean I'm not annoyed with you. Lucky for you, the night turned out okay or you'd be toast."

Turned out *okay?* She shook her head at the ridiculous understatement. The only word to describe what she and Ryan had shared was...perfect.

But now it was morning, and their time together was over. The sun was shining—

She froze and stared at the bright sunlight streaming through the window.

The storm was over. No more rain.

No more Ryan.

Her gaze flew back to the empty half of the bed where he'd lain and something that felt strangely like panic fluttered through her. Jumping up, she grabbed her robe from the floor and shoved her arms through the sleeves. Wrapping the material around her, she ran into the living area and skidded to a halt.

His drafting table was gone, as were all signs that he'd ever been there. Hot tears pooled behind her eyes and she impatiently blinked them away. So he'd left. So what?

Hollowness settled in her stomach. How could he have left without saying goodbye? He could have at least—

"Lynne? Are you all right?"

Her foolish heart jumped at the sound of his voice. Turning, she saw him standing in the doorway, dressed in shorts and a polo shirt, his skin and clothes both liberally splattered with mud. She forced a smile. "Seems I should be asking *you* that."

He looked down at himself and grimaced. "This place sure is hell on clothes. But at least my car is free."

"You dug it out?" She was proud of how calm and cool

her voice sounded, especially since her insides were churning.

"With Killer's help. He stopped by a couple of hours ago."

"A couple of hours ago? What time is it?"

"Almost noon."

She couldn't believe it. She never slept this late. Before she could reply, he continued, "The electricity is back on and the phone works again. The roads are still sort of muddy, but it's warm outside and they're drying fast." He toed off his muddy sneakers. "I stocked the fridge for you with the stuff from my cooler and tossed out anything that looked funky."

A golf ball-size lump lodged in her throat and she coughed to clear it. "Thanks. So, I guess that means you're all ready to go."

"Yes. But I'd like to shower first…if you don't mind."

"Of course not."

He walked into the bedroom, then she heard the bathroom door close. She clenched her teeth and fought the urge to stamp her foot. He'd been so polite, so civilized, not showing a single sign that they'd spent the night naked together.

Walking to the kitchen to make some much-needed coffee, she shook her head with bewilderment. How did people engage in casual affairs? How were they able to keep their emotions out of the mix? She'd thought she could keep her heart locked in another room, but she'd failed—miserably. The ache in her chest at the thought of him leaving proved it. Maybe she should ask *him*—he clearly wasn't experiencing any trouble.

It just proved it was best that he left—ASAP. Somehow she'd given Ryan Monroe something she'd vowed never to give another man: the power to tie her up in knots and cut her heart into little pieces. The sooner he walked out the door, the better.

Determined to be as cool as Ryan, she entered the bedroom and quickly dressed. It was difficult to force her disturbing thoughts of him aside while listening to the shower run, knowing he stood only a few feet away, naked and soapy, but she sucked it up.

Garbed in jeans and a T-shirt that read The Difference Between a Woman Who Wants Chocolate and a Terrorist Is You Can Negotiate With a Terrorist, she gathered a pencil and paper, returned to the kitchen, then started listing things she needed to do, workers and suppliers she had to call. She'd just taken her first sip of coffee when Ryan entered the room.

She peered at him over the rim of her cup and strove to appear calm—an effort that cost her. Fresh from the shower, dressed in a pale blue polo shirt and tan Dockers, he looked strong, masculine, and good enough to lick. His gym bag, presumably filled with his clothes, hung from one hand. In his other hand, he held a roll of his sketching paper.

"Would you like a cup of coffee before you go?" she asked.

"No, thanks." He crossed the room, then handed her the roll of paper.

"What's this?"

"You mentioned there were building lots available up here. I worked up some sketches for you, both new homes and renovation possibilities. Maybe you can use them to get your business started."

She stared at the roll of paper and fought the urge to cry. There was no way she could have afforded an architect— much less one from Taft, Hobson and Brown—to make sketches for her. Lifting her gaze to his, she said, "Thank you."

"My pleasure." He set his gym bag on the floor and stepped closer to her, until they almost, but not quite, touched. "Actually, this entire couple of days has been my pleasure."

Forcing a smile, she asked, "Bugs and all?"

Instead of smiling in return, he cupped her face between his hands and stroked his thumbs over her cheeks. "Bugs and all." He searched her face, his eyes serious. "I want you to know…" His voice trailed off, and he frowned. "Damn it, I don't know what I want you to know. Except that last night was…"

"Lovely."

The tension in his face seemed to relax a bit. "Yeah."

"And saying goodbye is awkward."

"I think 'difficult' is a better word."

Damn near impossible was closer to the truth. "But necessary."

"Is it? Maybe we could—"

"No." She shook her head and his hands slipped from her cheeks to rest on her shoulders. "We agreed it was only one night. Let's not tarnish the good memories by attempting to turn it into more than that…because we both know it can't be."

His expression was so intense, she held her breath, dreading, yet foolishly hoping, he'd dispute her words, prove her wrong. After what felt like an eternity, but couldn't have been more than ten seconds, he nodded. "All right."

She expelled her pent-up breath and forced a smile, ignoring the acute sense of loss flooding her. "Good luck with your project."

"You, too. Thanks for your help with Dracmeyer."

"No prob—" His mouth crushed down on hers, cutting

off her words. It was a hot, hard kiss that ended too soon, leaving her knees weak and her insides shaking. Before she could recover her equilibrium, he picked up his gym bag and walked out the door, closing it behind him with a quiet click.

9

CARMEN NEWBURY STOOD IN the center of the living area of the cabin and turned in a slow circle. Lynne watched her friend from the kitchen, anxiously awaiting the verdict. She'd worked like a woman possessed for the remainder of her two-week vacation, supervising the array of workers, then laboring long into the night hanging curtains, rearranging furniture, organizing the kitchen and bathroom with items that Carmen had received from her bridal showers, dusting, polishing and executing dozens of other small details. She'd completed the final finishing touches barely twenty minutes before Carmen arrived.

The result of her efforts surpassed even what she'd anticipated and pride washed through her. The cabin was perfect—warm, cozy, inviting and homey—yet practical and functional.

The navy, maroon, and cream plaid-covered sectional sofa was the centerpiece of the living room. A grouping of thick, pine-scented candles rested on the redwood coffee table along with a beautiful hand-carved mallard Lynne had discovered in an antique store.

A comfy maroon upholstered chair with a matching ottoman sat in the corner, directly under Dave's moose head, which Lynne had on second consideration decided lent a rustic air to the room.

Her gaze skimmed over the gleaming hardwood floors, but she scrupulously avoided looking at the hearth where the bearskin rug lay—an aching, knife-in-the-side reminder of her night with Ryan.

Not that she needed any reminders. The texture of his skin, his taste, his scent, were all so deeply embedded in her heart, she despaired of ever exorcising them from her memory. Heaven knew she'd tried, working herself to exhaustion, focusing all her energies on the cabin, but he'd constantly remained in the back of her mind, a phantom who invaded her every waking thought then drifted through all her dreams.

"Lynne, this is beautiful." Carmen's voice yanked her from her reverie. Carmen ran her hand over the back of the sectional, her dark eyes shining like a child's on Christmas morning. "I knew you'd do a great job—you had fabulous taste even back in high school—but I never suspected Dave's den-of-horrors cabin could look like *this*." She crossed to the kitchen and enveloped Lynne in a quick gardenia-scented hug. "The bedroom, the bathroom…all of it. It's absolutely perfect."

"I'm glad you're pleased."

"I can't wait to show Dave. I'm planning to drive him up here after work tomorrow, and we'll spend the weekend." She sent Lynne a saucy wink. "I can't wait to try out that bearskin rug."

Lynne forced a smile. "Sounds great."

Carmen raised a brow. "Yes, it does. You know, we haven't talked about anything except the cabin since I got home yesterday. So tell me…how did you make out with Ryan?"

She bit her lip at Carmen's phrase and resisted the urge to blurt out, *we made out great—in the bed, in the shower, on the bearskin rug.* "Fine."

When she didn't offer anything else, Carmen persisted, "That's *it?* You were alone for several days with a man who can only be described as gorgeous—a man with whom you shared unmistakable sparks at my wedding—and *fine* is all you give me? I want details!'' Grabbing her hand, Carmen pulled her toward the sofa. When they were both seated, she said, ''We're going to sit right here, and you're going to tell me everything.''

''There's nothing to tell.''

Carmen snorted her disbelief, then regarded her with a sharp speculation that sent heat creeping up her neck. ''Not likely. Something happened. I can tell. You're turning all blotchy, which means you either totally hated him…or totally liked him. And I think I know which one it was.''

A frustrated noise escaped Lynne. ''I didn't hate him. He was…nice.'' She nearly rolled her eyes at the lukewarm word. ''Very attractive. And very wrong for me.''

''Why do you say that?''

''Because I'm finished with relationships. Especially with men like him.''

''Oh? Good-looking, financially secure, straight guys?'' Before she could answer, Carmen continued, ''Maybe you've had it with relationships because you've never met the right man to have one with.''

''Ryan Monroe is *not* the right one.'' But even as the words passed her lips, fear that she was dead wrong skipped down her spine.

''And you know this because…?''

''He's a yuc. A fancy car-driving, suit and tie, Italian loafer-wearing city boy.''

''He's a honey.'' Carmen's eyes narrowed, and to Lynne's mortification, red-hot heat scorched her cheeks. Carmen's eyes widened to saucers. ''Ohmigod, you slept with him.''

She considered denying it, but decided there was no point. Carmen knew her too well, and her flaming face was a dead giveaway. Huffing out a long sigh, she said, "Actually, *sleep* had little to do with it."

"I knew it! I knew you two would hit it off. The minute I saw you together at the wedding, I said to Dave—"

"Whoa! You've got this all wrong. We had one night, and that's it."

"What do you mean 'that's it'? Was he crummy in bed?"

Lynne would have laughed at the ludicrous question if she'd been able. "No. He was…incredible."

"Incredible? Give me a number. On a scale of one to ten."

"Fifteen." When Carmen's eyes boggled, Lynne amended, "Fifteen thousand, four hundred and thirty six."

"And you *let him leave?*"

Lynne jumped to her feet and paced across the room, her low-heeled pumps tapping against the hardwood. "What would be the point of continuing when it can't go anywhere? There's no future for us. I want to move to the country, he loves the city. Neither one of us wants a long-distance relationship. I don't want *any* kind of a relationship. I want to concentrate on me. My career."

"And that's exactly what you've been doing for the last year and a half. Maybe it's time to crawl out of your cave and give another man a chance." Fixing a probing stare on her, Carmen asked, "Even if a relationship is out of the question—which I don't necessarily believe, by the way— why not just enjoy the sex? Good Lord, woman. How many fifteen thousand four hundred and thirty-sixes do you run into?"

"But that's the whole problem right there. I only spent one night with him—and it was enough to prove that it wouldn't, *couldn't,* be just sex for me."

"Maybe it wouldn't be for him, either."

Her friend's soft words, combined with the warm concern flowing from her gaze, halted Lynne's pacing. "He doesn't want a relationship any more than I do. And even if I manage to pretend it was nothing more than sex, how long before he got tired of me and left me with nothing but some hot memories and a broken heart? A week? A month?"

"Fifty years?" Carmen suggested quietly.

Lynne pressed her fingers to her throbbing temples. "Stop. You're killing me. You're a newlywed so you think everyone's destined to march down the aisle."

"Not true. But some people are destined to do just that."

"Maybe. But Ryan and I are not."

"If you say so."

"I *know* so."

But that didn't make it hurt any less.

RYAN SAT AT HIS DESK Friday evening and rubbed his tired eyes. The courier service had just picked up the sketches and blueprints for Leyton Dracmeyer's house. The author would receive them by noon tomorrow. Now all Ryan could do was wait—and hope Dracmeyer would give the green light.

Swiveling his leather chair around toward the window, Ryan observed the slow crawl of traffic winding its way down Commonwealth Avenue. The trendy Back Bay area was a mecca of upscale shops, restaurants and clubs, and Friday nights seemingly attracted every resident in the city to enjoy the nightlife. One of his co-workers had invited him to join a group of guys for dinner and club-hopping, but Ryan had turned him down. The mere thought of the singles' bar scene gave him a headache. His heart just wasn't into trying to meet women. And it was all *her* fault.

He dragged his hands down his face and for the hun-

dredth time in the past hour alone, pushed thoughts of her
aside. Damn it, his project was finished. He should be enjoying a night on the town, hoisting a few with the guys,
putting the moves on a good-looking babe. Instead, he sat
in his office, every corner of his mind filled, as it had been
for the past two weeks, with haunting images of a laughing,
curly-haired, blue-eyed woman who made every other female pale in comparison.

After leaving her at the cabin, he'd stopped by the salvage yard and managed to rescue nearly all of Dave's belongings. He'd arranged for the stuff to be delivered to a
storage unit in town, figuring Dave could go through it
when he returned from his honeymoon.

He'd spent the rest of his time off working on Dracmeyer's house—sketching, revising, until it was perfect. It
was, Ryan thought with pride, his finest work to date.

And Lynne was in every single line of the place.

He'd incorporated dozens of details she'd provided him
with, and many others had inspired still more ideas. He'd
researched Dracmeyer on the Internet his first night back,
but hadn't unearthed any information that Lynne hadn't already told him. In fact, he hadn't been able to dig up half
of what she'd given him. If Dracmeyer accepted the project,
he knew a huge chunk of credit belonged to Lynne.

Lynne. God, he had to stop thinking about her. But how?
He'd eaten lunch with Dave today and knew he and Carmen were heading for the cabin tonight. Clearly, Lynne had
finished with the redecorating. He'd given Dave the key to
the storage unit holding his furniture, and assured his friend
that he had every confidence that Lynne had done a great
job and not turned the place into the dreaded Camp Girly-
Girl. Dave had teased him a bit about "the decorator," but
Ryan had adroitly changed the subject to baseball and Dave
hadn't mentioned her again.

Yeah, like you need a reminder. His gaze settled on a group of young women waiting to cross the busy street. They all looked young and attractive, and he wondered if perhaps Lynne was going out tonight with her girlfriends.

Or with another guy.

A growl rumbled in this throat and he surged to his feet. The thought of another guy touching her pumped hot jealousy through him. Damn it, there had to be a way to get her out of his mind—and sitting here thinking about her wasn't doing the job.

The hell with this moping. He was young, single, had just typed "the end" on a major project—and he was going out to celebrate. He searched his desk for the piece of paper where he'd scribbled the name of the restaurant his co-worker had invited him to. Was it Biba's? Or—

"Hello, Yank."

Ryan jerked his head up and stared at the huge stranger filling the doorway.

"May I help you?"

A deep guffaw sounded from the giant. "Don't recognize me, eh? My mum always said I cleaned up right fair." He walked across the room to Ryan's desk then held out a ham-sized hand. "'Tis I, Killer, your Lexus-rescuing mate."

Ryan could only stare. This was more than a clean up. This was a freakin' metamorphic transformation. Gone was the Deliverance/Grizzly Adams dude with the wild hair, mustache, beard and denim overalls. This tall, dark, good-looking, clean-shaven guy looked like he'd just stepped off the cover of *GQ*. His dark hair sported a hundred-dollar haircut, and he wore an expertly tailored charcoal-gray suit, snowy shirt and silk tie. Gold cuff links winked at his wrists as did a discreet gold watch.

Ryan shook Killer's hand, not even trying to hide his surprise. "I never would have recognized you."

"Figured as much."

"What are you doing here?"

"Had business with my solicitor in the building across the way. Took a chance you might still be about." His gaze scanned Ryan's office and he nodded his approval. "Nicely done." He returned his attention to Ryan. "I'm on my way to sup on a sirloin then head out for a pub crawl. Care to join me for a piss up?"

"Ah, tempting as that sounds, I think I'll pass on the piss up."

"Oh, come on. Don't be a big girl's blouse. Let's go get pissed."

"Listen, no offense, but I can't work up much enthusiasm for going out to get *angry*. And what the hell is a big girl's blouse?"

Killer shook his head and made *tsking* sounds. "The problem with you Yanks is you can't understand English. A big girl's blouse is what you call a wimp. A wimp is a bloke who refuses to go to the pub and get pissed with his mate. Pissed *off* is angry. Pissed is drunk, you daft wanker."

Ryan snagged his suit jacket from the back of his chair and sent Killer a cool smile. "Well, mate. I'm no big lady's shirt, and I believe I'm in just a right fine mood to get pissed."

"Smacking, mate. Let's push off."

KILLER WAS FULL OF SURPRISES.

As soon as they stepped out of Ryan's building, a sleek, black Mercedes-Benz limo pulled to the curb. Ryan sent Killer a questioning look and the giant shrugged. "Can't drive when you're pissed."

The chauffeur drove to the Ritz-Carlton hotel where the maître d' greeted "Mr. Claymore" with the sort of deference usually reserved for heads of state. While they supped on "sirloin," which turned out to be English for porterhouse, Ryan learned that Killer had developed and sold several software programs for "stonking" amounts of money, thus enabling him to retire at the ripe old age of thirty-two. He loved the outdoors and, in spite of his wealth, preferred to live simply, but every once in a while he liked to "put on the dog."

After dinner they moved to the hotel's sumptuous mahogany-paneled bar. Not exactly the sort of atmosphere where Ryan would envision a "piss up," but the bartender greeted Killer like a long-lost friend and immediately poured two shots of whiskey for Mr. Claymore and his mate.

"Cheers," Killer said, raising his glass then downing the contents in one gulp.

Ryan followed suit, the whiskey scorching a path to his belly.

"Blimey," Killer said, indicating another round. "That'll put hair on your pecker."

Ryan tossed a pretzel into his mouth. "Yeah, that's just what I want."

Killer guffawed and slapped Ryan on the back, nearly dislodging the pretzel. The bartender placed two more amber-filled shot glasses in front of them. Killer reached for his, but instead of drinking it, he nudged Ryan with his elbow.

"Two dishy birds at the end of the bar, mate, giving us the eye. Let's go chat them up. I wouldn't mind ending the evening with a little rumpy pumpy with the blonde."

Ryan didn't need a translator to figure out what "rumpy pumpy" meant. He glanced down the bar. A Pam Anderson look-alike was regarding Killer with definite interest. Her companion, a knockout brunette, was giving Ryan a slow, thorough bottom-to-top ogle. When her gaze finally fastened on his, there was no mistaking the sensual gleam in her eyes. She was gorgeous, her endless legs and curves shown off to perfection in a short, black sleeveless dress. She even had curly hair.

She left him completely cold.

Picking up his shot glass, he tossed back the contents, enjoying the fire scorching his insides. "You go right ahead," he told Killer. "I'm not interested."

Killer simply stared at him. "Are you barmy? That brunette is positively cracking and that ogle she gave you could melt bricks."

"Not my type."

Killer's eyes widened, then he nodded slowly. "I see. Wouldn't have taken you for a shirtlifter, but I'm not one to judge. It makes no difference to me. We're still mates." He tossed back his whiskey.

"I'm almost afraid to ask, but what the hell is a shirtlifter?"

"You know, a bloke who fancies other blokes."

Ryan scrubbed his hands down his face, which was starting to feel a bit numb from the potent whiskey. Leaning toward Killer, he said in an undertone, "I'm not gay, you idiot. I'm just..." What the hell was he? Besides royally confused.

"Spoken for?" Killer guessed.

"Not exactly."

"But there's a lady you fancy."

An image of Lynne's smiling face filled his mind. "Yeah. But I wish like hell I didn't."

Killer nodded in clear male sympathy. "Know what you

mean, mate. But I'll bet you a fiver that the dishy brunette could help you forget.''

A series of pictures flashed through his mind like a slide show. Lynne wrapped in a shower curtain, threatening him with a pink razor; Lynne laughing, her big blue eyes teasing him over burned meals and bug fiascos; Lynne lying naked in bed, sighing his name, her body glistening after making love with him.

''If I thought she could make me forget for even two minutes, believe me, I'd go for it.''

''Well, I've got news for you, mate. If that posh bird can't take your mind off another girly, you're a goner.''

Ryan nodded slowly. Yup. That's what he was, all right—a goner. Because there was only one curly-haired woman he wanted and it wasn't the one sitting at the other end of the bar. Now all he had to do was figure out what to do about it. But one thing was crystal clear even in his rapidly clouding mind: something *had* to be done because the thought of never seeing Lynne again, never touching her or laughing with her, was simply unacceptable.

Considerably cheered by his plan—whatever the hell it was—Ryan ordered a beer. Killer grimaced, muttered something about ''piss water,'' then asked for another whiskey. When their drinks were delivered, Ryan reached for his frosty mug, noting how much he had to concentrate to wrap his fingers around the glass.

''I lunched with Lynne today,'' Killer remarked, grabbing a handful of pretzels.

Ryan's hand froze halfway to his mouth. ''What?''

''Lynne and I lunched together. At The Palm. Absolutely smashing food.''

Ryan carefully set down his untouched beer and stared with blurry vision at Killer—both of him. ''Lynne? *My* Lynne? I mean, Lynne Waterford?''

"The very one." Killer waggled his eyebrows and nudged Ryan with his elbow. "Now *she's* a tasty dish if I ever saw one. All those curves and big blue eyes. Makes a bloke want to just take a nice big bite."

Killer's words hit Ryan like a barrel of ice water, clearing the cobwebs from his brain. Pushing back his stool, he stood and glared at Killer.

"And did you?" he asked, barely controlling the urge to grab Killer by his silk tie.

"Did I what?"

"Take a bite."

Killer raised his brows. "I'm not the sort to kiss and tell."

Cold fury settled over him like a blanket of ice. "I suggest you rethink that policy, *mate,* or we'll be taking this outside."

"Blimey, sit your arse down before your eyeballs squirt blood."

Ryan glared at him through narrowed eyes. "I prefer to stand. What the hell is going on between you and Lynne?"

Killer popped a pretzel and regarded Ryan with speculative interest. "There's been no hanky-panky between me and Lynne. I'm just pulling your plonker."

Relief swept through him and his tense muscles loosened a bit. "So you and she never—"

"Are you off your trolley? She's my chum. You don't do the slap and tickle with your chums. Besides, she closely resembles my sister—not the sort of look that makes a bloke want to snog. But I can see where she'd appeal mightily to other fellows…such as yourself, perhaps."

"Perhaps."

His sharp gaze settled on Ryan for several seconds. "Well, then, you need to know that, even though we're mates, I'll plant you a facer if you hurt her."

"And I'll plant you one if you touch her."

They regarded each other for a full minute. Then Killer nodded. "Guess we understand each other. But you might want to quit fannying around and make your move. Noticed quite a few blokes giving her the look-over at lunch." He handed Ryan his beer. "Drink up, mate. We're not even halfway to pissed."

Ryan accepted the mug, draining half the contents to soothe his dry throat. Killer changed the subject to some property he was considering selling. They chatted for a few minutes, then Ryan excused himself to use the men's room. As he left the bar area, he glanced back toward Killer. A grin that could only be described as cat-ate-the-canary smug curved the Brit's lips. Warning bells jingled in Ryan's fuzzy brain. Clearly Killer was up to something.

But what?

ON MONDAY AFTERNOON, Ryan stared out his office window and raked his hands through his hair. He'd been waiting to hear from Dracmeyer all day, and the suspense was killing him. So much rode on the eccentric author's decision—his dreams for the arts center, a partnership, his career, his future. A humorless laugh escaped him. *Yeah, it's not like this is* important *or anything.* He turned and sizzled a heated glare toward the phone. *Ring, damn it!*

As if on cue, the instrument rang, nearly stopping his heart. He snatched up the receiver, then heard his secretary's smooth voice. "Mr. Dracmeyer is on line two."

"Thank you, Susan." Ryan forced himself to sit down. He drew a deep breath, then punched the button for line two.

And waited to hear his future.

TWO DAYS LATER, THE numbness surrounding Ryan's heart hadn't lessened. If anything, it grew worse with each pass-

ing hour. He stared out his office window at the dozens of
people streaming out of buildings on their way to lunch.
He supposed he should eat, but food held little interest.
Everything that had seemed so promising only days ago,
now seemed empty and hollow.

He ran a hand down his face. The partners at Taft, Hobson and Brown were singing his praises. Dracmeyer loved
the plans for his house. His bonus was assured, and he had
several leads on financial backing for his arts center project.
He should be ecstatic. Jumping up and down. Enjoying his
success. Instead, he was edgy. Unsettled.

Miserable.

Damn it, he couldn't continue like this.

He crossed to his desk and pulled a business card from
the top drawer. He stared at it for a moment, weighing,
deciding. But there really wasn't any decision to make. He
knew what he wanted. All he needed to do was figure out
some way to get it. He pondered for several minutes, then
a slow smile pulled at his lips. Grabbing up the receiver,
he dialed.

As soon as he heard the deep voice on the other end, he
said, "Killer, it's Ryan."

"Hallo, mate. Why the ring up? Wanting to go for another pub crawl?"

"And suffer another hangover from hell? No, thanks.
But I'd like to discuss something you mentioned during
our, uh, piss up. Can you meet me at my office sometime
today?"

SHE HADN'T HEARD FROM HIM since their one night together.

Late Friday afternoon, Lynne entered her office building,
trying not to dwell on her acute disappointment, but failing
miserably. No matter how hard she'd tried over the past

few weeks, she still couldn't squash the ridiculous hope that Ryan would call. Of course it was better that he didn't, that he honored their agreement. Still, a part of her had foolishly hoped their brief affair had meant as much to him as it had to her.

She pushed through the revolving door, leaving the noisy traffic sounds behind her. Forcing Ryan to the back of her mind, she made her way across the lobby to the bank of elevators, her heels clicking on the dark green and cream marble floor. Her meeting with the new owners of a South End restaurant had gone very well. They'd approved her final sketches, agreed upon the fabrics and light fixtures, and requested only minor changes to the plans. Her bosses would be very pleased as all systems were now go for the redecoration of the dining room. As soon as she returned to her office, she'd place the final orders for the materials. If everything went according to plan, the project could start late next week.

The elevator doors swished open. She entered the empty car, then pushed the button for the twentieth floor. Glancing at her watch, she heaved a sigh. Her phone calls would take less than half an hour. All her other job-related duties were caught up to date. There was no reason to work late, but she dreaded the thought of going home to her empty apartment. The lonely rooms mocked her and there was nothing there to occupy her, to keep her mind from dwelling on Ryan. She'd already cleaned the place to within an inch of its life, and every cabinet, drawer and closet was perfectly organized. Yes, over the past few weeks she'd ruthlessly micro-managed her job, her home—jeez, even her laundry was caught up. Every aspect of her life was filed, folded, faxed, fitted, finessed or fixed.

Except one.

The one that occupied every corner of her mind, all day,

every day, then kept her awake at night, haunting her
dreams even when she managed to fall asleep.

And during those long, lonely, sleepless nights, she'd
finally realized that she'd done exactly what she hadn't
wanted to do. She'd fallen in love. And with a yuc, no less.
Oh, she'd tried to talk herself out it—told herself these
feelings for Ryan were just lust, infatuation, or maybe in-
digestion—but it's hard to lie to yourself when your heart
is bashing you over the head with a bat screaming, *that's
not gastric distress, you ding-a-ling! You're in love!*

But what to do about it? *Nothing. It's over. One night
was all he wanted. If he'd changed his mind, he would have
called.*

Of course, she'd envisioned herself countless times picking up the phone and calling him, imagined dozens of conversations…

Hi, Ryan. Just called to see how you're doing.

*Hi there! I have an extra ticket to hear the Boston Pops
at Symphony Hall…*

Hey! Wanna catch the new James Bond flick with me?

*Guess what? I'm head over heels in love with you. I want
you in my life so badly my skin aches.*

She pressed her fingers to her temple and huffed out a
frustrated breath. She had two choices: she could throw
herself at a yuc who'd clearly closed the relationship door
after their one night together, or she could find a way to
get over him. Her pride balked at contacting him and risk-
ing rejection, but damn, could that hurt any worse than
what she was going through now?

The elevator *pinged* open. Stepping out, she walked
down the pale-blue, carpeted hallway leading to her office.
Juggling her portfolio and purse, she opened her office
door, bumping it closed behind her with her hip. She turned
toward her desk and froze.

Ryan stood by the window. Pale streaks of late afternoon sun spilled over him through the partially open vertical blinds, gleaming on his ebony hair. He wore a navy-blue suit, jacket unbuttoned, the sides pushed back by his hands casually tucked in the pants pockets. A stark white dress shirt, bisected by a red paisley silk tie, stretched across his broad chest. He leaned against the windowsill, his long legs crossed at the ankles, his feet encased in Italian leather tassel loafers.

God, he was beautiful. And *here.* Her heart flipped over, taking her stomach along for the ride. Pushing off from the windowsill, he stood straight, regarding her through serious golden-brown eyes.

"Hello, Lynne."

She opened her mouth to speak, only to discover, to her mortification, that it already hung agape. Snapping her lips together, she cleared her throat, but before she could say a word, her phone beeped twice, indicating the caller was the receptionist.

Somehow her feet propelled her to her desk. She murmured, "Excuse me," then lifted the receiver.

"Lynne," came Darla's hushed voice, "I tried to signal you before you reached your office, but I guess you didn't see me waving my arms at you." The receptionist went on, "I just wanted to tell you that that utterly glorious man in your office has been waiting for you for almost three hours. I told him you wouldn't be back until close to five, but he said he'd wait…as long as it took." A dreamy sigh drifted through the receiver. "I don't suppose there's any chance he's, like, your brother and you'd fix me up with him?"

Lynne slanted a glance at Ryan who watched her with an unfathomable expression. "Nope."

Darla sighed again. "I knew it. Well, I'm leaving in a

few minutes. I hope you and Mr. Glorious have a great weekend.''

Lynne hung up the phone, resisting the urge to tug on her suit jacket or pat her hair to see if any stray curls had escaped her chignon. Offering Ryan what she hoped was a casual, carefree smile, she said, ''This is a surprise. What brings you by?''

''Several things.'' He slipped his hands from his pockets and stepped closer to her. Her heart slapped against her ribs so hard she could feel the beat drumming in her ears. ''I spoke to Dave,'' he said. ''He's very pleased with your work at the cabin.''

She longed for a glass of water to cool her hot, dry throat. ''I'm glad. How did your project for Leyton Dracmeyer go?''

Something she couldn't decipher flickered in his eyes. ''I'm afraid things didn't work out quite the way I'd hoped.''

Sympathy flooded her, along with a healthy dose of resentment toward her literary idol. Moving around her desk, she walked toward him, stopping when only a few feet separated them. She reached out and squeezed his hand. ''I'm so sorry. I know how much that project meant to you.'' Standing closer to him, away from the sun's glare, she could see he looked tired. And sad. To fight the overwhelming urge to hug him, kiss him, comfort him, she forced a small smile. ''Dracmeyer's a great writer, but he clearly knows zilch about architectural talent. You can bet I won't be buying *his* next book.''

A ghost of a smile touched his lips. ''Thanks.''

Ryan stood before her, drinking in the warm sympathy flowing from her expressive eyes, absorbing the pleasurable tingle coursing through him from where their palms pressed together. God, he'd missed her. He hadn't realized how much until she'd walked into the room.

He inhaled, and her citrusy scent filled his head. It was all he could do not to groan. She smelled fabulous. And she looked...

Wow.

Her chestnut curls were ruthlessly tamed back in one of those prim styles that his fingers itched to mess up. She wore a conservative blue suit that exactly matched her eyes. The memory of the delights he knew lay hidden beneath her proper knee-length skirt and single-button jacket flashed through his mind, sparking a trail of heat.

She offered him a quick, nervous-looking smile and her dimples winked at him. "You didn't say why you're here."

"I'd like to hire you."

She stilled. "Excuse me?"

"I need a decorator and you come highly recommended."

She eased her hand from his, then stepped back several paces. He thought he saw disappointment flash in her eyes, but she quickly looked away. Circling around, she put her desk between them.

"Why do you need a decorator?" she asked, her tone cool.

"I recently purchased an investment property. It's in excellent condition structurally, but from a decorating standpoint, it's a disaster. I can't hope to rent it until it's fixed up."

"Surely a rental property only requires fresh paint and new carpeting. Why go to the expense of decorating the entire place?"

"Because it's on a lake and I may make use of it myself during the off season."

She stared directly into his eyes. "There are hundreds of competent decorators in Boston. Why me?"

"As I said, you come very highly recommended from Dave and Carmen—although your sales pitch could use a little work." He watched her closely, and it appeared her complexion paled.

Lifting her chin a notch, she said, "I appreciate the offer, but I'm afraid I—"

"It's only a few miles from Dave and Carmen's place," he interrupted smoothly. "Another decorating job up there might really get the ball rolling for your freelance career."

Interest, albeit reluctant, sparked in her eyes. "I see. What time frame are we talking?"

"I'd like you to start as soon as possible. I realize we'd need to work around your schedule, so the end date is flexible."

"And the budget?"

"Also flexible." He glanced at his watch. "It's only five o'clock. Why don't I drive you up to see the place? You can look it over and then decide if you're interested in the job."

She hesitated for several seconds. "I have some calls I need to make."

"No problem. While you're on the phone, I'll run out and pick up some sandwiches and drinks. Whaddya say?"

A tiny smile lit her lips. "I guess it couldn't hurt to look."

Relief raced through him and he expelled a breath he hadn't even realized he held. "Great. What kind of sandwich do you want? Wait—don't tell me. Let me guess. Peanut butter."

She laughed. "Actually, I prefer turkey and swiss on rye with lettuce, tomato, little bit of mayo."

"Got it." He crossed the room, sending her a salute.

"I'll be back." He left the office, closing the door quietly behind him.

Lynne plopped into her leather chair and whooshed out a long breath. Her pulse was jumping around like a kid on a pogo stick, and myriad emotions whipped through her with tornado-force fury.

She knew she should be elated at the possibility of another decorating job that could help along her freelance career—and she was—but the opportunity paled to insignificance compared to the prospect of spending an entire evening in Ryan's company.

She'd been disappointed when she realized he'd come to her office on matters pertaining only to business, but he'd lit a spark of hope in her that couldn't be extinguished. He could have chosen any decorator in the city, yet he'd picked her. And while it was crazy to hope that he cared for her as she did for him, perhaps, if they worked together...

Her mind told her heart to stop being foolish.

Her heart told her mind to sit down and shut up.

10

LYNNE SAT IN RYAN'S Lexus, listening to the smooth jazz flowing from the CD player, watching the scenery slowly change from congested to rural. She felt as if their one-night affair sat on the seat between them—an elephant-sized lump that couldn't be ignored, but no one wanted to mention.

In spite of her jumping stomach, she managed to remain outwardly calm and hold up her end of the conversation. They exhausted innocuous topics such as the traffic, the Red Sox, and all the new construction in the city. Then Ryan mentioned the Impressionist collection at the Museum of Fine Arts and they launched into a lively debate regarding their favorite artists. Finally, between the more stimulating conversation and leaving the city behind, her tension eased. Their discussion somehow segued into comedy, and they discovered a mutual love for old Abbott and Costello routines. They were only halfway through an impromptu rendition of ''Who's on First'' when Ryan turned off the main road onto a gravel-paved lane.

As they bumped along, she asked, ''Is your property right on the lake?''

''Yes. There's a dock and a boathouse as well.''

''Sounds wonderful. Just the sort of place to relax and unwind. I'm sure you won't have any problem renting it.''

"I'm definitely hoping it will get plenty of use," he replied.

He drove for several more minutes as dusk eased over the fiery-colored landscape, then parked the Lexus in a small clearing. "The cabin's about a hundred yards ahead, beyond those trees."

Peering through the windshield, she could see the burnished red and orange leaves reflected on the lake's mirrorlike surface. He walked around the car to open her door, then extended his hand to help her alight. Their fingers met and she fought to ignore the tingle that arrowed up her arm at his touch.

Instead of releasing her, he held her hand as they walked down the path. Colorful leaves crunched beneath their feet, and the pungent fragrance of pine scented the crisp air. She sent up a prayer of thanks that she'd worn low-heeled shoes because concentrating on her footing was impossible when all she could think about was the warmth of his palm pressed to hers...the pressure of his strong fingers surrounding hers...the remembered exquisite sensation of his clever hands roaming her body.

She ruthlessly pushed her thoughts away from that night, breathing a sigh of relief when they rounded a curve and the cabin came into view.

It was a lovely redwood A-frame structure with clean lines and a wraparound porch. In her mind's eye, she already envisioned an urn of geraniums here, a glider swing there. Ryan slipped a key from his pocket and unlocked the door. He waved her in with a gallant gesture, then followed, bumping into her back when she halted and gasped.

The view was spectacular. The entire rear of the cabin consisted of floor-to-ceiling windows. The lake glittered through the autumn-hued trees, a sparkling dash of shimmering blue. There was one huge main room with a fieldstone fireplace taking up the side wall. Sliding glass doors opened onto a deck that ran the length of the house. The kitchen area was compact, but contained all the essential appliances, along with a curved snack bar.

Turning her head, she noticed a wrought-iron spiral staircase leading up to a second level. Behind her, Ryan said, "That's the loft. The balcony overlooks the living area. C'mon. I'll give you the grand tour."

As they walked around, Lynne mentally jotted notes and filed ideas, clearly picturing color schemes, furniture and accessories. In addition to the main room and kitchen area, the bottom floor contained the laundry room, a guest bedroom and a full bath. They stepped outside onto the deck, and she hummed her appreciation. The view of the lake was gorgeous, yet enough evergreens surrounded the house to ensure year-round privacy. A covered hot tub sat in the corner of the deck, under the shade of a copse of towering pines. An image of her and Ryan sitting in the tub, naked, surrounded by moonlight and the sounds of the forest, popped into her mind. Her heart skipped a beat, but she firmly told her heart to get a life.

Returning inside, they climbed the spiral staircase. When she reached the top, she *ooohed* with delight. A huge skylight was set in the ceiling, directly above the spot where a bed would go.

"It would be just like sleeping under the stars," she said.

"There's another skylight in the master bath, too. Right over the tub."

She walked into the bathroom. A whirlpool bath, big enough for two, sat in the corner, directly under another huge skylight. She instantly imagined lying in that tub, surrounded by a cloud of bubbles, staring up at the stars. She pictured Ryan joining her in the warm, swirling water, their slippery, wet limbs entwining. He'd make slow, deep love to her, touching her everywhere, filling all the places in her heart and soul that had been empty since the day he'd left her at Carmen's cabin.

"So what do you think of the place?" His deep voice jarred her from her sensuous reverie. "Does it inspire any ideas?"

If you only knew. "Lots of ideas. It's a fabulous retreat. The abundance of windows gives it an open, airy feel, and the skylights are the perfect touch."

"So you think you can make it livable?"

"With this to work with?" she asked, waving her hand to encompass the entire cabin. "Are you kidding? Easily. But it's such a great place, anyone could do it."

"We really do need to work on your sales pitch." He leaned against the wall, then casually slid his hands into his pockets. He'd discarded his suit jacket and tie, and unfastened the top button of his white dress shirt. Her gaze zeroed in on the edge of his white undershirt peeking through the V, and she swallowed.

Just as she had a thing for a guy in glasses, she had a *huge,* inexplicable thing for the sight of a white undershirt showing at a man's throat when he unbuttoned his collar. Something about it just made her want to peel off all those layers of clothes to find out what was hiding beneath.

Of course, with *this* man, she already knew what was hiding beneath. And every time she thought about it, she suffered palpitations.

"So what do you think?" he asked.

I think I want to remove your clothes…with my teeth. I

think I want to be the mother of your children. And I know *I love you.* "What do I think about what?"

"Taking on the job. Are you interested?"

God, yes. The problem was she was interested in a whole lot more than the job. "I'd be crazy to turn it down, but let's talk about it. I have a pad and pencil in my purse downstairs. Why don't I sketch out a few ideas, then you can tell me if you're still interested in hiring me?"

"Oh, I'm interested," he said in husky tone that rippled a warm shiver down her spine. He pushed off from the wall, and her heart performed a triple somersault as he approached her, his gaze steady on hers. Instead of stopping and kissing her until her head spun—which would have been just fine with her—he simply snagged her hand as he walked by, entwined their fingers, then gently tugged her toward the stairs.

Back in the main room, she retrieved her pad and pencil, setting them on the snack bar. He stood next to her, close enough that she had only to reach out her hand to touch him. Close enough so that his crisp, clean, male scent surrounded her, urging her to bury her face in his neck and just breathe him in.

How could one man possibly smell so good? There was no way to avoid smelling him unless she held her breath until she passed out. Or unless she breathed through her mouth—but then she'd look and sound like a panting dog. Darn it, why couldn't a girl ever have a stuffy nose when she needed one?

And how was she supposed to concentrate with him standing so close? She could practically feel the warmth emanating from his skin. Skin she longed to touch. To lick. She shook her head to clear the image of her running her tongue down his abdomen. Good grief, she was losing her mind. If she didn't get her hands busy *now,* she was going to grab him and not let go.

Desperate to appear unflustered, she flipped through her pad to a clean page and remarked, "You know, Killer owns several cabins he rents out in this area, although I'm not sure exactly where."

"Actually, you're standing in one of them. And Killer doesn't own it any longer. I do."

She stared at him. "You bought this place from Killer? How did that happen? When? Why?"

"You sound like a reporter," he said with a smile. "Yes, I bought it from Killer. It happened because, as is customary with the sale of goods, I gave him money, and he gave me what I paid for in return. The deal was finalized this morning. As for why, I consider it an investment in my future."

Her mind buzzed with questions. "How did you know Killer wanted to sell one of his cabins?"

"He stopped by my office last week and we went out for a drink. He mentioned he was looking to sell. One thing led to another, and here we are."

Her amazement took a back seat as she imagined Ryan and Killer in a bar together. Women would hang on them like mold on cheese. Hot jealousy streaked through her at the thought of some sexy bimbette draping herself all over Ryan. "I didn't realize you and Killer were so chummy."

"We're mates." His golden-brown gaze probed hers. "He told me the two of you are mates as well—or chums, as he put it."

"Yes, we are."

"And that you've never been anything more than friends."

"That's true."

"Why not? He seems to have all the qualities women look for in a guy."

"Indeed? And what are those?"

"He's rich and good-looking."

She laughed. "Is that what you think women look for?"

"Isn't it?" Before she could answer, he asked again, "So why aren't you and Killer more than friends?"

She hesitated, searching his face for a clue as to what, if anything, was behind his question, but his expression appeared merely curious. "Even though Killer's a great guy, I've never felt that special spark with him. And don't ask me what the spark is, because it's impossible to describe. I just know when it's not there."

He reached out, tucking a stray tendril behind her ear, and her heart stuttered at the intimate gesture. "And when the spark *is* there…do you know that as well?"

Oh, boy, did she ever. And it was all his fault. He'd ignited a spark in her that had all but fried her circuits. She swallowed to ease her dry throat, then said, "Yes, I do."

"I know all about that spark, too," he said softly. "I felt it the moment I saw you."

She went perfectly still, then forced a small laugh. "That's because I was naked and I suspect you witnessed quite a peep show."

"I have to admit that seeing you step out of that shower nearly stopped my heart—"

"Ah-ha! I knew you were standing there the whole time!"

"But," he continued, "the *first* time I saw you was at Dave and Carmen's wedding. Seems I have a thing for curly hair, dimples and big blue eyes." He watched her closely. "I think you felt it, too."

She hesitated. This conversation clearly indicated he had

more in mind than her simply decorating his cabin. He wanted to resume their affair. God knows she wanted to as well—from a hormonal point of view—but damn it, there was a lot more than her hormones at issue here. She had no desire to spend the rest of her life picking up broken pieces of her heart after their affair ran its course.

"I can't deny I feel that certain spark with you," she said. "But this is only physical attraction. You'll be gone the minute you see another curly-haired, dimpled, blue-eyed chick."

"No. You see, I also have a thing for intelligent, talented, amusing, confident, kindhearted women. And I've been around the block enough times to know they don't grow on trees." His serious brown gaze probed hers. "Do you really think this is just physical attraction? Because I don't."

Her heart rolled in a slow somersault. "Perhaps not, but we haven't known each other very long."

"No, but how long does it take? I've dated women for months and haven't felt this spark or tingle or whatever you want to call it." He took her hand and gently squeezed her fingers. "The question is, what are we going to do about it?"

"Nothing." She eased her hand from his and stepped away from him. By God, he was scaring her. It would be so easy to agree to continue their affair, but she'd be insane to do so. She might as well just rip her heart from her chest and let a truck roll over it. "Look. Rekindling our affair is a bad idea. I distinctly recall that you're done with long-distance relationships. I want to move away from the city…and, let's face it, a country boy you are not." She paced in front of him. "Damn it, why aren't you like all the other yucs?"

"Yucs? What the hell are they?"

"Yuppie city slickers. You're supposed to be shallow. Want only instant gratification."

"Well, I'd be lying if I said I didn't want gratification from you. With you."

"You see? You're not supposed to be honest, either!" She halted, then spread her hands in a helpless gesture. "This would be just sex—"

"That's the point. I think we both know it *wouldn't* be just sex."

"And that scares me." Drawing a deep breath, she looked directly into his eyes and blurted out her fear. "I don't want to fall in love. I don't want to get hurt."

"So let's not hurt each other. But I've got to tell you, not being with you hurts." He tunneled his hands through his hair. "I'd made up my mind that I was through with relationships...at least, for the foreseeable future. I was tired of the games, the hassle, and being lied to."

He paused to take a breath, and she said, "I know exactly what you mean. If I'd thought the nuns would let me decorate the place, I'd have joined a convent."

"Exactly—except for the convent thing," he agreed "But then you know what happened?"

They stared at each other for several seconds, his question hanging heavy in the air.

"Then came you," they said in unison.

She stared at him in amazement, frightened yet elated. Impossible as it seemed, he felt it, too.

"I don't know why this is," he said, "and I don't know how. All I know is it's been magic from the very start. It's like playing tag."

She somehow found her voice. "Playing tag?"

"Yeah." He stepped closer to her, then reached out and touched her arm with a single fingertip. "You're It."

Ohmigod. She needed to sit down. And there wasn't a damn chair in sight.

"There have been several defining moments in my life," he said softly, his serious brown gaze steady on her. "Moments that changed everything in the blink of an eye. High school graduation, receiving my college degree, my mother's sudden death, completing my first project." He paused. "Meeting you."

She locked her knees to keep from slithering to the floor and grabbed on to the snack bar with one hand for good measure.

"My latest defining moment," he went on, "came several days ago. And you'll never guess where."

Probably she shook her head, but she wasn't sure. Anyway, she meant to. And she hoped the answer wasn't "at a strip joint" because then she'd be royally pissed.

"At the newsstand in the lobby of my office building," he said. "There I was, minding my own business, waiting in line to buy my *Globe* and a pack of gum, when I saw it."

She managed to swallow, then asked, "It?"

"The same issue of *Cosmo* that Waldo was tearing apart in the bathroom that first day at the cabin. I left the line and walked over to the magazine display. I felt like I was in some sort of a trance. I picked up the magazine and read the cover blurb, 'How to Touch a Naked Man—Caress His Secret Hot Spots and Drive Him Wild.' I vividly recalled reading that headline at the cabin and fantasizing you would."

"So your defining moment was realizing you wanted me to caress your naked hot spots? Not that that doesn't sound…promising, but I gotta tell ya, as far as defining moments go, that's a bit on the 'duh' side.''

He shook his head. "No, the moment came when I picked up the magazine. I held it in my hands and inhaled…and smelled you.''

Good grief, the man she loved was nuttier than peanut butter. Before she could say a word, he plunged on. ''That scent you wear—that citrusy, spicy cologne that drove me crazy—it was in there, in the magazine. I flipped through the pages, sniffing, trying to find it. And there it was, on page seventy-two. One of those sample pages. I breathed in, and it was as if you were standing there next to me. Only you weren't.

"I don't know how long I stood there with my nose buried between the pages, just breathing you in, but next thing I knew, some guy tapped me on the shoulder. He was looking at me like I was a pervert, and asked, 'Hey buddy, are you *smelling* that *Cosmo* magazine?' And *that* was the moment. That's when I knew.''

His face bore such a triumphant, expectant look, he clearly expected her to know what came next. "Knew what?'' she asked, utterly clueless. "That you like my perfume?''

He cupped her face between his hands and gently smoothed his thumbs over her cheeks. "That I love you.''

She went completely still under his gentle caress. For several seconds she forgot how to breathe. Then joy filled her, followed instantly by the certainty that she'd somehow misheard him. Clearly she looked all slack-jawed and buggy-eyed because he said, "I've surprised you.''

Holy cow, maybe he *had* really said he loved her. She managed to nod.

"Well, it surprised me, too. And let me tell you something—this love stuff is a real pain in the ass. Ever since I left you at Dave's cabin, I've been miserable. All I do is think about you. Day and night. Jeez, it's ridiculous. I can't sleep; I can't work; I can't even enjoy my success with the Dracmeyer project. Damn, my life's been a mess.''

So many thoughts and questions rocketed through her mind, she felt dizzy. But the overwhelming thought that pounded through the jumble was that he loved her. *Loved* her.

And she could definitely relate to being unable to sleep or work. As for his success with Dracmeyer—

Her brows shot upward then collapsed as she pressed her mental rewind button. What had he said about Dracmeyer?

Ryan watched her big, blue eyes stare at him while myriad expressions flitted across her face, ranging from dazed to stunned to confused. His heart beat in slow, hard thumps, as he wondered what she was thinking, and prayed she would say she returned his feelings. He'd thought long and hard about throwing his heart into her hands; had tried mightily to talk himself out of it. But, in the end, there hadn't been any choice. He loved her. He knew it. And he was willing to take the risk.

But now that the moment had arrived, he wasn't so sure. She didn't look ecstatic or even happy. In fact, her expression looked like she'd just found one of those big, green bugs with the hairy arms sitting on her dinner plate.

His hands slid to her shoulders, and he simply stood, watching her, waiting for her to speak. Nearly a minute passed before she cleared her throat, then spoke.

"What do mean 'your success with the Dracmeyer project'? You said things didn't work out the way you'd hoped."

Not exactly the words he'd hoped for. "They didn't.

Dracmeyer loved the house. The land is being cleared and construction begins next month. I received my bonus, impressed the bigwigs, and am working with several potential backers for my theatre project."

"But that's everything you wanted."

"I thought it was." Leaning forward, he brushed his mouth over hers. "But it didn't mean all it should have, all I'd expected it to…because I didn't have anyone to share it with. I didn't have you."

Her eyes grew misty. "Oh, Ryan."

Masculine panic set in. "Hey, you're not going to cry, are you?"

A big tear rolled down her cheek. "Of course not."

"Oh, man. Don't do that." He patted down his pockets, praying a tissue would magically appear. "I didn't mean to make you cry."

Another fat tear dribbled down her cheek. "I'm not crying."

"Right. And I'm the Prince of Wales." Giving up his search for a tissue, he gathered her into his arms, letting his shirt soak up her tears. Huffing out a long breath, he wondered what category these feminine tears fell under. Happy tears? That would be good. Sad tears? That would be bad. I-don't-love-you-back tears?

That would be very, very bad.

When she finally stirred in his embrace, he leaned back and looked into her drenched eyes that were swimming with emotion. His heart turned over and he lowered his mouth to hers, tasting the salt of her tears mingled with her own special flavor. She moaned, then wrapped her arms around his neck, pressing herself against him.

"I missed you," she whispered against his lips. "Every minute." She kissed her way along his jaw, interspersing her words with soft nips. "I must have picked up the phone a dozen times to call you."

"Why didn't you?"

"I'm a nincompoop." She leaned back in the circle of his arms, her expression warm and tender. "My defining moment occurred in my office. I was supposed to be sketching the living room layout for a client's loft, but I became lost in a daydream. When I snapped out of it, I realized the only thing I'd drawn was your name, over and over, with a big heart around it. That's when I knew I loved you."

He drew his first easy breath in what seemed like weeks. "You love me."

"Completely. And I agree with you one hundred percent. This love stuff hurts."

Elation exploded in him. "Only because we've fought it. Only because we've been apart. But I have a plan to deal with the long-distance problem."

"Ryan, that doesn't have to be a problem. I could stay in the city and still fulfill my dream of starting my own company."

"I'm so glad to hear you say that because I have the perfect assignment to kick off your freelance career."

"Oh?"

"How would you like to decorate Dracmeyer's house?"

She stared at him. Her mouth opened and closed twice, but no words came out. Finally she said, "You're joking."

"No. Dracmeyer's interested. You come very highly recommended from my firm."

"But...but..." She shook her head as if to clear it. "Good lord. A high-profile job like that would do more than kick off my career—it would launch it into orbit. What an incredible opportunity."

"Exactly. But I think I can sweeten the deal even more." Before she could question him, he crossed to the kitchen. He opened the refrigerator, then returned to her, holding a small multicolored shopping bag and a large gold-foil box. "For you," he said, handing her the box.

She nearly staggered under its weight, then blinked at the Godiva label. "Good heavens, what is this? A fifteen-pound box?"

"Twenty-five."

Her eyes goggled. "You bought me *twenty-five pounds* of Godiva chocolates? Talk about a sweet deal!" A laugh huffed from between her lips. "You realize it will take me forever to eat this. As much as I love it, I'll have to ration the calories out over the next fifty years so I don't gain a hundred pounds."

"Perfect. That's exactly what I want."

"For me to gain a hundred pounds?"

"No." He handed her the small shopping bag. "I want the next fifty years."

Lynne slowly shifted her gaze from the bag to his face. His expression was dead serious. With shaking hands, she set the heavy box on the snack bar, then opened the bag, pulling out a white T-shirt.

The front pictured a huge red heart and the words The One With The Most Chocolate Wins. Tears pushed at her eyes. Oh, God. This man was killing her. She turned the shirt over and froze. Emblazoned across the back were two words: Marry Me.

Before she could even attempt to recover, he reached in his pocket then held out his hand. "I'm hoping we can have the best of both worlds."

She looked down at the key resting in his palm. "What's that?"

"The key to this cabin. I meant it when I said I'd bought it as an investment for the future." He tipped up her chin with his fingers until their eyes met. "*Our* future. I didn't buy this place to rent it. It's for us. So we can split our time between here and the city."

The air seemed to leave the room, taking her voice with it. She had to swallow twice before she could speak. "I...I can't believe you did all this."

"I know what I want, and I want you. The question is—what do *you* want?"

She studied his very serious face, trying to assimilate all this, take it in. He not only loved her, he wanted to marry her, spend the rest of his life with her. It boggled her mind.

And it filled her with a joy like she'd never known.

Setting down her shirt and key next to the chocolates, she linked her hands together and cleared her throat. "Did I ever tell you how my parents met?"

Confusion flickered in his eyes. "Uh, no."

"They met at a wedding. My mother knew the bride, my father knew the groom." She smiled into Ryan's eyes. "They married three months later. They'll celebrate their thirty-second anniversary this fall. I think it only fitting I carry on the family tradition."

"Is that a 'yes'?"

"Yes. God, yes. Please, yes. Yes. Y—"

His mouth crushed hers into silence. Rising up on her toes, she poured all her heart and soul into their kiss. He ran his hands up her back, into her hair, scattering bobby pins onto the floor.

"I was afraid you were going to say no," he said, trailing hot kisses down her neck.

"Are you crazy? *I* was afraid I wouldn't be able to keep

my hands off you for the duration of the evening, and that if I made a move on you, you'd tell me to get lost.''

"Not a chance. Make all the moves you want. In fact—"

A deafening boom of thunder startled them, followed by a series of lightning flashes. Within seconds, fat raindrops splashed against the deck.

"Uh-oh," she said. "Maybe we should leave. Remember what happened the last time we were caught in a storm."

He waggled his brows. "Sure do."

Their eyes met. Tenderness, love and desire flowed through her like warmed honey. "Yeah, me, too. I fell in love...with the most wonderful man in the world."

"No. You fell in love with the luckiest man in the world."

"You know, you're very romantic for an architect."

He gently bit her earlobe, shooting heat straight to her womb. "You inspire me."

Trying to corral her rapidly evaporating concentration, she said, "We really should try to get back to town. The rain is coming down harder with each passing minute, and we don't want to get stuck here for God knows how long with no food."

"We have twenty-five pounds of chocolate," he reminded her, skimming his lips across her jaw, "and a fully stocked fridge, including a magnum of champagne."

She leaned back in the circle of his arms. "We do?"

"Yup."

"But there's no bed—or even a rug to sleep on."

"What happened to Miss I-Love-the-Country?"

"Nothing. I'd just rather have you in a comfortable bed for the weekend rather than on a cold, hard floor. I don't relish the thought of spending the next six months visiting a chiropractor.''

''Not to worry,'' he said, unbuttoning her suit jacket. ''Just like the Boy Scouts, I'm always prepared.'' He slipped her jacket down her arms, then turned his attention to her silk blouse. ''There's a queen-size, blow-up mattress in the trunk of my car, along with blankets and pillows— of the nonfeather variety, just in case Waldo stops by.''

''You're kidding.''

''I'm not.''

''But what about essentials like toothbrushes and toothpaste?''

''Got 'em in my gym bag in the car.''

''But I have nothing to wear.''

''Great!''

She fought to hide a smile. ''Food, champagne, instant bed, pillows, toothbrushes. You were very…confident.''

''I was scared spitless,'' he corrected, ''but hopeful.'' Their eyes met and he framed her face between his hands. ''Very, very hopeful.''

He lowered his head toward hers, but she pressed her palms to his chest, her gaze riveted just above his ear. ''Don't move, Ryan.''

He froze. ''God, I hate those words. What now? Hairy spider? Green thing? Snake?''

She reached up and pulled something from his hair. ''Twig.'' She held the small stick aloft. ''No legs, arms, or anything,'' she teased.

''Jeez. There goes another ten years off my life. Maybe I should rethink this whole country thing.''

Rising up on tiptoes, she gently bit the side of his neck. ''You're not backing out on me, are you?'' Her hands slid down to his belt. ''Because if you are, I won't share my

Godiva with you…and I have plans for you and that chocolate.''

"Not backing out," he assured her.

Another boom of thunder rent the air. Rain bombarded the roof, and the sky had darkened to slate. "Looks like we may be here for a while," he remarked. "Good thing I brought the rest of the essentials needed for a weekend in the country with you."

"The *rest* of the essentials? What else could we possibly need?"

"Twenty-five cans of bug spray." A slow smile eased across his face. "And four-dozen condoms."

HARLEQUIN®
Duets™

Welcome back to Nowhere Junction, Texas, where two women want to lay their hands on the perfect mate!

THE MAIL ORDER MEN OF NOWHERE JUNCTION

On sale July 2001
Duets #55

More Than the Doctor Ordered
by
Jacqueline Diamond

A Hitchin' Time
by
Charlotte Maclay

Available at your favorite retail outlet.

*Harlequin truly does
make any time special....
This year we are celebrating
weddings in style!*

To help us celebrate, we want you to tell us how wearing the Harlequin wedding gown will make your wedding day special. As the grand prize, Harlequin will offer one lucky bride the chance to **"Walk Down the Aisle" in the Harlequin wedding gown!**

There's more...

For her honeymoon, she and her groom will spend five nights at the **Hyatt Regency Maui.** As part of this five-night honeymoon at the hotel renowned for its romantic attractions, the couple will enjoy a candlelit dinner for two in Swan Court, a sunset sail on the hotel's catamaran, and duet spa treatments.

Maui • Molokai • Lanai

To enter, please write, in, 250 words or less, how wearing the Harlequin wedding gown will make your wedding day special. The entry will be judged based on its emotionally compelling nature, its originality and creativity, and its sincerity. This contest is open to Canadian and U.S. residents only and to those who are 18 years of age and older. There is no purchase necessary to enter. Void where prohibited. See further contest rules attached. Please send your entry to:

Walk Down the Aisle Contest

In Canada	In U.S.A.
P.O. Box 637	P.O. Box 9076
Fort Erie, Ontario	3010 Walden Ave.
L2A 5X3	Buffalo, NY 14269-9076

You can also enter by visiting www.eHarlequin.com
Win the Harlequin wedding gown and the vacation of a lifetime!
The deadline for entries is October 1, 2001.

PHWDACONT1

HARLEQUIN WALK DOWN THE AISLE TO MAUI CONTEST 1197
OFFICIAL RULES
NO PURCHASE NECESSARY TO ENTER

1. To enter, follow directions published in the offer to which you are responding. Contest begins April 2, 2001, and ends on October 1, 2001. Method of entry may vary. Mailed entries must be postmarked by October 1, 2001, and received by October 8, 2001.

2. Contest entry may be, at times, presented via the Internet, but will be restricted solely to residents of certain geographic areas that are disclosed on the Web site. To enter via the Internet, if permissible, access the Harlequin Web site (www.eHarlequin.com) and follow the directions displayed online. Online entries must be received by 11:59 p.m. E.S.T. on October 1, 2001.

   In lieu of submitting an entry online, enter by mail by hand-printing (or typing) on an 8½" x 11" plain piece of paper, your name, address (including zip code), Contest number/name and in 250 words or fewer, why winning a Harlequin wedding dress would make your wedding day special. Mail via first-class mail to: Harlequin Walk Down the Aisle Contest 1197, (in the U.S.) P.O. Box 9076, 3010 Walden Avenue, Buffalo, NY 14269-9076, (in Canada) P.O. Box 637, Fort Erie, Ontario L2A 5X3, Canada.

   Limit one entry per person, household address and e-mail address. Online and/or mailed entries received from persons residing in geographic areas in which Internet entry is not permissible will be disqualified.

3. Contests will be judged by a panel of members of the Harlequin editorial, marketing and public relations staff based on the following criteria:
   - Originality and Creativity—50%
   - Emotionally Compelling—25%
   - Sincerity—25%

   In the event of a tie, duplicate prizes will be awarded. Decisions of the judges are final.

4. All entries become the property of Torstar Corp. and will not be returned. No responsibility is assumed for lost, late, illegible, incomplete, inaccurate, nondelivered or misdirected mail or misdirected e-mail, for technical, hardware or software failures of any kind, lost or unavailable network connections, or failed, incomplete, garbled or delayed computer transmission or any human error which may occur in the receipt or processing of the entries in this Contest.

5. Contest open only to residents of the U.S. (except Puerto Rico) and Canada, who are 18 years of age or older, and is void wherever prohibited by law; all applicable laws and regulations apply. Any litigation within the Province of Quebec respecting the conduct or organization of a publicity contest may be submitted to the Régie des alcools, des courses et des jeux for a ruling. Any litigation respecting the awarding of a prize may be submitted to the Régie des alcools, des courses et des jeux only for the purpose of helping the parties reach a settlement. Employees and immediate family members of Torstar Corp. and D. L. Blair, Inc., their affiliates, subsidiaries and all other agencies, entities and persons connected with the use, marketing or conduct of this Contest are not eligible to enter. Taxes on prizes are the sole responsibility of winners. Acceptance of any prize offered constitutes permission to use winner's name, photograph or other likeness for the purposes of advertising, trade and promotion on behalf of Torstar Corp., its affiliates and subsidiaries without further compensation to the winner, unless prohibited by law.

6. Winners will be determined no later than November 15, 2001, and will be notified by mail. Winners will be required to sign and return an Affidavit of Eligibility form within 15 days after winner notification. Noncompliance within that time period may result in disqualification and an alternative winner may be selected. Winners of trip must execute a Release of Liability prior to ticketing and must possess required travel documents (e.g. passport, photo ID) where applicable. Trip must be completed by November 2002. No substitution of prize permitted by winner. Torstar Corp. and D. L. Blair, Inc., their parents, affiliates, and subsidiaries are not responsible for errors in printing or electronic presentation of Contest, entries and/or game pieces. In the event of printing or other errors which may result in unintended prize values or duplication of prizes, all affected game pieces or entries shall be null and void. If for any reason the Internet portion of the Contest is not capable of running as planned, including infection by computer virus, bugs, tampering, unauthorized intervention, fraud, technical failures, or any other causes beyond the control of Torstar Corp. which corrupt or affect the administration, secrecy, fairness, integrity or proper conduct of the Contest, Torstar Corp. reserves the right, at its sole discretion, to disqualify any individual who tampers with the entry process and to cancel, terminate, modify or suspend the Contest or the Internet portion thereof. In the event of a dispute regarding an online entry, the entry will be deemed submitted by the authorized holder of the e-mail account submitted at the time of entry. Authorized account holder is defined as the natural person who is assigned to an e-mail address by an Internet access provider, online service provider or other organization that is responsible for arranging e-mail address for the domain associated with the submitted e-mail address. **Purchase or acceptance of a product offer does not improve your chances of winning.**

7. Prizes: (1) Grand Prize—A Harlequin wedding dress (approximate retail value: $3,500) and a 5-night/6-day honeymoon trip to Maui, HI, including round-trip air transportation provided by Maui Visitors Bureau from Los Angeles International Airport (winner is responsible for transportation to and from Los Angeles International Airport) and a Harlequin Romance Package, including hotel accomodations (double occupancy) at the Hyatt Regency Maui Resort and Spa, dinner for (2) two at Swan Court, a sunset sail on Kiele V and a spa treatment for the winner (approximate retail value; $4,000); (5) Five runner-up prizes of a $1000 gift certificate to selected retail outlets to be determined by Sponsor (retail value $1000 ea.). Prizes consist of only those items listed as part of the prize. Limit one prize per person. All prizes are valued in U.S. currency.

8. For a list of winners (available after December 17, 2001) send a self-addressed, stamped envelope to: Harlequin Walk Down the Aisle Contest 1197 Winners, P.O. Box 4200 Blair, NE 68009-4200 or you may access the www.eHarlequin.com Web site through January 15, 2002.

Contest sponsored by Torstar Corp., P.O. Box 9042, Buffalo, NY 14269-9042, U.S.A.

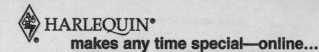

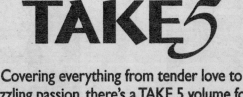